The Word Fulfilled

A Prophet's Tale

The Journey Begun
Book One

The Word Fulfilled
Book Two

The Prequel:
Ben Amittai: First Call

A Prophet's Tale
Book Two

❈

The Word Fulfilled

Bruce Judisch

OakTara

Waterford, Virginia

The Word Fulfilled

Published in the U.S. by:
OakTara Publishers
P.O. Box 8
Waterford, VA 20197

Visit OakTara at
www.oaktara.com

Cover design by Muses9 Design
Cover image, desert and camels © iStockphoto/Roberto Caucino
Cover image, map of Armenia © Clipart.com
Author photo © 2009, Collin McCann

Copyright © 2010 by Bruce Judisch. All rights reserved.

Scripture is taken from the King James Version of the Bible.

ISBN: 978-1-60290-225-1

The Word Fulfilled is a work of fiction. References to real people, events, establishments, organizations, or locales are intended only to provide a sense of authenticity and are used fictitiously. All other characters, incidents, and dialogue are drawn from the author's imagination.

To My Sister, Robin

Forever a best friend

WITH THANKS TO...

DR. JOHN WALTON, Professor of Old Testament in the Department of Biblical and Theological Studies at Wheaton College and Graduate School, for his scholarly work on ancient Mesopotamian lore. Excerpts from his *Ancient Near Eastern Thought and the Old Testament* (Grand Rapids, Mich.: Baker Academic, 2006) appear in this book by permission.

DR. DAVID CARNAHAN, author and friend, for his honest manuscript reviews of both this title and Book One, *The Journey Begun,* in A Prophet's Tale series.

JEANNIE, the wife of my youth, in whom I rejoice—and also a most supportive and constructive reviewer.

Finally, to RAMONA, JEFF, and the staff at OAKTARA for enabling this book to see the light of day.

Cast of Characters

HISTORICAL

Adad-nirari III—king of Assyria (811-783 B.C.)
Jonah (2 Kings 14:25; Jonah 1-3)—son of Amittai, prophet of Israel during the reign of Jeroboam II

FICTIONAL

MAJOR

Ahu-duri—Senior Scholar to King Adad-nirari III
Ianna—daughter of Mordac and Hani
Jamin—son of Obadiah and Judith; nephew of Hiram and Rizpah
Hani—Mordac's wife; Ianna's mother
Hiram—chief elder of the Jewish enclave in Nineveh; Rizpah's husband
Hulalitu—*naditu* priestess of Ishtar; Ianna's mentor
Zakir—senior court *tupsharru* (astrologer) to Adad-nirari III

MINOR

Abim—young Assyrian soldier
Akhyeshah—Jonah's guide from Damascus to Tadmor
Anardu—Assyrian soldier, leader of the guard detail
Iquisha—city magistrate of Nineveh
Issar-surrat—formerly Prahthah; now High Priestess of Ishtar
Jamal—caravan leader and Jonah's guide from Tadmor to Mari
Judith—Jamin's mother

Kasiru—court *baru* (haruspex—performs *extispicy*, "reading animal entrails for omens")

Mordac—Hani's husband; Ianna's father

Nurzani—court *muhhu* (casts lots and reads leaves for divination)

Obadiah—Jamin's father

Prahthah—*naditu* priestess of Ishtar; becomes the High Priestess Issar-surrat

Rizpah—Hiram's wife

Sasi—priest at the Temple of Marduk

Shalla—senior *naditu* priestess of Ishtar

Shera—*naditu* priestess of Ishtar

Suhru—young *ishtaritu* initiate

Thura—*naditu* priestess of Ishtar

Urdu—apprentice astrologer to Zakir

Zakheri—aide to Ahu-duri

Glossary

Baru—an Assyrian haruspex; a seer specializing in extispicy (reading the vital organs of sacrificed animals)

Enuma anu Enlil—(literally "When Anu Enlil"; more helpful, "In the Days of the God Enlil") a vast canon comprising thousands of astrological omens; used by ancient Assyrian astrologers to interpret celestial events and their meanings

Entu—a senior priestess of Ishtar, from which the High Priestess was chosen

Idiqlat River—Akkadian name for the Tigris River

ha eretz—literally, "the land"; Hebrew term for the Promised Land.

Ishtaritu—a young girl (or any woman) undergoing her carnal rite at the Temple of Ishtar; sometimes also used of a prostitute priestess of Ishtar

Ittu—an omen or sign

Kalakku—a flat wooden riverboat or raft used for commerce on the Euphrates and Tigris Rivers

Muhhu—an Assyrian seer specializing in divining communications from the gods through casting lots, reading leaves, etc.

Naditu—a temple priestess in service to Ishtar

Quppu—a small, round-bottomed boat made of animal skin stretched over willow branches; used for travel on the Euphrates and Tigris Rivers

Purattu—Akkadian name for the Euphrates River

Qadishtu—a temple prostitute in service to Ishtar

Tabiltu—Akkadian name for the Khosr River, which flowed through the center of Nineveh before joining with the Tigris River

Sukallu—a senior secular advisor to the Assyrian king; regent over a district of the kingdom and second only to the king in power

Tupsharru—an Assyrian astrologer

About Ancient Mesopotamia

How the Ancient Mesopotamian calendar relates to the modern calendar:

Month	Days	Equates to
Nisannu	31	March/April
Ajaru	31	April/May
Simanu	31	May/June
Du'ûzu	31	June/July
Âbu	31	July/August
Ulûlu	30	August/September
Tašrîtu	30	September/October
Arahsamna	30	October/November
Kislîmu	30	November/December
Tebêtu	30	December/January
Šabatu	30	January/February
Addaru	29	February/March

Ancient Mesopotamian days were divided into twelve "hours." The First Hour began at sunset. Below is an approximate chart of hours as they pertain to this story.

Hour	Equates to
First	7:00 P.M.—9:00 P.M.
Second	9:00 P.M.—11:00 P.M.
Third	11:00 P.M.—1:00 A.M.
Fourth	1:00 A.M.—3:00 A.M.
Fifth	3:00 A.M.—5:00 A.M.
Sixth	5:00 A.M.—7:00 A.M.
Seventh	7:00 A.M.—9:00 A.M.
Eighth	9:00 A.M.—11:00 A.M.
Ninth	11:00 A.M.—1:00 P.M.
Tenth	1:00 P.M.—3:00 P.M.
Eleventh	3:00 P.M.—5:00 P.M.
Twelfth	5:00 P.M.—7:00 P.M.

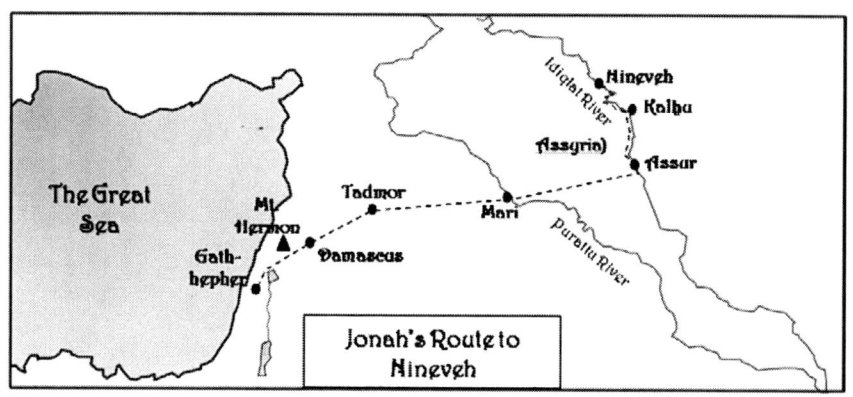

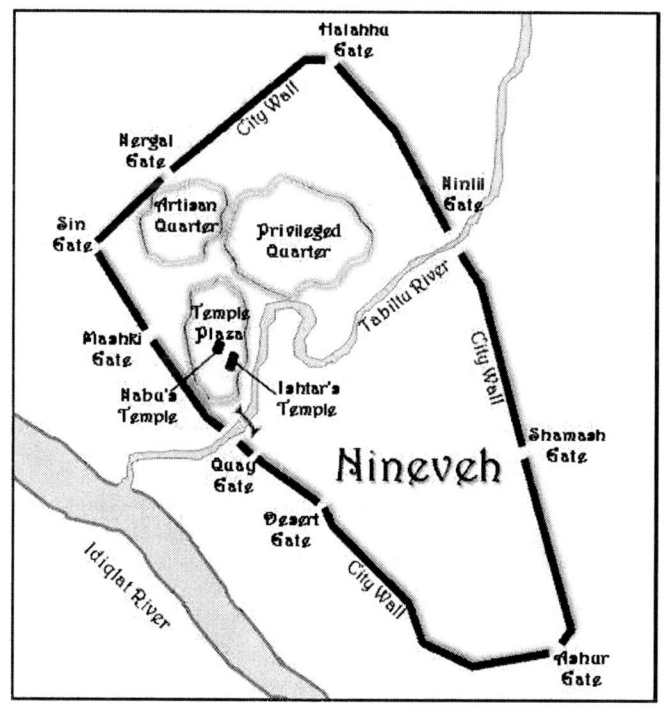

Prologue

The Jezreel Valley
841 B.C.

Sand and pebbles underfoot crunched as they circled on the riverbank. Abim gripped his sword and prayed the enemy soldier wouldn't notice his hand shake or his whitened knuckles. The Israelite was taller but appeared close to him in age, as neither of their beards had filled in. Like his own tunic, the warrior's showed no blood or damage of battle; the hollow look born of taking another man's life had not yet clouded his face.

The din of the fierce battle—the screams of the wounded and dying, the clash of sword upon spear—dimmed to a fuzzy echo. The rumble of horses' hooves and hiss of arrows—sounds that obsessed him only moments ago—now huddled in the recesses of his mind. Only two people filled his world: his opponent and himself.

True to his training, Abim focused on the Hebrew's shoulders. An attacker's face could deceive, his head feint, his eyes intimidate. But a dip of the torso or a twist of the neck would betray an attack. So he watched. He waited. And they circled.

Abim was among the new conscripts at the rear of the Assyrian column when the Israelites attacked. The enemy charge ripped through the center of the formation and severed them from their leadership. The untried soldiers broke ranks and scattered southeast through the valley, the only way open to them. Weapons clattered to the ground and were trampled, and men less swift on their feet fell with them. Dignity and honor bowed before survival.

The world shrank around Abim as he raced along the river. It became the wet gravel under his feet, the fallen logs he vaulted, the boulders he skirted. He hurdled a downed soldier, only to be overtaken by another warrior who shouldered him aside. The young Assyrian didn't know which way to go . . . only that he must flee. Although his heart pounded against his chest and his lungs threatened to burst, he was certain he could have run until he reached his home in Nineveh.

He turned a bend in the river and a barrage of screams shattered his thoughts. He skidded to a halt. The swarm of retreating soldiers had run into an enemy force hidden among the rocks and trees along the hillside. The Hebrews pounced and slaughtered the recruits in their tracks. Time came to a standstill. Abim gaped at the carnage piling up along the river before him. Only when an arrow embedded itself in a fallen tree by his side did his trance break. He wheeled and raced back up the valley the direction he came. He knew the enemy was ahead, but they were also behind. There were few choices.

He collided with the Israelite soldier when he rounded a rock outcropping. Stunned, they fumbled their weapons and toppled to the ground. His heart in his throat, he groped for his sword and scrambled to his feet just as the Hebrew regained his stance. They crouched and brandished their weapons only a few paces apart. Abim's pulse pounded in his ears and his vision tunneled. Aside from training, this was his first taste of combat since being forced into King Shalmaneser's army.

Skill in the art of war had always eluded Abim's intuition. The sword never settled well in his grasp, and the spear fit worse. His apprenticeship as an artisan had done nothing to imbue a warrior's heart in him, and army life, with its grit and austerity, held little attraction. But here he was, and this day's end would see if he would ever mix pigments for his beloved pottery again.

Neither man made the first move. Abim's eyes flicked to the Hebrew's face. The soldier looked no more sure of himself than Abim felt. His eyes were glazed, his jaw clenched in the same taut lines. Abim wondered if his own face was as pale as the Hebrew's.

A twitch in his adversary's eyes broke Abim's concentration. Then the Hebrew did what Abim least expected. He abandoned his defensive crouch and pulled himself erect. Abim searched the man's face, but he detected no guile, no trap. Abim hesitated, then straightened to match the Hebrew's stance.

When the Israelite lowered his sword, Abim knit his brow. Was that a smile turning the corners of the Hebrew's mouth? He lowered his own weapon, when he thought he heard a chuckle. The Israelite shrugged and laughed. He actually laughed! Despite his shock, Abim found himself unable to subdue a return smile. This was ludicrous; he knew it. Terror raged around them and the two enemies looked at each other with silly grins. The fearsome enemy that was the Israelite evaporated to reveal an ordinary man—one apparently with a sense of irony. It occurred to Abim that the young man opposite him wanted to live as much as he did. The hope in Abim fancied a refinement in the Israelite's mien. Maybe he even liked pottery.

The smiles faded, replaced by awkwardness. The Israelite gestured with his free hand. Abim shook his head. The Hebrew frowned and looked down, apparently at a loss. Suddenly, he raised his head and began to speak. An arrow tore through Abim's rib cage at the Israelite's first word.

The thin shaft radiated a bolt of searing pain through his abdomen, followed by a numbness that gripped his body. Wide-eyed, Abim dropped to his knees. His sword tipped from his hand and clattered onto the gravel. Through his stupor, he fingered the feathered notch that protruded from his side, as though not convinced it was real. He stared at a crimson stain that blossomed onto his tunic. His body stiffened, and his shoulders began to sag.

A pair of strong hands grasped his shoulders. The Hebrew knelt, easing Abim to the ground. His vision narrowed, and his breath chopped to short gasps. He reached under his tunic and tugged at a leather thong around his neck. The garment shifted to reveal a gold medallion clutched in the dying man's hand. Too weak to pull it over his head, Abim thrust the amulet toward the enemy soldier. The Hebrew's eyes widened, but he didn't move. Abim pushed the pendant into the Israelite's chest. Imploring the man with a final look, the young Assyrian laid his head back and died.

Stunned, the Israelite sat back in the wet gravel. His eyes welled up at the wasted young life, even if it was Assyrian. He turned the amulet over in his hand and stared at it. An ornate *menorah* etched into the polished surface gleamed in the midday sun. He shook his head. What was an Assyrian soldier doing with a priceless Hebrew heirloom? The man looked too young, too new to battle, to have spoils from a previous conflict. He looked back at his former adversary's face but met only a frozen stare. He eased the medallion over the fallen soldier's head, then brushed the man's lifeless eyes closed with his fingers. The Israelite looped the thong over his own head and tucked the pendant beneath his shirt.

He retrieved the Assyrian's sword and laid it across his chest. With a nod of respect, he picked up his own weapon and rose to his feet. He turned upstream and skirted a still pool of water trapped on the riverside by a low sandbar. It was there the Assyrian arrow found its mark at the center of his chest. His eyes bulged, and he crumpled into the dark pool. He was dead before the water settled around his body.

PART ONE

So Jonah arose,
and went unto Nineveh,
according to the word of the LORD.

JONAH 3:3

One

Nineveh, the Temple of Ishtar
Second Day of Šabatu
786 B.C.

A pungent haze of incense swirled about the lithe form of the young girl as she swayed to the monotonic chant of the temple priestesses. The primal throb of ceremonial drums and pop of tambourines, the tinkling of belled instruments and the hollow cooing of reed and clay pipes caressed her ears. She submerged herself in an atmosphere bloated with sound, smell, and sight.

A sheen of tears thickened and blurred her vision, birthing tears that spilled over the thick kohl lining beneath her dark almond eyes. Briny drops traced gray rivulets over cheeks stained with henna and powdered with ochre. Some droplets curled around the contours of her half-parted lips; others glistened on the tip of her tongue, where their muskiness assailed her taste. Charcoal smoke and incense fumes squeezed her throat and convulsed her chest. Her violated lungs fought for air and her brain slowly surrendered to the hypnotic effect of the frankincense and myrrh clouding the cella of Ishtar's temple.

Ianna reveled in her coming-of-age ritual. She and her sister initiates rocked and dipped to the mantra of the *naditu* priestesses paying homage to the Mother Goddess.

> *Praise the goddess, the most awesome of goddesses.*
> *Let one revere the mistress of the peoples, the greatest of the Igigi.*
> *Praise Ishtar, the most awesome of the goddesses.*
> *Let us revere the queen of women, the greatest of the Igigi.*

This was the day the young beauty had awaited for so long. Today, the only daughter of a prominent Ninevite family crossed the threshold into womanhood. As they became marriageable, young women across the land gathered under the tutelage of Ishtar's priestesses and gave themselves in sacred ritual to the Goddess of Fertility, Love, and War. After the ceremony, each would remain at the temple until a random traveler through the city selected her as a carnal partner. He would pay for the encounter, but she would accept his proposition regardless of the price, for it was the spiritual aspect of the rite that was important. Besides, the money went not to her, but to the temple and into the service of the adored goddess.

The young initiate was fortunate in her extraordinary beauty. Her time at the temple would be brief, perhaps only a night or two. Others less comely could look forward to a longer stay, indeed some waiting weeks or even months to catch an eye. After their inaugural night in a man's arms, a few would remain at the temple to become *qadishtu* and *ishtaritu*, priestesses and sacred prostitutes, destined to remain unmarried and childless in dedication to the Mother Goddess. Few alumni of the ritual, though, aspired to that level of devotion. Most would return home, marry and bear children, as Ianna knew she would.

For now, though, the temple ceremony was everything she dreamed it would be. Through her daze, she became aware of priestesses who specialized in ceremonial dance and song joining the festivities. They mingled with the novice devotees and, almost as a single organism, undulated their oiled and painted bodies with the swell and ebb of the music.

She is clothed in pleasure and love.
She is laden with vitality, charm, and voluptuousness.
Ishtar is clothed in pleasure and love.
She is laden with vitality, charm, and voluptuousness.

The young girl's movements slowed as her strength flagged into hypoxic lethargy. Her head swam, and her legs stiffened under the heady aromatic fumes that drugged her mind and body beyond their ability to respond. She closed her eyes, and her feet rooted themselves in place as she twisted and reeled with the musical reverberations in her ears. Finally, her oxygen-starved muscles succumbed, and she ceased all movement. Her arms settled to her sides.

> *In lips she is sweet; life is in her mouth.*
> *At her appearance rejoicing becomes full.*
> *She is glorious; veils are thrown over her head.*
> *Her figure is beautiful; her eyes are brilliant.*

Ianna didn't know how long she stood there when she sensed a delicate touch glide up her arms to her shoulders. She lifted leaden eyelids and peered through a glassy sheen at a *naditu*. Through the thick haze, the priestess sparkled with multiple necklaces, bracelets, and rings of gold inlaid with lapis, that set off an alluring light-blue tunic. Ianna tried to speak, but her lips, now encrusted with half-dried ochre, tears, and sweat, failed her. The priestess only shook her head and slid her fingertips back down the young girl's arms. Ianna lost focus, and the *naditu's* painted face began to fade. The young girl's knees buckled. The last thing she saw was the glint in the priestess's ebony eyes before everything went black.

Two

Nineveh, the Temple of Ishtar
Fifteenth Day of Nisanu

Ianna fixed a vacant stare at the mosaic fresco that framed the entrance to the Hall of the Ishtaritu. The late afternoon sun oozed through a narrow window high in the wall behind her and cast a hazy yellow swath across the faded tile chips. Her dull eyes traced the lower edge of sunlight as it edged up the frieze and released the ornate design into the solitude of dusk. The desire for similar release from the naked glare of life into the sweet anonymity of death wormed through her subconscious. She found herself in envy of the fresco and watched as it slipped into blessed obscurity.

She sat alone on the niche bench farthest from the statue of Mother Ishtar. The Matron regarded her with a thin, cold smile from her perch atop the back of a stone lion. Lately, Ianna fancied a mocking hue creep into the goddess's enameled eyes. Over time, she found herself withholding all but the occasional glance at the Mother Goddess, whom she once beheld with unrestrained adoration. That was months ago.

Two months and thirteen days, to be exact.

A lifetime, to be less exact.

She sat motionless and avoided eye contact with her Patroness. Shame tilted her torso forward onto stiff arms propped on the smooth surface of the bench. Her slender fingers fidgeted on the edge of the seat over which her delicate legs dangled listlessly, toes angled toward the floor they came short of reaching by a full hand's breadth. Once proud and erect, the weight of disgrace rounded her slender shoulders and slumped them into a posture more befitting a woman decades her senior.

Two novice *qadishtu* cult priestesses tittered through the doorway and drew up short at the sight of Ianna hunched in the shadows. Their cheeks flushed, and they fell silent as they hurried by. Once past, they stole furtive glances over their shoulders and shared clipped whispers. She knew they were too new to the temple to intend cruelty. They were simply curious. There were tales of a girl more beautiful than any of the others who passed through their rites but who could not consummate her initiation. For the others, the Temple of Ishtar was now a distant memory. Not for Ianna.

The tales were true. Ianna's beauty was the fodder of legend, a rare gem among the steady stream of Assyrian girls who coursed through the temple. No one understood why she had never consummated her ritual, least of all she.

The young initiate had dutifully, even enthusiastically, fallen in line with the other girls to avail herself as a temple virgin. Surely, she would quickly consecrate her blossoming womanhood in a holy act of devotion to Mother Ishtar. Then she would return to her family to live out a normal life, sanctified. But something had gone wrong. Terribly wrong.

She remembered the initiation ceremony like it was yesterday, at least until she passed out as the closing mantra was chanted and the brass gong fell silent. She awoke in these chambers, unaware how she got here. And here she remained. For two months. And thirteen days. Or was it fourteen now? It hardly mattered.

Certainly there were ample opportunities for Ianna to complete her ritual. Her exquisite beauty ensured that. As expected, she was the first maiden selected countless evenings as the men came out. But, for reasons far beyond her understanding, after they retired to her bedchamber and shared the prescribed ceremonial cup of wine, none of the men had been able to perform. Her own mortification was compounded by the humiliation of her partners, many of whom turned violent in their embarrassment.

"*What have you done to me? What is this curse? Whore!*"

She could only cower in fear and bewilderment, while one after another the men stormed from her chamber.

Her selection was rarer now. Word got around.

"Ianna?"

She jerked as her name scraped through the antechamber on a coarse voice. Her shoulders drooped further at the sight of Hulalitu. Her assigned *naditu* mentor stood across the room, hands propped on her ample hips. Even after months, Hulalitu's raspy voice sent a shudder up Ianna's spine.

"Ianna!" Her advisor would not tolerate being forced to a third summons.

"I'm here." The softness of Ianna's breathy tone overlaid Hulalitu's croak like balsamic myrrh on sandstone.

"It is late. There is an offering tonight. There will be men. Prepare yourself."

Ianna sighed and pushed off the bench. Her soft leather foot wraps padded over the smooth floor. She clasped her arms over her stomach as she made her way to her bedchamber. Her mind darkened.

So there will be men. So what?

"I saw Ianna today."

Hani tightened the last knot of the cable-stitch she hemmed on the sheepskin throw. She cut the mending twine with a flint knife and glanced at her husband, Mordac.

"She sat outside the temple. I saw her as I passed on the way to the marketplace. I couldn't approach her. That horrible priestess was at her shoulder again."

Mordac did not respond.

She laid the skin on her lap and looked at him. "She sat alone, apart from the other girls."

The silversmith kept his eyes lowered as he sorted a small pile of nuggets by size.

"Mordac—"

"I heard you." He sat back and rubbed his eyes.

Hani tightened her jaw. "They won't let me see her or speak to her."

"She should have come back home by now," Mordac mumbled.

"She should never have gone."

He narrowed his eyes. "We've discussed this. It's what is done."

"It's a travesty, what is done!" She glared back.

"Hani, you know the custom. If we are to maintain a proper place here, we must make certain . . . concessions."

His wife's eyes flashed. "Concessions? Ianna is our daughter!"

"I know that!" He slammed his hand on the table. "Don't you think I know that?"

"Sometimes I wonder." Her voice cracked.

"She should have been home right away." He rubbed his forehead. "It was supposed to be one day, just one day. Then she would be home, and we could forget it. Life could go back to the way it was."

Hani's shoulders sagged. "It can never be the way it was for a girl, Mordac. Not after the first time. It shouldn't be like this." Her voice softened. "It should be beautiful, like mine was."

Mordac's voice thinned. "It was supposed to be one day. Just one day."

"The moon has been through two full passages, Mordac. And it's halfway through a third." Her voice sliced the air like an arrow.

He furrowed his brow and went back to his nuggets.

Hani's voice dropped to a plaintive whisper. "What's happening there?"

Ianna sat motionless as Hulalitu caressed her silky black hair with an ivory comb.

"What's wrong with me?"

The *naditu* paused. "Nothing. Why do you ask?"

"You know why I ask." Ianna shook her head and splayed her

ebony tresses across her shoulders.

"Hold still!" Hulalitu frowned. She gathered her *ishtaritu's* locks together and smoothed them down her back.

Ianna persisted. "You haven't answered my question."

"Of course I have. Nothing is wrong with you."

The young girl swiveled and glared up at the *naditu*. "Then why am I still here?"

"Will you turn around and hold—"

"No, I won't!" Ianna folded her arms across her chest and met her mentor's frown. "This is senseless. I'm just wasting my time. I've been with countless men, but none have consummated me." Tears glistened in her eyes.

Hulalitu averted her look and tucked Ianna's hair behind her ears. "Maybe it's the men," she offered with a shrug. "Perhaps your beauty intimidates them."

"Oh, come now." Ianna scoffed. "Other beautiful girls have come and gone. None of them . . . failed." She choked out the last word.

"You haven't failed at anything." Hulalitu tipped her chin up with a finger. "There is more to this than beauty, more than . . ." Her eyes went distant, and she stopped. Her fingertips caressed Ianna's cheek.

"More than what?" Ianna's misty eyes beseeched Hulalitu's for some comfort, some believable assurance.

Hulalitu's hoarseness deepened. She averted her eyes again. "Mother Ishtar knows all. She will decide when the time is right, when the man is right."

Ianna's shoulders sagged at the lame reply. *Mother Ishtar.* It was easy to invoke the name of the Divine Mother when there were no real answers. Perhaps it was true, but it held no satisfaction.

Hulalitu cleared her throat and the edge to her voice returned. "Finished. Join the others. The men will arrive soon."

Ianna sighed and pushed up from the mat.

"And no tears. You'll run the color from your cheeks." Hulalitu turned her by the shoulders and nudged her toward the door. "Go."

※ ※ ※

Hulalitu slipped around the ornate tapestry into the small bedchamber assigned to Ianna. A goblet of wine sat on the floor next to the sleep mat. It was filled and ready for the ceremonial libation the *ishtaritu* would share with her partner before the ritual consummation.

She listened by the door. Satisfied no one was near, the *naditu* knelt beside the goblet. Lifting a vial from a small pouch tied to her waist, she uncapped it and stirred a measure of camphor powder into the red liquid. The anaphrodisiac disappeared into the wine, and Hulalitu wiped the rim clean to erase its telltale odor. She recapped the vial, then stepped back behind the tapestry and ducked through a low panel hidden in the wall.

This night, another man would find himself at a humiliating loss. Mother Ishtar was not ready to release Ianna.

Neither was Hulalitu.

Three

Nineveh, the Artisan's Quarter
Sixteenth Day of Ajaru

Jamin tied off the stack of woven mats and carried them to the back wall of the small workroom. He dropped them into a corner, where they exploded a billow of dust into the still air. He coughed and fanned at the gritty cloud. The heat, the dust—this city was insufferable! Whatever had possessed him to offer his labor to Uncle Hiram and Aunt Rizpah for the early season?

From the day he arrived in Nineveh, Jamin began to count the hours until he could return to his home in Aššûr. Unlike the well-appointed residence his parents enjoyed, his relative's home, like many others of the Jewish enclave in Nineveh, was tucked away in the poorer artisan quarter. The weight of the city seemed to press down on the ghetto, and its heaviness rolled down the streets from the ornate palaces and temples visible above the low rooftop of his uncle's simple home. The filth from the alleyways, the stench from open sewage ditches and animal pens—even the oppressive heat of the sun—settled low in the narrow passages between the sun-baked clay hovels. The neighborhood of rich dwellings that abutted the poorer quarter made the lowliness of his surroundings even more pronounced, and he longed for the comfort of his home. But he had committed to help his uncle and aunt, so relief from the suffocating backstreets was weeks away.

The boat trip up the Idiqlat River from Aššûr to Nineveh had been an adventure, giving him high hopes for his stay with his relatives. Lush vegetation and the cool river breeze fueled his excitement during the journey along the great waterway. He daydreamed of his uncle and aunt working among the reeds for their woven goods by its banks. His mind basked in its mild waters surging from the mountains that bordered Assyria to the northwest. He held fond memories of his family wading in the same river as it flowed past Aššûr.

Instead, he spent his days choking on dust in the sweltering backstreets, where many of the Hebrews displaced from *ha eretz* lived. He snorted his derision at the lesser Assyrian city. Nineveh, though large in its own right, did not match the splendor of Aššûr, which had enjoyed the resplendent attention of generations of Assyrian kings. As the former capital, Aššûr boasted a thousand of years of expansion and improvements, despite a period of subjugation to Babylon. Even when the second Ashurnasirpal moved the political capital to Kalḫu, Aššûr retained its importance as the religious center, for it was home to the chief national god of the same name.

Assyrian royalty only began to take serious notice of Nineveh in the past hundred years. The city's growth picked up momentum under Ashurnasirpal, and his successors maintained the pace. New construction and restoration projects were evident everywhere. Its massive walls pushed out to accommodate the flurry of activity reviving the ancient city, which seemed intent to renew its influence over Assyrian politics, religion, and society. The once despoiled Temple of Ishtar rose once again as a predominant feature of the cityscape, along with new temples to the moon god Sin and the sun gods Nergal and Shamash.

More temples were planned, of course, as there were a host of other gods to supplicate for protection and prosperity. The current king, the third Adad-nirari, had just completed work on a new temple to Nabu, the God of Wisdom and Learning. Now his workers busied themselves on the king's new palace not far from the temple plaza. Even so, Jamin doubted Nineveh would ever attain the splendor of either Aššûr or Kalḫu.

"Another hot one, eh Jamin?" Uncle Hiram stood in the doorway and squinted into the shadowed room.

"They're all hot, Uncle," Jamin muttered and barked another cough to clear his parched throat.

"Nineveh is not Aššûr, eh?"

A spark of guilt stabbed Jamin's thoughts. He wondered if he had grumbled aloud, or if his uncle was able to read minds. "It's all right, Uncle. Aššûr gets hot, too." He dipped his head, lest his eyes betray his discontent. "It's good to be here with you and Aunt Rizpah." Jamin meant it, despite his impatience with the city. "Our family misses you back home."

"And we miss you, as well. Perhaps a reunion sometime after the season . . ."

Jamin nodded. His uncle had proposed reunions with Jamin's parents for the past several years, but none had ever come to pass. Obadiah, Jamin's father and Hiram's brother, only shook his head when the subject came up. He said he doubted Hiram and Rizpah would ever step foot outside Nineveh again. Esteemed members of the city's Jewish community, their neighbors looked to Hiram for leadership and even brought religious and civil matters before him for resolution. He was not a judge in the Jewish tradition, but the enclave treated him as one. The weight of leadership rested heavily, but well, upon Hiram's shoulders, and it rooted his heart in the poor quarter. There, he and Rizpah were needed among *Adonai's* people, although they could have done much better for themselves, even prospered, if only they would return to Aššûr.

Jamin smiled. "Perhaps. After the season."

"But for now, we have work to do. Those mats are ready to be taken to market. Abijah will be waiting for them." Hiram stepped back into the alley and, with a wink, disappeared around the corner.

When his uncle had gone, Jamin settled against the wall and wiped his smudged forehead with his sleeve. He stared at the low ceiling and blinked in the flurry of dust motes his movement had roiled into the still air. No, Nineveh had nothing to commend it like Aššûr did. Except for one thing.

Jamin's heart skipped a beat at the thought.

Except for one person.

He squeezed his eyes shut.

The girl.

Four

Nineveh, the Temple Plaza
Seventeenth Day of Ajaru

Jamin lurked in the early morning shadows behind Nabu's temple. He wiped at the cold sweat on his brow, fidgeted, and glanced behind him. Skulking was not an inborn skill, and he was inept at it, which made him feel vulnerable. But he couldn't be caught. Not here.

The young Jew's route from the artisan quarter to the marketplace took him past the Mashki Gate and skirted the temple plaza. From there, it traversed a low bridge over the Tabiltu River, which bisected the city with its murky brown water. On his many journeys past the temple complex, he found his attention drawn to the magnificent Temple of Ishtar. The massive structure to Assyria's chief goddess dwarfed the lesser temples on the square.

Devoted to his worship of *Adonai*, Jamin was uncomfortable with the allure this heathen shrine held for him. He knew if his relatives were aware of these visits to the plaza, he would hear no end of it. His mind's ear burned from the nasal barrage Aunt Rizpah would launch. His chest could feel the poke of her stubby finger while she berated him for the curses he had surely brought upon their household. Uncle Hiram would stand to the side, shake his head, and ponder how many purification washings the errant lad should perform to remove the spiritual stench. His uncle would pronounce Jamin's sandals a total loss, as they had tread over defiled soil. Yes, they would have to be burned and replaced out of Jamin's own pocket as punishment for his wayward steps. Jamin half smiled at the mental image. He wasn't concerned about his faith or the temple square's impurity. After all, the entire city was pagan. What made this particular spot any worse? Besides, his interest was not of a religious nature.

He arrived behind the lesser temple shortly after sunrise. Staying to the shadows, he ducked behind a statue at the southern corner of the steps. The vantage point gave him a direct view across the street to Ishtar's temple. He leaned against the cool sculpture and let the small woven basket slip from his fingers. Yesterday, when Aunt Rizpah mentioned being short of cumin and coriander, Jamin pounced on the opportunity. He would go to the marketplace for her first thing in the morning. No, it was no trouble. He'd be happy to run the errand. It might take awhile, though, as he would want to shop the stalls for the best prices. He'd probably be gone until, oh, at least midday.

Jamin's conscience pricked him, but the story was half true. He would return with the herbs. How much time he spent shopping for bargains, though, was a weaker detail. This morning another matter would consume most of his time.

Ishtar's glorious shrine loomed across the narrow street against the pristine azure of the early morning sky. The brilliant aura from a morning sun lingering just below the roofline outlined its imposing edifice. Despite its beauty, the glare was an annoyance, for it would obscure the object of Jamin's interest in the recessed shadows of the temple's portico. He peeked around the base of the Nabu statuary and squinted into the light. He didn't have to wait long.

A subtle movement bumped up his heart rate. A flash of white glimmered between the columns, then disappeared. Jamin threw another glance down the street before tucking himself against the statue. His pulse quickened, and a familiar knot in his stomach tightened.

First, a few *ishtaritu* and *qadishtu* priestesses emerged, their pastel tunics vivid in the reflection of the sky. Then, one by one, and under the watchful eye of three *naditu* priestesses, the maidens who had not yet fulfilled their initiation rituals, wandered onto the steps to take the fresh morning air. They gravitated into small groups and tittered among themselves. The chatter stopped when three girls with small bundles emerged from between the columns. They hugged each other, several of their peers, then waved to the expressionless *naditu* who stood vigil.

After the last of their farewells, the girls hurried down the steps and set off up the road toward the affluent quarter of the city. These, Jamin surmised, were going home, their ritual devotions to Mother Ishtar completed the evening before.

Jamin searched the faces of the girls who still milled about on the steps. He craned his neck and squinted into the glow of the morning sun now poised to top the temple. When it did appear, it would blind him from the shadows of the portico. He prayed she would show herself soon, although he knew she would be the last to emerge. She would also stay to herself and avoid the cliques of prattling adolescents. The group seemed to be complete now, though. No other movement came from the portal leading from the shrine's inner sanctuary. He let his impatience override his vigilance against exposure and stretched his neck further. A sudden movement at the south end of the porch caught his eye, and he edged back against the statue.

The girl appeared from between the last two columns. As usual, a *naditu* was at her side, the same one who always seemed to be with her. His forehead tingled with another wave of heat. She was the most stunning creature he had ever seen. Her petite form stood out from among the other maidens like the immaculate Morning Star blazing its glory against a backdrop of lesser luminaries not worthy to share the same sky. Ebony tresses flowed across her slender shoulders and splayed over her sheer white tunic. Thin eyebrows drew graceful arches above her almond eyes, which, even at this distance, Jamin knew would be as breathtaking as the waist-long hair cascading over her lissome form. The morning light cast gentle shadows under high cheekbones tinged with blush and glowing through a flawless olive complexion.

As always, the girl remained aloof from the others. A heavyset *naditu* hovered at her side like a bothersome insect. The priestess leaned toward the girl's ear, her brow knit. Jamin saw the maiden shake her head and move to the end of the porch, her arms clasped across her stomach. The *naditu* frowned and propped her hands on her hips. None of the girls seemed to notice, though Jamin couldn't be sure, so focused was his attention on her. He soaked in her beauty and uttered a silent prayer of thanks that she held no small bundle to signal her departure.

It meant she hadn't yet completed the ritual. She remained untouched.

Jamin had no idea how long he stood there. Time, like everything else, faded in her ambiance. This was the fourth time he had seen the mysterious girl since he first cut through the temple plaza on his way to market. That first encounter still flushed him with a wave of embarrassment—and thrill.

It was three weeks ago. He chanced to pass Ishtar's temple after the bevy of initiates had already gathered. He glanced up as a flutter of giggles floated his direction from the temple porch. The girls closest to him glanced away when he looked, and the giggles spiked. He frowned and looked back down at the roadway. He knew who they were—*what* they were, for Ishtar had an even larger temple near his home in Aššûr. Years earlier, his mother and he had walked past it on the way to meet his father. She guided him to the opposite side of the street and whispered into his ear never to look at such girls. Their ritual represented the worst of Assyrian paganism, and to pay them any attention would surely lead a young man into ruin. He nodded but couldn't suppress a flitting look at the jewel-bedecked, colorfully dressed young women. But he was much younger then. Surely maturity had mellowed the young Assyrian Jew. He was in control. He could handle this.

Of course he could.

Jamin did not intend to look up at the temple. His gaze went there on its own. That's when he saw her, when his heart took up residence in his throat and hadn't reassumed its proper anatomical position since. The maiden sat on the stairs, her legs curled onto the riser beneath her. She kept her hands in her lap and fingered the hem of her tunic. His eyes ignored his conscience and lingered on this most glorious of beauties. And he got caught.

One moment her eyes were locked on her hem, the next moment on him. In that instant, her exquisite face burned itself into his heart. She neither smiled nor frowned. She just looked at him. He thought her visage sad—haunted, perhaps, was a better word. Her eyes betrayed neither annoyance nor invitation. She merely looked at him.

It was all Jamin could do to break his stare. Red-faced and, at the same time, heart-stricken, he found it difficult to swallow. He quickened his pace until he reached the end of the next building, where he slipped around the corner and leaned against the wall. He struggled to wrestle his heart and lungs back under control.

What's happening to me?

Jamin was no stranger to women. He knew plenty of young Jewesses in Aššûr. Several were quite comely, in fact. His father often asked why he had not settled on a suitable maiden, as Jamin had already seen nineteen summers. Most of his friends of the same age were married, many already with children. He usually shrugged off the question with a smile. There would be one someday, he would say.

But he never had a feeling like this before. Jamin fought the urge to steal another look, but it was a battle he lacked any desire to win. He edged to the end of the wall and peeked around the corner. The stair was empty. Disappointment flooded him. The other girls remained in their cliques, chatting among themselves. He couldn't have imagined her, could he?

Three out of five trips over the past two weeks conveniently planned for the same time of day proved he hadn't imagined her. Each time she held herself apart from the other girls, and each time Jamin felt himself slip further under her spell. He wanted to speak with her, to find out who she was and where she came from—and mostly why she was still here. One with beauty such as hers should have left with her little bundle long ago. That she was still here meant she remained a virgin. That was important, and Jamin clung to the hope. But how could he meet her without getting caught up in the violation that was her reason for being here?

Jamin leaned back into the shadows of Nabu's temple. Those questions would not be answered today. His heart heavy, he picked up his basket and trudged along the back wall, away from the road that passed by the Temple of Ishtar.

"He was watching again."
"I saw him."

"He's handsome."
"Very."
"I think he was looking at you, Suhru."
Suhru giggled.

Five

Nineveh, the Artisan Quarter
Twenty-first Day of Ajaru

Jamin listened to the steady cadence of Uncle Hiram's and Aunt Rizpah's breathing. At his suggestion, they retired early that evening in preparation for an early rise the next morning. There was still much to be done before they stopped work for the Sabbath, which began at tomorrow's sunset. The deep twilight in the house piqued his anxiousness at the hour. He didn't want to be late.

Satisfied they were asleep, Jamin sat up and pulled a hooded desert cloak from beneath his blanket. The garment hugged to his chest, he slipped through the window above his bed and eased himself to the narrow gap between the house and a small storage shed. He slipped to the front of the house and glanced both ways. The street was empty. Jamin stepped into the road. His head giddy with anticipation and his stomach in a turmoil, he set off at a trot down the cluttered alleyway toward the Mashki Gate.

He had wrestled with the idea for days and ran possible scenarios through his mind countless times before he settled on a plan. So much that was out of his control had to work in his favor. The timing needed be perfect. He would be careful to look like he knew what he was doing, which was far from the truth. Darkness and the cloak would help, so he felt sure he could get close to her. He was less sure what he would do once he was close. He'd sort that out when the time came. His heart left him no choice.

Jamin stopped short of the inner threshold to the city gate. There was no activity, no sound at all. Uneasiness creased his brow. He knew this was the right evening. He'd locked it in his mind as soon as he heard in the marketplace two days ago that a large caravan from Damascus approached en route to the spice markets in the East. They were to arrive this evening, before the gates to the city closed for the night. The western portal should be cluttered with camels and men by now.

Where are they?

Disappointment burned his forehead. The caravan's approach from the west made the Mashki Gate a logical entry point, but there were other entrances in the western wall. Perhaps the Quay Gate, or—wait! Of course! It didn't matter which gate they used. Their destination would be the open market square, where they could secure their animals and goods. There the travelers who desired to spend the night away from the stench of the camels could lodge in an inn that bordered the plaza. He would surely find them there.

Hope renewed, Jamin launched himself away from the wall and hurried down the street toward the Tabiltu River bridge. The route was familiar enough that he could set a brisk pace despite the darkness. He glanced to his left and squinted through the shadows at the smoky yellow halo framing the top of Nabu's temple. The plaza was ablaze with torchlight, a beacon to the ritual pleasures the Goddess of Love and Fertility offered male travelers to the city. Jamin gritted his teeth and quickened his pace.

He cut the corner of the plaza near the Tabiltu bridge and peered again over his shoulder. A hoarse shout averted a collision with two men who had stepped off the bridge.

"Watch your step, eh?" The man raised a forearm in defense.

Jamin halted just in time. "Sorry. In a hurry." He fought to settle his breath.

"What hurry?" a second voice chortled. "We have all night."

A wave of laughter rippled through the men close behind.

"Right." Jamin swallowed. "Sorry."

"He's young, Sheron. Give him some room."

Sheron chuckled. "That it, my anxious friend? This your first time?"

"Er, yes. First time." Jamin was glad the darkness hid the blush that rose to his cheeks.

"Well, come along, then. Stay close to Rimmon, here. You'll learn something." Sheron clapped Jamin on the back, and another chorus of sniggers filled the night air.

Jamin nodded and fell into step behind Sheron and Rimmon. He took advantage of the darkness to slip the cloak over his head.

The men from the spice caravan grew quiet as they trod the incline that led to the square. Torches blazed from stands patterned around the square; others poured out their light from holders attached to the sides of Ishtar's temple. The flickering yellow glow lent a jaundiced cast to the clay buildings that surrounded the courtyard. When they rounded the corner of Ishtar's temple, Jamin stopped in his tracks. He had dreamed of this time and time again over the past two days, but nothing he imagined matched the scene before him.

Along the top step of the temple, the virgin maidens stood shoulder to shoulder, hands clasped before them and their heads bowed. Shadows danced over their white tunics, and their delicate forms shimmered in the undulating light. Behind them, the *qadishtu* cult prostitutes clustered atop the risers, prepared for any of the men who did not find a desirable partner among the initiates. The scene sent a bolt of panic up his spine, and his throat went dry. *What am I doing here?*

"Go, man!" The hushed command filled his ear as the man behind Jamin stumbled into him.

Jamin lurched ahead, caught between the instinct to stare and his shame at the same impulse. He shook his head. Only one girl mattered. He had to find her before someone else did. Jamin forced his eyes down the line of girls and concentrated on their downturned faces. His fervor, and his anxiousness, increased when he couldn't spot her. He was sure he'd recognize her, but the dancing torchlight and the silhouettes of the men in front him played tricks on his eyes.

To Jamin's right, a man mounted the steps. His hand reached out, was met by the tentative hand of a maiden, and the two of them turned and disappeared into the darkness of the temple portico. Jamin began to sweat. What if she wasn't here?

"By the gods, look at her!" Rimmon's muted voice two paces to his left shattered Jamin's thoughts. He heard awe in Sheron's reply.

"I see her. Can you believe it?"

Sheron started forward, but Rimmon grabbed his arm. "I saw her first. Find another," he hissed.

Sheron turned on Rimmon. "You didn't see her first. You just spoke first. Let go!" He pulled his arm free.

Rimmon tried to slip past, but Sheron pushed him back.

"*Hoi!* Watch what you're doing!" A third man pushed Rimmon from behind.

"You watch what *you're* doing!" Rimmon stiff-armed the man in the chest. The man tripped over his own feet and slammed his back onto the pavement.

The commotion drew the attention of the other men. Some of the girls abandoned the decorum their *naditu* mentors warned them never to break and looked up wide-eyed at the ruckus. Stern hisses from the columns behind them snapped their heads back to a bow.

A cloaked figure slipped ahead of Sheron, who pushed off the man aiming a blow at Rimmon's jaw. The figure halted before the girl who had caused all the fuss. She remained still, her head bowed, apparently oblivious to the melee. Jamin peered from beneath his hood, his heart in his throat. Here he stood within reach of the splendid maiden whom for so many days he'd beheld in awe from the safety of Nabu's shadows. And he found himself at a loss at what to do next.

Jamin had no idea how long he stood there. He chastised himself under his breath for not thinking this through. Then he remembered the gesture of the man who had already made his selection. Slowly, he raised his hand toward the girl and prayed she wouldn't notice how it shook. He waited. There was no response. He wondered if an initiate was permitted to reject an offer and was about to lower it when he saw movement at her side. A graceful arm arced slowly toward his. His heart jumped as the first brush of her fingertips slid across his palm. He closed his fingers around hers. She turned and led him between the columns.

༒ ༒ ༒

"Sheron! Will you look at that?" Rimmon shrugged off a man who had grasped his shirt.

Sheron followed his friend's gaze in time to see the young newcomer disappear, hand in hand with the object of their quarrel. He wiped a dab of blood from his split lip. The two met looked at each other and broke into grins at the same time.

Sheron snorted. "Fast learner."

"Well, you told him to stay close."

Neither of them spoke. She led him down an ornate corridor lined with statues dedicated to Mother Ishtar and her sacred emblems. On one pedestal, the goddess stood with a lion at her feet, the great huntress of the northern cults. Daubed into a niche behind the statue was fresco that featured only her head and shoulders at a window, where she beckoned the viewer with a sensuous smile. A painted border of bug-eyed fish and pure white doves intertwined with oleander blossoms framed the scene. When they reached the end of the corridor, they turned down another passageway. Small doorways, some covered with damask hangings, others with ornate wooden panels, alternated on both walls the length of the hallway. Jamin jumped at a deep-throated laugh that penetrated a cloth partition as they passed. Two rooms further, he caught the breathy gasps of a gentle sob wafting through the fabric. His throat constricted. She led on, seemingly aware of nothing but her destination.

The girl stopped at the end of the hallway and pulled at a leather thong on a door panel. It swung open noiselessly. She released his hand and slipped inside. Jamin hesitated, then followed. The tiny room was bare except for a thick sleep mat, a small goblet, and a ceiling-to-floor tapestry that covered part of the back wall. A scarlet coverlet with an embroidered hem lay draped across the pad. At the end of the mat that abutted the wall, a small tufted pillow completed the ceremonial bed's adornment.

Jamin stopped by the door, mesmerized again by the maiden's beauty and seared with guilt for being in the pagan temple. The young girl stooped and lifted the cup. His eyes locked on the delicate hands cupping its bowl. She turned, dipped her head, and presented it to Jamin. He paused, unsure of his part in the heathen ritual, then accepted the cup. The maiden stepped back and eased herself onto the sleep mat. She bowed her head and nudged her shoulder out of the tunic.

"Wait!" His voice shattered the stillness like a thunderclap.

Startled, the girl raised her head in bewilderment.

Jamin hushed his tone. "I mean, wait a moment . . . please." He stooped and set the cup near the wall, then turned to face the young girl. When Jamin lowered his hood, a flash of recognition crossed her face.

"I've . . . seen you." Her first words brought his heart back into his throat. Soft and lilting, her voice caressed his ears like gentle strands from a golden harp.

"Yes. You have. I'm—"

"You're the man who passes by the temple on the way to market. You also watch from the shadows of Nabu's Temple."

Jamin's face reddened, and he averted his eyes.

Her brow creased. "What are you doing here?" The strands from the golden harp disintegrated into the crash of a tin gong. Her eyes flashed, and she drew herself up from the bed mat. One quick yank and the sleeve was back on her shoulder. "Is this some kind of joke?"

"No, I—"

"You aren't here to consummate me, are you? Who put you up to this?" She stepped toward him, her eyes on fire.

"Wait, I can explain—" A sharp crack cut him short as her right hand reddened his cheek.

He raised his hand to his face and stepped backward, his eyes wide. His foot grazed the goblet and tipped it over. The dull crack of silver against stone punctuated her malice, and the cup spilled its contents over the floor as the girl spilled venom into her words.

"How could you do something like this?" She clenched her teeth and took another step forward.

"I don't know what you mean—" He winced as her left hand raised a twin welt on the other side of his face.

"I've never been so humiliated in my entire life! Who do you think you are, coming here like this and making me a fool?"

"I didn't come to—" This time he caught her wrist on the upswing. "Stop it! Stop hitting me!"

Jamin had never been slapped. The sting on his cheeks released a rage he didn't know was in him. His anger launched a thousand images into his mind, none of them chivalrous. The last thought was the ugliest of all—that a lowly pagan harlot had dared to assault a chosen son of Abraham. He squeezed her wrist and stared her down, his face less than a hand's width from hers. Only when her eyes rounded and he saw her grimace did he regain control and ease his grasp.

Jamin's voice lowered to a growl. "Sit . . . down."

The girl stepped back. He held her arm while she lowered herself, her eyes still locked on his. He released her wrist, and she dropped it onto her lap. She lowered her eyes, and Jamin's heart lurched at the same empty expression he'd seen on her face so many times. She sat still, once again the mysterious maiden who pined alone on the temple steps.

Jamin stepped back. The adrenalin seeped away, and he fought his breath under control. He tried to assess what had happened. This was not what he planned, not at all what he envisioned their meeting would be like. He didn't know what to do next, how to rescue the moment—if rescue from such a disaster were possible.

The young girl shuddered, and a single teardrop spotted the front of her tunic. The translucent stain brought a sheen to Jamin's own eyes. He surprised himself when he moved to the bed mat and eased himself down. She stiffened and lifted her head but didn't look at him. Jamin raised the corner of his cloak and dabbed at another tear as it traced a path down her cheek. She flinched.

When he could finally muster his voice, it came in a hoarse whisper. "Yes, I am the man who goes to market and lingers in the shadows across the street. But no, I am not here to humiliate you or to make you the fool." He sighed. "If anyone is the fool, it is I."

She shifted but said nothing.

Jamin set his face. He had nothing to lose. "I don't even know you, so I don't know how this can be, but . . ." His voice fell to a murmur. "I've fallen in love with you. Yes, from the shadows across the street."

The girl turned toward him with a frown of disbelief. "How can you even—"

"I know! It's beyond reason." He settled more comfortably on the mat. "I'm not an idiot, regardless of what you may think, nor am I naïve." He looked into her eyes. "I'm not shallow about love. This doesn't happen to me. This has never happened to me."

She dropped her gaze.

Awkwardness pushed Jamin to his feet. He stepped to the wall and leaned his forearm against it as he searched for the right words. He turned his back to the wall and slid to the floor.

"You're also right that I didn't come here to consummate you."

The girl huffed and flipped her hair from her shoulder with a toss of her head.

"I came here to learn of you. Your name. Where you're from. What you like. What you don't like."

She glared at him. "I don't like being toyed with."

"Nor should you. Neither do I. I came at great risk tonight. If my family finds out where I am, I'll probably be disowned. I'm still not sure whether they know I'm gone, or what I'll tell them if they find out." Jamin rested his chin on his knees. "I didn't risk all that to toy with you."

Her intense eyes flashed to his and robbed him of his composure. The knot squeezed his stomach, and he swallowed in a vain effort to dislodge his heart.

Her gaze faltered; then she shook her head. "This is impossible. What were you thinking?"

Jamin chanced his first smile. "I was thinking that you're the most glorious creature I've ever laid eyes on. I was thinking that behind those piercing eyes there's something special, something different." He paused. "I was also thinking how sad you seem, sitting apart day after day from the other girls."

She looked away.

He continued, "I was thinking that, if I could somehow talk to you, it would settle my mind even if we never met again." Jamin measured his next words carefully. "Lastly, I was thinking how grateful I was you were still here, because that would mean you are yet untouched."

Her head jerked back, and the fire rekindled in her eyes.

Jamin cocked his head. "That's it, isn't it? That's why you're sad, why you stand aloof from the others."

"That is not your concern."

"You're right." The smile didn't leave Jamin's face. His eyes softened, and he held her look. "But what harm can it do to tell me? We'll probably never see each other again after tonight. To talk might help. If it doesn't, you've lost nothing by telling me."

She sniffed. "And what could you possibly gain from knowing?"

"My heart's desire."

She dropped her gaze back to the floor.

Jamin waited.

After several moments, she looked up and shook her hair back from her face. "All right. You want to know? I'll tell you." She set her jaw. "I'm cursed."

Jamin raised an eyebrow. "Cursed?"

"Yes, cursed. And it's not funny!"

"Of course it's not funny—if it's true. Why do you think you're cursed?"

"I've been here for over two months. I've lost count of the number of men I've received since my ceremony. Not a single one I've brought back to this chamber has been able to . . . perform. That is why I'm still here." She tipped her head back in defiance.

He pursed his lips but didn't reply.

"And, if you had come here to consummate me, you wouldn't be able to perform, either." She hurled the words at him like a challenge.

Jamin began slowly. "Is that what you really want? To be 'consummated'?"

The challenge turned to impatience. "Why do you think I'm here?"

"Why *are* you here?"

The impatience gave way to frustration. "Of course I want to be consummated. I've come of age. It's what is done."

"Is it?"

"What are you saying? You make no sense."

Jamin held her gaze. "Think for a moment. You've come to the verge of womanhood, the best and most fruitful part of your life. To celebrate, you lay vulnerable your most precious gift to a passing stranger who cares nothing for you. Now does that make sense to you?"

Her expression faltered. "It's not for me. It's for Mother Ishtar."

"Do you really think 'Mother Ishtar' cares?"

The girl flinched. "What do you mean by that?"

Jamin gauged his tone. "I mean, thousands of girls have been through these halls. There are dozens even now who await their chance to please 'Mother Ishtar.' Do you think she cares, or even knows, who they are?"

"She is the Matron—"

Jamin pressed his point. "Do you know any girls who have not submitted to this ritual?"

She set her face. "Yes. There are some. They are scorned for neglecting their sacred duty."

"Who laughs at them?"

"We do. The rest of us."

Jamin tested the edge of his advantage. "Has it occurred to you that they might be right, that they might be better off than you who laugh at them?"

Ianna's eyes flashed. "Mother Ishtar demands it of us—all of us."

"What does Mother Ishtar say? What does she do?"

"Well, I don't—what do you mean? What are you trying to say?" Exasperation flooded her tone.

Jamin softened. "Did you feel cursed before you came to this temple?"

She started. "No. I mean—"

"Maybe it's not you, then. Maybe it's this place. Maybe Mother Ishtar is not what or who you think."

The girl's eyes widened and darted around the room, as though the walls might collapse on them at any moment. "Don't say such things!" she hissed.

Jamin persisted. "You should know there is a God, one far stronger than Ishtar. A God who loves us and wants us to honor the miraculous bodies He has created for us—things Ishtar clearly doesn't want. All this God desires in return is our love and devotion."

The girl scoffed. "I know nothing of such a god. I've been given to Ishtar. It is the Mother Goddess I belong to. It's what is done!"

Jamin touched her shoulder. "I speak of the God of Abraham, Isaac, and Jacob. The only true God. Before Him, Ishtar is powerless."

She covered her ears. "Stop it. *Stop it!*"

"I only want you to see—"

"Please go!"

The ice in her tone dropped Jamin's heart from his throat to his stomach again. He rose and moved to the doorway, then paused. "There's nothing to keep you from going home to your family."

She shook her head. "I can't. I haven't—"

"You were seen coming to your chamber with a man. A man will be seen leaving. No one is here. No one will know what has or hasn't happened. If Mother Ishtar cares, she'll bring you back. If she does nothing, then you'll know."

Jamin lifted a silent prayer that something—anything—he said had made an impression.

Ianna tried to speak, but no words came. This was too confusing. Of course Mother Ishtar would know. Of course she would care. She was the Grand Matron, the goddess whose blessing would ensure a fruitful life for a young girl passing into womanhood. There was no goddess in Assyria greater than Ishtar, no god who held sway over her dominion. This young man was mistaken.

Love? Gods don't want love, they want obedience. Devotion? Gods want a devoted servant, not a servant's devotion. Wasn't that why the *Igigi* created man in the first place—to do their work for them, work they were tired of doing themselves? Of course it was. A god wanting love from a mortal man? Nonsense.

But, despite her resistance, the idea urged a gentle furrow to her brow. What if there was a god she hadn't heard of? That was possible; there were so many of them. Could there be a god who really did care for people? No, she'd have heard of him by now. Or would she? She wasn't a priestess; she didn't know gods. Her parents never instructed her on the pantheon of Assyrian deities during her childhood. The other *ishtaritu* initiates seemed to know so much more about them than she did. Perhaps this young man also knew something she didn't—as foolish as he might be, hiding in the shadows and coming here like this.

Ianna cradled her face in her hands, and confusion stabbed an ache deep within her head. Still the thought of such a god refused to release her imagination. *Should I ask? Would it only encourage him? Maybe he knows—*

She flinched as the door clicked closed.

Ianna looked up. Where the young man with the strange god stood a moment ago, the goblet lay on its side. Burgundy splashes on the wall birthed tiny rivulets down the masonry, as though they mocked her own tears. A viscous dark puddle crept from the cup toward her bed mat. She watched with stony detachment as the puddle of wine widened and reached the hem of the scarlet coverlet. The liquid surged into the loose weave and spread a dark stain through the costly fabric and into the sleep mat. The puddle thinned as the materiel sucked at the spill and drew the wine into its membranes.

Ianna felt her own energy sapping into the empty air of the chamber, like the wine dissipating into the cloth. She closed her eyes and released a slow sigh.

Ianna lowered herself onto her back and stared through half-shut eyes at the ceiling. She lay exhausted from months of disappointment, a life of unfulfilled expectations, a mind that overflowed with unanswered questions—and now by a curious man with answers that only gave rise to more questions. She rolled onto her side and curled her legs up to her stomach.

A quiet sniffle wafted into the air.

Ianna closed her eyes and drifted into a fitful sleep.

Hulalitu waited until she heard steady breathing before she stepped out through the panel behind the tapestry. The *naditu* eased herself onto the mat and stroked Ianna's hair.

She looked up and narrowed her eyes at the door.

Six

Gath-hepher, Israel
Twenty-second Day of Ajaru

"When will you return?"

Ehud and Sarah hovered behind Jonah's shoulder while he closed up his travel bag.

"I wish I knew." He stood and smiled at his brother and sister-in-law. "Hopefully, it won't be long. Only *Adonai* knows, eh?"

Jonah's niece, Miriam, dabbed at a tear on her cheek. She handed him a small parcel of food. "It's not much. There's some hard cheese, figs and dried meat. I filled a wineskin for you." Her voice caught. "I don't know how long it will last."

Jonah touched her shoulder. "Thank you, Miriam. This is fine."

Elias, Miriam's husband, managed a weak smile. "It's far to Nineveh. The road is well traveled, though, I hear. Perhaps you will meet someone to travel with. It would be safer."

"Are you scared, Uncle Jonah?" Jesse fidgeted by Miriam's side and fingered his mother's sleeve.

"Of course he's not scared," Jesse's twin, Joshua, scoffed. "He's a prophet."

Jonah laughed. "I'm not sure prophets get less scared than anyone else, Joshua. This one certainly doesn't."

Jonah secured the parcel of food to the belt of his cloak with a thong, then hefted his travel bag and his walking stick. He turned to survey the room a final time and nodded to his family gathered near the door. "Well, time to go."

Miriam sniffled and turned her head to her husband's shoulder.

"Well, take care of yourself and don't dally," Sarah huffed, her voice huskier than usual. "You still have unfinished chores around here."

Jonah smiled and hugged her with his free arm. "I'll miss you, too."

"Oh, stop it," she fussed. "You're wasting daylight."

Ehud clasped wrists with his brother. "She's right. Don't dally."

"I won't."

More embraces and Jonah was at the door. He turned back with a smile. "See you soon."

The door closed and he was gone.

Jonah plopped onto the small boulder and wiped the sweat from his forehead. His legs ached, and his lungs heaved in protest at the forced climb to the top of the ridge. The sun lingered just above the mountains, where it splayed vivid yellows and oranges into the light blue of the waning day's sky. He left Gath-hepher early that morning, and stopped only once at midday for a short rest and to nibble some cheese, meat, and a fig. He would have to pace his speed and his food, or he would never make it to Damascus, let alone Nineveh. He massaged his feet and wondered how much distance he had covered so far. Not that it mattered. He wasn't sure of the exact road to Nineveh, so keeping track of his progress seemed a waste of time. He would have to glean the way from others he might encounter who were better traveled than he. In fact, this boulder marked the farthest north Jonah had ever been.

He turned his eyes toward the east, and his breath caught. The Sea of Chinnereth spread before him like a shimmering blue carpet. Waves, roused by a gentle evening breeze, rippled over the shallow inland sea and sparkled in the bright sunlight as though *Adonai* had strewn crystalline chips across its sapphire waters. Mercifully, the incline down to the shores of the magnificent lake was more gentle than the slope he had just climbed. He breathed a prayer of thanksgiving for the respite for his body and the beauty for his soul that would close his first day of travel.

Beyond the lake lay the wastelands of the Arabian Desert. He knew vistas like this would be rare once he skirted the slopes of Mt. Hermon and entered the flatlands around Damascus. A prick of uncertainty chilled his spine and sparked a sudden urge to look back. Jonah shut his mind against the notion. There would be no more resistance to the road *Adonai* placed before him. The misadventures that marked his flight to Joppa and the pain of the losses he suffered during his return were still too fresh in his mind. He would not allow the slightest seed of a doubt to take root. God's will lay ahead, and it was the only road he would take.

His joints cracked their irritation as he rose from the boulder and shifted his bag. He planted his staff on the ground and took the next of countless steps into the unknown.

Seven

Nineveh, the Artisan Quarter
Twenty-second Day of Ajaru

"Wake up, Jamin. It's late, sleepyhead." Aunt Rizpah's voice bullied Jamin's sluggish brain into semi-consciousness. He cracked open an eye, then squeezed it shut against the next barrage.

"Come, come. It was your idea to go to bed early last evening so we could get an early start today. And here you lie. Up!" His aunt bustled out to fetch breakfast.

Jamin pushed upright on his mat. He propped his elbows onto his knees and gripped his forehead. Was it a dream, or did he really go to the temple last night? No, it was no dream. The encounter with the mystery girl loomed vivid in his mind. Every word, every look, every tear. He wondered if his face still showed red, and his fingertips went to his cheeks in search of the welts from the girl's assault.

Aunt Rizpah returned with a small flat board of cheese, bread, and figs in one hand, a small cup of goat's milk in the other. "Eat, eat. There's much to do before the Sabbath begins."

Jamin nodded and accepted the food.

"And be quick. Your uncle needs you."

When he was alone again, Jamin relived the encounter with the girl in his mind, like he had most of the night while tossing and turning just this side of sleep. He chewed slowly and searched his mind for any forgotten word or gesture that might have indicated she had understood something—anything—he had tried to say. But there was nothing. His plan was a dismal failure. Things were worse now than if he'd never gone. Before last night, she didn't know him. Now she hated him. Jamin sighed and threw the fig stem onto his plate.

"Jamin! Where are you?"

"Coming . . ."

"Hiram, I almost forgot. I promised Yulda I'd bring her a new mat. She's probably at the market wondering where I am. I need—"

"I'll go." Jamin jumped to his feet and grabbed a thick reed mat from the stack by the back wall. He was out the door before they could say another word.

Rizpah leaned out the door and stared at her nephew's figure as he disappeared around a bend in the street. "Now what do you supposed that was all about?"

Jamin hurried along the familiar route to the marketplace. When he reached the temple plaza, he ducked through the narrow lane behind Nabu's temple. This morning his prayers ran opposite to those he had raised during the past three weeks. Previously, he prayed she would be there. Now he prayed she would not. He hoped somehow his words had made it through to her, that she would have proclaimed her ritual act complete, packed her bundle, and gone home. Then he would be free to seek her out. Properly.

He rounded the back of the temple and dropped the mat as he slipped through the shadows. Breathless, he peered past the statue that had been his refuge over the past weeks. As always, white tunics milled about the steps of Ishtar's temple. His eyes flew over them, seeking her familiar form. When he didn't spot her, his heart went to his throat.

Jamin almost shouted for joy. Her usual spot on the steps at the end of the porch was empty. She wasn't—wait. His breath drained from his lungs. A glimmer of white flashed between the last two columns, and she stepped out from the shadows. Her head was bowed, her arms clasped to her waist. The pesky *naditu* leaned at her side and chattered in her ear. From the priestess's composure, Jamin judged she was scolding the girl. His jaw clenched, and he pounded the side of the marble statue with his fist. *Why didn't you leave?* His forehead burned with exasperation.

Jamin leaned further from the shadows for a better look. As he did, the *naditu* turned and stared directly toward his hiding place. He froze, caught in the open. Her glare bore hatred into his eyes.

Eight

Nineveh, the Temple of Ishtar
Twenty-fourth Day of Ajaru

"Hulalitu! You are summoned." The *naditu* motioned with her finger and turned away.

A prickle of fear scaled Hulalitu's back. She set aside her sewing and smoothed the front of her tunic with a nervous hand. A summons by Issar-surrat, the *Entu,* High Priestess to Mother Ishtar, was rarely a good thing. When she first came to the temple, her own mentor advised that it was safest to remain invisible in the Matron's service, to quietly go about one's duties beyond the notice of the High Priestess. What could this be about? Her practical knowledge of the hierarchy within the cult of Ishtar, and of this particular High Priestess, especially discomforted her.

The *Entu* of Ishtar was an exulted position, as high as any religious authority in the land. No one less than the king retained the prerogative to appoint her. It was normally a senior *naditu* that would ascend the dais of the *Entu*, but only after many years of service, and usually at the expense of her peers.

First, one had to gain admittance into the inner circle of senior *naditu* priestesses. Only those politically astute and adept at manipulation could hope to enter this privileged order. It was a risky ambition that required the aspirant to welcome the critical notice of the High Priestess herself. One misstep could mean dishonor, even banishment from the temple. To go beyond the circle and don the ceremonial accoutrements of the *Entu* put one in a position of influence unsurpassed among any other cult in Assyria.

Issar-surrat's ascension was notable in the temple annals. She arrived twenty years earlier as an ordinary *ishtaritu* dedicatee. She adapted immediately to the regimen of temple life and opted to stay on to become a *naditu*. From there, she gained prominence through manipulation and intrigue, where she pried open the door to the caste of the senior *naditu* only four years later by accumulating a significant following among the senior *naditu* council through shrewd pacts and promises. Gathering, or contriving, enough disparaging information on her competition positioned her ideally to inherit the sacred cap and necklace, and to grasp the ceremonial staff of ultimate authority when the reigning High Priestess, Xanathi, died unexpectedly six years later.

Hulalitu knew Issar-surrat well, for she had once been Hulalitu's own mentor *naditu*. Then she knew her as Prahthah, whose advice to remain invisible, while true enough, was also designed to suppress any competition in her quest for the throne of the High Priestess. Upon her ascension as the *Entu*, Prahthah changed her name to *Issar-surrat,* "Ishtar is Queen," lest anyone question her devotion to the Mother Goddess. It was this High Priestess who now summoned Hulalitu, a summons that tightened the *naditu's* throat.

Hulalitu knew Issar-surrat would not take well to waiting. So, despite her dread, she picked up her pace.

"Rise, *naditu*." Issar-surrat granted a thin smile to the prostrate Hulalitu.

"Gracious thanks, my High Priestess." Hulalitu kept her head bowed.

"It has been long since you and I have spoken."

"Yes, my High Priestess. Too long." A twinge of panic pricked her brow that she had been too familiar. If Issar-surrat sensed her discomfort, she did not let on but went immediately to the point at hand.

"You have a charge, a young initiate, I understand."

Hulalitu tensed. "Yes."

"A lovely girl, I'm told."

"She is . . . a fine girl." Nervous at the direction the conversation was going, Hulalitu struggled to keep the anxiousness from her voice.

Issar-surrat allowed a moment of silence to pass. A wave of heat flushed Hulalitu's cheeks. Now she was certain the scheming *Entu* perceived her discomfort.

"Yes, I am sure she is. Tell me, Hulalitu, when was her ceremony?"

Perspiration glistened on Hulalitu's forehead. The High Priestess was being too casual. It was obvious she knew the answer to every question she posed.

"I do not exactly recall, my High Priestess."

Issar-surrat's tone sharpened. "Do not be coy with me, *naditu*. When did she arrive at the temple?"

A bead of sweat scurried down Hulalitu's spine. "Nearly three months ago, my High Priestess."

"Three months." Issar-surrat's voice resumed its relaxed timbre. "So lovely a girl, yet she remains. Have not many who were much less comely already fulfilled their carnal rites to our Mother and departed to continue their lives in her honor?"

"They have, my High Priestess."

"Then why do you suppose she remains, Hulalitu?"

The *naditu's* voice wavered. "I . . . I am not sure. Perhaps the men are intimidated by her beauty?"

The weak reply hung in the air like an annoying odor. Issar-surrat said nothing, lending a tacit accent to the faux pas. Hulalitu kept her eyes downcast and wished she had said nothing.

"I see." Issar-surrat took on a playful tone, one a cat might use with a mouse. "My own consummation came only two nights after my initiation ceremony. Do you suggest I am less beautiful than this girl?"

"No! Of course, not, my High Priestess." Hulalitu croaked the words. "I only meant—"

"Never mind, Hulalitu. I know what you meant." A trace of condescension tinged Issar-surrat's voice. Hulalitu rankled at the knowledge that the High Priestess's benevolence only soothed the stir she had created herself. This was the Issar-surrat—the Prahtah—she knew so well.

"This girl, she has a name?"

"Yes, my High Priestess. Her name is Ianna."

"Ianna." Issar-surrat's voice grew reflective. "So close to Inanna, the Mother of our Babylonian sisters."

Hulalitu's growing fear sealed her lips.

"Perhaps she remains because the Mother Goddess wishes her to remain. Do you think?" Issar-surrat's tone became direct, her intention now clear.

Hulalitu could not respond. She never thought her intervention in Ianna's consummation rite would lead to this. She could not admit to the camphor powder she added to the ceremonial libation. This would violate a tenet ritual of the temple, one mandated by Mother Ishtar herself. But why would the High Priestess take notice of one lowly initiate among the hundreds who pass through every year? Why would she care enough to summon the mentor *naditu* for questioning?

Unless . . .

"You have no reply, *naditu?*"

"I . . . I don't know what stirs the heart of Mother Ishtar, my High Priestess." Hulalitu's heart was in her throat. She hastened to add, "I am sure, though, the girl's best interest lies with our Matron."

"'The girl.' You mean 'Ianna,' don't you?"

"Yes. Of course, Ianna." Verbalizing the girl's name stabbed Hulalitu's heart, a fact she was sure was not lost on Issar-surrat.

"And yes, you are correct. Mother Ishtar is interested above all in the welfare of her devotees. So am I. Therefore, Ianna will remain in the temple. She will assume the role of a *naditu*. See to it." Issar-surrat shifted on the chair. The audience was over.

Hulalitu didn't move. She stared at the foot of the High Priestess's dais. Issar-surrat knew. Somehow she knew Hulalitu had sabotaged Ianna's consummation ritual. She would also know why. Issar-surrat's decision to make Ianna a *naditu* would establish her as a peer and remove her from Hulalitu's control—perhaps even sever contact with her, if the High Priestess chose to send Ianna away to another temple in Kalḫu, or maybe Aššûr. Only if Hulalitu rose to the rank of a senior *naditu* could she hope to maintain any leverage over Ianna.

"My High Priestess—"

"You are dismissed." Hulalitu flinched at the ice in Issar-surrat's voice.

"But I—"

"You are dismissed!"

"Is there a chance I could become a senior *naditu?*" Hulalitu grimaced at her own words as they piled out and dropped flat onto the floor. No *naditu* ever nominated herself to the inner circle. This was unheard of, laughable. And that is exactly what Issar-surrat did.

The High Priestess's stifled smirk broke into a throaty chortle and then into a full-bellied laugh, which echoed throughout the chamber. "Why, Hulalitu." Issar-surrat lapsed into another fit of mirth. "You? A senior *naditu?* Come now, be serious."

Hulalitu lifted her tear-laden eyes to the High Priestess's chair.

Issar-surrat convulsed with laughter. "Why, I haven't heard anything as funny as this in, oh, I don't know how long!"

"I only thought—"

"*Dismissed!*" All levity disappeared from the High Priestess's voice. "See to the girl's—to Ianna's—ceremony. Without delay."

Hulalitu hid a quiet sob. "Yes, my High Priestess."

Issar-surrat's glare tracked Hulalitu's steps to the chamber door. The click of the latch echoed through her quarters and all went still. As the High Priestess eased herself back into her chair, a familiar shell of numbness slid up the back of her skull and over her brain. Her vision narrowed, and everything on the periphery went fuzzy. Her breath slowed; her arms went limp.

"Yes, my Mistress." Issar-surrat slurred the words through her trance.

"You have done well."

"Thank you, Mother Ishtar. The girl will soon be under my control."

"Your control? The girl will be under my control!"

"Yes, Mistress, of course. What is mine is yours." Issar-surrat flinched at a needle stab of pain in her temple.

"Indeed, it is. How good it is for you to remember that."

"Yes, my Mistress."

※ ※ ※

"Hulalitu, what is it?"

The *naditu* slumped in the doorway and gripped the jamb for support. Her face was blank, her cheeks wet with tears.

Ianna sat up on her bed mat. "What has happened?"

Hulalitu cleared her throat. "I have just returned from a summons."

Ianna knit her brow. "A summons?"

"To the chambers of the High Priestess."

The young girl cocked her head.

"Issar-surrat has taken notice of you." Hulalitu's voice tripped over a shallow cough.

"Of me? Why? How?"

"I . . . don't know how. You have found . . . favor in her eyes. In Mother Ishtar's eyes." The *naditu* folded her arms.

"Favor?"

"You are to become a *naditu*. I am to see to your ceremony immediately."

Ianna's face went white. "A *naditu*? How can that be? I have not yet even completed my *ishtaritu* rite."

"That is of no consequence. You are to remain in the service of Ishtar."

A wave of panic flooded Ianna's head. "I can't. I'm supposed to go home. Complete my ritual and . . . go home." Her voice choked. She rose and faced Hulalitu. "I never wanted to become a priestess. That was not why I came."

Hulalitu's face tightened. "It is an honor to serve Mother Ishtar. She has determined your fate. You will stay."

Tears spilled from Ianna's eyes. "No! I want to go home. You can't keep me here. I—"

A resounding smack filled the room as Hulalitu's hand found its mark. Stunned, Ianna dropped to the floor, her hand covering a rising welt on her cheek. She hung her head, and her body convulsed.

"You . . . you will remain in your chamber to prepare your heart and mind for the ceremony. It is tomorrow." The *naditu* pivoted on her heel and exited the room.

Hulalitu leaned against the wall outside the door. She closed her eyes against the quiet sobs that filtered through the gap under the wooden panel.

Nine

Nineveh, the Privileged Quarter
Twenty-fifth Day of Ajaru

Hani jolted at the rap on the door. She paused over the dried herbs she was sorting while Mordac napped in the back room. She wiped her hands on a scrap of cloth and pulled open the door.

"Are you the mother of Ianna?"

The young girl was dressed in a white tunic and held a small bundle in her hands. Hani recognized the garb as the same she had seen her daughter wear on the steps of Ishtar's temple. The girl was lovely, Ianna's age, Hani surmised. But she looked ill at ease.

"Yes, Ianna is my daughter. Who are you, please?" Hani tried to keep an even tone, but a sudden fear rooted itself in her stomach.

"My name is Suhru. I live at the end of this street."

"Of course. I recognize you now. Please, come in out of the heat." Hani stepped aside, but the girl only shook her head.

"Thank you, but I can't stay. I only came to tell you—" Suhru cleared her throat.

The fear rose to Hani's throat and gelled into a lump. "Tell me what, dear? Is this about . . . Ianna?"

Suhru nodded. She threw a furtive look over her shoulder, then blurted, "They're making her a *naditu*. It's all over the temple. I've just been released, but I wanted to let you know." She lowered her eyes. "They don't always tell the family."

Hani didn't understand. "A what? I don't know much of the temple. What does this mean?"

The girl's face flushed. "She's to become a full priestess of Mother

Ishtar."

Myriad thoughts raced through Hani's mind, and none of them comforted her. "I still don't understand. Please come in. I have questions—"

"I can't. I really can't." Suhru turned to go.

"No, please. You must tell me. I don't understand the temple rites. I never wanted Ianna to go there in the first place. It's just not right, the ceremony."

The girl reddened. "I must go."

Hani reached out and grasped the bundle. She pulled Suhru to her as the floodgates that restrained her anxiety burst open. Fears bottled up in her for months found their voice and tumbled out over each other.

"Please, you must tell me. What has happened to Ianna? Why has she not come home? I've tried to inquire at the temple, but no one will let me see her. She's been gone for months. Is this normal? Shouldn't she have been back by now? How long were you there? What are they doing with her? Is she well? She's not sick, is she?"

The girl tried to pull loose from Hani's grip. "I shouldn't have come here. We can't talk about what goes on in the temple."

"Suhru . . . *please?*" Hani's eyes brimmed. She stroked the girl's arm in desperation. "She's my only daughter. My only child."

Suhru eased her struggle to pull free. She glanced both ways along the street. "Maybe I could come in for just a moment. I should not be seen talking—"

"Yes, please." Hani pulled the startled girl through the door. "I have some herbal tea I can make—"

"No. No, thank you. I really can't stay." Suhru fidgeted and glanced back at the door.

Hani clasped her hands across her stomach. "What of Ianna? What of my daughter?"

Suhru dropped her gaze. "You know of the *ishtaritu* ritual, don't you?"

Hani stifled her reply out of respect for the young girl who had just completed her own rite of passage.

The girl blushed. "Of course you do. Well, Ianna, for some reason—reasons nobody can understand, she's so beautiful—has not completed her ritual."

Hani's heart leaped in spite of the fear that gripped her stomach. *Ianna remains untouched!* Perhaps there was still time to bring her home. There must be a time limit, some kind of rule she could appeal to that would free Ianna from her obligation.

Suhru cleared her throat. "The *naditu* assigned to her holds her close. No one has been able to speak with her, to find out what the . . . problem might be."

Hani nodded, still afraid to give her thoughts voice.

The young girl looked down. "We heard yesterday that the High Priestess believes Mother Ishtar smiles upon Ianna. She has called for a *naditu* ceremony for her."

Hani creased her brow, still unsure of what all this meant. "So, after this ceremony will she be allowed to come home?"

Suhru murmured, "Ianna will not be coming home. A *naditu* remains at the temple. For always."

The ball of fear that bulged in the back of her mind erupted and paralyzed her. Her voice was a hoarse whisper. "Not coming home? Ever?"

The girl nodded.

"Who is this? What's going on?" Mordac's mouth gaped in a broad yawn as he stepped from the back room.

Hani's vision tunneled. Her pulse pounded in her temples until she thought they would burst. Her breath cut to short rasps, and she turned toward her husband.

"*You!*"

Mordac scratched his neck, then paused. "What?"

Hani flew into the chest of her husband and nearly toppled him over. Mordac's eyes went wide as his wife gripped him by the sides of his head.

"You were the one who insisted Ianna go to the temple for that cursed ceremony! You said, 'It's what is done,' as though the honor of our only child meant nothing in the face of this cursed, vile, ritual!

What kind of father are you?"

Mordac tried to gain control. "Woman! You will not talk to me in that tone of—"

"Don't you dare talk to me!" Hani grabbed fistfuls of his shirt and pulled him to her face. "You've killed our daughter!"

"What are you talking about?" Mordac tried to pull loose from Hani's grasp.

"Ianna is to be a priestess! They're keeping her there! Do you hear me? Our daughter is never . . . coming . . . home!" Her fists pummeled her husband's chest with each of her choked words. He grasped her arms as she collapsed into sobs.

"Ianna . . . is . . . *dead* to us." A wail choked in her throat, and she fainted.

Mordac held his limp wife by the arms, still unsure of what just happened. Then he remembered the girl.

"Can you tell me what—"

The door closed, and the girl was gone.

Issar-surrat slipped the pale blue tunic over Ianna's head and the *naditu* ceremony was over.

"May you thrive in the service of Mother Ishtar." The High Priestess's lips curled in a half smile. She glanced at Hulalitu, who stood with the other *naditu* priestesses in the cella of Ishtar's temple. Hulalitu kept her eyes downcast during the entire ritual. So did Ianna, as she stood naked before the audience of priestesses until Issar-surrat incanted the homily of dedication and bestowed on her the tunic of her new status. Such public nudity would normally have been an unbearable embarrassment for her. Today, though, even the open exposure of her body failed to penetrate the stupor of dread at her induction into temple service.

She stared at the smooth floor of the ceremonial chamber, where her *ishtaritu* initiation ceremony had taken place—the euphoria of that ritual replaced by the disconsolation of this one. Issar-surrat turned on her heel and retreated to the rear of the room to supplicate before the statue of Ishtar. The white tunic that had served as Ianna's public wardrobe for the past three months lay flat at her feet, her hopes of returning home to a normal life lying with it.

The convocation of priestesses quietly broke up. Only the muted swish of their tunics and brush of sandaled feet over the floor broke the stillness. Ianna remained where she stood. The faces of her mother and father hovered in her mind, her father's more faintly than her mother's. The niche where she slept as a child loomed in the background of the vision. She knew her belongings—trinkets, memorabilia, her favorite woolen blanket—still lay neatly on her bed mat. Her mother's cheerful summons to breakfast resonated through her mind's ear, her father's guttural cough less so. Tears brimmed in her eyes. The images of the past vanished at the click of the latch on the cella door.

Ianna heaved a sigh and raised her eyes. The room was empty, but for herself and one other *naditu*. She looked at Hulalitu without expression. Her former mentor beheld her with an equally empty stare. After several moments of silence, Hulalitu cleared her throat.

"There will be duties to learn. I can help . . ." She bit her lip.

Ianna said nothing. She brushed a wisp of hair from her face and curled it behind her ear. She folded her hands in front of her and padded across the room to the chamber door. She felt Hulalitu's eyes bore through her as she passed but did not meet her gaze.

"Ianna . . ."

The door latched behind Ishtar's newest *naditu,* and the hall was silent.

Hulalitu took a deep breath to stifle a sob. She had intended to keep Ianna for only a week, maybe two. As the weeks came and went, though, she delayed Ianna's release for one more day, then another. She rationalized just one more measure of camphor powder; each dose was to be the last. But the beautiful young *ishtaritu* initiate had infected her, and there was no help for it. Life in the temple for Hulalitu was unimaginable without Ianna. She could care for the girl, yes, even better than her own family, she was sure of it. She suppressed the memories of the times she had denied Ianna's mother when she came to inquire about Ianna. Her mind blocked out the ashen pallor of helplessness in the woman's face, the haunted look in her eyes, and the choked pleas that had driven her to her knees the last two visits. No, Ianna was hers. It was meant to be.

Hulalitu's gaze settled on the wispy tunic on the floor. She stepped over to the puddle of sheer fabric, stooped, and picked it up. She rubbed the gauzy material between her fingers, then hugged it to her chest. Another sob convulsed her chest before she turned and left the silent hall.

When the door closed, Issar-surrat stepped from behind the statuary of Mother Ishtar. She narrowed her eyes at the closed door and stroked her cheek in thought.

Ten

Nineveh, the Artisan's Quarter
Twenty-fourth Day of Ajaru

Jamin jerked his head up. "I'm sorry. Did you say something?"

His uncle chuckled at him from his work mat. "Daydreaming, eh?"

The young man reddened. "Yes, I guess so."

He couldn't tell his uncle what he dreamt about—the young girl who languished in Ishtar's temple. The girl who, despite her verbal and physical assault that evening in her bedchamber, had captivated his heart beyond rescue. What was it about her? She was beautiful, of course, but he'd known other beauties. Why was this one different?

It was forbidden to marry outside *Adonai's* chosen ones, he reminded himself. Didn't Mosheh write that a man was to marry within the tribe of his own father? But this was Assyria. His father's family was brought to a land of exile, separated from the tribe of his fathers. Did all of the Law still apply?

His uncle's voice penetrated his musings. "I said we will miss you when you return to Aššûr. You have been much help to your Aunt Rizpah and me. This has been a good season at market, and it is yet early. We have you and your father's graciousness to thank for that."

"It's been an honor to be here. You are dear to my father, and you've become dear to me, too. We all wish you and Aunt Rizpah would move to Aššûr to be closer to family."

Hiram sighed. "Yes, that would be good. But there are others here who depend upon us. Our earnings help support those less fortunate than ourselves."

Jamin glanced around the hovel. *Less fortunate? How could that be?* "Their fortune is increased by your faithfulness." He smiled at his uncle.

Hiram chuckled. "Oh, I don't know about that. We keep each other afloat, praise *Adonai*, but not by much."

"I'll miss you and Aunt Rizpah, too." He meant it.

"Perhaps a reunion next year. Who knows?" Hiram shrugged and tied off the reed mat on his lap.

Jamin lapsed back into his thoughts about the young girl. She filled his world to the point he thought it would burst. Her almond eyes, her perfect lips, and her graceful figure all crowded his dreams at night and his thoughts during the day. The rock-hard lump in his stomach had not softened since he'd touched her shoulder before they parted that night. Although she had recoiled from his touch, he cherished the memory of his fingers across her silky skin, how the caress flamed the desire to spirit her away from the suffocating confines of the heathen temple. He needed to see her again, perhaps try to speak with her one more time. He couldn't leave the city with such a sour taste from their last encounter. But there was another possibility.

"Uncle, would you have any need of me during the rainy season?" Jamin tried to sound nonchalant.

Hiram raised a quizzical eyebrow. "Perhaps. Why do you ask?"

"I just wondered. There seems to be so much for you and Aunt Rizpah to do. I just wondered . . ."

"We harvest the reeds for our mats during the rainy season, when the plants are moist and supple. Then we cure the stalks and cut them to length. After that, we weave for the next season." His uncle paused. "So, yes, there is always work to be done."

"Perhaps upon my return to Aššûr, I can ask Father to spare me a little longer. I could come back after the heat?" Jamin kept his eyes on his work, lest he betray too much enthusiasm for the thought of returning to Nineveh. To the girl.

Hiram set aside his blade. "Something has changed in you."

A nerve twitched in Jamin's cheek. "Changed?"

"It was apparent to us shortly after you first arrived that you were not pleased to be here. We cannot offer the amenities of your father's house in Aššûr. We perceived you were anxious to return home."

Jamin could feel his cheeks flush. "I'm sorry if I came across as—"

"There's no need to apologize." Hiram's eyes creased behind the kindly smile Jamin had come to love. "No offense was taken. Your aunt and I knew before you arrived that a young man accustomed to the comforts of a city such as Aššûr would likely become restless in the poor quarter of a lesser city. Nineveh was great once, and she is on the rise again, but she cannot compete with Aššûr for comfort . . . or opportunity."

Hiram's emphasis on the last word did not escape Jamin's notice. A seed of alarm took root in the back of his head. He waged a hurried debate with himself whether to pursue his uncle's thought, or let it lie. The argument to pursue won.

"Opportunity?" He fought to keep his voice even.

Hiram chuckled. "Come now. You're a healthy young man. In the last message from your father, he voiced some concern over your resistance to marriage, despite arrangements they attempted. I told him your time would come." The elder man cocked his head. "Has it?"

The question brought a wave of heat to Jamin's forehead. "What do you mean?"

His uncle's smile softened the condescension in his sigh. "I mean that your impatience to return has not only waned but has been replaced by a notion to remain—and now return within the year. Our fortunes have not changed; neither have yours. There must be something that interests you—someone who interests you?—in Nineveh to cause such a change of heart. Am I far wrong?"

Jamin searched for the right words. "Uncle, it is true I come from a more . . . an easier life in my father's house. But here in Nineveh there is something I see that I don't see at home."

Hiram rested his arms on the finished mat. Jamin laid aside his trimming blade.

"There is a sense of community, of family, here that is lacking in the Jewish life of Aššûr. You have so little—" Jamin tripped over his words.

A gentle laugh from his uncle dissipated his embarrassment. "I understand what you're saying, Jamin. It's all right."

Jamin stumbled back into his explanation. "I mean, to the world it would seem that you have so little. Your home, while comfortable, is not one an ambitious man would aspire to have. Tomorrow's dinner is assured only by today's sale of a mat or a basket in a fickle marketplace. A season of poor weather, an illness, the Idiqlat overflowing its banks, a blight—any of these things could wipe out your means of earning a living with little warning."

Hiram nodded. "This is all true. We entrust our survival to *Adonai.*"

"You live on the edge of starvation, yet you freely give of what you do have to those who—how did you put it?—are 'less fortunate' than yourself." Jamin shook his head. "I see nothing of this in the Jewish community in Aššûr. Of course, everyone tithes to the fund for the Temple in Jerusalem. All give alms to the poor, but only from their excess. The first priority is for one to provide for his present comfort, then to bolster his savings to ensure continued comfort. Only then do they look beyond their own households. I wonder what would happen if hard times fell upon Aššûr. Would the Jewish community pull together, or would it fragment, while each sought relief for himself before he considered his brother?"

"And this is what draws you to Nineveh?" Hiram set his mat aside.

"I do like this, what I see. It is very . . . attractive." Jamin fell silent.

His uncle's voice dropped to a whisper. "I'm glad you are pleased."

Jamin returned to his work. Guilt over his evasion was eased by the fact that he had told his uncle the truth. The common bond within the Jewish community in Nineveh warmed Jamin's heart. The consideration families displayed toward each other had caught his attention, so what he told his uncle was true. It was attractive. Of course, he didn't reveal the whole truth behind why he wanted to stay, but Jamin could rationalize his decision to withhold information about the girl due to the hurt and confusion it would cause his beloved aunt and uncle. It wasn't deceit; it was protection.

That's what it was. Protection.

Jamin trudged to market, the reed basket slung over his shoulder. The sun, although past its zenith, hung high overhead, as if to delay its glide to the western horizon. He wiped his brow as he passed the Mishkal Gate, then glanced toward the Temple of Ishtar. He veered by habit toward the path behind Nabu's temple, but then he paused. There was little point in sneaking. The *ishtaritu* initiates would not be out, and, even if they were, it was clear from the girl's words and the *naditu's* ugly look that his hiding place had been compromised.

His mind flashed back to the night he had raced down this same road in his haste to find the caravan. He perked at the unexpected thrill of the escapade—and the fear that being discovered had brought into his otherwise mundane life. Then he grimaced at the memory of his disastrous encounter with the young girl. He remembered little of the trudge home, other than the misery that shrouded his mind as darkly as the night enveloped his body. What would happen the next time he saw her, when she saw him? An ache filled his heart—a strange blend of warring emotions that would only be eased at the next encounter, however it might turn out.

There would be no chance of spotting the girl along the road behind Nabu's temple, though, even if she were out. The other alternative was bold. He could pass in front of Isthar's temple, like he did the first time he saw her. It was a way to reassert his right to be there, not having to skulk behind pagan statues. This was a public byway, after all. He could use it anytime he wanted.

So he would.

Jamin turned onto the main route through the temple square. He kept his head bowed to the road, but his gaze flicked to the edifice of Ishtar's temple as he passed. He noted movement between the columns. Several figures loitered in the shade of the portico. Two of them leaned out from the porch and peered down the road in the direction he traveled. One wore the blue tunic of the *naditu* and the other a pastel of a *qadishtu*. He surreptitiously scanned the groups of women, but none of them wore the pure white tunics of the *ishtaritu*. Jamin returned his gaze to the road ahead and wondered why he had bothered to divert through the square. What was he trying to prove? And to whom was he trying to prove it?

As he reached the end of the steps, a movement by the last column caught his eye and he glanced up. She was leaning against the smooth white column, her ebony hair flowing over the back of—her light blue tunic! A *naditu?* She was no longer a lay maiden who awaited her ceremonial consummation, but a permanent priestess in the Temple of Ishtar.

How could this be?

Jamin stopped midstride. He dropped the basket from his shoulder and stared up at her, oblivious to the attention it drew from the other priestesses and passersby. The girl took no notice. She kept her gaze at her feet. For the longest time, Jamin stood immobilized by the horror of the pagan blue defiling the object of his desire. The next moment—he was not sure exactly when—her eyes were on him. Her face betrayed no expression, much like the first time she caught him staring at her. This time Jamin did not redden with embarrassment and drop his head. He reddened with despair. And anger.

The two locked eyes, and everything else in Jamin's world halted. He felt betrayed, although he knew he had no right to. She had made no promises. Quite the opposite—she had told him to leave, to get out of her life. But the short time Jamin had spent in her chamber gave him a skewed sense of ownership over her fate, or at least a vested interest in her life. He felt the urge to march up the steps, grab her by the arm, and drag her away. But he couldn't move. He could only stare.

The cough of a man passing by broke his stupor. The girl remained still, her expression unchanged. He searched her eyes, but there was nothing there. Slowly, Jamin cocked his head, the question unvoiced but obvious. She drew her head back, and he saw the trace of a single tear glistening on her cheek in the bright afternoon sun. He began to mouth the word *why*, but she pushed away from the column and stepped into the portico's shadows.

"It's not good to stare, boy."

The man's voice filtered through the deafening pulse in Jamin's ears. A stranger stood before him with the dropped basket in his hands. Jamin didn't respond.

The man pushed the basket against Jamin's chest and took him by the arm. "Come. It'll pass."

Jamin tottered forward as the man guided him toward the Tabiltu River bridge. He looked back over his shoulder, but she was gone.

Eleven

Aram, near Mt. Hermon
Twenty-fifth Day of Ajaru

The sun slipped behind the ridgeline of Mt. Hermon and left behind a sky ablaze with red and the cap of last season's snow tinged with magenta. The great mountain's shadow provided blessed relief from the heat of the desert floor, and Jonah paused to take in a deep lungful of the evening air.

He started early that morning after a lean breakfast of figs and a strip of dried goat meat. The road became more hospitable after he mounted the rise from the northern shore of the Sea of Chinnereth, and it leveled out on its trek toward Damascus. His achy joints welcomed the even terrain, another blessed relief from the hilly paths of northern Galilee. To the east, the Arabian Desert spread to the horizon, mottled brown and barren against the deep blue of a cloudless sky. Jonah knew he would soon enter this wilderness on his journey to Nineveh, but he hoped to delay the ordeal as long as possible. He hugged the lower slopes of the western mountains as he picked his way along the rock-strewn road. The heights gave him comfort born of familiarity from a life spent on the slopes around Gath-hepher. He knew when he lost sight of the highlands he would feel very much on his own.

Tonight, though, he would rest in the protection of Mt. Hermon's cool shadows. He stretched out beneath an acacia tree and massaged his legs. Travelers passing through Gath-hepher's valley from the north were few, and his knowledge of the territories outside Israel was limited, but he believed another day's journey should put him within sight of Damascus's gates. He pulled his cloak to his chin, and his mind worried over the road ahead. After Damascus came the open desert.

Tadmor would provide the next oasis. Then what? Perhaps, as Ehud had suggested, he might meet up with a caravan.

The staccato bark of a jackal from the hills behind him pricked a nerve on the back of his neck. He pulled his staff closer to his side and slinked down into his travel cloak. Yes, he decided, it would be good to meet up with a caravan.

Jonah jolted awake at the sudden onslaught of sunlight early the next morning. The daystar cleared the eastern horizon over the barren flatlands with a vengeance. The blazing orb drenched the slopes of Mt. Hermon with radiance, cascading its luminescence down the mountainside and into the niche where he had snuggled for the night. He blinked into the glare and struggled to sit up. His stiff back advised him against any sudden moves, so he paused to orient himself.

The main road lay a short distance to the east. From his vantage point, Jonah could see the ancient trade route pull away from the mountain, then veer into the desert on its course toward Damascus. Tonight there would be no cool place to rest if he did not reach the city gates before they closed. That worrisome thought prompted his decision to munch breakfast while he walked.

Jonah hobbled off on cramped leg muscles toward the main road. When he reached the beaten path, he looked back toward the south. He hunched his shoulders against one more urge to return to the comfort and familiarity of Israel, drew a deep breath, and turned his face north. Then he took the first steps into the hostile wasteland that would become his home for the next—well, who knew how long?

"The prophet leaves his homeland, Mistress."
　　"It is to his destruction."

"Your wish, my Mistress?"
"Watch and wait."

Twelve

Damascus
Twenty-seventh Day of Ajaru

Jonah slipped through Damascus's southern gate just as the night watch began preparations to secure the city. Jeroboam's raid, although several weeks past, still loomed fresh in the minds of the Arameans, and they went about their tasks in a terse mood. Elihu ben Barak, Jeroboam's senior commander and Jonah's lifelong friend, had gloated over how the Damascenes had been forced to watch camel loads and oxcarts of booty exit by this same gate. He believed, though, that the sting of defeat at the hands of a people Aram had oppressed not so long ago was worse than the loss of their treasure. He said Jeroboam accented the sting when he chose not to leave a contingent of soldiers behind. The surrounding nations would know for certain of Israel's resurgent power, and Jeroboam's decision to leave no military presence in the city enhanced the impression of Israel's confidence.

Elihu was certain the people of Damascus actually wished Jeroboam had left an encampment. Then there would at least have been someone to harass in retaliation. Jeroboam denied Israel's former tormentors even that small measure of revenge. The tense mood of the city was palpable from the moment Jonah walked through the gate, and it left him in a quandary.

He dithered whether to lodge at an inn. His speech would surely identify him as an Israelite, and he didn't want to invite another brawl like the one in Megiddo's backstreet tavern those weeks ago—especially since this time he would be involved rather than observing. He paused at the entrance of the marketplace to ponder his next move.

"You journey alone." The gruff voice came from his left.

He spun toward the voice.

"You travel beyond Damascus." The voice grew coarser.

Jonah stepped back and squinted into the deepening shadows. The voice addressed him in excellent Hebrew, but that accent . . . where had he heard that accent?

"Who . . . where are you?"

A shadow shifted and stepped away from the wall. In the dim light, it formed a massive figure easily a head and a half taller than Jonah and twice as wide. The stranger's face was all but lost behind a bushy salt-and-pepper beard. His brow supported a keffiyeh that was once probably white but now wore a crust of grime, as did the striped brown robe that swept the ground around his feet. A wide cloth sash girded his waist, from which hung a curved sword free of any scabbard.

"I say you travel beyond the city."

"I'm . . . not sure," Jonah stammered, his eyes glued to the weapon.

"Not sure? You do not know where you go?" The behemoth's guttural tone suddenly reminded the prophet of his friend, Moshe ben Gideon, who had died saving the lives of Jonah and his friends only a few short weeks back. It summoned a wave of sorrow, but the emotion broke over his sudden recognition at the stranger's accent. It was the accent of the young foreigner who had killed Moshe in his attempt to kidnap the young Leah. Jonah narrowed his eyes and took another step back. He glanced into the market square. It was now empty. The two of them were alone.

The stranger cocked his head and rested a casual hand on the grip of his sword.

Jonah tried to steel his voice. "I . . . I haven't decided yet. You haven't answered my question. Who are you?"

"I am Akhyeshah of Tadmor. A provisioner of caravans. I travel to my home from Moab, where I have found a wife." The man kept his eyes glued to Jonah's.

Jonah looked around. "Wife?"

Akhyeshah nodded. "I return when her bride price is complete. In three full passages of the moon. Not before."

Akhyeshah stepped toward him, and his bulk filled Jonah's view of the dusky sky. "We travel together."

"But . . . I haven't decided where I'm going yet," Jonah stammered as he shrank back from the towering man.

"You go beyond Damascus. You are of Israel. You should not stay in Damascus. They do not like you here." The whites of Akhyeshah's eyes were now all Jonah could make out in the failing light.

"But—"

"We stay at the inn tonight. I talk. You stay quiet. We leave in the morning." Akhyeshah turned and took two long strides into the marketplace. He stopped and looked back.

Jonah stood rooted in place, petrified at the thought of traveling with the giant. His size was fearsome enough, but the heavy weapon at his belt unraveled what was left of Jonah's nerves.

"Come. Now." Akhyeshah waited for Jonah to follow, then turned and strode across the open square.

Jonah picked up his pace, although he wasn't sure why.

The early morning sun threw an intense yellow beam across the room through a small window near the door. Jonah's eyelids twitched when the ray hit him full in the face. He groaned and turned on his side.

The inn was small, dirty, and crowded. There were no side rooms, so everyone slept in a common area on dusty straw mats that offered little protection against the stone-hard dirt floor. Jonah and Akhyeshah were the last boarders to arrive. The prime traveling season was underway, and the city was full. They had tried two other inns before this one, and now Jonah realized why Akhyeshah came here last. The two men took the only spaces left on the floor. When the first light of the morning splashed over Jonah's face, he also realized why this was the last spot claimed.

He squinted and struggled to sit. The previous night in the gulley at the foot of Mt. Hermon, as primitive as it was, was more restful than on the floor of this inn. He muttered and twisted around to look for

63

Akhyeshah, who had settled a short distance away. He was gone.

Jonah scanned the bodies sprawled across the floor. Throaty snorts and serrated snoring, punctuated by an occasional hacking cough, filled the room. An invisible fog of garlic, rancid wine, and other less pleasant odors permeated the air. He covered his nose, wondering how he'd ever been able to sleep through the noise and the stench.

He groped behind himself for his staff but felt only the cool dirt floor. He spun around and scoured the small space against the wall for his pouch of provisions. They were gone, too.

He muttered under his breath and cursed his timidity. Why had he let the stranger bully him? He was never going to make it to Nineveh at this rate. What little silver he brought with him was gone, along with his food. He struggled to his feet, intent to escape the stifling air and to find the man who stole his belongings, although he had no idea what he could do against that sword even if he did find the man.

Jonah tiptoed around and over men. Several lodgers stirred, and Jonah nearly stumbled over a bulky figure who flipped onto his back just as Jonah stepped over his outstretched legs. When he reached the door and yanked it open, the hinges squealed on their rusty pins and a brilliant swath of light flooded in. A chorus of shouts and curses from those nearest the door propelled him through the doorway. He slammed the door shut.

The side street in front of the lowly inn opened into the marketplace a short distance away. Jonah saw a flurry of activity between the low buildings. He looked both ways along the alley, but there was still no sign of Akhyeshah. Jonah set his jaw and made his way toward the market square. When he reached the end of the street, he stepped into the open plaza and paused, unsure of his next move.

"You sleep late. Time to leave."

Jonah jumped at the deep voice over his shoulder. He pivoted and saw Akhyeshah leaning against a shadowed wall. Two dates lay in the palm of his open hand, which he promptly flipped into his mouth. He stepped out of the shadow and the intense morning sun flashed from the blade of the sword at his hip. Jonah retreated a step. Akhyeshah was even more imposing in the daylight than he was in the dusk, if that were possible.

The huge man retrieved Jonah's staff and travel parcels from where they lay against the wall. He tossed them to Jonah, who fumbled his attempt to catch them. When he lifted the fallen parcels, he noticed the food sack felt bulkier than he remembered it being the day before. He glanced at Akhyeshah.

"I get more food. Tadmor is a four-day walk." With that, the big man grasped his own staff from against the wall.

"I can pay—"

Akhyeshah dismissed him with a wave of his hand.

"But—"

"Follow." Akhyeshah set a brisk pace toward the north entrance of the marketplace.

Jonah stooped to pick up his staff. He grumbled to himself, then hurried to catch up with the hulk, who had already reached the end of the square. His mind wavered between puzzlement and irritation at the unexpected turn of events and particularly at why he felt compelled to comply with the man's every word.

He jutted out his jaw. *I wonder what he would do if I said "no."*

Akhyeshah led the way along the ancient thoroughfare that bisected the city from north to south. Low buildings lined both sides of the narrow street, many in serious disrepair. They reminded Jonah of the derelict buildings he encountered in Megiddo's low quarter. He almost expected to see Ari, the crooked keeper of the tavern in which he had taken refuge during his flight to Joppa, emerge from one of the hovels. As they made their way toward the north gate, their surroundings improved. Newer and sturdier buildings, some with modern construction of stone and even occasional woodwork, replaced the teetering mud-brick structures of the inner city. Jonah's struggle to keep up with his companion's pace, though, gave him little time to admire the architecture.

The two men finally reached the gate. Akhyeshah diverted his path toward a well near the city wall. He lifted a water skin suspended across his chest on a leather thong.

"Nothing but desert to Tadmor. We need full water."

Jonah groped at his waist, but realized that the wine skin he left home with was gone. "I had a wine skin. I don't know what—"

"Wine skin? You need water." Akhyeshah shook his head.

Jonah reddened. "Perhaps back at the market I can buy a—"

"No time. We use mine." The big man turned and pulled at a rope lying on the edge of the well.

Jonah clenched his jaw. The abrupt dismissals were beginning to aggravate him.

Can't he even let me finish a sent—

"Pull." Akhyeshah thrust the end of the rope toward Jonah without looking back.

Jonah rolled his eyes but took the rope and looped it around his waist. As he walked backward, he felt the earthenware container grate against the inside wall of the cistern as it rose from the water level far below.

"Stop." Akhyeshah reached down and pulled the vessel over the lip of the well. Jonah returned and dropped the rope in a heap on the dirt.

Akhyeshah lifted the heavy clay container by the brim with one hand and poured its clear contents into the narrow mouth of the skin bladder. Jonah didn't see a single drop splash down its side, so steady was the man's hand. The flask filled, the giant tossed the earthenware container onto the pile of rope and plugged his water skin. In one movement, it was back over his head and resting under his arm.

"Come." The staff was back in Akhyeshah's hand, and he strode off toward the gate.

Jonah huffed, retrieved his staff, and set off after the hulk. "Can you slow down just a little?"

"He leaves Damascus."
"No matter. There are perils in the desert."
"Yes, Mistress."
"See to it."

Thirteen

Nineveh, the Privileged Quarter
Twenty-seventh Day of Ajaru

Mordac sat on a lush pillow, a tablet balanced on his lap. The markings in the soft clay blurred together through his weary gaze. The transaction notations had ceased making sense hours ago, and he had neither the energy nor the immediate desire to reconcile them.

Hani had not spoken to him since the day the girl came with the news about Ianna. He had seen his wife upset before, but her silence had never lasted this long. She went about her tasks listlessly, almost in a trance. He tried to comfort her, cajole her, berate her, but nothing he said made any difference. She never acknowledged he had spoken. This was not right. He was the master of the household. His decisions were not to be questioned. He had done what he felt was right when he sent Ianna to the temple for her coming-of-age ceremony. It was tradition. If they were ever going to fit into Ninevite society, they must comply with custom. Friendship would demand it. Membership in the trade guild would demand it. It's what was done.

Surely the girl was wrong. Ianna would come home. She had probably done something wrong, headstrong girl that she was. The temple had standards, expectations, as a temple should. When she satisfied those expectations, of course she would be able to return home. She just needed to be . . . not so stubborn. Lost in thought, Mordac started at Hani's voice.

"What will we do about our heritage?"

He looked up. She stood in the doorway. Her eyes were still red, and her shoulders drooped as they had now for three days.

"What?"

"Our heritage. With Ianna . . . gone . . . to whom will we bequeath the family treasure?"

He frowned. "My estate is not so great that—"

"Not your estate. Our treasure. *The* treasure."

Mordac leaned back and tapped the reed stylus on his leg. "I don't know. I haven't had time to think—"

"No. You haven't *thought*, have you?" Her sarcasm cut like a shard of flint.

Mordac tightened his jaw. "You will not address me in that tone. I have—"

Hani turned and disappeared through the doorway.

Jamin sprawled on his bed mat and stared through the window into the night sky. A half moon cloaked in a hazy aura lounged on the edge of the roof across the alleyway. Its dim light struggled to penetrate the thick night air. Any other time this moon might be silvery, mysterious. Tonight it was gray, tired. Half light, half dark, it appeared awkward in its role as the dominant night luminary. Jamin found it annoying.

Shine or don't shine. Stand strong or don't stand at all. It gradually occurred to him that his irritation was rooted in empathy with the moon's impotence. Like the half moon, powerless to alter its role in the natural order of the cosmos, Jamin felt half a man, equally powerless to affect anything in the natural order of human events—his own events. His heart burned bright for the girl, but his mind remained dark toward her. When she wore white, there was hope. The blue of *naditu*, though, seemed insurmountable, a pastel pinnacle that could not be overcome.

He rolled onto his side. For the hundredth time he asked himself what it was about this girl. Was it that she was the forbidden fruit, a child beyond the arms of Abraham? Would grasping for her mean his fall, as surrender to the fruit in the Garden of Eden had meant Adam's?

He frowned. No, there was something more to this. There had to be. There was a reason they had crossed paths, a reason she had captivated him so. Could God be behind this? He must be. There was no other explanation. Perhaps Jamin was to be the means of her rescue, the door through which she was to pass into the good grace of *Elohim Adonai.* But how?

The question bumped aimlessly through his mind. The tunic of a *naditu* had moved her beyond his reach. But beyond redemption? With God all things were possible, were they not?

All things . . .

Sleep crept over his benumbed mind from behind and nudged his eyelids closed. His chest settled itself into a rhythm of deep rest. The answer would come when it was ready. Not before.

Fourteen

The Arabian Desert, East of Damascus
Twenty-ninth Day of Ajaru

The road between Damascus and Tadmor traversed a landscape more barren than Jonah thought possible. To the east stretched desolate flatlands with only low dunes to break the horizon. A hot breeze lifted brown eddies of fine dust that swirled around the pair as they traipsed along the hardened path. To the west, forces of nature unremembered by man sliced deep clefts into the surface of the earth and intermingled them with ridges of rock that jutted up from the ground like broken teeth. In the distance, the land rose into the rocky foothills marking the eastern slopes of the mountains of Lebanon. Jonah focused his weary eyes on the variegated landscape to avoid being pulled into depression by the nothingness to the east.

Worse than the blandness of the terrain was the dust, the ubiquitous motes of grit that coated his cloak and assailed his eyes and nose. The granules squirmed beneath his collar and rubbed his neck and shoulders raw against the coarse cloth. Accursed land! Jonah tugged at the neckline of his cloak and glanced up at his companion.

Akhyeshah seemed oblivious to the heat and the dust. He threw the loose cloth of his keffiyeh across his face to filter the air and kept up a pace that seemed impossible to match. Jonah's heavier travel cloak, however, served him poorly in open desert. The dark fabric attracted the heat and trapped it against his body. There was no collar to protect his face, so he turned his head to the side and pulled the hood around to cover his mouth and nose. The twisted posture denied him the stability to walk a straight path, and it brought cramps to his neck and back. He had never been more miserable.

The days passed in silence, and today was no different from the others. Jonah plodded behind his guide in a stupor and wondered why Akhyeshah had approached him as a travel companion if he had no desire to socialize during the journey. Jonah's tentative attempts at conversation were usually met with a grunt . . . or no reply at all. He gave up on the effort after the second morning. One day melded into the next, until he was unsure exactly how long they'd trudged along the barren path. Time seemed to have forgotten him.

As the sun began its descent over the ridges to the southwest, Akhyeshah stepped off the main route. Jonah followed him until they found a small depression in the rocky soil that bordered one of the deep clefts. As he had done each night since they left Damascus, the Assyrian kicked aside several small rocks and peered around his resting place. Apparently satisfied, he grunted, settled onto the ground, and pulled his pouch of food onto his lap.

Jonah puzzled over the ritual, just as he had the previous nights. He shook his head and began his own search for a soft spot amid the stones strewn through the elongated hole. A small space less littered with rock on the shallow slope facing east availed itself, and he eased himself into it. He laid his walking stick aside and groped into his own bag of provisions for the evening meal. Jonah was surprised how much food remained after four days on the open road. True, they made a conscious effort to conserve their resources, but it seemed the pouch was no lighter than when Akhyeshah tossed it to him back in Damascus's marketplace. There was still a healthy stash of dates, dried figs, a block of hard cheese, and several strips of dried meat. What kind of meat? He thought it best not to ask.

As they chewed in silence, Jonah was struck anew by the utter quiet of the wilderness evening. In northern Israel, noises animated the night. Tree limbs scratched against the house as they stirred in the evening breeze. Choruses of insects serenaded a silvery moon drifting across the serene valley. The rustle of a nocturnal rodent as it rutted for food on the hillside filtered through his window. Here in the desert, the ambiance was as desolate as the landscape. Nothing stirred the night air, nothing broke the silence, save Akhyeshah's immense body shifting as he slept. Jonah almost wished his companion would snore—anything to break the absolute stillness.

What was magnificent, though, was the brilliance of the heavens. He thought the skies of Galilee were glorious, but they were nothing like this. Stars draped the heavens from horizon to horizon in a rich mantel with pinpoints of light that sparkled white—some tinged with blue, some with red. Jonah knew some of the stellar formations, but it was always difficult for him to pick out any but the most obvious ones. Tracing the Great Cross was simple enough, but the shape of *Kesil*, the foolish hunter Nimrud, eluded his imagination.

As a boy, he had complained in frustration when his father, Amittai, instructed him on the nuances of *Adonai's* celestial domain. Jonah said he thought man was silly to even try to sort out the stars. The amorphous mass of light above him seemed hopelessly random in its design—yet, as his father reminded him, there was purpose in all things God has made. *"Did not the psalmist write, 'He determines the number of the stars, he gives to all of them their names'? If Adonai gave each star a name, my son, there must be more to them than we know, eh? To have a name is to have essence, a reason for being."*

Jonah sighed and focused his eyes toward the east. The moon, although only at half fullness, cast a blue-white aura over the landscape that made a torch unnecessary to discern his surroundings. The lunar sheen reminded him of a night nearly seven years ago when the angel delivered his first call to prophesy to Jeroboam's court, the promise of *Adonai's* intent to restore His people Israel to the land. He remembered how the heavenly messenger's own aura scattered the light of the august heavenly bodies into the shadows, as glorious as they were. Here the moon and the stars held sway.

Thoughts of the angel dropped Jonah into a lonely mood. The last time the messenger appeared to him was on Joppa's beach. Was the angel still aware of him? Could he see Jonah here in the desert, outside the Promised Land? Would he ever speak again, or was the restored prophet now on his own? Jonah sighed and rolled onto his side. Sleep came slowly.

The morning light filtered an orange hue through Jonah's eyelids and stirred his restless subconscious from its wanderings. He winced and nudged his eyes open to slits as a shadow passed between him and the source of the light. His eyes shot open.

Akhyeshah knelt over him, his face set, his curved sword poised high above his head. He lunged and Jonah recoiled from the ugly blade as it flashed down toward his head. He twisted aside as Akhyeshah's sword shattered the ground a hand's breadth from his ear and peppered his face and neck with dirt and shards of rock. Wide-eyed, he rolled to his left and scrambled backward up the slope. He shielded his head with his arm from a second assault, but the attack never came.

Akhyeshah ignored him. The giant poked the tip of his sword into the deep cleft he had cut into the ground. He grunted and scooped a small pile of dirt onto the side of the blade. Then he straightened and extended it toward Jonah. Amid the debris on the sword lay the front half of a black scorpion, oozing a translucent viscous liquid from its severed abdomen. The carcass, easily three finger-widths in length, twitched twice, and then went still.

"Very poisonous." Akhyeshah flipped the blade over his shoulder. The scorpion flew from the sword and disappeared over the edge of the depression.

Jonah fought to get his breath under control. "How did . . . I thought—"

"Best to check the rocks before you sleep." Akhyeshah scraped the residue from his sword on a patch of loose dirt and replaced it at his side. He picked up his staff and climbed onto level ground.

"But—"

"Time to go. We eat and walk." With that he set off toward the road.

Jonah hustled to collect his staff and pouch. He struggled to calm his racing heartbeat as he hurried after Akhyeshah.

Jonah stumbled onto the main road fifteen paces behind Akhyeshah. He stopped, put his hands on his hips, and glowered at the giant.

"Wait!" Fatigue strained his voice. He was tired from nights of fitful sleep, tired from struggling to keep up with Akhyeshah, but mostly tired of being ignored. He felt like little more than extra baggage for the non-attentive Assyrian. What was the point of all this?

Akhyeshah turned and peered back at Jonah. He shifted, rested both hands on the top of his staff, and waited. The Assyrian's cheeks bulged from a handful of figs he'd stuffed into his mouth. Brown juice flowed into his beard as he chewed the fruit pulp. His dark eyes blinked but betrayed nothing. No irritation, no apology, no curiosity, nothing. That irked Jonah even more.

He stalked up to the big man and slammed the butt of his staff into the dust. "This is enough! We've been on the road for—"

"'Nuther day to Thadmor. We musht—"

"Stop it!" Jonah stomped his foot on the ground and flailed his hands. "Stop. Cutting. Me. Off! Will you, *please?*"

Akhyeshah's jaw stopped midchew. His eyes rounded, and he took a half step back.

The exasperated prophet narrowed his eyes. "Who are you? Who are you really?"

The Assyrian looked puzzled. "Hi amb Akhysha. Brofishoner of car—"

"I know, I know. 'Provisioner of caravans.' In the name of mercy, swallow that stuff, will you?" Jonah averted his eyes as Akhyeshah sucked the fruit pulp down his throat in one gulp and wiped his glistening whiskers with his sleeve. He lurched as a low belch rumbled up his throat and shattered the morning air, launching three nearby quail into the clear blue sky. Jonah cringed. He was certain he caught an echo off Mt. Hermon, four days to the south.

Akhyeshah grinned and patted his stomach. "Good figs."

Jonah shook his head. "Akha . . . Akhshayesh—"

"Akhyeshah."

"Thank you. Akhyeshah, I still don't know what to think about you."

"What is to think? Tadmor is small stop along desert caravan routes to the East. Caravans need supplies. Only one or two provide these things." He shrugged. "That is all. Nothing to think."

Jonah wasn't satisfied. "How did you find me? How did you know I was traveling alone? Why did you decide we should travel together?"

Akhyeshah cocked his head. "I did not find you. You were not lost."

"I meant—"

"I knew you were traveling alone because you were alone . . . traveling."

"I know, but—"

"I decided we should travel together because traveling alone—as you were—is not safe."

"But—"

"No more talk. Time to go. Another day to Tadmor, if we hurry." Akhyeshah clapped Jonah on the shoulder and turned on his heel.

His mouth agape, Jonah watched the giant twirl his staff and hum a tuneless air as he strode off down the road.

Fifteen

The Arabian Desert, Near Tadmor
Third Day of Simanu

Another day passed, indistinguishable from—how many days before it? Jonah lost track. The road ahead still looked the same as the road behind. Even their footprints disappeared in the dust swirls that erased any sign they had been there. The land to the right remained barren and parched. The land to the left had become the same. Everything was the same, the same, the same. Except his joints. They got worse. Ankles, knees, hip. They'd never recover from this ordeal, if, indeed, he ever completed it. The thought of going lame halfway to Nineveh popped into his mind. What would he do then? Just lie down in the dust and shrivel up? That would hardly be fair. *How irritating.*

Whatever possessed him to think he could walk the entire distance to Nineveh? Well, how was he supposed to know how far it was? He'd never traveled outside Israel before, save his short jaunt aboard the *Ba'al Hayam*—and he needed no reminder as to how well that turned out. Once, when he probed Akhyeshah how much further beyond Tadmor that Nineveh lay, all he got was a grunt. A grunt! That was it. *How irritating.*

Perhaps *Adonai* thought His prophet might have enough sense to procure a camel, or a donkey, or something to ease the road before he set off. Jonah stared ahead and grumbled to himself. It wasn't his fault. How was he to know? He could picture the angel's face looking down, sighing, shaking his head. The next time the voice decided to speak—if ever again—it would probably chastise him for not thinking ahead. Were prophets supposed to think ahead? Wasn't it the job of their angels-in-charge to tell them what was ahead? Of course it was. It was the angel's fault. Jonah gritted his teeth. *Great, I got a defective angel. How irritating.*

And this heat! It wasn't just hot; it was sweltering. Even his trusty travel cloak—a cloak that worked just fine back in Israel, thank you very much—turned against him. He yanked at his collar and sucked in a deep breath of hot, dusty, gritty, filthy, stifling, Assyrian air. He gagged. *How irrit—*

Jonah slammed into Akhyeshah and staggered back. The giant had stopped in the middle of the road and was surveying the sky from horizon to horizon. Finally, he turned, looked at Jonah, and sniffed.

Jonah bristled. "What?"

"We stop here. If we cannot find shelter, we build it." Akhyeshah pivoted and strode off the path.

Jonah hurried to catch up. "Already? It's only midday."

"We stop here."

"But there's plenty of daylight left. We could get much closer to Tadmor if we keep—"

Akhyeshah swept his hand from left to right. "There are ridges in the earth not far. We find shelter."

"But—"

"No 'but.' Follow me."

With that, the big man set off at a pace that forced Jonah to a trot.

They had only traveled a short time when they came upon a cleft in the terrain. It caught Jonah by surprise. The ground that appeared so flat from the road suddenly dropped off into a series of crevices similar to that in which he'd encountered the scorpion the day before. But these breaks in the earth were much deeper. Just beyond the crevices, more low rocky ridges jutted from the ground. He hadn't seen them through the waves of heat that shimmered from the desert floor.

Jonah came to the lip of the first crevice and began to loosen his travel pouch from his belt.

"Not here. Keep going." Akhyeshah plunged down the slope. He crossed the narrow floor and began to scale the other side.

Jonah creased his brow. "This should be fine. We slept in one the other—"

"Keep going," Akhyeshah barked over his shoulder.

Jonah heaved a sigh of frustration and stumbled down the side of the ravine. He scrambled up the far slope, the loose soil and rocks shifting so quickly beneath his feet that he had to pump his legs to make headway. When he finally topped the incline, Akhyeshah was already fifty paces ahead.

"Wait!" Jonah yelled after the big man as he disappeared over the edge of the next rift.

He jogged to the crevice and peeked over the edge. The gully was deeper than the last, its slopes steeper. Jonah scanned the bottom. Akhyeshah was nowhere in sight.

Jonah cupped his hands around his mouth. "Ayesh . . . Akhash . . . oh, why can't I remember that name?"

He huffed and lurched over the edge, half sliding, half falling down the slope until he crashed onto the floor of the fissure. His ankles wailed at the sudden stop, and he grimaced at a sharp catch that stabbed his lower back. He bent over and fought to catch his breath.

"More to go."

He snapped his eyes up to see Akhyeshah's head loom over the top of the far slope. Jonah squinted at him. "How did you—"

"Keep moving." The head disappeared.

Jonah limped across the ravine floor and began the arduous climb up the rock-strewn grade. When he gained the top, as he'd suspected, Akhyeshah was nowhere to be seen. The first of the toothy ridges rose only thirty paces ahead. He assumed that's where his guide had gone, so he trudged to the nearest cleft in the ridge and slipped through.

The valley between the first ridge and the next was flat and smooth, its surface blanketed with fine sand. He glanced to the left and spotted deep prints in the soft earth. Only Akhyeshah could have left the tracks, so Jonah followed them along the ridgeline.

After another twenty paces, he rounded a boulder and nearly tripped over Akhyeshah's legs. The giant had settled against the back of a rock outcropping and nestled between two boulders that framed a shallow niche in the low ridge.

Jonah stumbled to a halt. "Will you please explain what we're doing? Why are we stopping so soon, and what's the big hurry?"

Akhyeshah looked up at Jonah. "There is room here. Lie down."

Jonah stared at him. Then he surveyed the narrow space between Akhyeshah's bulk and the boulder. He looked back at the Assyrian and raised an eyebrow. "That's all right. I can find my own—"

"You will want to lie down." Akhyeshah squinted at him against the glare of the sky.

"Why would—"

A low rumble shook the earth beneath his feet and cut Jonah's words short. He slogged through the deep sand to a small cleft that slit the ridge a few paces away and peered through it.

A massive wall of sand rushed across the desert toward him. Earth and sky disappeared behind the monstrous brown cloud that obliterated everything in its path. It seemed to grow taller and darker with each moment. He stood mesmerized, until he realized the sand had just swallowed the road they had walked only moments ago.

Jonah scurried back to Akhyeshah's niche. His chest heaved. "What, in the name of—"

"You will want to lie down." Akhyeshah nodded to the space beside him, his voice barely audible above the roar of the sandstorm.

Jonah dove into the narrow gap beside the Assyrian. Akhyeshah shifted onto his stomach and covered his head with his robe. Jonah followed his cue.

When the leading edge of the storm hit the rocky abutment, Jonah thought the world had come to an end. Daylight disappeared and the ground shuddered under the onslaught. Sand, dust, and debris filled the air. The wind screamed over and through the rocks with such force it threatened to rip the cloak off his back. He stuffed his collar against his mouth and nose to filter air and clamped his eyes shut.

For what seemed an eternity, the maelstrom battered the earth around him. Rocks loosened above his head cascaded down and caromed off his huddled form. A heavy blanket of sand accumulated on his back and legs, and pinned him to the ground. Breathable air disappeared, and the relentless pressure of debris on his back squeezed his lungs.

Akhyeshah's voice came strangely clear through the chaos. "Tadmor is near. Over the next rise."

Jonah tried to reply but choked on the grit that invaded his throat. He buried his head into his cloak, shuddered, and blacked out.

Something tapped Jonah's forehead and jarred him awake. His right eyelid flickered open to see a pebble roll to a rest beside his nose. He clamped the eyelid shut against a grain of sand that slipped in and lodged itself against his eye. He tried to shift his body but couldn't move. Slowly, he lifted his head and shook it. A shower of fine sand flowed down the sides of his head. He pushed against the ground with his forearms and managed to free his shoulders. He shrugged off the thick blanket of sand with a twist of his torso.

Jonah sat up and brushed the grit from his face before he attempted to open his eyes again. When he did, the bright blue afternoon sky nearly blinded him. The air was still, the earth quiet. He squinted around himself. The events leading him here slowly reassembled themselves in his mind. The scramble for cover, the storm, Akhyeshah.

Akhyeshah.

Jonah swiveled and stared at the ground beside him. There was only sand.

The evening sun kissed the western horizon, stretching Tadmor's craggy shadow further across the sand dunes toward the eastern horizon. Twilight had painted the landscape a dull taupe by the time Jonah reached the city gate. He turned to look back along the road that led him here.

There was no evidence of the sandstorm. The sky had cleared, and the sun that had resumed its onslaught with renewed vigor now settled toward its nighttime rest. The road lay undisturbed—rutted and rock-strewn, as it had been for days. It was as though nothing had happened.

Most of his recollection after he lifted himself from the sand was fuzzy. He remembered little of the trudge back toward the road. He recalled the torturous climb through the ravines he had stumbled through in his haste to reach shelter from a storm he had no inkling was coming. The fierce blast of desert air sculpted elongated deposits of sand in the leeward walls of the rifts and left them treacherous to climb. The sandstorm left a different signature on the flatland, where the gale-force wind sandblasted the windward surfaces clean. Jonah shook his head. He wondered if such sandstorms were common in the desert, fearful he might be caught up in another without Akhyeshah's savvy to forewarn him.

Jonah was exhausted by the time he reached the roadway. He stopped and shaded his eyes to scan the path for any sign of his guide. There was none. No footprints. No movement.

"Tadmor is near. Over the next rise."

The husky words echoed through Jonah's mind, all that was left of his enigmatic, often annoying companion. The road ahead seemed impossible by himself, and Jonah longed for just one more clipped interruption, one more grunt that would mean he wasn't alone. Akhyeshah must have gone ahead, but why? Why would he suffer Jonah's belabored pace, when he could have made Tadmor at least a day faster on his own, only to abandon him almost within sight of the city? Akhyesha said he was from Tadmor. Perhaps Jonah could seek him out and ask why the intrigue.

With a sigh, he turned and stepped through the entrance to the city. What met his eyes fell far short of his expectations. The ancient oasis town was a shadow of its former glory. For hundreds of years, the city had enjoyed celebrity as an enabler of east-west trade. King Solomon had built up the outpost when he recognized its strategic importance, but the splendor he bestowed upon Tadmor was no longer evident. The settlement was now little more than a scattering of sun-baked mud huts. Sickly palm trees dotted the landscape with their pale fronds drooped against the yellow sky. Vegetation once flourished along a broad river that gave life to Tadmor, but now its decrepit trees scarcely survived over the parched remains of a river swallowed long ago by the desert sands. Stone rings lined the tops of wells dug along the ancient waterway and pockmarked the landscape like ulcers.

A few inhabitants took advantage of the cooler evening temperatures to sweep away the residue from the sandstorm. One man lifted a cover from the closest well and shook a cloud of sand into the air. He peered into the hole, Jonah supposed, to assess the storm's damage.

To his right, Jonah noticed a long wall, taller than the hovels that made up the village. In its shadow, he could see the shapes of camels shifting under their loads. Figures of men milled around the beasts, probably the drivers clearing their camp after the sandstorm. He hoped the caravan headed the same direction he was, and that he might be welcomed to join them. He would inquire the next morning, but, for now, all he could think of was rest. Nothing sounded better than to stretch out and put the day behind him in sleep. Even if there was an inn, which he doubted, his experience in Damascus tipped his decision toward another night under the stars.

Jonah found a niche in the wall not far from the caravan. A tapered mound of fine sand the wind had deposited through a breach in the wall would make a good bed. He set his staff and bags against the escarpment and began to settle. Then he stopped. He got back to his feet and kicked over the few rocks littering the ground near his resting place. Satisfied they harbored no threatening creatures, he settled back onto the sand. In spite of the unknown tomorrow would bring, he smiled to himself. *There. I've learned something, anyway.*

Sleep came quickly and completely.

"Who?" The man leaned toward Jonah from his perch on the caravan's lead camel.

"Akhyeshah. His name is Akhyeshah. He supplies caravans passing through Tadmor. You know, water and food." Jonah looked for a connection in the camel driver's eyes.

The man shook his head. "Never heard of him."

Jonah frowned. "Tadmor is not so large. Perhaps this is your first visit?"

"Been in caravans since I was born. Father led merchants to the east his whole life. So have I." He spit a red stream of areca nut juice onto the roadway. "I come through Tadmor once every two or three passages of the seasons."

"Then surely you've resupplied here."

"Every time."

Jonah creased his brow. "Well, how many suppliers are there in Tadmor?"

"Two."

"Two?"

"Two."

Jonah stared at the ground. "Two," he muttered.

"Two."

"Yes, I heard you. Two."

The man nodded. "Two."

Jonah rolled his eyes. "But no Akhyeshah?"

"Rashad and his cousin, Khalil. They do not get along." He shook his head. "But no Akhyeshah."

Jonah began to reply, but all thought deserted him.

The man broke the silence. "Sorry about your friend. Perhaps you travel to the East, also?"

Jonah mumbled, "Yes. I'm going to Nineveh."

The caravan leader flashed a red-stained toothy grin. "Ah, Nineveh. Nice city. Much rebuilding. You have been there before?"

"No."

"Ah. Come with us. We travel your road as far as Mari. Maybe farther. We see." He shrugged.

Jonah nodded, still lost in thought.

"You can help with the animals, and you will have company." The grin was back.

Jonah looked up. "Thank you. Perhaps I will." It was true it would be safer to travel with the caravan than on his own. His lack of wilderness savvy had nearly cost him his life twice already. He'd never have made it to Tadmor, if not for Akhyeshah, whoever he was. . . .

The caravan leader extended his hand. "I am Jamal."

Jonah grasped his wrist. "I am Jonah."

The man nodded. "Good. First, you must find good clothes."

Jonah raised his eyebrows.

"Your cloak. Good for the mountains. Bad for the desert."

Jonah looked down and slapped a cloud of dust from his sweat-stained garment. He shrugged. "I don't know. It's not so bad."

His new guide leaned back in his saddle and let loose a throaty guffaw.

"The prophet still travels."

"Yes, Mistress. But—"

"Is it your desire to join Edil in oblivion?"

"No! No, Mistress, I—"

"He, too, failed."

"I will not fail, Mistress. Please—"

"Be finished with it!"

Sixteen

The Arabian Desert, East of Tadmor
Ninth Day of Simanu

Jonah grumbled under his breath, "If *Adonai* ever made a mistake, it was in creating the camel."

Six days on the road since Tadmor, and Jonah resolved never to touch one of the beasts again. The morning they set out, Jamal pointed him to the animal over which he would have charge. His initial reaction was one of relief at no longer having to walk. He didn't protest the arrangement. In fact, he was encouraged. He had experience with donkeys and goats, which should serve him well. Besides, the animal looked docile enough. He was sure the dumb beast would acknowledge him as her master, and all would go smoothly. Instead, the first time Jonah moved into range, the animal spat a wad of cud down the front of his newly acquired lightweight desert robe. Their relationship went downhill from there.

When his camel didn't ignore him, she tried to bite him. Twin bruises still adorned Jonah's left shoulder, reminders of the time before he became wary enough, and quick enough, to avoid her powerful jaws. All this occurred before he had mounted the camel the first time, which was also nearly his last time.

He watched the other drivers goad their camels to their front knees to enable an easy mount. That looked simple enough. Jonah turned toward his beast and likewise tapped its front legs with the tip of his staff. Nothing. He tapped a little harder. Still nothing. The next tap was a swat, and it set the camel in motion. The enraged animal belted out a guttural bellow, veered sharply, and set off at a trot. The lunging beast knocked her would-be rider into a cloud of dust. His pained backside was surpassed only by his injured ego, bruised from the laughter of the other men.

When Jonah finally managed to get astride his mount, he wondered why he ever wanted to ride in the first place. The loping gait of the long-legged animal ground Jonah's hipbones together as he lurched forward, then backward with every step. By the time she had taken a dozen paces, Jonah was ready to climb down and walk the rest of the way. That was, if he could get her to stop. But it appeared that wasn't about to happen, either. So he sat. And he grumbled.

When the caravan halted in early afternoon of the first day, Jonah gratefully slid to the ground. He grimaced at the jolt when he landed.

"Good to ride, eh?" Jamal grinned.

Jonah frowned. "Jamal, I was thinking I would give the camel some rest. Maybe walk beside her this afternoon." Jonah rubbed his hip. "I don't want to tire her out."

The caravan master guffawed. "'Tire her out.' That is good!"

"Really—"

"You ride. Too slow if you walk." He shook his head and ambled away. "Tire out camel. I will remember that. Heh, heh."

Jonah sighed and glared over his shoulder at the animal. She ignored him.

Jonah hunched over and frowned at the disparate collection of mud huts and rocky ruins that was Mari. He couldn't believe his eyes. Was there nothing in this wasteland that even resembled civilization? Like Tadmor, the village was a little more than a broken reminder of the flourishing city it had been in ages past. Twice built, twice destroyed, the site never recovered from the final devastation the Babylonian King Hammurabi wreaked upon it a millennium earlier. Reminders of its former greatness jutted from the desert's surface. Great blocks of building stone and fallen pillars of massive buildings razed long ago had succumbed to the ravages of time, half-buried in a sea of sand that encroached from all directions. The great Purattu River skirted the eastern edge of the site, the only asset left to commend Mari as a waypoint. Jonah's heart sank when Jamal announced his intention to linger there. Here they would refresh their water supply and prod the river to augment their food supply with fish.

Jonah eased himself from the camel, then collapsed where he touched down. He sat in the dust, shoulders drooped, arms limp. After seven days on the back of this wretched beast, he was sure his backside would never be the same. It seemed every joint was permanently separated, every muscle stretched beyond hope. He suffered one day after the other with the hope that surely he would become accustomed to the gait, that his body would settle into the undulating rhythm. It did not.

Jonah slapped the ground by his side, and a cloud of dust billowed into the heat. He'd had it. He was not going to remount that wretched creature. He didn't care if he slowed down the whole world. Nothing would force him to ride. That was it. Done. Never again.

"We stay here four days." Jamal's jovial voice startled Jonah from his bruised ruminations.

Jonah glared at him from the dust. "Four days? Why?" He lifted his arms and gestured toward the collection of dilapidated mud huts. "There's nothing here."

"Ah, but there is. Water, fish, rest. Your camel carries you and cargo six days—"

"Seven days," Jonah corrected.

"Seven, yes, seven days. She will need rest."

"She needs rest? I'm the one who's too sore to move." He jabbed a thumb back toward the camel. "She's doing just fine."

A stream of cud shot over his shoulder and splattered onto his fist. He groaned in disgust at the brown scum sliding down his wrist and into his sleeve.

"Heh, heh. Must watch for that." Jamal sauntered back to his own mount, his chuckle fading into the suffocating heat.

Jonah sighed.

※ ※ ※

Jonah paced the embankment of the Purattu River and mumbled under his breath. For the fifth time that morning, he paused to fling a rock into the broad expanse. He took mirthless satisfaction at the hollow plop the stone made as it plunked into the water and sank out of sight. And for the fifth time, two men who fished from the river bank nearby turned and glared at him. He glared back.

The rings of wavelets that radiated from the splash glided downstream on the lazy current until they faded into the murky water. He folded his arms and sighed. *The river may be moving the wrong direction, but at least it's moving.*

Since he'd arrived in Mari the day before, his restlessness grew, although he couldn't explain why. Something, some sense of urgency, niggled at his brain and roused him even before the sun topped the horizon. His brief conversation with Jamal that morning echoed through his brain. . . .

"Are you sure we need to stay here four days? Why so long?" Jonah slouched upwind of the dung fire over which the caravan leader warmed a wedge of flatbread for his breakfast.

"We dry fish for travel. Takes time." Jamal lifted his bread from the heating rock and sniffed at it. He grunted his satisfaction and took a bite.

"But—"

"No 'buts.' We leave the river here. Much desert between Mari and Aššûr." The camel master glanced up from his breakfast. He held out a piece of the bread to Jonah and raised his eyebrows.

Jonah stared at the smudgy scrap. "No . . . no, thank you. I already ate."

Jamal shrugged and stuffed the morsel into his mouth.

Jonah frowned. "Wait—Aššûr? Isn't that east? I thought you said we were going north to Magrisu and then along the northern road to

Nineveh."

"Change plan. We go to Aššûr. The way is harder, but shorter."

"Then to Nineveh?"

"No Nineveh this trip. Aššûr. Then east to the mountains."

"But you said you were going to Nineveh," he protested.

"Said 'maybe' to Nineveh. Change plan." Jamal stood and wiped his hands on his robe.

"But I need to get to Nineveh."

The caravan master shrugged. "Then go to Nineveh. We go to Aššûr; you take *quppu* or *kalakku* upstream. Three days, maybe four."

Jonah creased his brow. "What is a *quppu*?"

"Small boat. Round. Made with skins. Faster than wooden *kalakku*, but *kalakku* is bigger. Flat. Carries much cargo." He shrugged. "Many *quppu* and *kalakku* on Idiqlat River. You find one from Aššûr to Nineveh."

Jonah dropped onto the sandy hillock and stared at the river. The Purattu crawled by, its subtle current hardly noticeable on the surface. But for the occasional reed or the indentation of a small eddy near the embankment to show its current, the river seemed to stand still. The thought of taking to the water conjured up memories of his ill-fated trip across the Great Sea aboard the *Ba'al Hayam*. He grimaced at the memory of the seasickness that overtook him the moment he stepped aboard. Would it be the same on a river? Surely a waterway as calm as the one before him would have no effect on his stomach.

He picked up another rock and hefted it a couple of times in his hands. He was about to fling it into the water when a stone whizzed by his ear and exploded a cloud of dust on the hillside behind him. After a belated duck of the head, he swung around to see one of the two fishermen grit his teeth and point at the rock in Jonah's hand. The other fisherman brandished a piece of driftwood.

Jonah dropped the stone. He averted his eyes back to the river and sighed.

Three more days.

Seventeen

The Arabian Desert
Fourteenth Day of Simanu

"This is impossible!"

Jonah squinted against the glare of the midday sun that reflected off the light sand. Dunes rippled in every direction, the smooth sand of the one they traversed broken only by the hoof prints of the camels ahead. He had never seen so forsaken a land, worse even than the wilderness he walked between Damascus and Tadmor. At least there he had a discernible road and a few rocks to divert his attention from the endless stretch of sand and pebbles. Here it was just sand. Nothing but sand, sand, sand.

Early yesterday, before they departed Mari, Jamal called the drivers together. The men circled around him while they chewed the last of their morning meal. He spoke in the Assyrian tongue, but then in halting Hebrew for Jonah's benefit.

"Follow close. Stay on trail. Do not stray left or right." The leader spat a stream of red juice into the sand. "Between the rivers, water is not far below the sands. A man breaks the surface and the desert swallows him up like that." He snapped his fingers.

Jonah stared, his mouth agape. He looked at the other drivers, shocked that none showed any concern.

"But . . . how do you know where to ride? How can you tell where the sand is thin?"

Jamal grinned, his chest puffed out. "Many times I cross this land. Only two camels have I lost." He held up a finger and a thumb. "Just two."

The other drivers nodded in apparent approval of his record.

"We stay to higher ground. Where there is no higher ground, we go slow."

Jonah's shoulders slumped.

He rode fourth in line. They forded the Purattu River at a stretch of narrows just upstream from Mari. Fortunately, a light rainy season left the river low, so the current created little problem for the animals. Still, the sight of the water roiling around the camel's legs brought a wave of nausea up Jonah's throat and forced his eyes to the horizon. Would this journey never end?

The worst began as soon as they regained the heights on the other side of the river. They topped the rise, and Jonah shielded his eyes against the glare and heat of the morning sun. The brilliance did not decrease even as the sun passed its zenith and moved behind him. Only when the sky flashed yellow and orange to signal the demise of another day, could he fully raise his eyelids. When he did, there was nothing to see but dunes devoid of vegetation, seemingly devoid of any life at all.

A day and a half east of Mari, he spied a lowland to the left of the trail. His eyes feasted on the diversity in the terrain, grateful for anything that broke the monotony of the dunes. The basin appeared completely flat. It lacked even ripples of sand like those over which he now traveled. He caught a glint of reflection from—could it be water? He leaned forward and squinted in the direction of the light. Pale, lime-encrusted puddles, tired remnants of the last rainy season, dotted the low-lying area. The puddles seemed to shrink before his eyes as the porous earth sucked at them from beneath and the arid air vaporized them from above.

Splotches of wetness lay amid a patchwork of dried mud chips, their jagged edges curled toward the sky as though beseeching the daystar for mercy from his relentless heat. The cracked earth stretched to the north until it disappeared into the waves of heat radiating from the baked ground. Was all Assyria like this? Little wonder it birthed such a harsh and cruel people, Jonah mused. If man tends to assume the personality of his environment, then the desert was an earthen Assyrian. It made sense to him.

The thought of the Assyrian people revisited in Jonah's mind the reason for this journey. *"YOU ARE TO GO TO THE GREAT CITY NINEVEH AND PREACH TO THE PEOPLE REPENTANCE OF THEIR SINS."* From the moment the angel reiterated his commission on Joppa's shore, the words clung to his mind and embedded themselves in his brain like an eagle's talons gripping their prey. He recalled many of the questions that sprouted in his mind during the trek from Joppa back to Gath-hepher: *How do I get to Nineveh? Who do I see and where do I start? Do I see the king first, like I did in Samaria? Will they understand me? Jamal has learned some Hebrew from his travels, and I struggle to understand him. What of the people of Nineveh? I know nothing of the Assyrian tongue.*

Jonah's troubled mind retraced the journey that took God's message of restoration to King Jeroboam in Samaria. Some of the same questions plagued that journey, but *Adonai* saw to His word. Jonah arrived at the court of the newly installed king in the wake of an assassination attempt and gained admittance into the court on the shirttails of Elihu, the war hero. That would not be repeated in Nineveh. A foreigner would be the last person granted an audience at such a time.

The camel yanked its head and took a stutter step. Absently, Jonah patted the beast on the side of her neck, then dropped back into his worries.

The old adage that you can't steer a donkey that is standing still resurfaced in his mind. Well, he wasn't standing still. He was moving. He was doing his part. But he had only been told what to do, not how to do it. Why did he feel no peace of mind? Why was the angel so silent?

The camel's bellow yanked Jonah back to the present. The beast sidestepped, then lunged forward. Jonah cried out at the sudden movement. His legs shot up and flailed in the air for balance. He grasped at the blanket on the camel's back, but his finger found no grip. For a brief moment, he teetered, then rolled off his mount and collapsed onto the trail in a cloud of dust.

Jonah sprawled on the sand and gasped to recapture the air forced from his lungs. A movement against his side caught his eye. He froze. From beneath his back, the rear half of a brown-and-tan patterned serpent writhed, its head pinned against the ground under Jonah's body.

Jonah squirmed onto his side, away from the twisting snake. He scrambled onto all fours and looked up. The viper, curved fangs bared, launched itself at Jonah.

The camel's bellow pulled Jamal's head around in time to see Jonah's animal lurch off the trail and lumber down the slope toward the parched lakebed—without his rider. He pulled his own mount aside and urged him toward the panicked beast. Ignoring the shouts of his fellow drivers, Jamal set an angle to intercept the camel. He kept an eye on the sandy flats that bordered the basin. His camel labored under the load of both cargo and rider that drove the animal's hooves deep into the sand.

The caravan master cursed under his breath. He leaned forward and urged his camel faster. The animals converged, and Jamal reached out for the lead rope. His fingers grazed the cord just as his own camel bellowed and pitched forward into the water-saturated flats. The beast roared in pain as his forelegs broke through the crust and sank. His knees snapped like twigs from the momentum and his weight.

Jamal flew from his seat and tumbled over the neck of Jonah's mount. He landed on his back on the lake berm, the air forced from his lungs. He sprawled out to even his weight over the surface of the sand and lay still, knowing any movement would embed him into the mire. Jonah's mount swerved to avoid Jamal's camel, but her momentum carried her broadside into the writhing animal. She stumbled and collapsed on her side over Jamal's outstretched legs.

Jamal's lower body sank into the quicksand under the camel's weight. Only his head, shoulders, and part of his chest still showed above the surface. The stricken caravan leader lifted his arm and reached out to grasp the hair on the back of Jonah's camel, but the beast was past hope. Only the side of her massive hump remained visible above the sand. Jamal became aware of the shouts of his fellow drivers, who had leaped from their animals and ran down the slope. They slowed to test the surface as they crept across the flats.

His body immobilized, Jamal turned his eyes toward his men. The caravan's second driver dropped to all fours, yanked off his keffiyeh, and crawled as close as he dared to his leader. He stretched forward over the crusted sand and whipped the light fabric toward Jamal's head. The end of the head dressing landed less than an arm's length from the trapped man. Jamal thrust his arm from the quicksand and groped for the material. The movement pushed his head and shoulders under the surface just as his fingers grasped the cloth.

"Pull! PULL!" Jamal's rescuer screamed at the men behind him. The drivers clutched his legs to their chests and scrambled backward. The man stared wide-eyed as Jamal's hand protruded from the sand, grasped onto the keffiyeh. The men pulled, and Jamal's hand rose from the quicksand to the wrist, then to the forearm. A patch of sand bulged where Jamal's head pushed back to the surface.

Sweat dripped from the rescuer's forehead and burned his eyes with salty sweat. The cloth began to slip between his strained fingers. He squeezed tighter.

As Jamal's brow broke the surface, his fingers stiffened, then went limp. The cloth slipped from his grasp, and his arm slid back beneath the surface. A final bellow from his injured camel broke the sudden silence, and she joined her master beneath the sands.

Jonah twisted his body away from the serpent's lunge. He scrambled to his feet and felt a strike on his shoulder. The snake squirmed in the air, suspended by a curved fang snagged in the loose fabric of the desert robe. He jumped to his feet and threw his shoulder back to dislodge the serpent. The move threw Jonah off balance, and he tumbled backward down the incline toward the lakebed.

He came to rest on his stomach in full view of the frantic scene at the edge of the dried lake. Jamal arced over a camel's neck—the camel Jonah recognized as being his own. A second beast stood knee-deep in sand and bellowed at the top of her lungs. Jonah watched, horrified, as his camel collapsed onto Jamal's body. After a moment, it occurred to him that neither Jamal nor the camels could get up.

As the sand sucked at the caravan leader and the trapped camels, three men raced toward them. Jonah watched the lead runner tear off his head covering and flatten himself against the sand, reaching out to Jamal. Then he saw Jamal's head sink beneath the sand. There came more shouts and more bellows; then all went quiet.

The caravan halted there for the day. Jonah hunched on the slope, his arms draped over his crossed legs. His glassy eyes fixed themselves on the stretch of sand that now betrayed no trace of the deadly drama he had witnessed less than an hour earlier. He had not moved from where he landed after he shook off the snake. The rest of the camel drivers huddled in quiet consultation. They still had precious goods to deliver. There would need to be a new leader. No one spoke out; no man volunteered. Every man there, save Jonah, had seen the desert claim men and beasts before. But this was Jamal. He was more than their leader. He was a brother.

There was also the matter of the snake. The desert viper was nocturnal, a night hunter, yet this one struck at midday. The two drivers behind Jonah who saw it lunge froze, shocked at the snake's appearance. But when they dismounted and ran up to kill the serpent, there was no sign of it. Scuff marks on the trail betrayed Jonah's struggle with the viper, but no telltale marks in the sand hinted where the snake may have come from, or where it may have gone.

Jonah sat apart from the others, his mind in turmoil. How could this be happening? He understood the misfortunes he met when he fled to Joppa. But why now, when he acted in obedience? Why the near-fatal encounters with the scorpion, the sandstorm, the snake—and if he had not been thrown from the back of the camel, certain death beneath the quicksand? And what of Jamal? He was innocent, merely a desert guide.

The questions niggled at him and birthed a dull ache in the back of his skull.

Eighteen

Nineveh, the Temple Plaza
Fifteenth Day of Simanu

Jamin eased himself onto the steps of Nabu's temple. Today he would neither lurk in the shadows, nor peek around corners. He didn't care if he was observed. This was his last day in Nineveh.

His desire to remain had not subsided, although with all that had happened at the Temple of Ishtar, he wasn't sure why. His uncle hadn't questioned him again about his renewed interest in Nineveh. He didn't want to chance the issue being raised again, so he abandoned the strategy of asking to stay longer, or return later.

Uncle Hiram was apologetic that he could only offer Jamin a paltry amount for his summer's work. Jamin refused the payment. It was his pleasure to help. He had learned much about the trade, and his time in Nineveh had been interesting. It had also frustrated him, but he didn't share that sentiment with his uncle. His mind was not on Aššûr this morning. His mind was where it spent most of its time. On the girl.

Jamin had not returned to Nabu's temple since he'd seen her in the blue tunic of a *naditu*. The ache in his stomach returned with every remembrance of the sight. Their disastrous first encounter should have dampened his feelings, even drowned them. He fancied the sting of her slaps still on his cheeks. Jamin ben Obadiah—a son of Abraham, chosen of the One True God—slapped by a heathen temple harlot! His forehead burned at the memory. But so did his heart. His desire, his concern, his—could it be called love?—for the young girl had not abated. Quite the contrary.

Why did she vex him so? She was pagan, hot-tempered, lacked common sense, stubborn . . . and probably a lot of other things. What was there to commend her? Absolutely nothing. Yet his feelings for her only grew. It was as though he was being pushed toward her, rather than pulled by her.

So here he sat, on the steps of Nabu's temple, in plain sight. And he didn't care. There was no movement between the columns yet, but Jamin was early. He wanted to be there when she emerged. He wanted to see her. He wanted her to see him.

Jamin shook off his disjointed thoughts and raised his eyes from the street. He was startled to see the steps of Ishtar's temple alive with white tunics. The *ishtaritu* initiates had appeared while he pondered. They clustered on the steps in small groups, as always. None of them looked his way, although certainly they'd seen him. More flashes of white, and some blue, showed from the shadows behind the columns. He searched the far end of the steps where she normally sat alone, but the space was empty.

Jamin heard cloth rustle, but before he could turn his head, someone settled onto the stairs beside him. He turned his head.

Uncle Hiram!

Hiram just looked ahead at the scene across the street.

"What are . . . how did you know—" Jamin stammered.

His uncle smiled. "Ours is a close community, Jamin. You've not been overly discrete."

Jamin reddened. "Then . . . how long have you known?"

"That's not important." Hiram looked back across the street. "Do you have a favorite?"

His nephew's jaw tightened despite his shock. "It's not like that."

"It's all right."

"No, it's not all right. You don't understand. I have not—"

"Calm yourself, Nephew. I know you haven't partaken." Hiram turned his head toward Jamin, a trace of the good-natured smile still on his lips.

Jamin creased his brow. "How can you be sure?"

"I would know."

Jamin's puzzlement was evident.

Hiram locked eyes with him. "There's a countenance. I'm not sure

I can describe it. A man who resolves to defer his desire until the marriage bed reveals his heart in other ways, other words and deeds." He patted his nephew on the shoulder. "And a violation of that intent is quickly betrayed."

Jamin looked down and struggled for the words to respond. After an awkward moment, he raised his eyes to meet his uncle's. "I question whether that bed will ever be mine."

"So there is a favorite." His uncle nodded across the street.

Jamin shook his head. "She shouldn't be there. I've . . . spoken to her. There's something different . . . I don't know." He clenched his fist. "She shouldn't be there."

He looked back across the street. The last of the *ishtaritu* had disappeared between the columns. He scanned the porch. It was empty.

Hiram laid his hand on his nephew's shoulder. "God knows the heart, Jamin."

"What do you mean?"

"Even the heart of a pagan. If there really is something different, there is always hope, no?"

"I don't know." He heaved another sigh. "I just don't know."

"Come. Time to go." Hiram pushed to his feet. He extended a hand to his nephew.

Jamin clasped his uncle's wrist and stood. He cast another look at the massive Temple of Ishtar. He sensed the goddess was gloating and daring him to wrest the treasure of his heart from her cold stone bosom.

His uncle's words rose again in his mind. *"Always hope, no?"*

I'm not so sure.

Hulalitu watched the two men descend the steps of Nabu's temple and turn up the road. She glared at them from behind her pillar until they turned a corner out of sight. Their voices had carried in the crisp morning air.

"So, 'Jamin,' is it?" Her hoarse voice grated against the smooth stone of the column. "We shall see what becomes of Jamin."

⁂ ⁂ ⁂

The early morning light had just broken over the roof as Jamin bade his aunt and uncle farewell. He threw his small parcel of belongings over his shoulder and accepted a pouch with some morsels of food from his aunt. He planted a kiss on her cheek, where a tear moistened his lips.

"*Shalom*, my nephew. You'll be careful. The Idiqlat is fickle." Her nasal twang was gone, replaced by a husky sniffle.

"I will, Aunt Rizpah." Jamin smiled. "I'll pass your love to my family. Perhaps I can return sooner, rather than later." He kissed her other cheek. *"Shalom."*

He gripped his uncle's wrist, looked into the older man's eyes, and nodded. They needed no words.

He strode down the alleyway and turned onto the road that led to the footbridge over the Tabiltu River. His uncle had arranged passage for him on the small boat of a friend heading downriver to Kalḫu.

Jamin didn't look at the temple as he passed.

Nineteen

The Arabian Desert
Nineteenth Day of Simanu

The last six days of the journey to Aššûr blurred together, as so many days had before them. Deprived of his camel, Jonah was forced to walk. Although there were extra camels laden with goods, none of the drivers offered to replace his mount. They kept their distance and eyed the Hebrew with distrust. The loss of their leader due to Jonah's mishap, paired with the mystery of the disappearing snake, placed him just below pariah on the social scale. He didn't care. Nor was he surprised to learn that he didn't miss their company. Instead, monotony became his travel companion.

The terrain was monotonous, the sky monotonous—and that was all there was to see. Day after day, just sand and the glare of the sun. Jonah retreated into his thoughts for refuge from the bleakness that surrounded him. He plodded along, allowing each foot its own freedom in the winless race to Aššûr. Gradually, his sluggish brain painted a scrim of northern Israel's vivid green over the dull taupe of the Arabian Desert. The lush Jezreel Valley nudged aside the barren wasteland in his mind's eye, and the Kishon River's springtime waters cooled his imagination. For hours of blessed delusion, he was back on his donkey cart, while his beloved Jezebel plodded a gentle pace along the familiar trails around Gath-hepher. Faint recollections of his mother's cook fire wafted ribbons of ethereal aroma around his brain and probed his inner senses with memories of roasted lamb and hot flatbread.

When sunset suspended the day's trek and interrupted his daydreams, he found himself resentful. He preferred the bliss of his mind's day wanderings to the stark and uncontrollable invasion of night dreams. So the cycle continued. Day after nameless day.

Yesterday there appeared out of nowhere a narrow riverbed. The river was dry, so it presented no obstacle to their progress. The caravan crawled through the cleft in the landscape and left it behind with little memory of its existence. Jonah never noticed the dry ford, for it, too, was obscured behind his blessed daydreams.

This morning, after the second thong on his sandal snapped both its binding and his thoughts, irritation took over. The knot he tied after the first break had rubbed a raw spot on his ankle, which now festered in the heat. He knelt to examine the damage, only to get kneed into the dust by the camel behind him. Rather than apologize, the driver just glared at Jonah and prodded his animal onward.

As he trudged mindlessly along the trail, Jonah's shadow crept further in front of him, stretched by a tired sun draining the last of its light onto the western horizon. His shadow climbed the rump of the camel ten paces in front of him and had just touched the back of its driver, when the caravan began to ascend a gentle incline. The subtle change in stride roused him from his trance.

The train of animals topped the rise and halted. Jonah limped toward the front of the group, then stopped in wonder at the sight spread before him. A vast river—the Idiqlat, he presumed—snaked through a low plain along a carpet of vegetation, the first foliage he had seen in days. The verdant green, even subdued as it was in the shadows of the fading day, hurt his eyes, such was its contrast to the desert grays and browns that had dulled his senses for so long. To the south a small tributary converged with the great river and nurtured a vast field of reeds, rushes, and low brush between itself and the larger waterway. To the north, the buildings of a great city gleamed in the late afternoon light. They shone a vibrant white, not yet grayed by the evening shadows that encroached from the western ridgeline. On the outskirts of the city, disciplined rows of orchards, vineyards, and other crops, framed with irrigation trenches, melded in with the wild vegetation along the riverbanks.

Jonah devoured the sight. He was unable to break his stare even when the caravan began its trek down the slope toward the city. A rough nudge from the cargo bag on a passing camel broke his stupor, and he fell into step behind the beast, though he still craned his neck for another view of a civilization he almost forgot existed.

The caravan reached the city gates as the evening's shadows topped the parapets. The lead driver signaled for a halt. They would spend the night outside the city, but in the protection of its proximity. Although Jonah would part company with the caravan here in search of transport upriver to Nineveh, he decided to remain in familiar company for one last night. Tomorrow would be soon enough to explore the city on the final leg of his journey.

Jamin stepped off the *quppu* onto the sandy bank of the Idiqlat River, his small bag of belongings slung over his shoulder. He glanced up at the familiar Temple of Ashur, which shone its brilliance in the waning rays of sunlight, a grand reminder of the city's former prominence as the Assyrian capital. Although King Ashur-nasirpal had relocated the political capital to Kalḫu seventy-five years earlier, the great structure dedicated to the nation's patron god ensured the spiritual capital would remain in Aššûr. The massive edifice dwarfed the promontory on which it stood, and bowed only to the shadow of a lofty ziggurat that loomed a short distance to the southwest. The stepped tower provided Ashur a convenient avenue to descend to the city at his pleasure, as similar ziggurats across Assyria did for their gods and goddesses. There, the principal gods of the *Igigi* and lesser deities of the *Anunnaku* pantheons would find ample stores of sustenance, gathered and dedicated to them by the humans they had created from the clay of the Mesopotamian delta for just that purpose.

Jamin ignored the heathen temple. He had suffered his fill of such places in Nineveh, and his heart still ached. It rankled him that so much wealth and grandeur were dedicated to these idols. These were the weakness—indeed, the downfall—of any heathen nation, no matter how great it might be among men. He knew it was only a matter of time before Assyria would collapse into rubble along with the shrines of its impotent gods. Such was the fortune of those who put their trust in wood and stone.

The journey downstream from Nineveh should have taken a little over two days, half the time it took to ply the river upstream. There was an unexpected delay in Kalḫu, though, where the boat owner put in to repair a persistent leak. As his fare for passage, Jamin was to help with steerage, but most of the time he just bailed water from the narrow, curved bow. Although he was anxious to get home, he was grateful to have the seam patched and get some relief from the back-bending chore of sloshing water out of the prow.

The prolonged journey did give Jamin more time to think. It also allowed returning to Nineveh to grow from a niggling idea to a full-fledged urge. The next step would be obsession, and he knew he wasn't far from it. But what would he say to his parents? What reason would he give to leave again so soon? He was old enough to be on his own. Surely he didn't need their permission. Still, their blessing was important to him, and he knew they would never bless the reason for the urge—all right, now it was an obsession. He sighed and shook his head as he made his way along the familiar streets to the Jewish enclave.

"Shalom, Son! We've missed you!" Judith pushed to her tiptoes and hugged her son. She planted a big kiss on his cheek.

Jamin smiled and reddened at the attention. *"Shalom*, Mother. You are well, I trust?"

Obadiah grasped his son's wrist. *"Shalom*, Jamin. Yes, we are well."

His mother beamed at him. "Supper will be ready soon. We weren't sure what day to expect you. This is perfect. Tomorrow we celebrate your father's birthday."

Obadiah raised an eyebrow at his wife. "Celebrate? We talked about this."

She smiled sweetly. "Yes, we did."

Jamin laughed. "I remembered your birthday, Father. I wanted to be home in time. It's good I left Nineveh early, though. We had to put in at Kalḫu for repairs. I was afraid I'd miss it."

"Give me your bag. Is there much to be cleaned or mended?" She tugged at the tie string and peered into the musty sack.

"I cleaned everything before I left Nineveh, but I'm afraid the boat was dirty."

"No matter." His mother touched his cheek. "It's wonderful you're finally home."

Jamin swallowed and forced another smile. His resolve to broach the subject of returning to Nineveh began to melt in the glow of his mother's adoring eyes.

Obadiah pulled his son aside while Judith dumped the contents of the bag in the corner of the room. "So, how are Hiram and Rizpah?"

"I'm sorry, Father, I should've told you. They're doing very well. They send their love."

"And did you learn much of their trade?"

"I learned a great deal in Nineveh." *About a lot of things.* Jamin averted his eyes, fearful they might betray his thoughts.

Obadiah cocked his head. "A great deal, eh?"

Jamin's cheeks tinged pink. He never could get anything by his father; he should know better by now than to try. "You know, about their craft, yes—but also about the community, the city. Nineveh is growing. Getting bigger . . . a lot of building . . . and things. There is much to learn . . . about Nineveh." He rolled his eyes inwardly at his rambling.

Obadiah smiled. "Do you want to talk about it?"

"Talk about what?"

"Talk about why your face is the color of the sky at sunset and your forehead glistens like a spider's web with the dew of dawn?"

"I hurried from the river to get home. I guess I'm a little overheated." Jamin tried to smile and did it poorly.

"Jamin, I'm your father."

Jamin's shoulders slumped, and his gaze dropped to his feet. His words rolled out on a heavy sigh. "Why can I never get a thought past you?"

Obadiah smiled again. "I just told you why. I'm your father." He glanced toward his wife. "Let's go outside."

The two men stepped through the door, chased by Judith's exhortation not to go far. Supper was nearly ready.

His father's opening deflated Jamin's chest. "What's her name?"

"Wha—who?"

Obadiah struggled to stifle a laugh. He failed.

Jamin bristled. "What's so funny?"

The elder man sniffed back another chortle, and his eyes glistened. "Son, it's all over your face. You want to go back, don't you?"

Jamin put both hands on his hips. "How can you know? Maybe it's not that at all. Maybe I'm just . . . maybe it really is just the heat. Maybe—"

Obadiah brought the back of his hand to his mouth to block another laugh. He slapped Jamin on the shoulder. "It's all right, Son. It happens to the best of us." The next chuckle escaped before he could get his hand back up.

"It's not funny!"

Obadiah forced a straight face and tried to blink away the moisture in his eyes. "All right, all right. No need to get upset."

Jamin drew himself up. "Maybe it's not a girl at all."

Obadiah tilted his head, and the corners of his mouth quivered involuntarily.

"All right!" Jamin flailed his hands. "It's a girl! Are you happy now?"

Obadiah bent double, and the guffaws now poured out unrestrained.

Jamin narrowed his eyes. "I hate it when you do that."

"Sorry." His father gasped for breath and raised his hands to signal a truce.

Jamin crossed his arms and waited for his father to regain control. He hoped it was painful.

"So." Obadiah sniffed and brushed a tear from the corner of his eye with a knuckle. "What's her name?"

"I don't know."

His father stared at him. "You don't know?"

"Not yet."

Obadiah searched the ground at his feet for the right words. When he looked back up, his brow was knit. "Where did you meet her, Son? What family is she from, what tribe?"

Jamin ground his jaw. "It's a long story, Father. I don't have those answers yet."

"Is that why you want to go back?"

"Yes." Jamin's eye twitched. It wasn't the whole truth, but it wasn't a lie, either.

Obadiah raised an eyebrow. "She's not . . . you didn't . . ."

Jamin reddened. "No. It's nothing like that."

The elder man pursed his lips.

"Please believe me, Father. I've never given you cause to distrust me, have I?"

Obadiah shook his head. "No, you haven't."

Jamin frowned. "I'll need help telling Mother. I don't think she'll understand."

"How soon do you want to go?"

"Soon. When I can find another boat going upriver." Jamin paused. "Father, Uncle Hiram said he could always use the help. I will be useful there."

His father smiled. "I know you will, Son." His face grew serious. "We will want you back soon, though. We deserve some answers."

"I know, Father. Thank you."

The door swung open and Judith's smiling face poked out. "Supper!"

Twenty

Aššûr
Twentieth Day of Simanu

Jonah peered through the western gate as the portal opened for another day of commerce. A narrow road led across a thin strip of ground enclosed on both sides by rubble walls faced with sun-baked brick. The newer outer wall stood proud and strong against the morning sky, while the inner wall sagged under the weight of its age. The older structure featured pockmarked, decaying brickwork with variegated signs of patching and refurbishment applied at intervals throughout the centuries. It looked tired. Jonah sighed and empathized with the decrepit bulwarks as his old joints reminded him of every step he had taken across the desert.

Once through the gap, he found himself on a modest street in a residential area. Private houses lined both sides. Most of them appeared new. He walked toward the city center, where the size and newness of the buildings diminished. Older quarters now assumed prominence, most neglected and some in serious disrepair.

The street dead-ended into a broader avenue after it entered the inner-city district. Jonah stood at the convergence of the two roads, and pondered which route would take him to the riverside. To the right, a row of low structures wound around a bend. To the left, he could see the tops of taller buildings above the low houses. Their silhouettes girded the morning sky, aglow with the aura of a brilliant sun that crowned the eastern hills.

Jonah decided the larger buildings meant a business area, which would more likely lead to the primary waterway that supplied the city with irrigation, sustenance, and, most importantly, transportation. He turned to the north and plodded along the boulevard.

Soon the road broadened into a large square bordered by a low wall on the left. The buildings he had keyed on came into view, and he stopped in his tracks. Spaced along a wide avenue through the plaza were pillared structures that could only be temples. Pagan temples. Jonah set his jaw and pressed forward. The road forced him to pass between the heathen shrines.

As he came abreast of the first building on his right, movement between the columns caught his eye. He glanced up the steps and slowed to a stop. On the portico milled a bevy of women clad in varying degrees of immodesty. The prophet's jaw dropped at his first encounter with temple prostitutes. He stood mesmerized at the bizarre sight, his stare broken only when one of them turned and flashed an alluring smile at him. Heat flooded his head when she raised a hand and beckoned. It suddenly occurred to him what she was. Jonah had heard of cult prostitutes, a *qerashah* in his own tongue, but had never seen them in such numbers or so brazenly displayed in public. He knew from lore that, in Israel, cult prostitutes veiled themselves and lured their victims in a much more subtle fashion. Here, in Assyria, they flaunted themselves openly and shamelessly. He tore his gaze from the woman and lurched ahead to distance himself from the vile shrine.

His path took him between more buildings, which he assumed also to be temples, although their steps were devoid of women. Finally, he came to a walled complex that looked more like a palace than a temple. The upper terraces of a stepped tower rose above complex. He recalled the mental image he had formed of the Tower of Babel, when, as a young boy, his father told him the story of man's frustrated attempt to equal himself with God. The ziggurat rose darkly into the morning sky, a stark reminder of how far behind he had left the Promised Land.

The road forced Jonah to the left where it led between the walled complex and the largest temple in the plaza. He skirted the wall and found himself perched atop a rocky slope that dropped off to the Idiqlat River. Jonah stopped to catch his breath, unsure of where to turn. He scanned both directions and glimpsed a narrow road tucked against the wall to his right. The path led downward along the face of the hill and then leveled out by the river. He took a deep breath and set off toward the water.

The road opened into a courtyard of another even more imposing temple that commanded the high ground above the great river. He reckoned this one to be quite important, given its size and position on the promontory where the Idiqlat River wound around the rock bluff from the west and continued its unhurried journey southward. He shook his head in disgust at the heathen monument.

Jonah turned his attention to the waterfront. Countless landings stretched along the peninsula and disappeared around the bend of the headland. Boats of various sizes and shapes tethered to trees and boulders along the bank sent gentle ripples into the quiet current of the river flowing past. He tried to guess which might be the *quppu* and which the *kalakku* that Jamal had spoken about. There were too many that seemed to fit both descriptions, though, and he gave up any attempt to identify them. It didn't matter anyway. He intended to find the largest, most stable barge he could find, no matter how long it took to get to Nineveh.

With a glance at the sun ensconced in the eastern sky, he picked his way down to the river.

I hope someone here speaks Hebrew.

Jamin finished his breakfast quietly. News of his intent to return to Nineveh had not set well with his mother the evening before.

"You remember today is your father's birthday."

Her subdued tone pricked his heart. "Yes, Mother."

She opened her mouth to continue, but then stopped.

Obadiah glanced up. "Judith, I know this is difficult, but Jamin is right. He has his life and he needs to live it. He can't stay in our house forever." He reached for his wife's hand, but she shifted just beyond his reach. Her moist eyes remained on a morsel of bread she was fingering into crumbs.

"Mother, I won't be leaving for another couple of days. Tomorrow at the earliest. I'll look for passage upriver this morning. I don't know how soon I'll find something." Jamin's voice beseeched at least her acquiescence, if not her blessing.

"How long will you be gone this time?" She brushed the remains of the bread crust from her tunic.

"I don't know. Not long, I hope. I'm just not sure." Jamin threw a pleading look at his father.

Obadiah shrugged.

"I'll see to your travel bag." His mother rose from her seat and padded to the back of the room. She stopped near Jamin's sleeping niche and stooped to pick up his blanket. She kept her back to the men while she folded the blanket.

Jamin cleared his throat. "I'd better get down to the river. It may take awhile to arrange passage."

His father nodded.

〽〽〽

Jonah's quest for a boat went poorly. The few boatmen who stopped to listen just shook their heads at his words. He tried to gesture, point at the boat and then the river, and to over-enunciate "Nineveh . . . Nin-e-veh . . . Ninnn-ehh-vehh." That usually resulted in an annoyed scowl and a turned shoulder.

By midmorning, having experimented with every possible way to gesticulate and pronounce "Nineveh," Jonah was at his wit's end. How was he supposed to preach repentance in a land where he couldn't even arrange a simple boat ride? He flung a rock into the water, and his words grated with exasperation. "This is impossible! What am I even doing here?"

"Excuse me. Are you an Israelite?" Jamin paused on the hillside path to address a slight, white-haired man.

The man looked startled. "Yes. Do you speak Hebrew?"

Jasmin twitched an eyebrow at the silly question. "Yes. I'm a Jew. I live here in Aššûr."

The old man rose from the boulder, relief all over his face. *"Halelu-yah!* I didn't know there were Hebrew-speaking Jews in Aššûr."

"There is a community of us who follow *Adonai* and retain the old language. My name is Jamin." He stepped closer and held out his hand.

Jonah grasped his wrist. "I'm Jonah. I've been sent by *Adonai* to preach to the people of Nineveh."

"You are a prophet?" Jamin's eyebrows shot up. He'd heard of prophets, but living in Assyria afforded little opportunity to meet one.

"I am. Well, I'm supposed to be." Jonah frowned. "I came by caravan as far as Aššûr, where I intended to take the river to Nineveh. But I can't seem to arrange passage. I don't speak the Assyrian tongue."

Jamin knit his brow. How does one prophesy to people when he can't speak their language? He took another look at Jonah. Nothing in the frail-looking man before him fit the mental image Jasmin had formed of a prophet of God. A holy man who carried the word of the Living God would be robust, confident, strong, exuding purpose from every pore in his body . . . wouldn't he? Jasmin looked again.

Jonah fidgeted, sniffed, and scrubbed a sleeve across his nose. A self-conscious smile touched his lips for a second, then he stared at the ground, exuding awkwardness from every pore in his body.

Jamin shrugged. "Perhaps I can help you. I'm seeking passage to Nineveh, too."

Jonah's eyes lit up. "I would be very grateful. I can work for my passage." His voice faltered. "I'm afraid I don't have much silver."

"No matter. Boatmen have little use for silver. They barter in labor and goods. We should be able to find someone going north within a day or two."

Jonah nodded, his relief evident. "I'll let you do the talking."

"That would be good."

It was midafternoon before the two men found a small *kalakku* bound for Kalḫu the following day. Jamin arranged passage for labor, and they agreed to meet at sunrise. They would seek another boat for the final leg of their journey to Nineveh from the capital city.

Jamin offered his family's house to Jonah for the night. Jonah was grateful to accept, and the men backtracked across the city. Jamin pointed out the sights and explained some of the history of the ancient city. The massive temple and ziggurat on the promontory were dedicated to the principal Assyrian god, Ashur, he explained, as they climbed toward the city center. When they reached the top of the hill, he confirmed Jonah's impression that the walled complex was a palace—actually more than one palace, constructed by various kings through the centuries. He pointed out the one built by the first King Adad-nirari over five hundred years earlier.

Jamin named each of the temples along the road that led away from the palace complex. The large temple on their right was dedicated to Anu, the ancient king of the Sumerian gods, and the storm god, Adad. Across the road to their left was the temple of the sun god Shamash, and the moon god, Sin. A few paces more put them beside Nabu's temple, which shared a courtyard with the larger shrine to Ishtar.

Jonah threw a glance at Ishtar's temple, and the heat returned to his cheeks from his encounter with the *qadishtu* that morning. Jamin grew quiet, as well. The portico was vacant in the high heat of the afternoon. Jonah marveled at the plethora of idols in which this nation placed its trust. The message of repentance he held for Nineveh could have benefitted Aššûr, as well. Maybe it would.

They crossed the plaza and turned up the boulevard leading to the western-gate road. Jamin led his guest back into the newer quarter. He halted before a neat, modest house.

Introductions between Jonah and his parents broke his mother's glum mood. She was agog, and somewhat flustered, that a prophet of the Most High God was in her home and would spend the night. Her parents eagerly, but respectfully, plied Jonah with questions about events back in Israel. Few travelers from the Levant passed through

Aššûr, and they were hungry for news and gossip.

Jonah told them what he could. He related Jeroboam's ascension to the throne, God's promise of restoration to *ha eretz*, and Israel's resurgence in the Promised Land of their forefathers. Obadiah sat back and beamed with pride at the news of the renewed Israel. He asked of Elisha, the great prophet. Jonah quietly told them of the prophet's death over twenty years previously, and that he was buried in his hometown of Dothan. A moment of silence settled over the room, and Obadiah muttered a quiet prayer over the memory of the holy man.

After a larger-than-usual supper in honor of their guest and Obadiah's birthday, they retired early to rest for Jamin's and Jonah's departure at first light the next morning.

Jonah jerked when Jamin nudged him from his slumber in the predawn. His mother fussed by lamplight while she stoked the cook fire to heat some flatbread, determined that her son and their special guest begin their journey with a good breakfast and a full sack of provisions. Obadiah placed Jonah's staff and their travel bags against the front wall, then unbolted the door.

After a tearful hug, Judith kissed her son on his cheek. She exhorted him to be careful and to return soon. She smiled at Jonah and nodded her appreciation for his choosing to grace their home with his presence and for lifting their hearts with news of their homeland. Obadiah grasped both men's wrists and bade them farewell. He blessed them with a prayer for safe travels.

Jamin led again through the familiar streets, lit only by the dim glow of a three-quarter moon low in the sky and the burgeoning glow of early dawn to the east. They walked in silence, each occupied with his own thoughts.

Jonah pondered how he would ever communicate with the people of Nineveh.

Jamin pondered how he would ever communicate with just one

certain person in Nineveh.

Both men were still at a loss for ideas when they arrived at the riverfront.

Jamin mentioned how fortunate they were to find passage so soon, as upriver navigation on the Idiqlat River was rare. He explained to Jonah that most goods going north traveled overland in caravans. River craft coming downstream were often dismantled at their destination, the wood from the frame sold, and the skin coverings hauled back north in caravans to be reused by the boat builders.

He related how the Idiqlat's lazy current between Aššûr and Kalḫu permitted the flat-bottomed *kalakku* to be towed upstream, usually by oxen that walked a path along the riverbank. Jamin told Jonah their odds of finding a boat would normally have been worse so soon after flood season. In springtime, the river often overflowed its banks without warning. The early rains sometimes washed away paths, destroyed crops and villages, even changed the course of the river itself. This year's rainy season had been lighter than most, though, and the water level was elevated but not dangerous.

Khalil, the boat owner, was a wiry little man. How old the boatman was, Jonah couldn't guess. Years of exposure to the sun had turned his dark skin leathery, but his eyes still held the glint of youth. He spoke little, although he wasn't unpleasant. There was just little to be said.

The trio pushed off into the river shortly after sunrise. The *kalakku* rode the water smoothly tethered to two yoked oxen that plodded along the western bank. Jamin explained that, although Kalḫu lay on the eastern side of the river, the Idiqlat had no large tributaries that fed it from the west that would block the oxen's path. The same was not true of the eastern bank.

The barge carried sacks of early barley for beer, small amphorae of sesame oil, grapevine roots to transplant, and sundry other consignment items. Tucked along the stern were the men's personal bags and supplemental feed for the animals, should they be unable to forage at any point along the way. Khalil took the helm and applied just enough counter steerage to keep the oxen's pull from veering the *kalakku* toward the riverbank. The oxen knew the path and didn't require a lead. Jamin shifted the cargo to ensure a balanced load. At midmorning, he glanced over his shoulder at Jonah, who sat hunched over on a sack of barley near the gunwale. Ashen-faced, he held his head in his hands and fixed a blank stare at the passing riverbank. His stomach had lurched the first time before they even cast off the bowline. It hadn't stopped lurching since.

They moored across from Kalḫu just before sunset two days later. Khalil and Jamin spent the night on the *kulakku*, but Jonah offered to go ashore and keep an eye on the oxen. The boatman said that wouldn't be necessary, but Jonah insisted. Khalil shrugged and mentioned something about snakes. Jonah didn't care about snakes. If he didn't get off the water soon, he was sure he would die anyway. His stomach settled the moment his foot touched dry land.

 Early that morning, Khalil left Jamin and Jonah to watch the craft while he made his way to the city to arrange a ferry for his cargo. He would inquire about craft bound upstream for his passengers' continued journey to Nineveh. The two men watched the capital city come alive in the morning light. Kalḫu sprawled over the landscape, its palaces and temples every bit as impressive as Aššûr's. A ziggurat rose above the city's skyline. It reminded Jonah of the tower beside the great temple back in Aššûr. He wondered for a moment to which god this monument was dedicated, but then decided it didn't really matter. He preferred to avoid the temples anyway, and was glad to stay behind—on shore. Jamin tidied up the barge and waited for Khalil to return.

 The swarthy boatman reappeared before midday. He leaped with a smile onto the boat from the sandy embankment. "Good news for you. I go on to Nineveh. More cargo."

 Jamin was overjoyed, Jonah less so. He had secretly hoped they wouldn't be able to find another boat and that they'd have to go overland. It was only a little over one day's trek on foot anyway. By boat it would be a full two days, maybe more. Two days on the water. Two days hunched over the side.

By sundown, their cargo was offloaded and a new shipment of dried herbs and spices, as well as three large timbers cut for the king's new palace in Nineveh, were loaded. The herbs and spices could have gone overland, but the timber's length and width presented a problem. River transport would be ideal, and the boat owner was very happy with the generous fee he received from the king's vizier to hasten the materials north. He lashed the timbers together and attached the lead rope to the rear of the *kalakku*. The beams rested in the calm water astern the barge.

Early the next morning, they re-harnessed the oxen and prepared to cast off. Jonah took a long look at the boat's deck before he stepped aboard. He told himself how silly it was to be sick. The boat was stable, the water was smooth as glass—in fact, if he closed his eyes, he was sure he would barely detect any movement at all. That's what he would do. He would close his eyes. Then he could imagine he was anywhere but on a boat. Jonah set his jaw, measured the pace to an open spot amid the cargo, and closed his eyes.

His stomach lurched as soon as his foot touched the deck.

Twenty-one

Afloat the Idiqlat River, North of Kalḫu
Twenty-fourth Day of Simanu

"It is a different river every year." Khalil leaned over the stern and scanned the surface of the water.

"How so?" Jamin sat on his clothes bundle and chewed the stub of a reed he'd plucked from the shallows downstream.

"Floodwaters change the riverbed every season. Silt changes the channel every day. It is not always possible to take a boat this far north." Khalil nodded toward the water. "Her current is stronger than her sister's, the Purattu. Yes, the Purattu is much easier to boat. The Idiqlat, she is fickle."

Jamin's eyes followed Khalil's gesture toward the expanse of water. On the surface, the river seemed tame enough. But spring storms in the mountains to the north could raise the water level in short order. He had heard stories of whole villages flooded, caught unawares by the bloated river. He threw a subconscious glance upstream.

Khalil grinned at Jamin's anxiousness. "Enki smiles on us this year. The God of the Rivers has calmed the Idiqlat. Just for us." A toothless grin stretched his mouth. "In Kalḫu, I met two friends. They boat the Idiqlat and just came from Nineveh. They tell me the river is good for travel north. The king will have his timber, no?"

Jamin nodded. He looked over at Jonah, who was sprawled near the bow. "How soon will the king have his timber?"

"By nightfall."

"That's good."

They arrived at Nineveh late that afternoon. As at Numrud, Khalil tied off the boat and left Jamin in charge while he saw to business across the river. The ferry would take the spices to market, while another *kalakku* towed the timber beams across the river and up the mouth of the Tabiltu to the staging area for construction on the palace.

"You must stay at my uncle Hiram's house while you're in Nineveh. He and Aunt Rizpah will be honored by your presence. They can also introduce you to the city's Jewish community." Jamin bent over Jonah's supine form.

The queasy prophet squinted from beneath an arm draped across his forehead. "When do we get there?"

"We're here."

Jonah peered over the gunwale. The *kalakku* floated motionless at its mooring. Across the water, Nineveh's western wall rose from the rocky desert floor not far from the riverbank. A tributary pushed through a gap in the fortification and spilled muddy water into the Idiqlat. Branches from a single westward road punched holes through the city wall, their gates still open for perhaps another hour. The tops of great buildings rose above the wall and glistened beige in the late afternoon sun. One of the structures appeared to be either new or newly restored, and scaffolding rose beside another. He guessed the scaffolding belonged to the palace for which their timber was destined.

He pushed himself to his knees and grasped the gunwale to steady his balance and his stomach.

"How do we get over there?"

Jamin shrugged. "We can either take the ferry across with the spices, or walk up to the ford and take the road."

"Let's take the road."

When Kahlil returned, the two Jews bade him farewell. The boatman grinned at Jamin as they clasped wrists. "You work hard. Maybe we travel together again."

He just grunted when he clasped wrists with Jonah.

The two men scaled the riverbank and made their way upstream to the ford. Jamin had difficulty keeping up with Jonah, whose energy revived at the feel of solid ground beneath his feet. They reached the Mashki Gate as the sun touched the western horizon. Jamin led the way through the gate and turned up the familiar road to the artisan's quarter. He forced his eyes away from the temple plaza.

Jamin stood in the narrow alleyway and tapped on his uncle's door. Jonah fidgeted behind him, with his staff propped against his shoulder. He twisted his travel bag with nervous fingers.

The door opened a crack. "Jamin!"

The door flew open, and Rizpah swooped into her nephew's arms. She squeezed his neck until he began to gasp. "You're back! So soon?"

She spotted Jonah over her nephew's shoulder and released her grip. Uncle Hiram appeared in the doorway, and Jamin introduced his traveling companion.

"This is Jonah ben Amittai. He's from Israel."

"Israel?" Rizpah's hand covered her mouth. Hiram smiled.

"My Uncle Hiram and Aunt Rizpah." Jamin nodded toward his relatives.

"*Shalom.*" Jonah grasped Hiram's wrist.

They echoed his greeting.

"Uncle Hiram. Jonah has come to Nineveh with a message. He is a prophet of *Adonai.*"

Uncle Hiram broke the stunned silence first. "Come—come in. Please." He glanced at his wife. "Rizpah, you'll need to move. Rizpah?"

She apparently didn't hear her husband.

"Rizpah. Let the man in." Hiram threw an apologetic look at Jonah and tugged his wife's arm.

Rizpah stared over her shoulder, her mouth agape, while her husband guided her into the house.

Jamin smiled red-faced at Jonah and gestured to the door.

A flustered Aunt Rizpah managed to pull together a modest meal for her family and guest, while the men settled on reed mats in the small front room. They sipped herbal tea still hot from an earlier brewing. Uncle Hiram tried not to appear too curious about Jonah and his message, so he turned the conversation to news of the homeland. Jonah repeated the tidbits he had passed on to Jamin's parents, which seemed to satisfy his host. Aunt Rizpah kept an ear bent from the cook fire as she worked. Despite her distraction, she clipped only one finger with the knife she was using to trim a string of dried figs.

Uncle Hiram's curiosity finally won out. "You mentioned a message for Nineveh? Am I permitted to inquire . . . ?" His voice dropped, not sure how prophets delivered their messages, or if it was all right to ask.

Jonah looked up. "Yes, it's fine." He repeated the message the angel gave him on Joppa's beach, and added that the city had forty days to repent before the Lord, or it would be destroyed.

His words hung in the air like a dark cloud.

"Destroyed?" Hiram stared at the prophet. He turned his eyes toward his nephew. "Did you . . . know this?"

Jamin stared at Jonah just as intently. "No, I didn't." He set his half-eaten fig down.

Jonah kept his eyes on the mat. "I am to preach repentance to the city, but I'm not sure how. I don't speak the language." He looked up and flushed at his hosts' horrified expressions.

Rizpah glanced up from her work. "What was that, Hiram? I didn't hear you."

Hiram repeated his question and Jonah's answer. His wife dropped the blade and settled onto the floor. Her eyes drilled into her husband's. "All of Nineveh?"

Jonah glanced at her. "Yes. Unless the city repents, it will be destroyed."

Hiram cleared his throat. "How?"

"I don't know. The angel didn't say. Only that it would be destroyed." Jonah's eyes beseeched his host's. "I'm only the messenger."

Hiram drew himself up and released a slow exhale. "Forty days is not much time for a single man to warn a city this size—even if he did speak the language." He glanced over at Jamin. "We can help."

Jamin cocked his head. "Help?"

Hiram set his face. "We will convene the Council." He glanced at Jonah. "The Council is the group of elders who watch over the interests of Nineveh's Jewish population. You can deliver the message to them. They can then pass the word to their families. We have retained the tradition of our native tongue, so we speak both Hebrew and the language of Assyria. We can spread the news much faster throughout the city. That's the only way we'll have time to reach all the people."

"But will it do any good? Will the people repent?" Rizpah's voice was small.

"We have no control over that. We can only deliver the message. The rest is up to *Adonai.*" Hiram addressed Jonah. "You will need to lead. The people must see you and hear you to know the message is indeed from *Adonai*, and that we have not gone crazy in the head."

Jonah nodded. "When do we start?"

The Council met at midday in a corner of Nineveh's marketplace. Business and community gatherings like this were common events in the open square, and no one took particular notice of the group. Hiram was grateful for the anonymity. He knew the message would not be received with calm by anyone who might overhear their parley. To make sure, they would speak only in Hebrew.

Jonah sat to Hiram's right, the place of honor. The remaining thirty-nine elders sat in two concentric semicircles. Hiram, Jamin, and Jonah occupied the open end of the U-shaped gathering. Hiram hadn't told Jonah he was the senior elder of the Council, and Jonah was impressed with the measure of deference the others showed his host.

Hiram greeted each of the elders personally with the traditional wish for peace and a kiss on both cheeks. When everyone had taken their places, he rose in silence, his eyes fixed on the ground. This was a grave posture, and the Council grew quiet. The business at hand must be serious.

"Thank you for coming on such short notice. Please forgive me if I forgo pleasantries, for today we have a matter of great urgency to discuss. I ask you to listen carefully, and consider fully your response to what you are about to hear. We will need to decide on a course of action quickly."

Murmurs spread through the group. Rarely was Hiram this solemn.

He continued. "The man seated to my right is Jonah ben Amittai. He arrived at my house yesterday evening. He comes from Israel."

The buzz rose, and several of the men leaned over and whispered to those seated next to them. Jewish visitors were rare in Nineveh—especially one who had come directly from *ha eretz* and whose presence warranted a convocation like this.

"What can this be?"

"Has something happened to the Temple?"

"Has Jerusalem fallen?"

Hiram gestured to Jonah to stand. Jonah rose to his feet and surveyed the gathering, wondering how he would present news that their city was doomed.

Hiram raised his hand and the whispers dropped. "Jonah has a message for us, for the city of Nineveh, from *Adonai*. He is a prophet of the Most High God."

All conversation died in an instant. Every eye stared at the white-haired man who fidgeted beside their leader. The only sound was the rustle of activity from the market vendors' stalls. That sound, too, faded into the background in the presence of an emissary of God.

Hiram nodded at Jonah and took his seat.

Jonah scanned the eyes that bore into him from every face in the Council. He prayed for the words and the strength to deliver them. "Sons of Abraham, I bid you *shalom* from the land of our forefathers, *ha eretz*, the Land of Our Promise. Many of you have heard of Israel's recent resurgence—how she has reclaimed lost land and thrown off the yoke of oppression under which we have suffered for so long."

Most heads bobbed in affirmation.

Jonah continued. "I am the man who, six years ago, delivered *Adonai's* message of deliverance to King Jeroboam at his court in Samaria."

The murmurings rose again, excitement more evident in this round of whispers.

"Yes, I heard of a prophet."
"Can it be the same?"
"It must be!"

"I have been given another message from *Adonai* through his angel. This time it is not for Samaria, but for Nineveh." He paused. "I wish the message was as joyous this time as it was six years ago."

His last comment cut the murmurs short. Brows furrowed, and the men leaned forward.

"The angel told me to preach repentance to the great city of Nineveh, for its evil has come up before the Lord."

Not a man moved.

"If the city does not repent of its evil ways in forty days, complete destruction will befall it at the hands of *Elohim Adonai*, the Lord God."

Jonah fell silent and waited for the reaction. He did not have to wait long.

With a single voice, the Council burst into shouts of dismay and disbelief.

Jonah stood his ground.

Hulalitu shifted her stance beside the spice-seller's booth. She clutched her basket to her stomach and strained to hear through the hubbub. The cluster of men who sat nearby babbled and waved their hands in the air. The hubbub drowned out the words of the stranger who stood before them.

The *naditu* arrived on her weekly trip to the marketplace just as the group gathered near the booth she now shopped. She wore a plain cloak over the distinctive priestess's tunic as she always did in public. Hulalitu detested the sidelong glances of passersby and the nervous looks the temple garb sometimes drew from the laity of the city. The common garment was an easy solution, although the other priestesses at the temple would not approve of the disguise. Service to Mother Ishtar was an honor, and most of the *naditu* priestesses reveled in the attention their appearance drew. But the disguise would serve her doubly today, as she knew her tunic would stifle the men's conversation. She edged closer.

The white-haired man in the center of attention was curious enough, but what drew her attention was the unfamiliar language. People from many lands had settled in Nineveh, but seldom did they gather publicly in large groups and speak in their native tongues. What drew her suspicion most, though, was the young man seated next to the speaker. It was the man who had tried to steal Ianna away from the temple that night, the man with silly notions of a strange god. He had confused her precious Ianna, brought her to tears. Hulalitu clenched her teeth. What was his name? Oh yes, hadn't the old man on the steps of Nabu's temple called him "Jamin"—the same old man who led this gathering? If Jamin was part of this, nothing good could come of it. He would bear watching. They all would.

By this time Hulalitu had reached the outer ring of men. She stayed in the shadow of the wall, but now she could hear more clearly. She frowned again at the foreign tongue.

A man seated near her jumped to his feet and stalked to a spot only few paces away. He leaned against the wall with his head bowed. An idea grabbed her. It was improper for a woman to speak unbidden to a man in public, but she had to try. There was nothing to lose.

"Please forgive me, sir. May I have a moment?"

He jerked his head. "What is it, woman? Why do you approach me?" His face was dark.

"It is with the best intentions, please, sir. I am not here to proposition you. I have only a question, and I will leave you." She kept her head bowed in respect and tugged the collar of her cloak closer to her neck. It would be disastrous for him to glimpse her tunic, as he would surely take her for a temple prostitute.

He narrowed his eyes. "Very well, what is it?"

"Please, sir, I hear the voice of your speaker, but do not understand the language. What could he be saying that distresses you so?"

"Him?" The man gestured with a thumb over his shoulder. "Hah! The end of the world, that's what!"

She lowered her voice. "I don't understand."

The man snorted. "He fancies himself a prophet. He preaches destruction upon the city at the hand of the God of Israel."

Hulalitu's downturned face warmed, but she kept her voice even. "Destruction? From a god of Israel? What does a god of Israel have to do with Nineveh?"

He turned to face her. "Not a god, woman, *the* God. *Elohim Adonai*, the God of Abraham. If He determines to destroy, He will destroy. Make no mistake about that."

It was all Hulalitu could do to subdue her anger. How arrogant for a foreign god to think he could have his way in Assyria with impunity! She forced calm into her voice. "But what of the gods of Assyria? What of Ashur, Marduk, or Ishtar? Surely they will not allow this to happen."

The man snorted. *"Adonai* is the only true God, the God of all nations, of those who recognize Him as well as those who do not. Assyrian gods are nothing but stone idols. They are powerless before Him."

Hulalitu nearly lost control. She came a breath away from slapping the man for his blasphemy. Instead she backed away, her head still bowed, her voice raspier. "Thank you, sir. I leave you now."

The man turned and strode back to the Council.

Hulalitu hurried to the far side of the spice booth to collect herself. She gripped her basket until a reed snapped against her whitened knuckles. The furious priestess took a deep breath and strode across the marketplace toward the Tabiltu River bridge. When she reached the far side, she glared back over her shoulder at the assembly. She took a hard look at the strange prophet of this arrogant god. But she took a harder look at the young man who now stood at his side.

Twenty-two

Kalḫu, the Royal Observatory
Twenty-fifth Day of Simanu

Zakir focused his gaze through the observation hole in the roof. He shook his head, then bent back over his lunar charts and stared at their symbols and notations in the flickering light of a small oil lamp. He shifted through several clay tablets until he found one marked at the top with the symbol of the Moon God, Sin. His finger traced the wedged glyphs that forecasted the moon's trajectory and phase. It stopped at a symbol halfway down the right column. He lifted his head and peered back through the sky hole. His bushy eyebrows twitched.

"Urdu, come here a moment, will you?"

The junior astrologer slipped to his master's side. "I am here."

Zakir pointed to a small wooden board on a low table, its wax inlay half-filled with pressed notations. "You annotated the log that Sin rose pure this evening at the expected time."

"I did, Master Zakir."

"Of course you did, boy. It is right here. But look now." Zakir stepped from the circle etched onto the floor beneath the sky hole.

Urdu took his mentor's place and peered upward. He squinted to adjust his eyes, then arched a puzzled brow.

"What do you see, Urdu?"

"Sin has faded. It appears his face has grown dim. I also see . . ." Urdu concentrated on the orb. "A dark cleft on his side." The apprentice lowered his eyes. "He has lost his roundness."

Zakir tapped his finger on the Simanu tablet. "A dark cleft, yes. How do you explain that?"

Urdu shook his head. "I don't know. I've memorized the chart, as you instructed. My annotation was correct. Sin rose when, where, and how he should have. I don't know why . . ." Urdu's voice faltered. He returned his gaze to the observation portal.

Zakir nodded. "There is a pattern to the dimming of Sin. No need to worry. You will learn it. However, it is not always seen well, so it is not always predictable. Rarely does his face go dark, any part of it. When it does, we watch for other *ittu*."

Urdu dropped his startled eyes to his master. *"Ittu?* You mean omens? Could this mean something?"

Zakir replaced the Simanu tablet. "By itself, it might signify nothing. But if other signs follow, we must be vigilant."

"But his face is not dark, merely dimmed. Perhaps it is part of Sin's course."

"True, Sin has his course and he does dim. However, tonight's shadow is unpredicted. And do not ignore the dark cleft. As you know, Simanu is the month of Sin. He should be strong; he should stand proud in the skies. That he does not may mean he is displeased."

Urdu fidgeted. He had aspired to be an astrologer since he was a young boy. The art of reading the skies to discern the will of the gods had always fascinated him. Honor awaited in the king's court for the man who could interpret signs of the deities and recognize their moods, which he knew were varied and unpredictable. Now, faced with his first possible *ittu*, he found himself unnerved.

"If he is . . . displeased, then what do we do? How do we determine what causes his displeasure?" Urdu was visibly shaken.

Zakir chuckled and shrugged. "We never know the source of the gods' displeasure; we only read the signs that tell us they are displeased. Theirs is not to reveal themselves to us. We are mere mortals. Perhaps they argue among themselves. Perhaps someone has transgressed a vow, insulted a priest or priestess, or failed to provide for a god's needs at his shrine. Who knows?"

"Then what do we do? There must be some reasoning in this."

"Reasoning? Why?" Zakir glanced up at his apprentice. "The gods need no reason. They are the gods. Here, let me show you something."

Zakir turned to a row of earthenware urns against the wall. The rolled ends of new leather scrolls protruded from the mouth of each urn. He scanned along the row, then pulled a short scroll from the fourth pot. "I think . . . yes, here it is."

The old astrologer loosened the jute binding and spread the parchment over the table. He mumbled as he ran his finger down the Aramaic characters stained into the hide. "This is from an old clay tablet—" He glanced up at his assistant. "I have asked Remuttu, the senior scribe and an old friend, to rewrite the old language records from the clay tablets into the new language on these parchments we have begun to receive from the west." He held up the cured animal skin and tossed it lightly from hand to hand. "Much easier to handle than mud bricks, don't you think?"

Urdu began to reply, but Zakir laid the parchment back down. "Such modern innovations." He smiled and shook his head. "What will they think of next?"

The senior astrologer continued his search. "It is a prayer by a forgotten sage of an age long past. He mused, as you do, at the fickleness of the gods. His conclusion is here somewhere on this—yes, here it is. Let me read it to you."

Urdu peered over the old man's shoulder at the scroll. "I don't recognize the writing."

Zakir nodded, still squinting at the text. "It is new to me as well, so I must read slowly. Remuttu has instructed me in its use, but my mind is old. I do not grasp as well as I once did."

Urdu smiled. He knew no man of any age in the entire land whose mind was as sharp as his mentor's. He was certain Zakir would digest this new tongue with little effort. And he was not disappointed.

Zakir scratched his nose and began, "It's entitled 'Prayer to Every God':

'The transgression I have committed I do not know;
The sin I have done I do not know;
The forbidden thing I have eaten I do not know;
The prohibited place on which I have set foot I do not know;

> *The god whom I know or do not know has oppressed me;*
> *I am troubled, I am overwhelmed, I cannot see.*
> *Man is dumb; he knows nothing;*
> *Mankind, everyone that exists—what does he know?*
> *Whether he is committing sin or doing good, he does not even know.'"*

Urdu opened his mouth, but Zakir silenced him with an upraised finger. "And farther down there is more from a similar tablet. It is . . . here:

> *'I wish I knew that these things were pleasing to one's god!*
> *What is proper to oneself is an offense to one's god,*
> *What in one's own heart seems despicable is proper to one's god.*
> *Who can learn the reasoning of the gods in heaven?*
> *Who could understand the intentions of the god of the depths?*
> *Where might human beings have learned the way of a god?'"*

Urdu leaned back as the old man straightened. Zakir rerolled the scroll, tied off the twine, and returned it to the urn.

The young astrologer frowned and stroked his wispy beard. "If there is no way to discern the cause of a god's distemper, what is the value in what we do?"

Zakir chuckled. "My son, it makes what we do all the more valuable. If one knew the source of a god's displeasure, he could ensure he does not arouse it by doing or saying only the right and proper things. But, as one does not know such things, he can only seek to appease the offended god when the need arises. To know when the need arises is the job of those such as the *muhhu,* who seeks communication with the gods, the *baru,* who reads the entrails of sacrificed animals for good and bad signs, and—most importantly, of course—we *tupsharri,* who are the first to see omens in deviations from the normal cycles of the heavens."

Urdu did not look convinced.

Zakir continued, "And there are many others. There are those who read signs in the earth—"

"I understand, Master. I know of these seers." Urdu knit his brow. "But what good is an omen if we do not know which god is offended, or what has occurred to offend him?"

Zakir waggled his finger. "The god and the offense are not important. What is important is the king."

Urdu's brow wrinkled again. "The king?"

"Of course the king, boy. The dispositions of the gods reflect on the king and his court. The legitimacy of his reign is measured by divine affirmation of his decisions and his plans. We seek good omens that affirm the king, as well as bad omens that portend problems for him. That is why we are in the court's employ." The elder *tupsharru* took his apprentice by the shoulders and gazed into his eyes. "King Adad-nirari relies on us—you and me, Urdu—to ensure his reign is stable and his legacy strong. We watch, we advise, and we warn. If we do that well, our job is secure. It is up to the king's religious advisors to counsel him on which gods to appease and how to appease them."

Urdu nodded, and Zakir released his shoulders. The senior astrologer moved back to the observation circle and peered through the cleft. "So, now, back to where we were. What action do we take based upon what we have seen this night?" Zakir glanced over at his apprentice.

The young astrologer thought for a moment. "You said we have too little to act upon with only the dimming of Sin, although the cleft in his face is more troubling." He raised an eyebrow. "We watch for more signs?"

Zakir smiled. "You learn quickly, boy. More dangerous than delaying an advisement is rushing one."

Urdu nodded, but he still couldn't shake the uneasiness in the back of his mind.

Twenty-three

Nineveh, the Temple of Ishtar
Twenty-seventh Day of Simanu

Hulalitu pressed her point with the High Priestess's aide. "I must speak with her. It is of great importance."

"Issar-surrat is not to be disturbed. She rests."

"But I have—"

"Come back before the evening meal. Perhaps then." The senior *naditu* pulled the embroidered scrim across the doorway. Hulalitu heard the attendant's soft sandals pad a gentle rhythm across the smooth floor.

She heaved a sigh and turned away.

Issar-surrat tossed on her sleep mat. She kicked aside the scarlet silk coverlet draped over her bare legs. The seed of a headache centered low in the back of her head sprouted into a hundred thorny tendrils that clamped down and gnawed at her brain. The onslaught had cut short her preparations for the evening rites and drove the High Priestess to her chamber. She left three senior *naditu* priestesses to finish. Issar-surrat gripped her head and dropped onto the luxurious mat without shedding her robe.

Her eyes quivered beneath her kohl-lined lids.

"You have arranged for the girl?"

Issar-surrat jerked her head. "Yes, Mistress. She has . . . learned quickly as a *naditu*."

"Her time is coming."

Issar-surrat grimaced as another bolt of pain shot through her temples. "Yes, Mistress. I've ensured her preparations . . . have been thorough. She will not . . . disappoint."

"No, she will not disappoint. But she needs more power for her task."

"More power, Mistress?"

"Of course. The threat is great. The defense must be greater."

Issar-surrat tried to lift her head, but an unseen weight pressed it further into her pillow.

"You have named her as your successor, no?"

"It was recorded . . . four days ago, Mistress. Although I do not see why—" The weight on her head cut off her words. Issar-surrat struggled, but her neck sank deeper into the pillow. The rich cushion billowed and puffed up against the sides of her head.

"And you are sure the king will assent?"

"All has been . . . arranged, Mistress."

"You have done well enough, Issar-surrat. You have been compliant. Perhaps you will not be forgotten."

"Forgotten? What do you mean—"

The fringes of the pillow folded over her face. Issar-surrat's thick fingernails tore at the fabric as the cushion closed over her mouth and nose. Her legs flailed and sent the coverlet into the air. Muffled screams pushed through the bulging pillow but melted into the heavy air. The priestess's back arched and slammed to the mat where she writhed and fought for breath. Gradually, the struggle abated to a twitch, then to stillness.

Her left arm slipped from the pillow and slapped against the floor. As though on cue, the cushion deflated. It released the dead priestess's face and flattened against the mat under her head. Streaks of kohl smudged Issar-surrat's powdered cheeks and splayed streaks of charcoal gray away from sightless eyes.

Mother Ishtar would have a new High Priestess by nightfall.

Ianna sat on the floor of the cella. The *Entu* ceremony had concluded at sunset. The hall was empty; only the subdued hiss and snap of the torches broke the stillness.

The ornate robes of the greatest religious authority in Nineveh lay piled around her diminutive figure in a rumpled heap. The gold cap and bejeweled ceremonial staff lay on the floor by her side. A heavy, multi-strand necklace, now removed from her neck, draped over the cap and staff. She sat with her elbows propped onto her knees, her chin pressed into the palms of her hands. Through her foggy mind, she tried to reconstruct the series of events that had led her to this lonely spot on the floor. . . .

Ianna's dramatic rise to the most exalted position an Assyrian woman could attain surprised her more than anyone. Issar-surrat's sudden death stunned them all, but preparations had to be made quickly for her replacement. The post of High Priestess could not be vacant. Issar-surrat's foresight in naming her own successor quickened the process, as extraordinary as the act was. The king's assent to her nomination documented on a clay tablet bearing his seal lay next to her body. Its contents shocked the senior *naditu* council, but nothing could be done. The King's decision was final. No sooner had the High Priestess's body been removed from her bedchamber than the tight-lipped council of senior *naditu* priestesses met and began their preparations for a hurried ascension ceremony.

The astonishment at her summons before the council still numbed Ianna's mind. The solemn pronouncement that she would assume the ultimate position in the cult of Ishtar left her speechless. She was not alone in her reaction. The strained resentment that clouded the council room was palpable. Shalla, the presiding senior *naditu,* refused to make eye contact with the High Priestess designee. It had been assumed by everyone, not least by her, that Shalla would be Issar-surrat's eventual successor. After the charge for Ianna to prepare herself for the ritual, the taut-jawed *naditu* adjourned the council without ceremony and stalked out of the meeting hall, her disdain undisguised.

When the news of Ianna's ascension raced through the temple, Hulalitu retired to her chamber and did not reemerge. Her absence from the rite—an absence that should have earned her at best a severe censure, at worst banishment—was noticed. But no censure came. Those in the position to impose the sanction were too occupied with their own violated egos to bother with a formal reprimand for a lesser priestess who only did what they all wished they could have done.

Ianna's own shock rendered her impervious to the reactions of others. She plodded from the council summons to her chamber in a daze. The young *naditu* entered the room, sank to the floor and stared at the wall. She took no steps to prepare herself for the ritual—if, indeed, she even knew what steps she should take. When the senior *naditu* escort came to her door to convey her to the cella, they found her in the same bewildered state in which she left the council meeting.

The walk to the cella was a blur. The door opened in front of her, and a wide yellow swath spilled into the dim hall from the room ablaze in torchlight. Someone took her arm and guided her to a marked spot on the floor in front of the great statue of Ishtar. A whisper in her ear, a slight nod, and she lay prostrate before the Mother Goddess, for how long she had no idea.

The words of the mantra incanted by the assembly jammed in her ears against the shell of numbness that encased her brain. Another tug on her arm raised her to her feet, where she turned to face the gathering. She didn't know how large or small the crowd of witnesses was. Their forms blurred together in a pastel smear, punctuated by flashes of silver and gold that glinted in the flickering torchlight. They had no faces.

A few terse, hushed words—who knew how many?—from Shalla, and the heavy robes of the High Priestess suddenly pressed down on her shoulders. An unseen pair of hands draped the festooned gold chain around her neck. Another pair lifted her arm and pressed the short staff into her listless fingers. After an indeterminable pause, a single voice began the final chant of dedication to Mother Ishtar. Something in her told her to turn and face the statue. She did so with unfocused eyes. Other voices joined the chant. She stood dumb.

Her next memory was the dull thud of the massive chamber door, and she was alone. . . .

Ianna sighed. She wrinkled her brow at a sudden prick in the back of her skull. She sensed, more than felt, the jab expand into a numbness that slid over her brain, where it sent twinges of needle pricks into the skin under her hair. The sensation enveloped her head like a thorny sheath. Her eyes rolled back in their sockets as her eyelids slid closed. Her breath came in short gasps

"You are the chosen one. Prepare to meet your Mistress."

Ianna shook her head and pressed her fingertips to her brow.

"Speak your readiness, your desire, to serve the Mistress."

The new High Priestess forced her eyelids open. She touched her fingers to her temples and massaged her throbbing head. The numbness began to recede, but then clamped down and dug its claws deeper. She grimaced.

The silky voice hissed, *"Speak your desire to serve!"*

Ianna moistened her dry lips with the tip of her tongue and took a deep breath.

The voice screeched in her mind's ear, *"Now!"*

She gritted her teeth. "Who is speaking? Where are you?"

Ianna jerked her head as the ethereal shell snapped and disappeared. The seizure cleared, and the vestiges of a headache lurked behind her forehead. She squinted into the muted light. The statue of Mother Ishtar hovered over her shoulder, her enameled eyes bearing down on her new supreme servant.

The High Priestess collected the accoutrements of her office and pushed to her feet. She stretched the stiffness from her joints, replaced the necklace around her neck, the cap on her head, and padded to the door.

She turned to glance once more about the cella, faded now with the glow of the dying torches. Then she opened the door and stepped into the corridor.

Mother Ishtar glared at the door from her pedestal.

"The girl is difficult. She resists."
   "Leave her to me."

Twenty-four

Kalḫu, the Royal Palace
Twenty-eighth Day of Simanu

King Adad-nirari scrutinized the plans for his palace in Nineveh. Ahu-duri, the Senior Scholar and the king's closest advisor, fidgeted on the far side of the low table while the king muttered under his breath.

"How near are we to completion?" The regent didn't look up from the drawings.

It was the first question the king asked and the one Ahu-duri feared the most. "We are on schedule, my lord."

Adad-nirari raised his eyes, but his head remained bent. "That is not what I asked."

Ahu-duri cleared his throat. "The work on the Temple of Nabu took longer than expected, my lord. Materials are slow coming in, but we are making progress."

The king narrowed his gaze. "I do not—what is that?"

Ahu-duri didn't answer. He thought his eyes were playing tricks on him. A clay dish with two styluses at the corner of the work table began to clatter and bobble. The floor beneath his feet undulated as though he stood on water. He gripped the table and jumped when the clay dish tottered off the edge and shattered on the floor. Everything around him moved while he fought to stand still. The vizier never felt so helpless, so out of control. He stared wide-eyed at the king.

Adad-nirari's face was set. He gripped his side of the table, willing it to stand still. The king muttered the word absently, as though it was an afterthought. "Earthquake."

The tremor ended as suddenly as it began. Ahu-duri held onto the table, his equilibrium not yet convinced the floor had settled. For a moment, neither man spoke. Shouts rose from the streets below and spilled into the room through the high windows.

The king finally looked up. "Report back to me on any damage. We will resume this discussion later."

Ahu-duri nodded and hurried to the door. Once outside the chamber, the advisor heaved a sigh of relief, despite his raw nerves.

Urdu rose from the floor. He clutched a jumble of parchment rolls that had spilled from an overturned urn. The quake only lasted moments, but the documents stacked against the wall needed little encouragement to collapse and jitter across the floor. Thankfully, none of the stellar instruments or clay tablets was damaged. He righted an urn and eased the parchments back into it just as Zakir burst into the room.

"What's broken? Is there any damage?"

"No damage, Master. Only a mess." Urdu retrieved the hinged writing board and set it on the stone table.

"The city will be in an uproar. It's been long since the earth has moved in Kalḫu." Zakir took a deep breath and reached out to steady a stack of tablets.

Urdu didn't reply. He stroked the log with an absent expression.

"You are all right then? Unhurt?"

"Yes."

Zakir steadied the tablets and stared at his apprentice. "What are you thinking?"

Urdu just shook his head and continued to stroke the wooden pad.

"Come, come. Out with it." Zakir grasped his assistant's wrist. "I think the lunar log has sufficiently recovered from its trauma."

The young astrologer pushed aside the wooden palette. He turned and leaned against the table, his arms folded across his chest. "I'm trying to make sense of this. Two nights ago Sin darkened his face. Now the earth shakes."

"And . . . ?"

Urdu shrugged. "You spoke of omens."

Zakir nodded. "Yes, I did."

"What does it mean?"

"You do well to think in such a way. It is discomforting, no?"

Urdu persisted. "I want to know what it means."

The senior astrologer turned to face his assistant. "As do I."

"But, if we don't know—"

"Urdu, the gods create such omens not as explanations, but as hints. There is no vapor in the air, no secret formula, that details the exact meaning of omens. It is not that easy." Zakir eased his back against the table beside his apprentice.

"But there are ancient writings, adages that give the meaning of signs, are there not?"

Zakir smiled. "Yes, of course there are. The *Enuma Anu Enlil*, our collection of celestial omens. How much of it have you read?"

Urdu tinged red. "I know I was supposed to begin my study of them, but I'm afraid I've not yet started."

Zakir nodded. "I have read it all. Those stacks of tablets in the corner are a small part of it. And, in my humble opinion, it is useless."

"Useless?"

The master astrologer shrugged. "Guesses. The musings of men who strain beyond the limits of their wisdom."

Urdu's shoulders sagged. "But, if the *Enuma Anu Enlil* are useless, what can we know of the *ittu* at all? How are they omens if they cannot be read?"

"That man fails to understand them does not mean they are not omens. There are things that can be discerned, things upon which we can act. It is the difference between their meaning and their significance."

"How so?"

Zakir stroked his beard. "Well, take today's earthquake. The writings have much to say about their meaning, and they vary greatly. If the earth shakes in the month of Nisanu, there will be a revolt against the king. If in Du'uzu, the king will be exalted in the lands of his enemies. If in Tisritum, we will have a curious combination of prosperity and hostility in the land. If it occurs at night, it means devastation in the land. Oh, I could go on and on."

"And the significance?"

"Ah, yes, the significance is much more useful. When the earth shakes, we know Nin Ur, the God of the Earth, has begun to march. So, we know which god has been moved to action. We do not know whether he is pleased or displeased—which would be the meaning of his movement—but we know he moves. That is the significance." Zakir pushed away from the table and crossed to a stack of clay tablets beside the *Enuma Anu Enlil*.

Urdu shook his head. "But isn't discerning his mood of most importance?"

"Why?" Zakir selected an ancient tablet near the top of the second stack and blew a layer of dust from it.

"So that we know what we should do, of course."

"Whether he is pleased or displeased does not change our response. In either case, we appease him. If he is displeased, we appease to assuage his anger. If he is pleased, we appease to bolster his good graces. Appeasement is always the key. Then, who knows? Maybe he will hear and relent in his evil intent, or increase his good intent."

Zakir squinted at the tablet.

"What do you have?" Urdu frowned at the brick of dried mud.

The elder astrologer brought the tablet to the table. He eased it down and brushed the remaining dust from its surface. As the writing became clearer, Urdu creased his brow. He had never seen symbols like these, nor had he observed a tablet with its contents organized in such a fashion. The nameless scribe of a distant age who pressed his stylus to this clay had separated the surface into three parallel columns. Each column was divided into several rows, which formed blocks into which symbols were grouped. Centered at the top of each block were two large symbols. Urdu noted the glyphs were repeated in successive blocks, but in different combinations. Beneath the dual-symbol headings, several more markings appeared, grouped in rows reading right to left.

141

"Master?" Urdu glanced at his mentor.

Zakir's face was set, his eyes intent. He traced his finger down the center column, then stopped four blocks from the top. He nodded and looked up at Urdu.

"This is the Chart of the Gods. It has been long since I have consulted it."

"I don't recognize the writing."

"It is very old. Let me explain. These symbols represent the principal gods of the ancient order." He pointed to the large markings at the top of the first block. "The sign in each block reveals the relationship of the gods whose symbols are paired at the top. This is an early symbol for the sun god, Shamash. Paired with him in this block is the King of the Gods, Ashur."

Urdu nodded his head. "I see. I think I understand what you're saying. The dimming of Sin by itself was not sufficient to discern any meaning."

"Significance, not meaning." Zakir held his finger up to accent his point, but kept his gaze on the tablet.

"Significance, then." Urdu rolled his eyes.

"Words are important, boy. Use them well." Zakir's tone teased, but his face betrayed no levity.

Urdu continued. "The earthquake by itself, although more disturbing, was also a single sign. Am I right that one of these blocks is dedicated to the Sin—Nin Ur relationship, and by that we might be able to determine what the two omens together might mean—I mean, signify?"

Zakir smiled without looking up. "I knew there was a good reason I chose you among all the other apprentice candidates." He pointed back to the fourth row in the second column. "Here they are."

Urdu crowded Zakir's shoulder. "What does it say?"

The old astrologer squinted. "It has been long since I've read these symbols. Let me see . . . Sin, among the luminaries, is closest to Nin Ur, the Earth. He is perceived here as a nephew, of sorts. This symbol means 'good' and indicates that they are close." He straightened and stretched his stiff back.

"So, what does that mean?"

Zakir raised his eyebrow.

Urdu sighed. "Signify."

Zakir buried his smile behind a sniff. "Most of the writings that identify a close relationship between two gods or goddesses imply concurrent activity is significant—more significant than deities who have no close relationship, but less significant that those who are at odds, noted by the 'bad' sign . . . here." He pointed to a block several rows down the tablet. "This is the block for Ishtar and her sister, Ereshkigal, the Goddess of the Underworld. Very bad blood there."

"Why is 'bad' more significant?"

Zakir glanced at his apprentice. "More dangerous than collusion among the gods is war among them."

Urdu thought for a moment. "So, what do we do?"

"The significance, in counsel with our brother seers and their observations, should lead us to the meaning." Zakir tapped the surface of the tablet. "We have enough now to report to the court. The earthquake will have King Adad-nirari's attention. He needs to know of Sin's involvement. We cannot ignore the ancient record."

Urdu smiled at his mentor. "But I thought you didn't trust the writings."

Zakir shrugged and returned the smile. "Well, we must start somewhere, must we not?"

Twenty-five

Kalḫu, the Royal Palace
Thirtieth Day of Simanu

"What is it?" Ahu-duri frowned at the rap on his chamber door. He bent over his writing board and examined the marks pressed into the wax by his staff scribe. These were the last notes from the damage report. Too little sleep since the tremor left the vizier's eyes burning and his nerves frayed. To gather information like this in a city as large as Kalḫu was difficult. The city walls needed to be inspected, as did the levee that bordered the Idiqlat River and dozens of other critical points. The last report came in less than an hour ago, and he hurried to finish his findings for the king, whose demands for them had increased in both frequency and volume over the past few hours.

The door cracked open, and his adjutant's nasal voice grated into his ears, which sparked new life into an old headache. "Visitors for you, Vizier. The senior court astrologer seeks an audience."

"Now? Can it not wait?"

"Zakir believes it to be important, Vizier. Something about the earthquake."

Ahu-duri straightened and rubbed the grit deeper into his eyes with the palms of his hands. "All right, all right. See them in."

A moment later Zakir and Urdu entered the chamber and stood by the door. They awaited the signal to approach.

Ahu-duri gestured them in with a wave of his arm. "Come Zakir, please. My apologies, old friend. The king's demand for his damage report is at a fever pitch. I am just finishing up."

"I understand." Zakir approached. Urdu followed close behind with two writing boards clutched to his chest. "My sincerest apologies for the interruption, but we may have some more information for your report." He glanced at the disarray on the vizier's table. "Not that you want any more information."

Ahu-duri's smile was appreciative but lacked mirth. "What do you have?"

Zakir turned to his apprentice. "I do not think you have met Urdu, my new apprentice."

Urdu bowed.

"Welcome to the court, Urdu." He turned back to the senior astrologer. "Forgive my manners, Zakir, but I am afraid I have little time for pleasantries. What is it you have for me?"

Zakir signaled Urdu, who laid a waxed board on the table and opened the hinged cover. "As you know, we rarely report to the court unless summoned. However, there may be more to the earthquake than physical damage."

The vizier knit his brow. "Meaning . . . ?"

Urdu shifted the log in front of his master. Zakir ran his finger down the first column of markings until he reached an entry from the previous week. "Here it is. We observed an anomaly in Sin last week. His phase was full, but after he rose, he faded and lost a portion of his visage to darkness. This is rare, but not unheard of. Most notable, though, is that it occurred during Nisanu, the month over which he presides. You see, when Sin—"

"Zakir, my friend. Please." Ahu-duri held his hands up and forced a weak smile. "You know I trust your mastery of all things celestial. I fear, though, my present task permits me no time for tutelage in the art of astrology. Please reach your point soon."

"Of course. Certainly. I am sorry." Zakir nodded. "Sin's dimming, by itself, was not worthy of mention. However, his relationship with Nin Ur is strong. The earth shakes when Nin Ur marches. The two *ittu* together could mean displeasure among the gods."

"And, therefore, with the king."

"That should not be discounted out of hand." The seer raised an eyebrow.

145

Zakir had Ahu-duri's full attention. "So, you believe these to be *ittu*, signs of something more to come?"

The astrologer shrugged. "Perhaps. We should seek corroboration."

"Such as . . . ?"

Zakir grew thoughtful. "At the next sacrifice to Marduk—which is later today, I believe—it might be good to have Kasiru examine the beast's entrails. If he sees anything out of the ordinary, we could then summon the *muhhu* to cast their lots. Perhaps they can petition the gods for the meaning behind these signs."

Ahu-duri paused. "Do you think your present concerns warrant the king's attention?"

The senior astrologer smiled. "That, my friend, is for you to decide. I have reported what we observed and have recommended how we might proceed to validate them. It is your job to advise the king."

"You are right, of course. My fatigue is speaking for me." Ahu-duri sighed and rubbed the back of his neck. "My mind is in a bit of a fog right now."

"You might reserve what we have told you until you discern the king's mood," Zakir offered. "If he seems receptive, you could mention it. If not, today's sacrifice is not long off. To wait for further *ittu* should not hurt."

The vizier nodded. "Good points. Thank you."

"We will take our leave now and let you get back to work." Zakir patted his friend on the shoulder. "Get some sleep."

"Hah! Sleep? What is that?" Ahu-duri muttered and returned to his report.

The astrologers let themselves out.

King Adad-nirari scowled at the writing board. He raised his bloodshot eyes at Ahu-duri and dismissed the report with a wave of his hand. "I have no intention of reading all this. Tell me what it says and keep it short."

The vizier shifted his stance. His fatigued brain felt so sluggish, he wasn't sure he could string together three coherent words, let alone summarize details it had taken him over two days to compile. He recognized the signs of one of the king's headaches, though. This was no time to dither.

"Well?" Adad-nirari cocked his head.

"My lord, there appears to be no serious damage from the earthquake. The city wall is intact; the few superficial cracks that appeared have already been repaired. No leaks have been noted along the levee. Several buildings show stress from the tremors, but none have collapsed. They are being repaired, as well. All should be back to normal within, oh, two weeks, at the longest."

Ahu-duri paused, but as he considered where to continue, it struck him that was about all there was to it. His shoulders slumped. To be able to summarize the entire report in so few words depressed him. This was the most painstaking work he had done since he became the vizier, and he was sure it had taken at least two years off his life.

"And the people?"

Ahu-duri snapped from his thoughts. "I am sorry, my lord. The people?"

The king sighed and rubbed his forehead. "Of course. What of the people? What are they saying? How has this affected them? I can replace buildings, but reassuring the populace is another matter."

Ahu-duri reddened. He was so preoccupied with the physical damage that it never occurred to him to gauge any trauma the earthquake may have inflicted on the citizenry. His conversation with Zakir rushed back into his head. Would the people be thinking of omens, of the displeasure of the gods, too? Of course they would. And of course the king would be concerned. His regime, his legacy, everything he worked for during his reign would find its legitimacy in the eyes of the people through the *ittu* of the gods. He better have an answer for this question. There would be no excuse not to.

"The streets are calm, my lord. My sources report no discontent among the people."

The king leaned back in his chair. "But it is yet early. Fear takes time to foment into discord."

Ahu-duri nodded his agreement. The fewer words the better.

Adad-nirari squeezed his eyes closed. "Convene the court seers. Tell them I want a report on what they have observed."

The Senior Scholar bowed. "It is timely for a convocation, my lord. Zakir will have his celestial observations. The sacrifice to Marduk is taking place even now. I have already ordered the *baru* to perform an extispicy. The animal's organs should support any other signs there may be."

The king opened his eyes to slits. "You already thought to do that? Good. You're looking ahead, Ahu-duri."

The vizier felt a pang of guilt at taking credit for Zakir's idea, but now was no time for trivial confession. "Thank you, my lord."

"Have them convene in the anteroom to my chamber before the evening meal."

"Yes, my lord."

〽️ 〽️ 〽️

Kasiru slipped the blade of his ceremonial knife under the hide of the sacrificed ram's belly. He slid it to the groin and opened a clean slit the length of the animal's abdomen. His practiced hand then drew a quick slice across the torso that extended across both sides of the rib cage. "Now, peel back the skin. We will examine the intestines first, then the stomach. The liver we will save for last."

Kabti, his apprentice, took Kasiru's instruction and folded the lower two flaps over the animal's haunches. He turned his head from a musky odor that billowed from the gaping hole.

"You must get used to it sooner or later, boy. I suggest sooner."

Kabti nodded but didn't speak. The boy's pale face hinted to the senior *baru* that he'd likely lose his apprentice before the day was out. The next few moments would either confirm or allay his suspicion.

Kasiru gave a cursory scan over the exta lying in the animal's opened carcass. As senior haruspex at the Marduk's temple in Kalḫu, he had performed thousands of extispicy rituals. He led a group of seven seers who regularly examined the exta, or vital organs, of sacrificed lambs, sheep, goats or rams, usually by request from the king or another prominent citizen who faced a dilemma or a critical decision. The ritual was always the same. After he performed multiple purification rites, the *baru* would lay the supplicant's petition before Shamash and Adad, the gods who governed divination. Then they would pray for a decisive sign to be revealed within the sacrificed animal. Today's request had come from the king's vizier, although he gave no reason for it.

Kasiru lectured his young assistant as he patted the flaps of hide away from the incision. "Normally, we begin with the liver, the most vital of organs. There is a strict method we use to search for markings, or anomalies. You will learn it. Then we move to the gall bladder, kidneys, breastbone, stomach, and intestines for corroborating omens."

Kasiru glanced at Kabti for any sign of understanding. Nothing yet. He frowned. "Today, however, we began with the intestines, as it is better to test your powers of observation there. The animal's colon holds many signs: weapon-marks, holes, request-marks, fissures, foot-marks, cysts, and many more telltale anomalies you will also learn. The order in which we examine the exta is not as important as that we examine them well."

Still no hint of comprehension in Kabti's glassy eyes.

Kasiru pursed his lips. "Before we touch anything, be attentive to the whole of what we will see, not just the parts. While you might think it's best that there be no anomalies at all, what we hope to see is regularity and wholeness on this side." He gestured to the right of the body cavity. "But not so regular on this side." He moved his hand to the left. "Here there should be some malformation for a positive reading."

Kabti stared at the mass of entrails that wound their way through the animal's abdomen.

The *baru* raised an eyebrow. "Kabti?"

The apprentice flinched but didn't look up.

Kasiru shook his head. "Now, move around here and tuck your hands under both sides of the intestines. Good. Now move them here, like this. We must not break the organ open and spill its bile, or it will spoil the reading. Well, go ahead . . . slowly—no! . . . That's right. Now lift. . . . I said lift. Kabti, are you all right? You don't look—by the gods, turn your head!"

Fortunately, Kabti missed the carcass.

Kasiru sighed. "Go home, boy. I will finish up here."

Without a word, the ashen-faced youth staggered to his feet and stumbled off. He held his blood-soaked hands at arm's length in front of him.

The haruspex looked around for any of his associate *baru* seers, but they had gone to clean instruments and dispose of remains from earlier rites. He repositioned himself at the ram's side and glanced over his shoulder toward the altar. "Sasi, some help, please?"

The temple priest laid his swabbing cloth on the half-cleaned altar and joined Kasiru. He steadied the carcass as the *baru* reached into the hollow. Kasiru shook his head while he worked. "I don't know where we get our apprentices, Sasi. Kabti was a disaster from the moment he set foot in the temple."

Sasi chuckled. "Kabti's father is intent on his son becoming either a priest or a seer. And since only the king can appoint priests, that leaves seer. He'd already bumbled through four failed apprenticeships before they sent him to you. Zakir has forbidden him to come near the observatory just on reputation."

Kasiru grinned and shook his head. "Zakir is a wise man. I can just see the boy fumble with a stellar measure. It would be in pieces on the floor before he ever got it up to his eye."

Sasi glanced up at Kasiru. "The boy emptied his stomach on purified soil. Will that affect the reading?"

The *baru* shook his head. "Prayers have already been said and the animal opened. His discharge did not touch the beast. All should still be in order."

The priest nodded.

Kasiru lifted the entrails and untangled them, careful to note their original configuration and not to disrupt any twists or marks. He traced its surface with his fingertips, lingered over bulges and probed hollows. Finally, he piled the tubular organ on the ground beside the ram's corpse.

"Nothing here. Everything appears as it should."

Sasi took the cue and peeled back the upper two flaps of hide. Kasiru squinted into the cavity as the stomach came into the light. He performed the same fingertip examination over the surface of the organ, but he didn't shift it from its position.

"Nothing of note," he concluded. "Except . . ."

"I was just going to ask," Sasi interjected. "The color?"

"Yes, exactly." He looked up at the priest. "What do you see?"

"Well, extispicy is not my art, but the stomach seems off-color. It looks to me to have a gray tinge." His eyes questioned the senior *baru*.

Kasiru nodded. "You are correct. The surface is discolored. Notice, it becomes more so toward the top. We may need to open it." He slipped his hands around the top of the organ and began to shift it to the lower part of the abdomen.

"I did notice that." Sasi leaned closer as the entire stomach slid into view.

Kasiru smiled. "Have you considered a change in careers, Sasi? I appear to have an opening for an apprentice—by the gods!"

Sasi jerked his head. "What? What is it?"

For a moment, Kasiru said nothing. He stared at the shaded hollow above the stomach, then slowly removed his hands from around the stomach. When words came, his voice was low. "Pull the hide back farther."

Sasi complied, and then he, too, went still as the liver came into view. Normally a dark reddish-brown, the principal organ of the ram appeared piebald gray and black, and mottled with white lesions.

Kasiru found his voice first. "It's diseased. I've never seen one this bad. This wasn't a sacrifice; it was a mercy killing."

The odor of rotten tissue wafted from the cavity, and Sasi turned his head away. Kasiru pushed the stomach back into position. "Burn this. Everything. Now."

Sasi nodded. He stood and shouted to two priests who stood by the temple door. "Bring wood. And fire. Quickly!"

Kasiru rose to his feet and inspected his hands. He whitened at the sight of decaying liver tissue that lodged beneath his long fingernails when they scraped the surface of the diseased organ. Sasi nudged Kasiru's shoulder and nodded toward a stone basin near the altar. Both men crossed to the cistern and scrubbed their hands. The clear water turned to a putrid pale red swirled with shreds of gray flesh.

Sasi looked up at the *baru*. "What does it mean? Do you know?"

Kasiru shook his head. "I suspect, but I'll need to confer with others before I am certain. The diseased ram and the earthquake together worry me. Have we heard anything from Zakir?"

Sasi shook his head.

"I wonder if there have been any signs in the heavens. If so, the king needs to know."

"Kasiru!" The call came from a temple steward at the doorway. "The king's vizier summons the court seers at the palace."

Sasi frowned. "Something's wrong."

Ahu-duri scanned the group of advisors though bleary eyes.

Zakir and—what was his name? oh, yes—Urdu were at the front, still laden with the writing boards he carried earlier that day. Kasiru stood close behind them. The *baru* leaned forward and whispered something into Zakir's ear. Ahu-duri thought he saw the senior astrologer's brow crease at one point, but Kasiru stepped back a moment later without a response. Two *muhhu* stood off to the side, the shorter one—presumably the junior diviner—carried a cedar box. Ahu-duri recognized the container as one in which the seers kept the instruments of their trade: various lots of wood, bone and ivory they would cast before the gods for divine direction. They might also scatter dried herbs and tea leaves to discern patterns, as well as employ sundry other articles to attract the attention of a particular god or group of gods. The art fascinated Ahu-duri, and he wondered if he might not have undertaken divination, had he not become Adad-nirari's Senior Scholar.

Ahu-duri stifled a yawn, then addressed the small assembly. "Thank you all for coming on such short notice. As I'm sure you've gathered, the king is concerned over the recent earthquake. He has asked me to convene you to advise him on its significance—if, indeed, there is any significance. I must caution you of one thing, though. The king suffers from one of his severe headaches. It is abating, but his temper remains short. When he questions you, be succinct." His eyes flicked involuntarily toward Zakir, whose own eyes twinkled in return. He subdued a smile and continued, "The king will address you in turn. Zakir, you will be first, followed by you, Kasiru. Again, please be brief."

The vizier turned to the door and rapped twice, more gently than usual out of respect to the king's condition. A muffled "Enter!" slipped out beneath the heavy wooden panel. Ahu-duri pulled it open and the group followed him into the king's antechamber. They remained clustered in the entryway while the royal advisor approached the king.

"Your chief advisors have assembled, my lord."

Adad-nirari sat with a cloth draped across his forehead. The windows were curtained; the room's only light flickered from four oil lamps and what little daylight slipped past the heavy fabrics. A steward removed the cloth and dipped it into a bowl of water on a small table beside his chair. He replaced it on the king's forehead and stepped back.

"My lord?"

"Yes, yes. Just a minute." Adad-nirari gritted his teeth. "Curse this head of mine!"

Ahu-duri glanced at the group by the door. "My lord, perhaps it would better tomorrow—"

"Nonsense. Continue." Adad-nirari pressed the wet cloth against his skin and let the cool water stream down his temples onto his neck. He nodded, and the steward stepped forward. He removed the cloth and laid it over the bowl. The king tilted his head forward and squinted at the assembly across the room.

"I assume Ahu-duri has informed you of my reason for convening you today. Therefore, I will dispense with formalities. Zakir, what have you for me?"

The astrologer signaled his apprentice to stay put and stepped forward. "My lord, it pains me to see you in such . . . pain."

Ahu-duri rolled his eyes and shot his friend a warning look.

Zakir missed the cue. "I pray for your quick recovery from—"

"Yes, yes. Thank you, Zakir. What say the heavens, man?" The king grimaced at his own raised voice.

"Of course. My apologies, my lord. Three days before the earthquake, we observed an anomaly in the face of Sin. A darkening, my lord, that is unusual for his phase."

"And this means . . . ?" Adad-nirari tapped his fingers on the table.

"By itself, probably nothing, my lord. However, the occurrence of the earthquake so soon after Sin's dimming—and the close association of Sin and Nin Ur—give me pause to consider. Before I go any further, though, my lord, it may be good to hear Kasiru."

"Very well." The king lifted his hand in a weak gesture, then let it flop back onto the arm of the chair. "Kasiru."

The *baru* stepped to Zakir's side. "Good health to the king, my lord. May your days be forever. My—"

Adad-nirari silenced him with a wave of his hand. "Kasiru, I know this is your first visit to my chambers. Save the honorifics for the formal court. I need to trust your counsel. To begin with a shallow wish we both know will not come to pass does not further my confidence in you. Tell me only the truth, not what you think I want to hear." He grimaced at another stab of pain. "And be brief."

Kasiru reddened, then nodded. "My apologies, my lord. There appeared a most disturbing sign after today's sacrifice to Marduk. The sacrificial ram was diseased—badly diseased. He was likely near death even before the knife ended his suffering."

The king leaned forward, his eyes wider at this news. "And your interpretation?"

Kasiru glanced at Ahu-duri, and then continued. "As Zakir has explained, by itself, it has minimal significance. However, paired with Zakir's observation and the earthquake, I fear there may be discord among the gods. Why, I do not know. But something is surely afoot."

Adad-nirari leaned back, but his eyes remained locked on Kasiru. "Sin, Nin Ur, and now Marduk. When is the next ram sacrifice?"

"Two days from now, my lord."

"You will perform the rite again and report back to me immediately."

"Yes, my lord." Kasiru glanced at Ahu-duri, then stepped back.

"Nurzani."

The senior *muhhu* stepped forward. "My lord?"

"I know your art requires more time. How long before you might have communication from the gods?"

"It's difficult to say, my lord. The gods answer at their own pleasure and—"

"Two days. You have two days. Come back with your report then." Adad-nirari closed his eyes.

"But my lord—"

"Zakir and Kasiru, you return also. I desire your full counsel before I decide upon a course."

Nurzani threw a worried look back at his colleague, who hugged the wall by the door. He turned a pleading face toward Ahu-duri. The vizier avoided eye contact.

"Go. All of you. Two days. Be back." The king flinched at another pang and raised a weak hand to his steward. The aide leapt forward and doused the cloth in the bowl. He pressed it to the king's forehead and squeezed another stream of cool water down his face and neck.

The audience was over.

Twenty-six

Kalḫu
The Second Day of Du'ûzu

Zakir and Urdu hurried from the observatory at the last possible moment before the appointed time to appear at the palace. Nothing in their past two days of observations revealed anything extraordinary in the heavens—that is, what they could see of the heavens. What was extraordinary was the weather.

This time of year the Assyrian skies were normally clear and provided no relief from Shamash's withering heat. These skies during the past day and a half, though, were overcast. The clouds blocked Shamash's direct onslaught, but they trapped the heat low and engorged the land with humidity. Life in the observatory was insufferable. No breeze stirred the air, and the two *tupsharri* could scarcely breathe in the confined space, let alone concentrate on their calculations. Soaked with sweat, their tunics clung to their bodies like sodden shrouds. The cloud cover prevented them from any further observations of the skies, which pushed their moods even further downward. Urdu complained incessantly, and Zakir wondered if he might not kill his apprentice before the heat did.

When the cloud cover finally broke, they went fairly giddy. They stood in the doorway, flapping their arms in the renewed draft that coursed through the opening. Zakir slapped his assistant on the back and confessed how close he had come to strangling him. Urdu replied he'd been so miserable, he probably would've let him. They worked in haste to make up for lost time, but to no avail. The heavens had nothing further to say.

Zakir and Urdu hurried into the palace courtyard and stopped to catch their breath before they reported to the vizier. Once revived, the two astrologers crossed to Ahu-duri's quarters at the side of the main palace entrance. The Senior Scholar met them at the doorway.

"There's no hurry. You're the first to arrive."

"Good. We were not sure when the king would be ready to receive us." Zakir took another deep breath.

The three men walked toward the king's chamber. Ahu-duri confirmed they would gather in the same anteroom they had two days prior.

Urdu spoke up. "I hope the king feels better."

Ahu-duri nodded. "The ache subsided yesterday evening. The residual pain should have passed by now."

"Does he get these headaches often?"

The vizier shook his head. "Not often. This one was particularly bad, though."

Zakir glanced at his friend. "Another *ittu*, you think?"

Ahu-duri returned a tight smile. "I'm just a political advisor. To read the *ittu* is your job."

The astrologer laughed. "Point taken."

The men met up with the *muhhu* seers when they reached the door to the anteroom. Nurzani looked uncomfortable.

Ahu-duri nodded his greeting. "Are you ready for our audience?"

Nurzani glanced at his associate, then shook his head at the vizier. "Nothing. Absolutely nothing. The gods are silent. We performed several rituals, and just when it seemed the lots began to fall in a meaningful array, everything came apart. Neither were there any patterns in the herbs. It's as though the gods toy with us."

Ahu-duri shrugged. "Well, the king's health is better. Perhaps he'll give you more time."

"It's our only hope," Nurzani muttered.

When Ahu-duri reached the antechamber, he turned and squinted into the sunlight over their shoulders. "Where is Kasiru?"

Zakir shrugged. "He will be along."

The vizier narrowed his eyes. "He better be. You don't keep this king waiting." Ahu-duri signaled the group to remain and knocked twice. At the king's reply, he opened the door and slipped in.

After a few moments, the Senior Scholar reappeared in the doorway. "He's nearly ready." He scanned the outer courtyard once again for the *baru*, but there was no sign of him. Ahu-duri shook his head.

"Enter!" The king's voice rang stronger than it had two days earlier. The vizier pulled the door open, threw one more glance over his shoulder, then herded the group into the king's presence.

King Adad-nirari looked up from the waxed board on the table. "This is a good report, Ahu-duri. Keep me apprised on these repairs."

"Yes, my lord."

The king straightened and sized up the group of advisors huddled by the door. His eyes stopped on the senior *muhhu*. "Well, what do we have, Nurzani? What say the gods of these events?"

Nurzani stepped forward. "My lord, I—"

A sharp knock interrupted the diviner's report. Ahu-duri frowned. He caught Zakir's eye and muttered, "It's probably Kasiru."

The king's voice was harsh. "Enter!"

The door swung open and a temple priest stood on the threshold, a palace steward at his side. The priest stumbled forward as the steward pushed him into the room and closed the door.

King Adad-nirari narrowed his eyes. "Who are you?"

Dirty sweat streaked the priest's puffy face, and his chest heaved. "I am . . . Sasi, my lord. A priest at the Temple of Marduk."

Ahu-duri frowned. "Where is Kasiru?"

Sasi's eyes went vacant. "He's dead."

"What do you mean 'dead'?" Ahu-duri stared at the priest.

"There is really only one thing he can mean by that, eh?" Zakir murmured to his friend. He walked over to Sasi and clasped his shoulder. "Collect yourself, man. How did this happen? Kasiru was with us only two days ago. He seemed well enough."

Sasi took a deep breath. "Yesterday morning I came across him outside the temple where he interviewed a new candidate apprentice. He complained of aches. Then, around midday, he came to the altar as I was preparing for the evening rituals. He said he felt feverish, and that he decided to take to his quarters early." The priest hacked a rattled cough.

Zakir patted him on the back. "Did he attend the evening ritual?"

Sasi shook his head. "No, but that's not unusual. There was nothing that demanded his attendance. His rite takes place after the sacrifice."

"And then . . . ?" Ahu-duri appeared at Zakir's side.

"He didn't meet with his new apprentice at the appointed time this morning. The boy found me and asked what he should do, so I had him clean the instruments. I thought Kasiru would be along shortly and I had duties to perform, so I went about my business. I forgot all about it until just a short while ago. I went to check back on the boy. When I found no one in the *baru* work area, I went to see if Kasiru was still at his quarters. He didn't answer my knock, so I peered though his window. That's when I saw him. He was dead."

"You could tell he was dead through the window?" Ahu-duri cocked his head.

"I saw him on the floor beside his sleep mat. I called to him, but he didn't move. So I went back around to the door and went in. He was face-down. His eyes and mouth were open. There was a red stain on the floor by his nose." Sasi shuddered at the memory.

Zakir spoke softly. "You're sure then, Sasi?"

He stared wide-eyed at Zakir and stammered, "I didn't touch him, but I've seen death before, Zakir. Yes, I know death." Sasi wiped the sweat from his upper lip.

King Adad-nirari's voice came over his vizier's shoulder. "Excuse the priest, Ahu-duri. Send him home."

"Yes, my lord." Ahu-duri glanced at Sasi and gestured toward the door.

When Sasi left, Zakir turned to Urdu. "Go back to the observatory. Prepare another observation for tonight."

His apprentice stared at the closed door. "Yes. Uh . . . certainly."

"I'll be along soon." The senior astrologer raised a sympathetic eyebrow. "Try to forget this."

Urdu turned his eyes toward his master. "You can't be serious—"

"Urdu . . ." Zakir jerked his head toward the door.

His apprentice nodded and hurried out.

At Adad-nirari's hint, Nurzani dismissed his assistant, too, and the king was left alone with his senior advisors.

The regent edged around the table and settled onto his chair. He propped his forearms onto the table and surveyed the small group. "I want your impressions on what has happened. We will start with you, Nurzani."

The news of Kasiru's death hung heavy in the air, and the *muhhu* took a moment to respond. "My lord, the gods have been silent. I wish I had something to report, but I do not." He shrugged and glanced over at Ahu-duri.

"Is that normal?" The king was thoughtful.

"No, my lord. Not at all. There has been no discernible pattern in the lots or the leaves."

Adad-nirari raised his eyebrow at the seer. "Perhaps that, then, is the answer."

"My lord?"

"Clearly the gods are disquieted. We do not know why, and they have apparently chosen to withhold that information." The king turned to Zakir. "Two days ago you spoke of a connection between the earthquake and the dimming of Sin. That means Nin Ur and Sin are active. The diseased ram is further sign of discontent among the gods. Do we have any idea which?"

Zakir furrowed his brow. "Only from the ancient records. Ea, the God of Wisdom, has the ram as his symbol."

"You say 'the God of Wisdom' . . . but that is Nabu, the god whose temple I have just finished restoring in Nineveh. He is the patron god of my family." The king begin to pale.

Ahu-duri stepped up. "My lord, I'm sure—"

"How can you be sure of anything?" Adad-nirari was hoarse. "Have I angered Ea by honoring Nabu?"

160

"The cult of Ea is ancient," interjected Zakir. "Nabu is Ea's grandson."

"Is that good or bad?" The king shook his head. "This is too complicated."

The astrologer hesitated. "We need to determine the relationship between Nabu, Sin and Nin Ur, my lord. Unfortunately, my records are at the observatory."

"Get them. I want an answer by sunset."

When the door closed behind Zakir and the *muhhu* seers, Adad-nirari slumped in his chair. "I do not have a good feeling about this."

"My lord, we must not assume too much until Zakir—"

"Look at the signs, Ahu-duri! Sin, Nin Ur, Ea, perhaps Marduk, and who knows what other gods are upset at me."

"It may not be you, my lord." Ahu-duri was unnerved. He had never seen the king fret like this.

"Who else could it be? This is not a lesser god who grumbles at some commoner's misstep. These are the high gods, whose favor or displeasure determines the fate of the realm." Adad-nirari slammed his hands on the table. "The kingship lives or dies by the pleasure of the gods, Ahu-duri, you know that."

Ahu-duri opened his mouth to speak, but then stopped. The king was right. The vizier had no argument, nothing to comfort his master.

"Sin dims, Nin Ur quakes, the ram of Ea is diseased—and now the *baru* of Marduk who examines the ram is dead." The king's face went pale, and his voice faltered. "Could Ea have killed him?"

"My lord, this still does not mean you are to blame. Have you not honored the gods? Have you not rebuilt their temples, improved our cities to their glory, expanded their fields for planting to maintain them? Assyria has prospered under your leadership." Ahu-duri shook his head. "No, there must be another explanation."

Adad-nirari's voice dropped to a murmur. "It does not matter who is to blame. Their wrath falls upon the king. Upon me."

"Then perhaps we need another king until their wrath is assuaged."

Ahu-duri glanced at his liege.

"Do you mean—"

"Yes, my lord. We may need to consider the *ugu lugal.*"

Adad-nirari sat back and stroked his beard. "It has been long since the ritual of a substitute king has been invoked in Assyria."

Ahu-duri nodded. "Since we adopted the tradition from the people from the Westland ages ago, we've installed a substitute king only a few times. The omens are strong, though, my lord. If wrath comes, we must avoid it falling on your head. You are too valuable a king."

Adad-nirari raised his eyebrows. "A substitute king reigns one hundred days. Do you think that will be long enough to ensure the gods' wrath has passed its full measure?"

Ahu-duri creased his brow. "The timing must be right. We must watch the signs closely and install the *ugu lugal* at the latest possible time. That will allow for his reign to span the worst. We need to start soon, though, to identify a candidate. We also need a substitute queen to replace the Queen Mother, Sammuramat."

The king nodded. "How long do you think it will take?"

"Six or seven days, perhaps, to compile a list of candidates. It will also require time to arrange for the proper ceremony to transfer the evil omens from you to him. There may be suitable candidates among the local nobility, but we may draw from the commoners, as well. It is your decision." Ahu-duri frowned. "I fear there may not be time to convene the full council of advisors, my lord." The vizier drummed his forearm with his fingertips

"What are you thinking, Ahu-duri?"

Ahu-duri looked up. "I think we should look outside Kalḫu, my lord. In fact—"

"Yes?"

"We may want to relocate the substitute king's throne, too." The vizier creased his brow. "If wrath comes, it would not do well to have it fall upon Kalḫu, the seat of your kingdom, any more than upon you personally. Although the tradition calls for the substitute's throne to be here, we might consider installing him in another city—Aššûr, perhaps, or Nineveh."

Adad-nirari leaned forward in his chair and leveled his gaze at Ahu-duri. "What you say has merit. Is Nineveh is far enough from Kalḫu, do you think?"

Ahu-duri nodded slowly. "And your palace in Nineveh is nearly complete, my lord."

"Then there is a suitable throne there."

"Yes, my lord."

The king set his face. "So shall it be. There will be a king in Nineveh."

Twenty-seven

Kalḫu, the Royal Palace
The Ninth Day of Du'ûzu

Ahu-duri paced the room. He found himself in the awkward position of knowing too much and too little. The gods were active, probably angered. That he knew. Sin, Nin Ur, Marduk, and perhaps Ea all showed signs of discontent. What he did not know was why. And what if other gods were involved? And what might the remedy be for the discontent? And might even more serious events be in the offing? And when would be the proper time to act?

The "and"s kept him awake at night.

As Senior Scholar, it was his duty to have more answers than questions. He felt sure he failed that duty in this crisis. He hoped his suggestion to invoke the *ugu lugal* had not been premature. He should have thought it over, slept on it, before he gave the idea a voice. It seemed appropriate at the time, but he did not realize all that was involved until later, when he had researched the extraordinary ritual.

Adad-nirari hadn't revisited the subject since their discussion after Kasiri's death, although the vizier's estimate of seven days to draw up a list of candidates had passed. It would only be a matter of time before—

A knock at the door shattered his concentration.

"Enter!"

The door opened, and a palace steward slipped into the room.

"The king calls for you."

Ahu-duri nodded, and the steward disappeared back through the doorway. The chief advisor gathered his wits, then hurried out the door toward the king's chambers.

Here it comes.

Adad-nirari wasted no time. "What have you done regarding the *ugu lugal?*"

Ahu-duri cleared his throat. *Does he read my thoughts all the time, or just when they're stuck?* "I have given the matter great thought, my lord."

The king raised an eyebrow. "It has been seven days since my decision to proceed. Surely you have done more than just think about it."

Ahu-duri coughed. "Yes, my lord. I only meant it has been at the forefront of my mind since we discussed it. I can offer names, but the decision is ultimately yours. A relative—a cousin or even a brother—would be best to take your place for the prescribed period."

The king leaned forward. "Neither of which I have. We both know this. Come to the point."

"Yes, my lord. As I cautioned during our last discussion, I have had no opportunity to consult with the *sukallu* council, or any of your other senior advisors. They are spread across the kingdom attending to matters in their own districts, and there is no time to convene. Therefore, I can only say what seems best to me."

"Please do."

The vizier continued. "As you have decided that Nineveh will host the substitute king, I recommend he be a local man, a native of Nineveh. That will make a clean separation from anyone or anything having to do with your realm."

"Agreed."

"The construction on your palace proceeds nicely. You could travel to Nineveh to inspect the work and consult with city leadership to identify a substitute."

Adad-nirari sat back and stroked his beard. "I am not of a mind to travel at this time." He looked up. "I will invest you with the authority to make the assignment. I already approved the new High Priestess of Ishtar by proxy upon the recommendation sent by the temple. That is unusual, but the precedence has been sent. I will likewise give you my seal and you can act in my stead."

"But my lord—"

"You have family in Nineveh, do you not? You know the city?"

"Yes, my lord, I grew up in Nineveh, as you know. My brother is a stonecutter who works on the palace. I have a sister there, as well, but—"

"That settles it, then." The king stood. "Prepare a tablet that announces your purpose and authority. I will seal it. I want you in Nineveh within three days, your selection made, and the *ugu lugal* installed within seven."

"Three—yes, my lord." Ahu-duri's chest deflated. He bowed and started for the door.

"And Vizier."

He turned back toward the king. "My lord?"

"Do not neglect a single detail. All needs to be in order."

"Yes, my lord."

֎ ֎ ֎

Hulalitu sat on her sleep mat, her head propped in her hands. Sleep had become more elusive the past two days, which left her body aching and her mind sluggish. Fatigue decayed the turmoil of Ianna's ascension to High Priestess into a puddle of vague resolution. She resolved revenge for the wrong done her, for the loss of her precious Ianna, but she lacked a focus for her anger. Issar-surrat was the most responsible, but she was dead, beyond touch—not that she was touchable while alive. Hulalitu's mind churned.

An image flashed through the grayness, faint at first, indistinguishable in form. Slowly, its features morphed into—was it a face? Still, she could give the face no name. She pressed her forehead against the palms of her hands and adjured her addled mind to solidify the image. Its features gelled into the visage of a man, a young man. Her brow creased. It was not a young man; it was *the* young man. The man called Jamin.

She narrowed her gaze into the gloom. That was it. The interloper Jamin was to blame. She was sure of it. Things began to come apart after his devious attempt to lure her Ianna from the temple. Her young *ishtaritu* had become more distant, less responsive since that evening. Hulalitu's jaw tightened. Yes, this could all be traced to that night, to Jamin. She would exact her revenge—oh yes, she would.

But how?

Twenty-eight

Nineveh, the Privileged Quarter
Eleventh Day of Du'ûzu

Mordac slammed his hand against the wall. He fumed at the guild's audacity. What more could they want? He followed every rule to the letter, attended every event, participated in every festival, no matter how distasteful. He contributed more than his share to the common good—that is, what portion made it past the guild leadership's pockets.

His was a model Ninevite family, he had made sure of that. He prodded Hani to keep their home in the upper district spotless. They dressed impeccably, chose their causes carefully, and never created a public scene—or even allowed themselves to be caught near one. Not an important civic event went by at which they were not seen in attendance. To cover all exigencies, they bowed a knee to every god and goddess that he thought might make a difference. Ianna had complied with every demand he made, as a good daughter should. Hani, though, was less helpful. If she opened her mouth, if he sensed any resistance at all, he cut her off with the reminder that he was the head of the household and his decision meant the end of the discussion.

That's what is done. That's how one keeps order. Yet unspoken attitudes could be discerned, as Hani's must have been. Yes, this whole incident was her fault.

He was sure he had the timing right. It would never be better. He had taken great pains to position himself as a prime candidate and, when a seat of control in the jeweler's guild became vacant, it was only natural that he be the one to fill it. But what was the response to his self-nomination? Sutharu, the leader of the guild, just shrugged with a trace of a smile. "We'll allow the seat to remain vacant for the time being. There's really no need for it."

No need for it? Couldn't the fools see the guild collapsing around their ears? Their own greed and self-serving policies had sucked the coffers dry. Members threatened to bolt left and right. Soon there would be nothing left but a shell. Mordac could turn it around, though. He had plans—great plans. They could join forces with other jeweler's guilds in Kalḫu, even as far as Aššûr, and, through collective agreements, control the prices of jewelry throughout the region—maybe even in all of Assyria. They all would gain from such a federation and from his leadership. But because of the short-sighted idiocy of a select few, everything he had worked for—they all had worked for—was now in jeopardy.

It just wasn't fair. It wasn't supposed to work this way.

As the afternoon wore on, his frustration heated to the boiling point. "By the gods—"

"'By the gods'? Really, Modac, have you fallen that far?" Hani stood in the doorway.

"Don't start on me!" he snarled. "I'm not in the mood."

"What is it now? Does Sutharu's wife still resist your advances?"

He swung on her. "I am not after Hara. How many times do I have to tell you that? Sutharu is the chief of the guild, and it is expedient to handle him smoothly—and his wife."

"Curious way to put that." She crossed her arms.

"You will not—"

"Dinner is nearly ready. That's all I had to tell you." She turned to go.

The look on his wife's face, the days of caustic avoidance, the loss of his daughter, and the weight of his failures at the guild all bore down on Mordac beyond his ability to bear. His chest tightened, and the flat finality in Hani's voice finally snapped something inside him. The realization that he was now alone, completely alone, bent him until he was sure his spine would snap. Hani could not turn her back on him. She was all he had left. He forced the words out through clenched teeth. "Wait. Hani . . . wait. Please."

Hani stopped at that last word. It was a rarity on his lips. Indeed, it hadn't been used in this household for years. She turned back, her face a blank.

Mordac's head was bowed. He cupped the back of his neck with his hands.

She waited.

Finally, her husband released a slow exhale and straightened. He fixed a plaintive look on her. "I'm sorry. I'm . . . sorry."

Hani jolted. *"I'm sorry"?* She didn't remember that phrase ever crossing his lips. Even if she wanted to respond, no words availed themselves. What was he up to now?

His eyes flicked to a cushion against the wall. "Can we sit? Just for a moment?"

She shifted in the doorway but made no move toward the cushion.

Mordac nodded. He settled himself stiffly onto the soft seat. With a heavy sigh, he rested his elbows on his knees and wrung his hands. His blank stare glued itself to a spot on the floor as he struggled for the right words. "So much has happened. Even in just the past few passages of Sin—"

"The moon, Mordac. It's only the moon." Hani sighed, her face still a mask.

He looked up at her. After a moment, he nodded. "The moon," he repeated.

The softness in Mordac's broken voice awakened vague memories of a man she once knew. It was the voice that soothed her fears as a young wife, that strengthened her to endure a broken family, and that gave her hope of a secure future in a foreign land. Where had that voice gone? Where had that man gone?

Hani struggled to pinpoint the event in their lives that triggered the change in him. But, as so many times before, it eluded her. It had happened, though, for he had indeed changed. Gone was his passion for right, replaced by passion for success. Gone was zealousness for faith, crowded aside by jealousness for social standing. Friendships melted into associations, affection into avarice, until she no longer knew the man who slept beside her fewer and fewer nights as the years passed.

Then there was Ianna. The damage Hani had suffered during the long labor and traumatic delivery resulted in four miscarriages over the next three years. Then she ceased even to conceive, until her husband's desire for intimacy went as dry as her womb. Mordac never seemed to recover from the fact that there would be no son to ensure his legacy. A man's life continues only as long as his name lives and is spoken by generation after generation. An only daughter would do little to ensure that. So Ianna did not exist because she embodied the end of his existence.

Hani's eyes misted at the memories of Ianna as she crawled to her father's lap, only to be brushed aside at her first touch like a bothersome insect. Her mind's ears rang as Mordac's voice roared for her to hush the crying child. Ianna's sobs only pushed to a higher pitch, her face pressed against her mother's shoulder. Hani would plead with her husband, try every angle to break down the wall he had built, but her words fell on deaf ears. *"If I cannot establish my legacy through this family, I will establish it in this city,"* was his reply.

So he immersed himself in Nineveh—its culture, society, and economy. And, to his credit, he built a comfortable life for his family. Through guile, shrewd business deals—albeit not always ethical ones—and political maneuvers, he increased his influence in the trade guild and among their new circle of friends. No, they couldn't be called friends. They were associates. But, lately, his ambitions seemed to have stalled. The guild leadership held him at arm's length, regardless of how he pandered to them. His contributions were much more welcome than his participation. Today, things came to a head. She knew Mordac chanced everything by openly nominating himself for a position of leadership in the guild. And the worst happened: Sutharu publicly and unceremoniously denied him.

Hani had never seen her husband so irate. He slammed through the door and barged into his workroom without a word. She backed against the wall as he stormed past, purple veins bulging in his neck and forehead. She feared the curses and crash of tools and supplies in the back room would go on all afternoon.

But before her now sat a subdued, defeated Mordac, a Mordac she had never seen before. She wasn't altogether sure it was a bad thing.

He sat silently as though mesmerized by the spot on the floor. Hani turned to slip out, but something held her there, something she didn't understand. It was strong enough to give her pause, but not yet strong enough to draw her closer to him.

She thought she saw a bemused smile curl his lips, although his face remained taut, his eyes hollow. "Solomon was right, wasn't he?"

Hani blinked. "Solomon?"

His eyes flicked to hers. "Vanity. All is vanity. Man toils, but gains nothing. Generations pass, seasons pass, but nothing really changes. There is no real gain." He locked his gaze onto hers. "I had dreams once. We had dreams. Do you remember?"

Hani's eyes brimmed. Her throat tightened to cut off any words that might have offered themselves, though none did.

Mordac shook his head and returned his stare to the floor. "There are so many forks in the road. How does one ever really know which one to take? How can one know where they lead? You think you know. You decide. You move forward. You find yourself farther back than where you started."

Hani moved across the room and eased herself onto the cushion. "Perhaps when our dreams changed to your dreams." Her voice was soft, firm, but without condemnation. She sensed Mordac's state to be fragile, but platitudes and false assurances would not help. "When we began, we chose our roads together. Somewhere that changed."

He nodded slowly. "I wanted what was best, I think. I don't even know if that's true anymore."

He flinched as she laid her hand on his arm. "I think you did."

He shook his head. "No, I'm not so sure. I got lost somewhere. I don't know where or why. A man can't do what's best if he's lost. A lost man has no goal, no sense of direction. If his goal was in sight, if his senses were about him, he wouldn't be lost. Does that make sense?"

Her eyes misted again as his right hand slipped over hers. His fingers seemed cold against her skin, and she felt them tremble.

His voice dropped to a whisper. "I built a livelihood but have no life. I married a wife but have no mate." He paused. "I sired a daughter but was never a father . . . Ianna."

Hani's heart leaped at his mention of their daughter's name. It was the first time Mordac had ever voiced it. To him she was always "the girl," or "your daughter," but never had he spoken her name.

He lifted his hand and began to massage his shoulder. "I wonder where she is."

Hani cocked her head at him. "She's at . . . the temple, Mordac."

"No, I know that. But . . . I wonder where she is in her mind." Mordac pulled himself erect on the pillow, and Hani's eyes widened at the beads of sweat on his forehead.

"Mordac. Are you—"

"Perhaps there's still something I can do." He barked a short cough. "We have silver . . . gold. We could redeem her, perhaps—"

Mordac gripped his shoulder and grimaced. His breath dropped to short, erratic gasps.

"Mordac!"

He turned his head and looked wide-eyed at his wife. He worked his jaw, but no words came out.

"Mordac!"

Hani jumped up as her husband's eyes rolled back in his head. She grabbed his shoulder but lost her hold as he pitched forward. Mordac's head cracked on the hard-packed earthen floor, and he pulled into a fetal position. His head twitched, and he went still.

Hani froze. She stared at her husband's inert form. Her chest began to heave until it broke the adrenalin grip on her throat. Her scream shattered the still of the late afternoon in Nineveh's privileged quarter.

Twenty-nine

Nineveh, the Privileged Quarter
Twelfth Day of Du'ûzu, the Sixth Hour

Hani eased herself onto Ianna's sleep mat, her eyes red and swollen. She stared at nothing, while she caressed the folds of her daughter's blanket. The house was so quiet, so . . . dead.

Mordac's death was little more than a blur, a surreal dream that hovered just beyond her mind's reach. She thought she remembered somebody scream, then someone pounded on the door. Suddenly there were people in the room, and two men carried something out, something large. A woman whispered in her ear; Hani had no idea what she said. Hani had merely gazed into the woman's face, and that's all she remembered until she woke this morning. Alone.

Hani spent the morning in a daze, her blanket clutched to her chest. At midday, she found herself with a piece of flatbread by the cold cook fire. She wasn't hungry, but it was time to eat, she thought. The crust of bread went no farther than the back of her throat before she gagged it back up. Now she sat on the floor of the main room next to Ianna's sleep niche, and tears poured down both cheeks. She wasn't sure why.

Ianna.

The thought of her daughter sparked in her mind. She crawled to the light scrim that covered the alcove and nudged it aside. Leaning her back against the cold clay wall, she buried her head in her daughter's woolen coverlet. She fancied Ianna's fragrance in the fibers.

Her blurry gaze fell on the small collection of her daughter's belongings. A hand-fashioned doll Hani made when Ianna turned five years old leaned precariously to the side, propped up against an earthenware bowl. The bowl brimmed with an assortment of stones her daughter had collected on the banks of the Idiqlat and Tabiltu Rivers over the years. Atop the pile perched a small brooch of silver and lazuli lapis, a gift she had asked Mordac to make for their daughter's seventh birthday. It was his only begrudging acknowledgment of Ianna's existence that Hani could recall. She picked up the trinket and turned it over in her hand. Surely there had been other times that Mordac...

Mordac. Where was—

Something in her mind told her not to finish the question. She obeyed.

Hani fingered the piece of jewelry, and her mind wandered back to the day Ianna was born.

It was a long labor, a difficult one. When it was over, Sari, the midwife, told Hani she had passed out three times near the end, but Hani didn't remember that. Finally, somewhere in the darkness of the second night, through her pain and fatigue, she became aware of a tiny bundle on her stomach. She vaguely remembered she had pushed, then lay back from the birthing position after uncountable cramps, screams, and convulsions. She squinted at the bundle through glazed eyes. In the dim lamplight, it looked vivid purple, save a large splotch of ebony-black—was it hair? The bundle lacked any discernible features from her angle of view. She could barely feel its weight on her depleted abdomen. But she did notice there was no movement. Hani laid her head back onto the thin mat. *Stillbirth? All this, and my baby is dead?*

Sari knelt over the tiny form and worked feverishly to clear its airways. She pinched and slapped the bundle to prompt an acknowledgment of life. Hani could hear her cluck and coax the infant to respond. Finally, Sari sat back on her ankles.

Hani's parched lips quivered on a face pale from the loss of water and blood—and from fear. "S-sari?"

The midwife looked at Hani. She reached out to brush a wisp of sweat-drenched hair from the exhausted woman's forehead. Then she smiled. "It's a girl, Hani. A beautiful girl."

Hani's eyes flew back to the bundle. "But, is she—"

A flicker of movement cut her words short. Nineveh's newest citizen flailed her feeble arm in the still air of the early morning. Hani's eyes welled up, and she choked back an involuntary sob. Her eyes again met Sari's, and she managed a weary grin. "A daughter."

Sari tied off the umbilical cord and began to swab the baby. "Yes, a lovely daughter. She fought birth, no?"

Hani nodded, then frowned. "I hear nothing. She does not cry."

"She is silent, true, but wait until you see her eyes, Hani. I have never seen such depth in a newborn's eyes. She is very much alive, yes, very much." Sari wrapped the infant and nestled her to her mother's shoulder.

Hani twisted her body for a better look. "Is she whole? She's so tiny—" She grimaced as a cramp gripped her abdomen.

"You must lie still, Hani. You still have the afterbirth to pass." Sari loosened the infant's cloth and shifted the baby to Hani's breast. "Yes. She has the right number of fingers and toes. Her head is pressed, but that's from the strain of birth. It will correct itself."

Hani prodded her nipple with a fingertip against her daughter's mouth until the infant settled into a soft suckling. She couldn't take her eyes from the beautiful, blotchy, miraculous, misshapen face of her new daughter. "Welcome, my young one, my . . . daughter," she whispered.

Sari smiled. After she poured a cup of water and urged Hani to drink, she moved to the foot of the mat. The practiced midwife frowned and tugged gently on the umbilical cord. "Come, come. Let's not be difficult."

Another cramp overtook Hani's abdomen and then eased, and Sari rose to dispose of the last evidence of birth.

Hani jolted from her fixation on the baby. "Mordac. He doesn't know." She looked up at Sari.

The midwife smiled. "I'll tell him."

Sari rose and limped on stiff joints into the main room. The light of dawn crept down the narrow street, where Mordac sat outside the door, his head lolling as he fought drowsiness.

"Mordac?"

His head jerked and he struggled to his feet.

"Sari! What—is Hani—is everything—"

Sari smiled. "She's fine, Mordac."

Relief relaxed his face, but anticipation squeezed his voice. "Is it—"

"Mordac, you have the most beautiful daughter I have ever delivered. She is perfect. Her . . . Mordac?"

Mordac's face clouded over. "A daughter? A girl?"

"Yes, a daughter," Sari said softly. "A very lovely daughter."

He stepped back and dropped his gaze.

"Hani asks for you." She searched his face, but it was blank. "Mordac?"

His eyes flicked up to hers, and he muttered under his breath, "Yes. I just need to . . . I'll be there. A daughter . . ."

Sari cocked her head and turned toward the door.

Hani looked up when Sari stepped back into the niche. "Sari?" She looked past the woman. "Is Mordac—"

"He'll be right in." Sari smoothed the front of her tunic and avoided eye contact with Hani. "He just needs a moment."

Hani nodded and returned her attention to her baby.

Two hours later, long after Sari went home, Hani and her baby drifted off to sleep. Alone.

※ ※ ※

Hani wiped the latest of countless tears from her cheek. She began to replace the brooch, then stopped. She turned it over in her hand once more, then closed her fingers over it and pushed herself up from Ianna's sleep mat. She set her jaw. Her mind was made up.

The linen cloth over the entrance to Ianna's sleeping niche rippled as Hani slipped back into the main room.

"S̲ʜᴇ ɪs ʀᴇᴀᴅʏ."

Thirty

Nineveh
Twelfth Day of Du'ûzu, the Ninth Hour

News of the royal delegation's imminent arrival spread quickly. The city magistrate whipped his staff into action, caught off guard by only a half-day's notice. This was unheard of. The Senior Scholar, closest of the king's advisors, en route to Nineveh with no advance warning? He fumed as he fired instructions to his first assistant. This was a serious breach of protocol. How was he supposed to prepare properly for the king's emissary when he had no word of when or why he was coming?

Ahu-duri sighed as he planted a weary foot on the dusty road in front of the king's nearly completed palace. He hated to travel. Especially on land. To ride the great river was one thing, but to rock to and fro on the back of a smelly, insolent camel was another. Time was short, though, and his mission afforded him no choice in conveyance. So he rocked to and fro. And he scowled.

The caravan's entrance through Nineveh's Ashur Gate went unnoticed to the vizier. There was so much to do and so little time. He didn't know whether to blame his headache on the task at hand or the camel.

"Good health and long life to you, Vizier." The magistrate's narrowed brow belied any sincerity in his greeting. Surrounded by his closest advisors, the city official dipped his head in perfunctory respect.

Two scribes stood ready with waxed wooden boards to record any instructions the king's legate might utter. Four slaves supported poles from which banners of light fabric shielded the delegation from the midday sun.

"And to you, Iqisha."

Ahu-duri's brusque reply stoked the magistrate's irritation. The vizier's apparent disinterest in the trouble he had gone to in preparation for this no-notice visit added to his annoyance. The Senior Scholar didn't even look at him. Instead, his eyes darted around the new palace complex. Iqisha gritted his teeth. This was not going to be a good visit.

Ahu-duri barely heard the magistrate's greeting. The king had levied a last-minute order for a progress report on the palace upon the delegation's return. The vizier was caught short at how the construction languished. He shook his head. Adad-nirari would not be pleased.

Iqisha's high-pitched voice snapped his train of thought.

"To what do we owe the honor of your presence in Nineveh, my lord?"

Ahu-duri glanced down at the magistrate, still bowed before him. He sighed and wiped the sweat from his brow with a sleeve.

"A matter of urgency for the king, Iqisha. My sincerest apologies for the lack of forewarning. Please let us forego the usual protocol. I need your help. Where can we speak in private?"

Ahu-duri reclined in the corner of a walled garden that adjoined the new palace. He didn't want to stress the magistrate's services any more than necessary, so he decided his entourage would stay in a completed part of the complex for the few days they were in the city. True, these were more austere accommodations than he was used to, but the stay here would give the vizier greater opportunity to inspect the building.

He slipped a morsel of cheese into his mouth and chased it with a sip of wine as he reflected on the day's activities.

The meeting with Iqisha earlier that afternoon had gone as well as could be expected. The city magistrate received the reason for Ahu-duri's visit with calm, but the vizier noticed him pale as he digested the king's intent to designate Nineveh as the source and the seat for a substitute king. The royal advisor didn't blame him. It was a serious issue that his city and one of his citizens was to become the target of wrathful gods for over full three phases of Sin. Iqisha chanced a curt reminder to his visitor that Nineveh had just begun to enjoy a period of renewal. Was it really a wise move to lift the city to the attention of displeased gods? Ahu-duri reminded him that the king's decision was just that, the king's decision. He omitted the fact that Nineveh's selection was his own idea. That would only complicate an already strained visit. His aide's grating voice interrupted his ruminations.

"Sincerest apologies, my lord. You have a visitor." Karehi threw an irritated glance over his shoulder toward the courtyard gate.

"A visitor?" Ahu-duri frowned.

"Yes, my lord. A woman. I told her you were at rest, but she insisted. She says . . . she says she's your sister." The steward averted his eyes.

"Oh. Of course. Please see her in."

The man tinged red at the cheeks. "It's just that she's a—"

Ahu-duri's mouth lifted into a thin smile. "Yes, I know. And I do have a sister in Nineveh."

The aide's eyes widened. "Of course, my lord. I didn't mean to imply—"

"See her in, Kaheri."

"Certainly, my lord." The aide spun on his heel and hurried back the way he came.

Kaheri returned a moment later with the woman. She stood with her head bowed while the steward presented her.

The vizier nodded. "You may go, Kaheri. Oh, and bring another cup of wine."

"Yes, my lord."

181

Ahu-duri rose to his feet. "Sister, it has been a long time."

She kept her head bowed. "Thank you for receiving me, Brother. I know you're busy and—"

"Nonsense, and you need not be so formal. Come, sit."

The woman raised her head and ventured a smile at the second most powerful man in the realm. "Thank you." She settled onto a low stone wall that bordered one of the courtyard's floral plots.

Kaheri returned with the wine and another small plate of fruit and cheese.

Ahu-duri nodded and the aide left them alone. His sister lifted a grape and fingered it as she pondered how to begin.

"I only just heard you'd arrived in Nineveh. The whole city wonders what brings a king's delegation to us."

Ahu-duri raised an eyebrow. "I am sure they do, and rightly so. It is a matter of great urgency."

She cocked her head.

He shrugged. "The word will come out officially tomorrow, but there is no reason you cannot know now. There has been a series of bad omens over the past several days. Sin dimmed unexpectedly, Nin Ur has shaken the earth in Kalḫu, a ram sacrificed to Marduk was diseased—and worse, the *baru* who performed the extispicy fell ill and died. Very bad omens indeed."

The woman's eyes widened. "We have heard none of this. What of the other gods? What of Nabu, of Ishtar?"

Her brother shrugged. "That is all we know. The gods have not answered the *muhhu* through the lots or the leaves. But enough has happened that King Adad-nirari has decided to invoke the *ugu lugal* tradition to avoid any coming wrath."

"The substitute king? That is serious. He must indeed be concerned. But why does that bring you to Nineveh?"

"To avoid the anger of the gods falling on Kalḫu—especially while we recover from the effects of the earthquake—the king decided to select a candidate from Nineveh and install him here."

The woman grew thoughtful. "Do you know who that will be yet?"

The vizier shook his head. "King Adad-nirari has entrusted me with his seal to make the selection. I have seven days to complete my task and report back to him. The king has no relatives here. We may have to select a commoner if no nobleman can be found who is suitable, or who cannot buy his way out of it."

"A commoner." She knit her brow. "Is that done?"

"Rarely, but there is a precedent."

The woman paused, then a subtle smile touched her lips.

Ahu-duri cocked his head. "Something amuses you?"

She shook her head. "Please let me know when you begin your search. I may be able to help."

Her brother frowned. "My search has already begun. How could you help?"

The smile on her face broadened. "There may be a common solution to both of our problems. Don't let it distract you now. I'll be in touch with you."

Ahu-duri shrugged. "All right. So, tell me, Sister, how are things at the temple under the new High Priestess?"

Hulalitu smoothed her light blue tunic over her thighs. "They have been . . . interesting."

Thirty-one

Nineveh, the Artisan's Quarter
Thirteenth Day of Du'ûzu

Jonah roused before daybreak from a night that offered little rest. Fragments of the Council meeting still littered his dreams, and a morass of worry sucked at his spirit.

The Council had convened twenty days earlier. The tumultuous meeting broke up with a consensus to carry *Adonai's* message to the city, but with a broad range of mixed belief and emotions. Jonah couldn't blame them. Nineveh had become the only home many of them had ever known. The generation that lived through the exile had nearly passed away, and personal knowledge of the Promised Land passed with them. Their children and grandchildren carried only secondhand memories of Jerusalem and the Temple through stories handed down from their parents. They honored their homeland through prayers and tithes, but more out respect to their parents than through any fervor of their own. For them, Israel became a land of revered mystery, a legend.

But Nineveh was known, familiar. It was home. And now the God of Israel intended to destroy it—or so said this odd, white-haired stranger. Reactions ran through the gamut of emotions.

"*Nonsense! What has the God of Israel to do with Nineveh?*"

"*Are we being punished for adopting this heathen land over the land of our forefathers?*"

"*Are we to die with the heathens, or will God spare His chosen people, from His wrath?*"

Despite formal agreement among the elders, the message seemed to have stalled. Of course, there had been a few responses. Word came that some families had packed and left the city, as Lot and his family left Sodom before its destruction. Others conducted purification rituals as true signs of repentance—what details they could remember of them without the guidance of a formal priesthood. But from most of them, there was silence. Confusion, skepticism, uncertainty of expectations, ignorance of how to repent, all took their toll. Twenty days had now passed, already half the time allotted for the city to repent.

Jonah knew from his experience six years earlier that, even in the face of serious odds, *Adonai* would see to His word, and that it would yield the desired results. Of that he was certain. It was the desired result itself about which he was less certain. Had God intended to destroy the city all along? Why send a message to the people to repent if their fate was already sealed?

Members of the Council had grilled Jonah over the past few days with questions like these and many others, and he found himself woefully short of answers. All he could tell them was that the city needed to repent. His responsibility and theirs stopped when the message was delivered. He said the rest was up to *Adonai*, which was completely true, but emotionally unsatisfying. Most of the elders left with grumbles on their tongues.

Word of the prophet spread through the Assyrian population, as well, but with less impact. Assyria was a land of many gods, so to absorb one more presented little problem for anyone. Of course, the message of destruction was unsettling, but that was a matter for the *Igigi* to sort out with this new god. It had little to do with them.

That is, until news of the king's delegation spread through the city. Their mission, and the omens that prompted it, crashed in on their comfortable world and threw all but the most irreligious into turmoil.

"Sin has dimmed in the skies?"

"Nin Ur has shaken Kalḫu?"

"Marduk has killed a baru*?"*

"What? They seek a substitute king?"

Now things were serious. First came news that a new god threatened the city with annihilation. Then their own gods sent ominous signs of discontent through the heavens and the earth. Those who had heard of the intrigue at Ishtar's temple, of the sudden death of the High Priestess and hurried ascension of an unexpected replacement, added this event to the list of worrisome signs. Now the king took drastic measures to avert their wrath from his own head. What wrath? What did he know that they didn't? Were the gods at war with this new god, or was their discontent directed at the people of Assyria? They heard that the *Igigi* refused any revelation to the *muhhu* diviners. Only this new god offered any remedy or gave them any hope to escape the wrath. All they needed to do was repent, whatever that meant.

The Jews who spread the message through the city said their god was angered by the city's evil. What evil? The Ninevites were just being themselves. They acted the same as they had for centuries. What was this new standard against which they were being measured, one that judged them to be evil? How were they to know the exact things of which to repent?

Quarter by quarter, news of the omens, the substitute king, and the prophet's fateful declaration spread through the city. It gained momentum with each hour that passed. As the word fanned out, questions over details went unanswered. Speculation resulted and spawned embellishments. The embellishments birthed mutations of the message, which, when they rebounded and collided in the marketplace and over evening meals, produced more confusion. Confusion led to fear. Fear to paralysis.

Hiram burst through the front door, shattering the late-morning quiet. Jonah had just fielded a fresh list of questions from a small group of elders and was at rest. He jolted at his host's entrance. Jamin emerged quickly from a back room.

"You've got to do something. This is out of control."

Jonah rose to his feet. "What do you mean?"

"The whole city is in an uproar. No one knows what to do. I was nearly trampled in the marketplace by people who wanted to know about this god, and why he was going to overflow the Idiqlat River and swamp the city." Hiram leaned against the doorframe to catch his breath.

"Who said anything about a flood?" Jonah asked.

"Oh, that's not the only story around the city. Some people ask if the invading Urutian army has been spotted yet; some wonder when Ishtar became this god's consort and if she's in on this. Still others hope the *ugu lugal* can repent for all of us."

Jonah shook his head. "What is an *ugu lugal?*"

Hiram waved his hands. "Never mind that now. The point is, you have to get out there and address this. There will be no repentance if the people don't understand what to do. There are too many rumors and not enough answers."

Jamin spoke up. "I'll go with you. I know the city. We need to find a place to speak where it will have the most impact."

Hiram nodded his agreement. "The marketplace is a shambles. You'll never be heard there."

"The temple plaza." Jamin's voice was subdued.

Hiram shook his head. "Surely you're not serious, Nephew. The bastion of paganism is no place to pronounce the word of *Adonai.*"

Jamin gave his uncle a serious look. "That's exactly where the word of God should be heard, Uncle. The people think the omens are part of this prophecy. Complicity by false gods with the intent of the true God settles in their minds. We need to stand in the midst of their sanctuaries and expose them for exactly what they are: idols, impotent before *Elohim Adonai.* We must separate them from the message, or they will only gain legitimacy in the eyes of the people. Then the confusion over repentance—over what and to whom—will be all the greater."

Hiram appeared thoughtful.

Jamin pleaded with him. "Uncle, there's no other place. You said yourself the marketplace is in turmoil. We need to send messengers to the marketplace first, then as far throughout the city as we can. The prophet of *Adonai* will speak in the temple square. It's not as large as the marketplace, nor as open, but it's large enough. The cluster of buildings in the temple plaza might even help contain the crowd."

"Contain the crowd?" Jonah asked.

Hiram paused in thought, then nodded. "You're right. I'll have the elders—as many as I can find—spread the word that the prophet will speak in the temple square today at the twelfth hour. That will give us time to get the word out. It will also leave only a short time then until nightfall. That should help subdue any severe reaction by the crowd."

Jonah paled. "Severe reaction?"

Hiram set his face. "We haven't much time. Have Jonah on the steps of Nabu's temple before the twelfth hour."

Jamin retreated to the back room to leave Jonah with his thoughts and to deal with thoughts of his own. The aftermath of Jonah's prophecy had left him no time to seek out the girl. The few times he did pass the plaza, he never caught sight of her. Once or twice, he spotted groups of priestesses on the portico, but her distinctive figure did not show itself among them.

Never far from the front of his mind, though, was the quandary of how to get close to her, how to talk to her. If Nineveh was to meet its fate at the hands of *Elohim Adonai*, he must spirit her away from the city to save her from certain death. As a plan formulated in his mind, he pushed away the guilt that came with it.

His advice about the merits of the temple square as the best place for Jonah's address was true. The hope flowered in his mind even as he spoke, though, that a commotion such as the one the prophet was sure to raise would draw attention away from the priestesses, who would surely emerge from the temple. If he could edge through the crowd, he could watch for her. Then he could slip up behind her, appeal to her, and convince her to leave.

For her own safety.

With him.

He would have to face the problem of exactly what to say when the opportunity arose. He just hoped he'd be able to spot her in the crowd. Right now, he needed to deal with the twinge of guilt he felt at leading his uncle along with an ulterior motive of his own.

※ ※ ※

Hiram managed to reach half the elders through their families by the sixth hour. The messengers dove into the crowd at the marketplace and spread the news of the prophet's pronouncement. Excitement mounted as the word went throughout the city. The streets filled with men, women, and children streaming toward the temple square from every direction.

News of the rising pandemonium reached both the Temple of Ishtar and Adad-Nirari's new palace at the same time.

Thirty-two

Nineveh, the Temple Plaza
Thirteenth Day of Du'ûzu, the Twelfth Hour

Jonah and Jamin hurried past the Mashki Gate and pressed through the shadows of the city wall. People passed them on the road to the temple plaza, but those who saw him did not recognize the prophet in the subdued light. When they reached the path behind Nabu's temple, Jamin pulled Jonah aside.

"This leads around the back of the temple. There's a niche behind a statue where we can wait until it's time."

Jonah puffed from his efforts to keep up with the younger man. "You seem . . . to know the area well."

Jamin nodded grimly. "Yes. I know the area."

He led the way as the two men hugged the wall of the temple and slipped around the corner to the cranny behind the statue. From there they could see the crowd amass in the temple square. Families struggled to stay together as the multitude swelled into every empty space. Some fathers lifted their children to their shoulders to protect them from being trampled. A few boys climbed onto the fountain at the plaza's center and reveled in all the excitement. The throng began to surge up the steps of the temples, in search of some vantage point to see and hear the prophet. As the mass bulged toward the steps of Ishtar's temple, the portico came alive with pastel tunics. Priestesses swarmed down the steps in a vain effort to hold the crowd back from their sacred shrine.

Jamin glanced at Jonah. Even in the shadows, he could make out the prophet's worried look. He began to wonder if this was such a good idea. What if Jonah wasn't up to it? His bent shoulders didn't inspire much confidence. Indeed, he seemed to shrink into his robe. Would his thin voice even be heard over the crowd? Jamin began to scramble for an alternative plan, just in case, but the activity on the steps of Ishtar's temple across the road cut his thoughts short. He squinted into the mass of priestess and sought the splay of black hair and petite form of the girl he loved.

The girl he loved.

He had expressly denied himself even the tacit voicing of that fact, but now it thrust past his emotional defenses and planted itself in the forefront of his mind. The phrase heated his forehead and pumped new fervor into his suppressed feelings. The strained looks of admonishment and defiance he and the girl exchanged at their last encounter, his frustration at the hopelessness of the situation and her apparent apathy toward it, did nothing to subdue his heart. She frustrated him, allured him, repulsed him, and melted him. He simply loved her. And he still didn't know why. The mental image of her face launched his heart into his throat, and his stomach ached more than ever.

He shook his head in an effort to dislodge the warring emotions that tore at his mind. They presented a distraction he couldn't afford, not now. He faced a critical situation that affected his life, the lives of his loved ones, and countless others in the great city. He had to focus. But the unbidden emotions battled hard for survival. They refused to subside, impervious to every effort he could muster against them. So he gritted his teeth, swallowed past his love-sick heart, and tightened his stomach against the titillating nausea.

And he searched for her again.

"I thought you might be here." Uncle Hiram's voice jolted Jamin from his thoughts.

"Oh, Uncle." Jamin looked over his shoulder at the older man, who was inspecting Jonah. Hiram looked as concerned for the prophet as Jamin felt.

"Jonah, are you all right?" Hiram gripped Jonah's shoulder.

"Yes. I'm . . . yes."

Jamin reckoned Jonah's face seemed a shade paler than the last time he looked, if that were possible.

Hiram nodded. "It's time."

The urgent knock echoed through Ianna's chamber and roused her from her thoughts. She stood and donned her ceremonial cap.

"Enter!"

Thura, the *naditu* in attendance at the chamber of the High Priestess, stepped halfway through the doorway, protocol forgotten in the midst of worry.

"The situation worsens, High Priestess."

"Worsens?"

"People now fill the plaza. We tried to clear the portico, but we cannot keep the crowd back." Thura threw an anxious look back over her shoulder.

Ianna frowned. "So, the rumors of the prophet's appearance in the plaza are true."

"Yes, High Priestess. They appear to be."

"Very well. I will be along shortly."

Thura disappeared. In her haste she forgot to close the door.

Ianna retrieved the ceremonial staff lying on the dais. She took one step toward the door but stopped short at bolts of pain that arced over her brain. She staggered and grabbed her head. Her eyes flickered under their clenched lids.

"Tread carefully. The prophet must be stopped, but you—"

Ianna shook her head and forced her eyes open. She cringed at the burning in her head. "Stop it! Leave me! I know what to do," she sputtered between clenched teeth.

Their grip tightened and fought to hold, but the High Priestess bore every ounce of will she could muster against them. "Leave me!"

The tentacles snapped back over her brain. A trail of serrated claw marks scored her mind and left a dull ache behind her eyes. She set her jaw.

I know what to do!

Ahu-duri paused in his dictation. He raised a finger to the scribe who sat poised with his waxed board.

"What is it, Kaheri?"

The aide gasped for breath. "The crowd, my lord. It grows. The temple plaza overflows."

The vizier frowned. "Are they unruly?"

Kaheri shook his head. "No riot has been reported, my lord. But tension builds. The rumored prophet is to speak soon. There is no way to tell how the mob will react."

Ahu-duri nodded. He dismissed the scribe and rose to his feet. "Assemble a squad of soldiers. I want to hear what this so-called prophet has to say."

"Yes, my lord."

※ ※ ※

The murmur of the crowd swelled as the three men stepped from behind the statue of Nabu. People shifted and jostled for a better view of the celebrated prophet. Jamin and Hiram guided Jonah to the center of the portico that overlooked the plaza. Jonah surveyed the sea of faces and closed his eyes.

Hiram leaned toward him and whispered, "The elders and others have spread out through the crowd. They will translate what you say for the many who do not speak Hebrew. Speak slowly. Give them a chance to interpret and the people a chance to comprehend."

Jonah did not respond. He stood motionless, his lips voicing a silent prayer: *Lord God of Hosts, I am beyond my ability. Calm my fears,* Elohim Adonai, *for they are as great as I am small. Steady my heart; it threatens to burst in my chest. Grant me the words to say, as You did before the king in Samaria. Make the people receptive. The message is Yours. Hide me behind it. May Your word accomplish Your will.*

Jonah opened his eyes. The crowd quieted until not a whisper or shuffle of feet could be heard. He scanned the multitude. Every eye bore into his face; every ear bent toward his lips.

He took a deep breath. "People of Nineveh, you know from ancient lore of the cities of the plain, of Sodom and Gomorrah."

A brief murmur rippled through the crowd as the elders repeated his words in Assyrian.

"You have heard of those great cities being destroyed by fire, by brimstone that rained from heaven."

The commotion increased as some in the crowd began to connect his words with the rumors they had already heard about their own city.

"Their destruction came as punishment for their iniquity. They were lovers of idols, violent and immoral in their treatment of each other." Jonah paused to allow the people to assimilate his words. When the murmurs of the elders ceased, he continued, "Their destruction came at the hands of the one God, the true God, the God of Abraham, Isaac, and Jacob. *Elohim Adonai*, the Lord God of Hosts, sole Creator of Heaven and Earth."

The murmurings arose at this proclamation of one God. For millennia their culture had created and taught a pantheon of gods, many of whom played active roles in the creation of the heavens, the earth, and man. Yet, they had also heard of the cities of the plain. But this was the first they'd learned of a single God who had delivered the cities' destruction. The notion of one all-powerful God was a strange one.

Jonah waited for calm to reclaim the crowd. He surveyed the assembly before he delivered his crucial point. "This same God has turned His eyes toward Nineveh."

The murmurs billowed to a roar. Bewilderment, disbelief, fear, and anger all swept through the assembly. The interpreters bore the brunt of the backlash. The pagan Ninevites pushed and shouted down the Jews among them. More than one elder suffered jabs to the body.

Jonah lifted his arms for calm. The noise subsided as people pointed toward the prophet, and their curiosity overcame their anger. Jamin and Hiram exchanged nervous glances, ready to whisk Jonah away at the next sign of serious trouble.

"I know you wonder why such a fate should befall Nineveh. The answer is simple. You share the transgressions of the cities of the plain."

More grumbles rolled through the mob.

Jonah's voice found new strength. "Nineveh is known for its wrongful dealings, even among her sister cities. Your army is notorious for its wanton atrocities, senseless destruction, and mercilessness." His voice cracked in remembrance of his own experience in the Jezreel Valley. "And," he gestured around the plaza with his arms, "the temples you have raised in this very square are sufficient testament to your idolatry. Therefore, you will share the fate of the cities of the plain."

He expected another outburst from the crowd, but there was only stunned silence. He could see seething frustration on the faces of those gathered nearest, anger that had not yet found its voice. He took advantage of the moment of quiet. "But all is not lost. There remains a chance for you to escape this fate."

The tension vented and left an uneasy silence over the crowd.

Jonah's voice rose to a fever pitch. *Elohim Adonai* will forestall His judgment over your city if you repent and turn from your evil ways. You must abandon your idolatry. You must denounce the false gods you have created and proclaim Him the One True God. Tear down these temples! Fall on your face before Him, if you hope to live."

The anger found its voice and exploded in a roar.

"What? Tear down our temples?"

"Who does he think he is? We know of no such god!"

"What proof is there of what he says?"

"Ashur will protect us! No one is greater than Ashur!"

Those elders too slow to evade were shoved to the ground and forced to shield their heads from punches and kicks. Others managed to escape to the fringes, where they cowered behind statues and around corners of the temples. Those closest to Nabu's shrine surged toward the steps. Hiram and Jamin slipped to Jonah's side and grasped his arms.

Sudden shouts from the south end of the plaza rose over the hubbub. Heads turned and the crowd separated as a squad of soldiers pushed into the square. They formed two ranks and drove a wedge into the mob. The squad stopped at the foot of Nabu's temple.

From between the soldiers stepped a tall man in the regalia of a royal advisor. His unexpected appearance silenced those closest to the squad. He mounted the steps flanked by four guards, and an uneasiness settled over the plaza. The dignitary stopped a pace away from the prophet and gazed intently at the white-haired foreigner.

Jonah returned an even look.

The official pursed his lips. "Are you the instigator of this riot?"

Jonah was surprised at the official's flawless Hebrew, but his tone was steady in his response. "I have merely delivered a message."

"I see. And your message, Israelite, did *it* instigate this riot?"

"The people have reacted in accordance with their hearts."

Jamin and Hiram shifted as the royal official circled Jonah, his dark eyes appraising the foreign seer from head to foot. "Perhaps you can repeat your message for me, Israelite. I arrived in time to hear something about tearing down temples. I trust there is more . . . ?"

A sharp feminine voice cut into Ahu-duri's inquiry. "I heard enough."

All eyes turned toward the voice. Behind the squad of soldiers and surrounded by a cluster of priestesses stood a figure in the ornate robes of the High Priestess of Ishtar.

Jamin started at the woman's voice. A guard on the second step blocked his line of sight, so he shifted his stance to peer past the soldier.

A familiar petite figure mounted the stairs and rose into his view. Her black hair streamed from beneath a gold cap and flowed over her slight shoulders. Her fiery eyes were fixed on the prophet.

Jamin's jaw dropped. His vision tunneled, and a rush of lightheadedness threatened to drop him. *The High Priestess? How could that . . . when did she . . . the High Priestess?* Jamin could only stare.

Hiram narrowed his eyes at this most heathen of priestesses. He glowered at the imperiousness of her stride as she ascended the stairs and drew herself up beside the royal dignitary. Here stood the symbol of everything wrong with this city—the very reason it stood under the judgment of *Adonai*. He prayed for the earth to open up beneath those cursed feet and swallow the holy harlot for all to see the wrath of the Lord revealed. He knew Jamin would feel the same. But a glance at his nephew prompted a double-take.

Jamin's face was pale; his jaw was dropped.

What is the matter with—oh, no! The conversation Hiram had shared with his nephew on these very steps only a few days ago echoed through his mind. *This couldn't be the girl. Not the High Priestess! What could he be thinking?*

The *Entu* of Ishtar drew near, and Ahu-duri bowed in deference to the most powerful spiritual figure in Assyria, aside from the king himself. But his eyes remained riveted on her extraordinary beauty. *So, this is the new High Priestess of Ishtar. She's so young. So beautiful. Her eyes are like—no!* He shook the notion from his mind and flushed involuntarily, lest his face betray his thoughts. He cleared his throat.

"You know something of this man, then, High Priestess?"

The High Priestess halted two paces from the foreign prophet. She addressed the royal advisor in a low voice but did not shift her eyes from Jonah. "He preaches death and destruction upon our city at the hands of a foreign god, my lord. He calls our gods—the great Ashur, the Mother Goddess Ishtar—false idols. Yes, he incites the people to riot, an understandable reaction to the blasphemy that we should abandon all we hold holy and dear." Her eyes intensified. "He insists we bow to this unknown foreign god."

Ahu-duri looked at the prophet, then back at the High Priestess. "So you consider him a threat?"

"Threat?" She sneered. "Not to Mother Ishtar, certainly. But to Nineveh? Well, my lord, look around you. What do you see?"

The vizier's eyes flicked over the restless mob. Several men were down, obviously victims of assault. Subdued mutters floated above a sea of terse faces. It made for a volatile mixture—one that could ignite at any moment with the least provocation. Something needed to be done.

Ahu-duri glanced at his senior soldier. "Seize him. Bring him to the palace."

※ ※ ※

Two soldiers reached for Jonah, and Hiram rushed forward. "No! He is an emissary of God! We must heed his message."

Jamin shouted, "Uncle! No—"

The soldier struck without warning. He brought the butt of his spear up and thrust it into the elder man's midriff. Hiram dropped to his knees and gasped. He teetered, then collapsed onto his side.

Jamin rushed to his uncle's side. The soldier raised his spear again and Jamin rammed him with his shoulder. The guard toppled backward down the stairs into the crowd below. A woman screamed as two other soldiers raced up the steps.

"Take them!" Ahu-duri snapped.

Ianna sidestepped the soldiers, but her robe caught underfoot on the riser. She stumbled forward and collided with Jonah. The impact caught the prophet off balance and toppled him backward over Hiram's prostrate body. Ianna teetered, then collapsed over him.

"Stop!" Ahu-duri warned the soldiers off with his hand and grasped the arm of the fallen High Priestess.

The soldiers stalled their advance at the command.

Ianna reddened at the spectacle she had created. No one here would forget such an indignity suffered by the High Priestess of Ishtar. She fought to right herself and regain some measure of decorum.

Ianna propped her hand against the downed prophet's chest as the royal advisor lifted her other arm. Her palm settled against a hard object beneath his robe. As she pushed away, the object slid across his chest and dropped out through the neckline.

As Ianna righted herself, she caught sight of a large gold medallion affixed to a leather thong that lay beside the prophet's head. Two soldiers jerked Jonah to his feet. The dignitary steadied Ianna, then hastened to remove his hand from her hallowed arm. Her eyes fixed themselves on the pendant that now dangled outside his robe.

Her lungs heaved in humiliation. She dared not make eye contact with anyone but flipped her hair back and straightened the ceremonial cap on her brow. She needed something—anything—to divert attention from her embarrassment. The medallion flashed as it twisted in the torchlight, and its glint caught her eye.

Ianna drew herself up and glared at the prophet, who stood with his arms pinned by two soldiers. She stepped forward with a challenge in her eyes. Then, with a thin smile, she dropped her gaze to the amulet.

Jonah's eyes widened as she reached for his heirloom. The guards held him while he watched the heathen priestess lift his priceless treasure away from his chest. She inspected it front and back.

"Well, now, what is this?" Her eyes toyed with his. "A charm, perhaps. For good fortune?"

Jonah struggled against the soldiers' grasp.

"But it appears your fortune has run out today." She cocked her head and pouted.

Ahu-duri's gaze flew between the medallion and the High Priestess.

"And so you won't need this." With a flick of her arm, she flipped the thong over his head and drew it from his neck.

The panic on the prophet's face raised a smug smile on Ianna's. Slowly, she lifted the thong and looped it over her own head. She guided the medallion down and let it drop against her robe. Its weight pressed against the silky material over her bosom and accented her delicate curves.

Her gaze went back to Jonah's. "There, now, it looks so much better with my finery than hidden away under a dirty shirt." Her eyes turned to Ahu-duri and caught him staring at the front of her garment, possibly at the amulet. "Don't you think so, my lord?"

His startled eyes met hers. "Yes! Of course, High Priestess. It was meant for such a . . . robe . . . as yours."

His flushed face was not lost on her.

She turned to throw one more smirk at the prophet when she caught a movement behind the soldier on his right. A young man bent over the prostrate form of the man the soldier's spear had dropped. As he raised his head and gazed into her face, she recognized him as the same man who had entered her chamber weeks ago, the same man who confessed his love for her, who tried to convince her to flee from the temple unconsummated. The man who told her of a God who loved her.

This god? The god of this prophet? A god who would destroy an entire city?

They locked eyes . . . for how long she didn't know. Long enough, though, for her to read hurt, sorrow, and—could it still be?—love in his eyes as his agonized gaze bore into hers.

A harsh command from Ahu-duri for his troops to take the prisoner away broke their silent exchange. Ianna blinked and straightened her shoulders. She averted her eyes and hardened her heart. With a flourish, she pivoted and descended the stairs. Her retinue of *naditu* priestesses fell into step behind her, then followed her across the road and up the steps of Ishtar's temple.

As the servants of Ishtar disappeared into the building, one blue tunic lagged behind. Hulalitu peered from behind a pillar as the soldiers muscled the cursed prophet down the steps of Nabu's temple and along the street toward Adad-nirari's palace. The crowd began to disperse.

The two men who had attended the prophet remained alone on the portico of Nabu's temple, both now forgotten by the soldiers. The younger man—Jamin, she remembered—helped his elder comrade to his feet, but the old man remained bent over from the jab of the guard's spear. Jamin gave his uncle a moment to regain his breath. He spent that moment with his gaze locked onto Ishtar's temple and the darkened porch her Ianna had just entered. After a moment, Jamin resumed his attention to the injured man. He straightened him, and together they limped around the corner and out of sight.

From her earlier vantage point among the priestesses on the stairs of Nabu's temple, Hulalitu saw the look Jamin gave Ianna when their gazes met. More importantly, she saw Ianna's expression.

Hulalitu gritted her teeth.

It was time to act.

Two rough hands shoved Jonah through the low door of the small prison chamber. He stumbled across a dirt floor, collided with the far wall, and collapsed. His eyes rolled back in his head, and his world closed in on him.

Thirty-three

Nineveh, the Royal Palace
Fourteenth Day of Du'ûzu, the Tenth Hour

Ahu-duri propped his cheek in his hand and stared absently at the cup he held over the garden wall. He tipped it slowly and watched the last dregs of wine trickle over the rim and soak into the soil around the roots of a newly transplanted oleander.

He sighed. *It should feel honored. How many plants merit a taste of the king's wine?* He pursed his lips and laid the empty vessel on its side by the tray of half-eaten fruit and cheese. Sometimes wine just didn't taste good.

The vizier settled back on his cushion and retreated deeper into his thoughts. Yesterday's events weighed heavily on him. All this ugly business with the foreign prophet and calming the agitated citizenry of Nineveh stole precious time from the reason he came to the city. Adad-nirari wanted his substitute king, and he wanted him soon.

Ahu-duri mentally kicked himself for ever suggesting it. His inquiries to the upper class of the city yielded no results. They all had the resources to purchase the services of a surrogate, and the vizier was not ready to settle for a mercenary just yet. He snorted at the notion. *A substitute-substitute king. How silly is that?*

"My lord?" Kaheri's high-pitched voice pierced the vizier's tranquility.

Ahu-duri threw an annoyed look at his aide. "What is it?"

"A visitor, my lord. The same woman who says she is your sister."

Ahu-duri rolled his eyes. "It *is* my sister, Kaheri. See her in, will you?"

"Yes, my lord."

The vizier rubbed at a headache that lurked behind his temples.

"Greetings, Brother." Hulalitu stood at the center of the walkway, her head bowed.

Kaheri lifted an eyebrow at the priestess and backed away.

"Sister." Ahu-duri nodded. "Please sit."

"Thank you." She settled herself onto the low wall.

Ahu-duri took the initiative and addressed something that had bothered him since the scene in the temple plaza.

"Your new High Priestess is quite lovely, is she not?" He searched his sister's eyes for any reaction to his words. He knew she had been among the retinue of priestesses in the square. The mental lapses the enchanting High Priestess evoked in him still seared his forehead. He wondered if anyone noticed the effect she had on him.

Hulalitu paused, as though caught unaware by the question. Her voice assumed an added gruffness in its reply. "Yes, my brother. Very lovely."

There was nothing in her tone to indicate she had noticed anything out of the ordinary in his notice of the High Priestess. He relaxed. "It was a tense moment yesterday."

"It was, Brother. In fact, it is about yesterday that I would like to speak to you."

He raised an eyebrow. He wondered if perhaps she had noticed something after all. "What might that be?"

Hulalitu took a deep breath. "When we last spoke, you mentioned your quest for a substitute king."

"Yes."

"How goes your search?"

Ahu-duri rose and paced the path, his arms crossed. Finally, he turned toward her. "Not well, actually. Not well at all."

She looked down at her feet. "It is a weighty task."

"Very. Why do you ask?"

Hulalitu looked up, her eyes intense. "You said there was precedence for a commoner to become the *ugu lugal.*"

He nodded slowly. "There is."

"I know of one who would be the ideal candidate, if I may be so bold." She paused.

"Really. Who, and why is he ideal?"

His sister took a deep breath. "You saw him yesterday in the temple square."

"Yesterday?"

"Yes. He was with the prophet." She studied his face.

Her brother furrowed his brow.

She continued, "He was the young one, the man who shouldered your soldier off the steps."

"I don't understand. How could this man possibly be a suitable substitute king?"

Hulalitu leaned forward. "He must be known by the citizens to have taken a prominent role in the assembly. He showed courage and loyalty to his uncle when he protected him from the soldier." Her voice picked up tempo. "He is young, vibrant—clearly one the people could accept on the throne as a substitute. He is just what you need."

Curious, Ahu-duri asked, "His uncle? How did you know that was his uncle?"

Hulalitu's cheeks tinged pink. "He . . . he has been to the temple plaza before. They both have. This is how I know of him."

"So these two were here before the prophet came."

She nodded, and her words rushed out. "This is how I know he would serve well as the substitute king. The details are not important right now, only your mission. I offer you a solution to your problem."

Ahu-duri paced as he thought over his sister's words. The choice of a commoner was not optimum, but it was acceptable, if done correctly. He had come up short in his search for anyone of nobility. And his sister was right. This was a potential solution.

Only four days remained for him to make his selection and send word back to the king. That meant only two days for the selection and two days for the scribes to record the decision and transport the sealed proclamation back to Kalḫu. He would stay in Nineveh and see to the *ugu lugal* installation, while others made preparations in Kalḫu for Adad-nirari's solitude, hidden away from the notice of the gods.

He turned suddenly when a thought germinated in the back of his mind. "The young man. Do you know his name?"

"His name is Jamin." A note of hope lifted her voice.

"Jamin. A Hebrew name, I think, which explains his presence with this prophet of Israel. But—"

A new thought gave the vizier pause. He smiled as the notion blossomed. Yes, this might work well, after all. If the young man was a Hebrew, his selection as the substitute king may avert the wrath of his god of destruction, this god of Israel. That's what the substitute king was supposed to do: to protect the rightful king from the wrath of the gods—any gods. Whether that meant to absorb it or forestall it didn't matter.

Of course, there would be no destruction from this god. It was a dream concocted by a vagabond who had spent too much time in the desert sun. But the people's belief that there would be destruction was what was important.

Ahu-duri's face lit up. Yes, this might offer the best opportunity to quell the unrest that gripped the city. And if the prophet's threat did have some substance, Jamin's presence on the throne would surely appease the Israelite god, even if only for one hundred days. That should be plenty of time for the god to tire of Nineveh, perhaps even to return to Israel.

He smiled to himself. Everything seemed to come together—except one thing. "This man. Is he married?"

Hulalitu's face fell. "I don't believe he is. Is that important?"

Her brother tapped his chin with a fingertip. "It would help. We need a substitute for the Queen Mother, too. A marriage could be arranged, though, if necessary."

"I'm sure a suitable wife could be found."

Ahu-duri went silent while his mind raced through the implications of such a decision. After a moment, he nodded to himself. It was his best option. Even if Adad-nirari did not approve, it would be too late. The selection would be made; the king's seal would be on the declaration.

"Brother?" His sister looked hopeful.

"Your idea has merit, but I must think it over. I will decide before nightfall."

Hulalitu leaped to her feet. In three steps she reached her brother and threw her arms around his neck, abandoning the protocol due the Senior Scholar. She drew back an instant later in shock.

Ahu-duri smiled. "Do not worry, Sister. I am glad you came. It has been wonderful—and profitable—to see you again."

She bowed her head. "Thank you. It's been good to see you again, too."

"Back to the temple with you." He signaled Khaheri, who waited across the garden. "I have work to do."

The aide saw Hulalitu to the gate, careful to keep his distance from the priestess of Ishtar.

PART TWO

So the people of Nineveh believed God, and proclaimed a fast,
and put on sackcloth, from the greatest of them
even to the least of them.
For word came unto the king of Nineveh,
and he arose from his throne, and he laid his robe from him,
and covered him with sackcloth, and sat in ashes.

JONAH 3:5-6

Thirty-four

Nineveh, the Temple of Ishtar
Fourteenth Day of Du'ûzu, the Eleventh Hour

"There is a visitor, High Priestess." The *naditu* bowed from the doorway.

Ianna tucked Jonah's gold amulet beneath her robe. The ornate *menorah* and the beauty of its workmanship had captivated her. She found herself unable to resist the urge to handle it.

"Who is it?"

"A woman. She would not say her name." The priestess kept her eyes lowered and extended her hand. "She gave me this."

"You bother me with an unknown—" Ianna's voice caught.

In the priestess's palm laid a small brooch of pure silver that framed a setting of lapis lazuli. Her eyes filmed, and she shuddered a short cough. She steeled her voice to reply.

"Leave it on the brazier stand. Bring my . . . the woman in."

The *naditu* bowed and slipped back into the antechamber.

When the door closed, Ianna stepped down from the dais. She approached the waist-high stand on which a blackened charcoal brazier awaited the next cold season. The brooch perched on the corner of a slate surface that protruded from beneath the grate. It glimmered in the subdued light, the lapis seeming to emit its own ambiance. Ianna blinked away a tear at the childhood memories the jewel elicited. She reached a tentative hand out for the piece but withdrew it when the hasp on the chamber door clicked.

Hani stood by the doorway, her hands gripped at her waist. Even across the room Ianna could see her mother shiver as she beheld her daughter in the robes of the *Entu* of Ishtar. Ianna's face began to flush, but she shook away the heat. She stepped back from the brazier and faced the door.

"Mother." Her voice was flat. She would betray nothing.

"Ianna . . ."

Her mother's frail tone sparked another wave of emotion, and this one nearly broke her. To deflect it, she turned and ascended the dais to the High Priestess's seat. She eased herself onto the scarlet cushion and looked down at her mother.

"You wanted to see me?"

Hani took two tentative steps forward. "I've wanted to see you ever since you first came to this . . . place."

Ianna frowned. She had heard of no attempted visits by her family. She had assumed they'd forgotten her—or, at least, she was certain her father had. "What stopped you?"

"I was never permitted. A woman, a priestess, I assume—she wore a blue tunic—told me it was not allowed."

"A priestess?"

"Yes. She had a low voice. It sounded like . . . like it hurt her to talk."

Hulalitu. Ianna clenched her jaw. "I know of no such priestess," she lied.

Her mother stared at the floor and said nothing.

Ianna cleared her throat. "Is there something you wish to speak to me about?"

Hani looked up, tears brimming in her eyes. "It's your father. He died. I thought you should know."

A pang of guilt-tinged anger pricked Ianna's forehead. Guilt that she subjected her mother to such coolness in the face of her sorrow. Anger at her father for dying . . . for living . . . for everything. It was he who insisted she participate in the carnal ritual of Ishtar, despite her mother's objections, and nothing had gone right since she'd stepped into this temple.

Now he was gone. Gone before he ever saw where his bull-headedness had led. Gone before he knew the humiliation she had suffered during her months as an unconsummated *ishtaritu*, her despair when she was sucked deeper into the Ishtar cult as a *naditu*, and now her fatalism as the very High Priestess of Ishtar.

She looked back down at her wounded mother—another of his legacies—who cringed at the foot of the dais. "I'm sorry for your loss."

"*My* loss? Ianna, he was your father."

Ianna's cheeks burned at the rebuke. "And what kind of father was he? What kind of father was he *ever?*"

She knew her words bit deeply into her mother's sorrow, but they had been pent up far too long and now burst like a flashflood over a sand levee.

Her mother's eyes hardened. "You will not speak ill of your father."

Ianna bristled. Her few weeks as High Priestess had already accustomed her to universal subservience. She was to be feared, not resisted—and certainly not reprimanded. She leaned forward. "I will overlook your tone. My father meant nothing to me."

She expected her mother to back down at the flash in her eyes.

But Hani returned her daughter's glare. "And I will overlook yours."

Before Ianna could reply, Hani reached over and snatched the brooch from the brazier stand. "This was a gift from your father. He made it with his own hands. He wanted only the best for you—"

"Hah!" Ianna jumped to her feet and strode down to her mother. "The best for me? Then tell me, Mother—" she lifted her arms and gestured about her chamber—"why am I here? I'm here because of him! You think a mere trinket atones for this?"

Hani flinched at her daughter's tirade but did not back down. "You have—"

Ianna cut her mother short as a thought leaped into her mind. "This seems to be a week for jewelry, Mother." She smirked as she yanked Jonah's gold medallion from beneath her robe and held it in front of her mother's face. "What do you think of this? Not silver, but real gold, do you see?"

The medallion twisted at the end of its thong. The *menorah* etched into its surface seemed to leap off the surface of the pendant.

Ianna glared at her mother.

Hani, face ashen, stared at the gold disk. The lapis brooch dropped from her fingers and clattered to the floor.

"Mother . . . what—?"

Her mother's voice was barely audible. "Where . . . did you get that?"

Hulalitu paced the floor in her small quarters. Her heart sagged in her chest until she thought it would flatten under her fear and shame. Since Ianna became the High Priestess of Ishtar, the *naditu* rarely emerged from her chamber. The other priestesses grumbled at the duties left unattended in her absence. Knuckles rapped on the wall outside her room, but they went unanswered. Rebukes barked through the door met with no response.

Never known for her social acumen, the morose priestess retreated even further into herself since the *Entu* ceremony put Ianna out of reach forever. Not that it made any difference in the young girl's attitude. She had all but ignored her mentor since her *naditu* ceremony, and that was only the beginning of a breach between the two that widened with each day.

Everything happened so quickly. Hulalitu's head still spun over the course of events since Ianna first came to the temple. As hard as she tried to get close, her young charge never warmed to her as she had hoped, as she had intended. Ianna's distance only served to prolong Hulalitu's decision to use the camphor powder one more time, and then one more. She was sure she could win the maiden's heart, given time. But time dwindled, and finally died, shrouded in the light blue tunic of the *naditu*. And all because of Issar-surrat's interference.

Issar-surrat! Hulalitu's mind growled the name. Her own mentor *naditu*, even after becoming High Priestess, seemed intent to ruin Hulalitu's life at every opportunity. Now, before her own untimely death, she'd named Ianna as her own successor and destroyed any chance of Hulalitu's happiness. No High Priestess ever named her own successor! There were protocols for that, a process instituted by Mother Ishtar herself and endorsed by no one less than the king. But nobody protested at the pronouncement of Ianna's advancement to the exalted office of High Priestess. Why? It was as though Issar-surrat still controlled the temple even from the underworld.

Now Hulalitu struggled with a notion that took seed in her mind one restless night and grew to an obsession over the past two days. She didn't know what prompted the thought. It was certainly not a decision she would ever have reached on her own. But it was there, and it gave her no peace. The seed sprouted and took firm root in both her conscious and subconscious. It fed the guilt and the fear that now oppressed her. The notion told her to confess. Confess everything.

That she had something to confess in the first place birthed the guilt. The fear came from the sure retribution that her now all-powerful former charge would bring upon her head for such a vile transgression. Ianna could have her executed for what she'd done when she subverted the sacred rite of the *ishtaritu*. And if the attitude Ianna now displayed toward Hulalitu was any indication, execution was a certainty. But this new fearsome notion burrowed into her brain and would not let go.

Today it was worse than ever. The urge spawned a pain in her head, which in turn spawned a lump in her stomach. The discomfort drove her to pace her room. Finally, after hours of emotional turmoil, something broke.

It snapped like a cord stretched too tight, and the bolt of pain it fired through her head dropped her to her knees. She tipped forward until her forehead met the floor, and she grasped her arms around her stomach. She tried to cry out, but no sound escaped her throat. Another pain exploded in her forehead, and her eyes rolled back.

Hulalitu retched and passed out.

"SHE IS READY."

※ ※ ※

Hulalitu's eyelids quavered. She opened her eyes to subdued light beneath her chamber door. She didn't know how long she had lain there, but a sore abdomen hinted at cramps that lasted perhaps hours. She pushed herself up, and her hand smeared through the half-dried bile that stained the small rug. Her brain was too numb to react to the violation, and she settled both hands onto her lap where she slouched.

The debilitating pain that drove her to the floor lingered as an ominous throb in the back of her head. It threatened to burst again unless Hulalitu obeyed its impulse and did so quickly. It left her no choice. She didn't think she could survive another onslaught like this. She would confess. It was time. Nothing else mattered anyway. Ianna had been her hope, her future. Now that future was gone. What did it matter that she would die? For all purposes, she had already died at the *Entu* ceremony.

Hulalitu pushed to her feet and stumbled toward the door. She didn't stop to smooth her tunic, brush out her matted hair, or wash her fouled hand.

※ ※ ※

"Well, look who's come back to life." Shera pursed her lips as Hulalitu's haggard figure approached. She glanced at her companion, who turned and surveyed the *naditu*.

Thura frowned at the delinquent priestess. "Well, are you ready to pick your duties back up, Hulalitu?" she huffed. "It's been extra work for all of us while you've been doing . . . whatever you've been doing."

Hulalitu ignored both the rebuff and the sarcasm. "I need to see Ian . . . the High Priestess." Her hoarse voice cracked from the strain and the nauseous residue that coated her throat.

Thura raised her eyebrows. "Oh, you do, do you? Looking like that?"

Shera stifled a snort. "Yes, I'm sure she would be quite happy to receive—by the Mother Goddess, what is that smell?"

Hulalitu self-consciously slipped her rancid hand behind her back. "I must see her. Now. It's important."

"Oh, important is it?" Thura dipped her head in mock respect. "Well, shall I summon her for you?"

Hulalitu remained stoic. "She will want to—"

"She will want to slap you silly for this intrusion, that's what she'll want to do." Thura took a step toward Hulalitu. "Who do you think you are to demand an audience—to demand anything—of us?"

Hulalitu persisted. "She—'intrusion'? What do you mean 'intrusion'?"

"If you must know, she already has a visitor. So you'd have to wait anyway."

"Who is with her?"

"I don't know. She didn't give her name. Just an old woman—why am I even telling you this? It's none of your business." Thura stepped to within a pace of Hulalitu.

"Perhaps if you were to go clean yourself up, she'd be finished when you return." Shera wrinkled her nose. "You certainly can't go in while you look or smell like that anyway."

Hulalitu met Thura's glare but decided not to antagonize the two priestesses any further. There was no way to win. Besides, she had another idea. "Very well, I'll return later." She pivoted on her heel and walked away.

"Cleaned up, perhaps?" Shera threw after her as she rounded the corner.

"I'll clean you up, you . . . ," Hulalitu muttered.

She picked up her pace at the corner of the Hall of the *Ishtaritu*, then hurried to the end of the corridor and stepped into the tiny room once assigned to Ianna. The priestess stepped behind the tapestry on the back wall and nudged aside a small panel. She crouched and slipped through the portal into a narrow passageway inside the wall.

Hulalitu moved quietly along the pitch-black tunnel. She was one of only three who knew the secret passageways by heart, having discovered them early in her stay at the temple. An elder *naditu* who had taken a fancy to the young Hulalitu had told her of rumors that such hidden corridors existed. The idea of secret hideaways intrigued the inquisitive young girl, and she set out on a quest to discover if the legend was true. It only took her and two equally adventurous friends three weeks to discover the hidden panels in two of the carnal initiation chambers. The excited novices swore never to reveal their secret to anyone.

Over the next two months, whenever they could sneak away from their duties, the trio explored the dark tunnels throughout the temple. Much to their thrill, there were outlets in rooms other than just the bedchambers. It was to one of those outlets Hulalitu now made her way.

She counted twenty-five paces, slowed, and began to trace her finger along the stone wall to her left. Two more paces and her fingertips brushed the smooth surface of another panel. She nudged it on the top right corner and it slipped aside to reveal a low opening like the one through which she had entered the tunnel. Hulalitu eased herself onto all fours and squeezed through the portal. She struggled to clear the wall cavity, her waistline more robust than the last time she used it.

Hulalitu drew her legs up behind herself and rolled to her side. She rested a moment from her exertion before she rose to her feet. As expected, she found herself huddled in a narrow space between the High Priestess's dais and the rear wall of the *Entu's* chambers. From her hiding place, she could hear muffled voices around the corner of the platform. Although she couldn't make out what they were saying, she recognized one of the voices as Ianna's. It sounded strained.

Hulalitu crawled to the corner of the platform and peered around its base. She couldn't see who was there, but the voices were clearer now. The second voice sounded familiar, but only vaguely—no, wait. It was the woman who had come to the temple to see Ianna several times since the girl arrived as an initiate. She said she was Ianna's mother.

Hulalitu narrowed her eyes.

Thirty-five

Nineveh, the Temple of Ishtar
Fifteenth Day of Du'ûzu, The First Hour

"Your father decided it would be best not to tell you until he felt you were old enough to understand everything." Hani sighed and squeezed her moist eyes shut against the weight of her heart and the burden of her secret.

The evening shadows sneaked across the floor from the corners of the High Priestess's chamber. They slithered up the walls, where they obscured the frescoed hall behind the dull gray of twilight. Although the worst of the day's heat had waned, the air in the room remained heavy, as though pressed down upon by another presence, one unseen. The two women sat on the lower steps and spoke in hushed tones.

The gold amulet lay in Ianna's lap, its leather cord entwined around her slender fingers. Hani stared at the medallion but made no attempt to touch it.

"I don't understand. You recognize this pendant. What is it, and why is it important? It's beautiful, and obviously costly, but I don't recognize the design."

Hani's lips twitched. "It is costly; you're right about that. Invaluable, really. But not because of the gold."

Ianna cocked her head. "Tell me—"

A soft tap at the door interrupted her. Ianna rose to her feet and whisked the heirloom behind her back.

"Enter."

A swath of yellow light invaded the room as the door opened. Thura stood in the doorway with a torch. "Shamash sets, my High Priestess. I thought you might need light . . ."

She faltered as she spotted her High Priestess's visitor sitting motionless on the steps of the dais.

Ianna was curt. "Very well. Light the torches and leave us."

"Yes, High Priestess."

Thura hurriedly touched her flame to four torches affixed by iron braces to the walls near the door. She moved to the side of the dais to light the two torches at the rear of the chamber.

Hulalitu raised her head and stared at the wall above her. One of the two unlit torches hung a scant five paces from where she hid. Thura would surely spot her. She began to scoot backward, further into the shadows between the platform and the wall. The panicked *naditu* craned her neck toward the secret portal and hoped beyond hope she could reach it before Thura lit the last torch.

She blinked at a burst of light that flooded the back corner of the chamber and shrank into the shadows. Hulalitu wriggled in the tight space, hoping the noise of her sandals against the floor would not betray her.

Thura's muffled footsteps grew louder. Hulalitu threw another look over her shoulder. There was no way she could reach the opening in time. In desperation, she tucked herself into a ball and held her breath.

The torch appeared around the corner of the dais and illuminated Hulalitu's hiding place in a blaze of light. She cringed and squeezed her eyes shut against the inevitable.

"That will do, Thura." Ianna's voice cut short the *naditu's* steps.

Hulalitu chanced a quick look up. Thura stood a mere seven paces away, her torch poised to light the final fixture. A glance to her left would put the skulking priestess fully in her view. As though she heard Hulalitu's mental pleas, Thura turned to her right and retraced her steps.

Shadow once more engulfed the niche. Hulalitu released a long, silent sigh.

When the door closed behind the attendant, Ianna returned to the steps. She eased herself down beside her mother and replaced the pendant on her lap.

Hani lifted her head, and she and Ianna locked gazes. Time slowed. The hiss of the torches receded into the background, and the room faded away. Only her mother remained in view. Ianna watched shadows from the flickering torchlight dance along the contours of the elder woman's face, where it animated every careworn wrinkle and highlighted every blemish. Ianna's breath caught short. A thought arose that had never occurred to her before. Her mother was beautiful.

The world would take no second glance at Hani. It would judge her plain, unremarkable. But in this moment, there was no purer beauty, no greater serenity than in this woman. It was more than her mother's face, though, that caught Ianna's attention. She peered behind her mother's eyes, and what she saw unnerved her. Fear and love, pain and joy—a hundred other mismatched emotions wove themselves into an intricate tapestry of the woman who was her mother. What kind of life could stitch an embroidery of such contradictions?

A thousand questions crowded the back of Ianna's mind. They chipped away at the shell around her heart until first one crack appeared, and then another.

The young High Priestess had no idea how long she remained lost in her mother's gaze, but the treasured stillness now became a weight that pressed down on her heart and her mind. A tightness worked its way into her throat, and she struggled to swallow past it. She felt the need to say something, to get some kind of affirmation of what she sensed. Lost in her quandary, she wasn't ready for what came next when her mother's soft voice broke the silence.

"You should know something. My name is not Hani."

"Your grandfather was a master craftsman, a goldsmith by trade. The landed and royalty alike sought his work not only in our homeland, but from abroad." Her mother shifted on the stair.

Ianna folded her hands in her lap, her face intent.

"One day, many years ago, a stranger stopped by your grandfather's house. Your father was very young, but he remembered his mother ushering his older brother and him from the house while his father spoke with the man. Your grandmother stayed outside with the boys while the men visited well into the evening. When the man finally left, your grandmother took the boys back inside and sent them straight to bed. Your father and uncle stopped at the top of the loft ladder and huddled together while they listened to their parents below. It wasn't long before the voices grew louder, more terse, and finally broke into an argument."

The elder woman's eyes grew distant. "It seems the stranger had offered your grandfather a position of prominence and enough silver and gold to ensure a comfortable living for the rest of their lives."

Ianna nodded. "That sounds very wonderful. Why an argument?"

"The position was in a foreign land, away from the home and family your grandmother loved. Your grandfather insisted it was best for the family, that it was a blessing they should not turn down. She tried to dissuade him, but he was adamant. They would leave, and that was final. Your father remembered his mother burst into tears and refused to go. The next thing he heard was a smack, then a thud on the floor."

Ianna's eyes narrowed.

Her mother swallowed and continued, "The boys heard the door slam and scrambled down the ladder to find their mother huddled on the floor in tears. They tried to comfort her, but she wouldn't stop crying. Her sons sat vigil by her for the rest of the night. Their father didn't return.

"The next day, around midday, your grandfather finally came home. He called the boys and told them to help begin with preparations to leave. He had purchased an oxcart and two animals, and they would leave with a group of travelers the next day. When they asked where they were going, he ignored them."

Ianna jumped in. "Where did this happen? What was—"

Her mother silenced her with an upraised finger. "Their trip was a perilous one. Your grandfather knew that. As they neared their destination, a band of Assyrian soldiers attacked their caravan. Several travelers were killed. Your grandmother was among those who died."

Ianna's eyes misted. "I thought Grandmother died in childbirth."

Her mother blinked a tear from her own eye. "That's what your grandfather wanted people to think. He refused to take responsibility for her death and thought the childbirth story would silence further questions."

"What happened then?"

"The soldiers began to loot the wagons. When they came across the jeweler's tools in your grandfather's cart, they questioned him. Their leader recognized his name by reputation and decided to take your grandfather and the boys back to their garrison. Their commander apparently thought such a renowned artisan in his custody might make good leverage for his own advancement, so he brought them all back to Assyria. Here, in fact, to Nineveh."

Ianna rubbed her forehead. As a child, she had learned almost nothing about her heritage. Now her family's entire life story poured out before her, and none of it was what she expected.

Her mother touched her daughter's forearm. "Are you all right, dear?"

Ianna started. She had not been called "dear" since she left home. The endearment sounded odd, out of place in this temple—especially in the sterile deference she was now accorded as the High Priestess. She searched her mother's eyes. The compassion and love in them, also strangers in this place, ushered a tear onto her cheek.

She brushed it away. "Please go on."

"Your grandfather never recovered from your grandmother's death. Although he hid the real story from others, it ate at him over the years. He retreated slowly into himself, hardened by the guilt he tried to deny, until he was little more than a recluse. Still a brilliant goldsmith, but a broken man."

An edge returned to Ianna's voice. "And my father became a jeweler like his father."

Her mother nodded. "Your father became a jeweler and his brother a potter. Before your grandfather died, he made a special gift for each of his two sons." Her voice grew fainter. "Gold medallions that were to be passed down through their respective families. Gold medallions on which he embossed the great symbol of the life, the land, and the faith he had left behind in search of greater wealth and fame."

"Your uncle Abim was forced into the army under King Shalmaneser. He left with the army on his first foray to the west . . . I don't know exactly where. He never came back." Her voice quavered. "He so loved his pottery."

Ianna put her hand over her mother's, which still rested on her forearm. "I never knew my uncle."

Her mother stared at Ianna's hand on her own, her voice now a whisper. "He was my husband."

Hulalitu crouched behind the dais, mesmerized by the tale. She shifted and grimaced at an arc of pain that shot through her cramped leg muscles. She had no idea how long she hid but noticed the charcoal gray of her niche had given way to an inky blackness that was held at bay only by the yellow glow from the torches. Her muscles screamed to move, but she dared not chance any noise that might betray her presence. To remain still, though, was no longer an option. Her leg muscles burned, and the pain overcame her ability to concentrate on the faint conversation.

The stocky *naditu* struggled against the tight space to push herself to her knees and steadied herself against the wall. She rose to her feet and stiffened her legs. Her knee joints popped, and the sound echoed into the chamber from her niche. To her ears, it was like a clap of thunder.

The voices went still.

Ianna stared at her mother. The question reached her lips, but her breath failed to push it any farther.

Her mother sat motionless. The only movement in the room, save the flickering of the torches, came from a tear that streamed down her cheek.

"I don't understand. My father then . . ." Ianna's whisper faded.

Her mother shook her head. "No, Abim was not your father."

Hulalitu stifled a sigh of relief as the elder woman's voice resumed, although now more quietly. She edged closer to the corner of the platform, but the women's hushed tones were lost in the sputter of the nearby torch. She leaned out from behind the platform. Neither woman was visible around the front of the podium. Hulalitu paused, wracked with uncertainty, but only for a moment. Despite the risk, she couldn't bear to lose the rest of the story. Her decision came quickly.

The *naditu* slipped around the corner of the platform and sidled along its wall until she reached the staircase. The voices grew clearer. She surmised the women must be on the steps. Hulalitu turned her back to the platform and slid to the floor. From here she could hear every word.

"Abim did not return with the remnant of the army. There were stories of a battle that had gone poorly. Many men were lost. Abim, we feared, was one of them."

"Then my father . . . ?" Ianna pressed for clarification.

"It is the custom among our people that, if a married man dies, it's the duty of the next older brother to take the widow as his own wife. Your father honored the law, and I entered his house." She drew a deep breath. "He was not my Abim, but I learned to love him."

"'Our people'?" Ianna cocked her head.

Her mother nodded. "The home your grandfather left was Jerusalem." She reached over and lifted the medallion from her daughter's lap and traced its surface with a fingertip. "This emblem is called a *menorah*. It is the symbol of the Hebrews. You are a child of the God of Abraham, Isaac, and Jacob, Ianna. You are a Jewess."

The God of Abraham, Isaac, and Jacob!

Ianna's fragmented thoughts flew back to that evening when the young man in her bedchamber told her of such a God. A God, he said, who valued her. A God who loved her and wanted only her love and devotion in return. Although such a notion had struck her as foolish, to be discarded as sheer nonsense, she recalled that something in his words would not leave her. Could it be that this God was in the young man's words themselves, that the words carried a power released the moment they were uttered? Did gods do that? Did they work that way?

She felt no such tug on her conscience when she chanted the prescribed devotions to Mother Ishtar. Could the man have been right? Ianna remembered telling him she was cursed. She also remembered that she had no answer when he asked if she ever felt cursed before coming to this temple. The answer now sprang to the forefront of her mind. No. She had never felt cursed until she crossed the threshold of this shrine.

She squeezed her eyes shut. What was happening to her?

Her mother's voice penetrated her troubled mind. "Before your father was Mordac, he was Mordecai, a Jew of the tribe of Judah. Before Hani, I was Hannah, a Jewess of the same tribe. My family was displaced to Nineveh in an exile many years ago. When your father lost his brother, Abim—his name also shortened from the Hebrew name Abimelech—his heart was broken. Your grandfather died within a year, and I think something in your father snapped. His heart hardened. He blamed God for the loss of his home and his family. He determined then to live without God, to meld into Ninevite society and establish his legacy here. That's when he changed our names, even the name of his late brother. He wanted to obscure our Hebrew roots, so we would better fit our new Assyrian identity."

Hannah's voice dropped further. "It also drove his desire, his need, for a son to carry on his name. After many years of trying, I gave him a daughter, but my labor was very difficult. I could never carry a child to term again. He withdrew from me more with each failed pregnancy."

Ianna's mind reeled. There were so many more questions she needed to ask, but she had no idea where to begin.

"Your temple ceremony was all part of fitting in. It was—" her voice caught—"'what is done.'"

Ianna slumped against the steps, her strength ebbing with every word her mother spoke. The disparate fragments of her life finally came together. She felt anew her father's distance, the perpetual sadness latent in her mother, her own lack of self-identity, of self-worth in a family and a world that never seemed at peace together. Her jaw tightened at the realization of what she was in the light of what she was meant to be. Because of her father's weakness, her family had lost everything it could have been in his quest for what it could never be.

Hannah shook her head. "I didn't want you to come here. Your father insisted. I begged him to reconsider. I told him this is not the way for a child of the Promise. Your body, your soul, your very life belong to God. I told your father the ritual was a travesty—that your first love should come in the arms of your husband in the sanctity of your marriage bed. Like mine was." She looked back up at Ianna, fresh tears on her cheeks. "Not in the arms of a stranger, not in this . . . this pagan brothel they call a temple." She hung her head. "I should have fought harder. I should have . . ."

Ianna closed her eyes, at a loss for a meaningful word of solace for her mother.

"Your father and I expected you back within a day or two. That's all it should have been. I secretly prayed I could make it up to you, that God would somehow forgive our idolatry, our transgression. Also, that He might heal you of this foul act."

"When you didn't return after a week, I came to the temple. I tried to see you more than once but was turned away. I began then to believe that we were under judgment. We turned our backs on God, so He left us to pay for our error. When I was told they made you a priestess, and that we had lost you, I was certain He had forsaken us. We allowed—no, we forced—you to surrender your precious virginity on the altar of a heathen goddess, an idol. For that, surely there is no forgiveness; there is no healing."

"Mother?" Ianna touched Hannah's arm.

"We lost . . . I lost all hope of ever seeing you again. I believed if I came here with the brooch, something tangible, that you might relent and see me." Her mother's hand trembled under Ianna's touch.

"Mother, there is nothing to heal."

Hannah looked confused. "What do you mean?"

"I was never consummated."

Her mother shook her head, puzzlement evident in her eyes.

Ianna's cheeks tinged pink in the glow of the torchlight. "Over the months I received many men in my bedchamber, but none was able to follow through, to perform. I don't know why, Mother, but I remain a virgin."

Hannah's face broadened in joy and disbelief. "But how, then, can you be here, in this room as the High Priestess? I don't understand."

Both women jumped at the hoarse voice that split the air.

"I am to blame for that."

Ianna leaped to her feet, the fire back in her eyes. The gold medallion clattered to the floor. Hannah twisted in her seat and gaped in the direction of the voice.

"What are you—how did you get in here?" The High Priestess drew herself up, her jaw clenched as Hulalitu rose into view beside the stairs.

The *naditu* kept her eyes on the floor and clasped her arms across her waist.

Hannah pushed slowly to her feet. "You . . . you're the priestess who turned me away when I tried to visit my daughter."

Hulalitu nodded but didn't look up.

Ianna stalked around the edge of the platform to within a pace of her former mentor. She bore down on the cringing woman, her hands jammed onto her hips. "I could have you banished for this," she growled through clenched teeth.

"Ianna . . ." Her mother's voice barely pierced her fury.

"How dare you enter these chambers unannounced! I demand to know how you got in here. Now! Before I have you dragged out and beaten," Ianna seethed as she unleashed all her pent-up emotion at the silent priestess.

Hannah's voice sharpened. "Ianna."

"Answer me when I speak to you!" Ianna raised her arm and threatened a backhand across Hulalitu's face.

Her mother's shout froze her. "Ianna!"

The irate *Entu* spun and glared at her mother.

Hannah's voice softened. "Ianna . . . look at her."

The High Priestess swiveled her head back toward the silent *naditu*, her eyes mere slits. Hulalitu had not moved, even under the threat of Ianna's hand. She stared at the floor, and her body shuddered in the sudden stillness. A single tear fell from her cheek and disintegrated into a ragged splotch on the floor.

Ianna's chest heaved and she lowered her hand, but her face remained hard. With a deep breath, she settled back on her heels.

Hannah exhaled. "Perhaps she can explain. If we let her."

Ianna's eyes remained on Hulalitu. "She *will* explain."

Hulalitu appeared frozen in place until Hannah stepped forward and touched Hulalitu's hand. Then the *naditu* jolted and lifted her eyes. She stared at Hannah, then broke her stance with a shallow cough.

Hannah clasped the priestess's hand and motioned to the steps. "Come. Please sit down."

Hulalitu took a half step forward and glanced toward her High Priestess but didn't make eye contact. She allowed herself to be led to the steps, her hand limp in Hannah's.

Ianna did not move but watched her mother and Hulalitu settle onto the stairs. Anger, pride, and the imperiousness even her short time as High Priestess fostered in her kept her from joining the other two women where they sat. She stood with her arms crossed and waited.

Hannah released Hulalitu's hand. "What is it you need to tell us? What do you mean you are to blame for Ianna's presence here?"

Hulalitu swallowed. "Perhaps I should start from the beginning."

༄ ༄ ༄

Fourteen-year-old Hulalitu sat quietly on her sleep mat four weeks after her *ishtaritu* ceremony. Her consummation in the arms of a nameless stranger had come six nights after she came to the temple. She had remained because there was nowhere else to go. Her parents had left for Kalḫu to be near their son. They did not send for her.

Prahthath hovered over the young girl, her hands on her hips. "What do you mean? What are you telling me?"

The young *ishtaritu* flinched. "I have not yet stained the cloth. I should have with Sin's full face. He has gone dark now."

"Are you sure?" her mentor's voice rasped.

"I am."

"What were you thinking, you fool! You do not come for your ceremony when you are fertile. You plan your initiation rite around that. You knew that."

"But I—"

"But what? There is no 'but'!" Prahthah spun on her heel and paced the room.

Hulalitu pleaded, "My womanhood began late. I thought I knew my cycle, but it has not been regular—"

"Nonsense!" The *naditu* stomped her foot. "Do you know what this means? It's a disgrace to conceive during your initiation to the Mother Goddess. And it disgraces not only you, but me as your mentor." She rolled her eyes. "How could you do this?"

Hulalitu began to cry. "I—"

"Oh, stop it! Shut up, do you hear me?" Prahthah glanced over her shoulder toward the corridor. Her voice lowered. "Have you told anyone?"

"No."

"Don't. We'll take care of it."

The young girl sniffed back a sob and frowned. "What do you mean?"

"There is a mint herb that grows in the West. Zithralu keeps a store of its oil for cases like this."

Hulalitu stiffened. "Do you mean—"

"It's fortunate you're fat. Your condition isn't noticeable yet."

The *ishtaritu* dropped her gaze to the floor.

"No, we should be able to contain this until the oil has had its effect." Prahthah nodded to herself. "I'll see to it. Stay to yourself, and don't talk to anyone about this. Do you understand me?"

Hulalitu gave a slight nod but didn't raise her eyes.

Over the next three months, Prahthah brought small quantities of pennyroyal oil mixed with wine for Hulalitu to drink. When there were no results, she began to suspect the truth—that Hulalitu could not bring herself to end the pregnancy. The young *ishtaritu* secretly emptied the laced wine anywhere she could. Although she knew it would destroy her status at the temple, even prompt her eviction, she marveled at the new life in her. The thought of her own child, someone who could give her the love her own parents withheld, overwhelmed her. She was determined to have the child, no matter the consequences. When Prathah questioned her, she merely shrugged and suggested she might be immune to the drug's effects.

Prahthah's frustration grew with Hulalitu's waistline. Zithralu began to resist dispensing so much of the rare oil for one girl. It was seldom included in the goods of caravans that passed through Nineveh, and she could only spare so much. Prahthah had depleted her stock, and Zithralu began to threaten exposure. To add to the problem, Hulalitu began to thicken noticeably, despite her already ample girth. Prahthah was grateful the girl didn't carry the child in front, as so many others did, nor, mercifully, did she miss any duties from nausea. They could count on the impression of simple weight gain for a while, but not much longer. Still, Prahthah couldn't afford to risk the impact this would have on her aspiration to become a senior *naditu*. Something would have to be done, and soon. As Hulalitu approached the end of her second trimester, Prahthah made her decision.

Late one night, the *naditu* slipped into Zithralu's work area and emptied a vial of the toxic extract into a goblet of wine. It was three times the normal dosage, but Prahthah didn't have time to worry about that. Under the guise of celebrating the young girl's first season at the temple, Prahthah brought the poisoned wine with a plate of fruit and cheese to the girl's small chamber. Suspicious at first, Hulalitu relaxed when she saw her mentor take a deep draught from her own cup. Hopeful that the attempts to abort her baby had finally ended, the *ishtaritu* smiled, took a bite of cheese, and followed her mentor's lead with a deep drink from her goblet.

"I took one more swallow of the wine, and a sharp pain—something like I'd never felt before or since—racked my body. I fell to the floor, curled into a ball, and emptied my stomach. Before I passed out, I remember seeing Prahthah slip out the door."

Ianna stepped around the front of the dais and lowered herself onto the step beside Hulalitu. Her face had softened, and her moist eyes glistened in the torchlight.

"When I awoke the next morning, I couldn't speak. My throat was on fire, and my stomach convulsed the entire morning. The pains started two days later. Of course, the child was stillborn." Hulalitu raised wet eyes toward Ianna. "It was a girl. She already had a mat of hair." Hulalitu lifted a finger and stroked a tress flowing over Ianna's shoulder. "Dark hair."

Ianna didn't flinch from the touch.

Hulalitu dropped her hand to her lap, and her voice turned to gravel. "She was beautiful. Would have been . . . beautiful." She hacked a cough. "Prahthah slipped my daughter's body to a priest from another temple. He tucked her into the woodpile when he prepared the evening burnt offering. She swore the priestess-midwife who attended me to secrecy, and then, to be sure, had her moved to another temple. Aššûr, I think."

The *naditu* smiled wistfully. "I used to sing. I had a . . . beautiful voice, they told me. After that day, no more. The vomiting, I guess." Her smile disappeared, and she dropped her gaze. "I used to sing," she whispered.

Hannah took the priestess's hand into her own and caressed her wrist. Several moments passed before Ianna broke the silence.

"But what does that have to do with me?"

Hulalitu lifted her head. "When I saw you at your initiation ceremony, I knew you were her."

Ianna wrinkled her brow. "Knew I was who?"

Hanna nodded and laid her hand on Ianna's arm. The young girl's eyes flicked toward her mother.

Hulalitu murmured, "My daughter. You were my daughter . . . would have been my daughter." She surveyed the beautiful priestess through glossy eyes. "She would've looked just like you." She reached out again. "Just like you."

Ianna sat back, her eyes wide.

Hulalitu coughed and steeled her voice. "Yes, I'm to blame. Camphor powder."

"What?"

"Camphor powder. I mixed it in the ceremonial wine, the libation cup, in your bedchamber. It renders men impotent." She dropped her eyes again. "That's why none were able to perform."

Ianna's face reddened.

The *naditu* nodded. "It wasn't you who failed. It was my doing. I couldn't let you go." She leaned forward and her eyes pled with Ianna's. "It was only supposed to be for a few days. Then maybe a week. Just one more time. But I couldn't stop. I couldn't bear to lose you . . . again." She flashed a glance at Hannah, before she lowered her gaze. "I'm so sorry. I kept your daughter. I turned you away when you tried to see her. I needed to be . . . a mother."

Neither Hannah nor Ianna knew what to say. The sputter of the torches offered the only sound in the quiet chamber.

"Issar-surrat found out," Hulalitu muttered.

Ianna jerked her head up.

"Who?" asked Hannah.

The *naditu* glanced at Ianna's mother. "Prahthah went on to become High Priestess. She changed her name to Issar-surrat."

Hulalitu looked back at Ianna. "I don't know how. She must have put it together. She knew I had requested to be your mentor. She heard of your beauty, and yet your . . . your failure to be consummated. She must've seen through me. That's when she decided you should become a *naditu*. That would make you my peer and remove you from my charge." The priestess tipped her shoulders. "She could've had me banished for subverting the *ishtaritu* ritual. I guess she thought it would be a worse punishment to lose you, yet have you remain in my sight in the temple." She shrugged. "Perhaps it was retribution for tricking her during my pregnancy. I don't know for sure."

Ianna found her voice but didn't know what to ask first. "But High Priestess? Me? How—"

"I know nothing about that, I promise you." Hulalitu shook her head. "I don't know why she named you as her successor. That is never done. The king always chooses the High Priestess. She must have known he would agree, but," the pleading look returned to her eyes, "I don't know how or why. You must believe me."

It was the third hour of the new day before the three women parted. Hulalitu replaced the panel over the secret portal, and Ianna saw her former mentor to the main door of the chamber.

"We will talk again. I still have many questions."

Hulalitu nodded. She reached a tentative hand toward Ianna, then stopped as her eyes locked on to the High Priestess's vestments. She began to withdraw, but Ianna took her hand and gave it a gentle squeeze. The *naditu's* lips twitched with the hint of a smile, and she slipped into the dark hallway.

Ianna returned to her mother. The elder woman held the gold medallion across her palm and probed a deep dent in its surface with a fingernail. She shook her head.

"I still don't understand. You say this came from a prisoner? Someone here in Nineveh?"

Her daughter nodded. "He was imprisoned yesterday. I found it around his neck."

"Why were you at the prison?"

"I wasn't—it's a long story, Mother. I'm not sure I understand all of it yet." She closed her eyes against a sudden weariness.

Hannah touched her face. "I'll go now."

Ianna nodded.

Her mother paused. "I'm so glad you agreed to see me. None of this would have happened. There would still be so much unknown if you hadn't agreed . . ." She looked into her daughter's eyes.

Ianna embraced her mother. She felt the older woman's hands squeeze her shoulders, and a quiet sob shook her back. Hannah gently caressed her daughter's hair, then she stepped back.

"I would like to visit this prisoner. Do you think that would be possible?"

Ianna glanced down at the amulet in her mother's hand. "Yes. I can arrange that. I'll send word."

"Thank you," her mother said. "And . . . may I have this? Just for now?"

Ianna smiled. "Keep it. You should have it. Perhaps it will shed light on what happened to my uncle."

Hannah closed her fingers over the precious heirloom.

Ianna led her to the chamber door. "It's dark, and you don't know the temple. I'll see you to the door."

As they reached the hallway, Hannah turned. "I may not be able to do this at the door." She placed her hand on her daughter's cheek and touched a light kiss to the other one. "I miss you."

Ianna blinked back a tear. "We'll see more of each other, Mother. Much more. I promise."

The two women stepped into the hallway, and the door clicked shut as the last torch sputtered and died.

Thirty-six

Nineveh, the Temple of Ishtar
Fifteenth Day of Du'ûzu

Ianna remained in her bedchambers the entire morning. The revelations of the night before echoed through her mind and raised more questions as the day wore on. Tentative taps at her door went unanswered; daily rituals were left unattended. Her mind struggled to understand the pieces of her life handed to her so unexpectedly, to assimilate who she was and where she came from. The string of events—the heritage that brought her to Nineveh, the rejection of faith that brought her to the temple, the guile and intrigue that brought her to this room—refused to set themselves in order.

And in the background lingered the face of a young man with irrational love in his eyes and an irrational God in his words. She tried to reconcile the God of love and acceptance he had described to her with this God of destruction His prophet preached. It should have been easy to reject one such as He, given the obvious contradictions in His nature. But, for some reason, thoughts of Him would not let her rest.

Perhaps the reason she couldn't dismiss him was the discovery that this was also the God of her heritage, the God her father supplanted with his desire for prestige among his Ninevite peers. What would life have been like if she had known all along? How would it have been different?

But, still—*one* God? How could only one God rule over the heavens, the earth, and the affairs of man? If there was only one God over all creation, how could He know she existed, let alone care for her? She was but one person among all the people of the earth. The gods she knew were not personal. Their history was one of intrigue and a struggle for power within a tumultuous pantheon. But could one God know what it meant to be individual and unique? Was it possible this God could see into the heart of a single young girl—and would care to do so? Could He really know her hurts, her desires, her innermost dreams?

Ianna winced at a stab of pain in the rear of her skull. She recognized it.

"Your thoughts, girl. Keep them only on me."

She frowned. "They've never been only on you."

"Fool! All you are is because of me."

"Yes, and I hate what I am."

"You are my High Priestess! All power is yours; power that comes only from me! Look around you. All bow to your every wish; you are the law. Your word alone cast our enemy into prison. You are mine. My realm is the world, and you are its keeper."

Ianna narrowed her eyes against the pain. "I *do* look around me. I see a life twisted and torn by deceit, ruled by lies, served by those who hate me. I see a realm of suspicion and fear." She steeled her will. "And I see walls of cold clay guarded by statues of dead stone. I see the prison, and it is around me, not the prophet."

"Silence! I nurtured you! I gave you your glory, your power. You will—"

"I will *nothing!* Away with you! I deny you, I detest you, I cast you to . . . to . . . God! To the God of Abraham, Isaac, and Jacob!" Ianna's heart throbbed until she thought it would burst from her chest. She screamed her defiance, oblivious to the tears that flowed down her cheeks. "To the God of my fathers. To . . . to . . ." She pounded her fists on the floor and sobbed her frustration. "Oh, God, I don't even know your *name!* Who *are* you?"

"ADONAI. HIS NAME IS ELOHIM ADONAI."

The still small voice enveloped her brain with warmth and evaporated the vile fog from her mind. It dissolved the pain and restored a peace she hadn't known since she entered the Temple of Ishtar. Her lungs ceased their convulsing, and Ianna lay prostrate with her cheek against the cold floor. She swallowed and grimaced at the dryness of her throat.

"*Elohim . . . Adonai?*" The name rolled from her tongue. It massaged her lips, soothed her ears, and settled her mind. She released a heavy sigh. "I don't know You. I should know You. I want to . . ."

"YOU ARE HIS CHILD."

Ianna rolled onto her back. She squinted into the twilight that now overtook the room. Her voice shook with unresolved emotion and unanswered questions.

"How can I be a child of the God of Israel, while I serve as the High Priestess of Ishtar?"

"IT IS FOR A PURPOSE YOU ARE HERE. THE TIME IS NEARLY FULL. SOON ALL WILL BE REVEALED."

"But—"

"REST NOW."

Ianna closed her eyes. She drifted into sleep while the gentle words from her new God made her bed, and the face of a young man ushered in her dreams.

"SHE IS READY."

Thirty-seven

Nineveh, the Artisan Quarter
Fifteenth Day of Du'ûzu, the Eleventh Hour

Aunt Rizpah paused with her pestle over the dried cumin seeds and frowned at the quiet tap on the door. Her house had known no peace since Jonah arrived. The elders met daily; gawkers loitered in the narrow street outside the house that harbored the prophet; her husband and nephew ran in and out at all hours. All the commotion wobbled the delicate balance of life in the poor quarter. Nothing was the same since the prophet arrived.

Granted, life began to settle after the soldiers took Jonah away. She felt guilty in her relief at the gradual return to normalcy, given the price it carried. Personally, she still wasn't sure what to think of this message of destruction anyway. How did they know Jonah was genuine, that he had really been sent by God? She had never heard of this prophet from anyone who passed through the city from the West. Nobody in the community had heard of him—even those who spent more time in the marketplace than she. Wouldn't there have been some forewarning before a prophet with such a terrible message showed up on her doorstep?

Another tap roused her from her thoughts. She sighed and set aside the pestle. She brushed dried bits of herbs from her hands and opened the door.

"They aren't home. There's an elders' meeting—" Rizpah stopped short at the sight of a hooded figure in a full-length cloak.

The stranger stood silently with hands clasped at the waist.

Rizpah raised an eyebrow. "May I help you with something?"

The head lifted to reveal a face of such uncommon beauty that

Rizpah was actually startled. She stared at a young girl's dark almond eyes, delicate cheekbones, and unblemished olive skin. A wave of ebony hair swept a graceful forehead from beneath the hood, accenting her face as a delicate border might frame a costly tapestry.

A hesitant silence fell between the two. Then Rizpah's cheeks reddened as she realized she was staring. "I'm sorry. Please forgive me. I wasn't expecting . . . visitors."

The girl shook her head and returned an apologetic smile. "The fault is mine. I hope I'm not intruding."

"No, please. Won't you come in?" Rizpah stepped back from the doorway.

"Thank you. Just for a moment. I won't keep you." The girl slipped into the room, and Rizpah latched the door behind her.

"I have hot water. May I offer you some herbal tea?"

"Thank you. That would be very nice." The tentative smile flashed again.

Rizpah retrieved two cups and reached for a small bag of tea. Her visitor eased her hood off her head, and Rizpah stole another look at the silky black tresses that spilled over the girl's shoulders. She forced herself not to gape at the exquisite maiden—at least she assumed she was a maiden. Rizpah suddenly felt quite plain next to her, almost unworthy to share the same room. She shook the thought away as silly.

Rizpah ladled hot water into the cups. She turned and mustered a smile. "We have not met. Are you . . . of the artisan's quarter?"

The girl's eyes dipped, and a tinge of pink colored her cheeks.

"No, I live not far from here." She looked back into Rizpah's face. "My name is Ianna."

The two women settled onto a thin mat against the wall, their fingers laced around their earthenware cups. Neither spoke for a moment. Rizpah wondered how to inquire as to the reason for the visit without appearing too blunt. Ianna seemed to struggle with her own thoughts. Twice her lips quivered, as though she wanted to speak, but then fell still again. Her apparent discomfort troubled Rizpah's heart, and she searched for a way to soothe her guest's nerves.

"I hope the tea is not too strong," she offered.

The girl appeared startled. "No, it's very good. Thank you." She dropped her gaze, then looked back up, fervency replacing her hesitancy. Words tumbled out. "Tell me of God, the God of Israel. Of *Adonai*. Please."

Rizpah lowered her cup to her lap as she fumbled for a response. "I don't understand. Tell you of God?"

"Yes, of *Elohim Adonai.*" Ianna's hands shook, sloshing drops of tea onto her cloak.

Rizpah swallowed. "There is so much. I don't know where to begin."

Ianna reached out and grasped her hostess by the wrist. Her eyes pleaded beyond her words. "Start from the beginning."

The elders' meeting lasted longer than expected. Jonah's arrest had thrown the Jewish community into turmoil. Nothing made sense. Questions flew from all directions.

"What do we do, Hiram?"

"If Adonai is truly in this, how could the prophet be arrested?"

"Who will carry the message now?"

"Not me! We are being watched. My family cannot afford for me to be imprisoned, too."

Jamin tried to help his uncle calm the assembly, but to no avail. His own mind was in pieces. The horror of Jonah's arrest, the ugly mob scene in the temple square, and the demands of the elders all weighed on him. But the burning image of the girl he loved in the robes of the High Priestess of Ishtar pushed all else aside. It tore at his heart every time the incident resurfaced in his mind. Numbness had overtaken his brain at the first sight of her on the temple steps. Then, through the shock, he remembered her gaze on him after the assault on his uncle. It was all such a blur, he wondered if he had imagined that part. The encounter seemed lifted out of time. She had stared at him not three paces away; then she was gone.

A sudden quiet of the assembly roused Jamin from his thoughts, and he scanned the group of men. They all stared past him. Jamin turned around.

Two squads of soldiers stood shoulder to shoulder in an arc. Their formation hemmed the Council into a corner of the marketplace. For several moments, neither the soldiers nor the elders moved. Finally, a movement to his left pulled Jamin's attention. An older soldier, presumably the leader of the troops, strode to the front and centered himself before the group of elders.

"There is one of you here named Jamin," the commander bellowed. "Identify yourself."

Jamin froze. How did they know his name? What could they want with him? He threw a panicked glance over his shoulder toward his uncle, who returned the startled look.

"I said, identify yourself!" The soldier's voice rasped to a growl.

One of the elders behind Jamin hissed at him, "Speak up. You want them to slaughter us all?"

A hand shoved him in the small of his back, and Jamin stumbled forward. He stopped five paces away from the soldiers.

The commander looked him over. "That you, boy? I've seen you before."

Jamin couldn't speak; he could only stare into the eyes of the soldier.

"I remember now." A taut smile pulled at the commander's jaw. He jerked his head at two of his men. "Take him."

When Jamin regained his senses, he was being hustled out of the market square, his arms pinned to his sides.

"The people entered His promise, and the Lord God fought for them to occupy the land." Rizpah paused. She had recited the story of her God and her people for over an hour.

Ianna sat spellbound. She had never heard such a tale of a god who interacted in the lives of people like this God did. She shook her head as Rizpah related how time and time again the people rebelled against Him and forsook the covenant He established through a man named Moses. A covenant? Imagine a God who would reveal Himself to mortal man. Even more shocking was the notion that one would enter into a covenant with them. The gods she knew expected to be served without question. Why should the *Igigi* reveal themselves? Man was of no consequence, other than to provide for their needs. But the God of her heritage needed no sustenance, no provision, no one to do His work for Him. He didn't want the labor of their hands; He wanted the willingness of their hands. This God didn't force blind obedience; He revealed Himself so man would desire to be obedient. He didn't want to be appeased; He wanted to be loved—loved as He loved them.

Love? From a god?

But didn't that make Him weak? To seek the hearts of man rather than to coerce them? Perhaps not, she reasoned. Perhaps it took a more powerful God to grant His people the power of choice. He would know some would reject Him, yet He still maintained His sovereignty over all. Ianna struggled to sort out the paradoxical nature of this God.

"Are you understanding this, or is it too much?" Rizpah's voice interrupted Ianna's thoughts.

"Yes . . . and yes. I understand all you've told me, but this God you describe is difficult to grasp. There are still so many questions, but I'm not sure how to ask them."

Rizpah smiled. "Yes, the 'what' is straightforward. It's the 'why' that gives us fits, no?"

Ianna's face lit up. "Yes, exactly. What this God has done, how and with whom He has acted, is clear. But why He chooses to act this way puzzles me. It seems so strange."

Rizpah cocked her head. "You know, you still haven't told me anything about yourself. Where do you live and what brought you to this house? Why does our God interest you?"

"I—"

The door slammed against the wall, and Hiram barged into the room, red-faced and out of breath. Rizpah jumped up. Her cup flew to the floor and shattered into a splatter of wet herbs and clay shards.

"Rizpah! They've taken Jamin. He's—" Hiram stopped in his tracks at the sight of Ianna. His mouth fell open.

Ianna shrank back at the sight of the old man the soldier assaulted on the portico of Nabu's temple.

Rizpah looked at her husband, then at Ianna. "Hiram?"

He raised a finger at the High Priestess of Ishtar. *"You!"*

The soldiers led Jamin through the arched gateway into the garden courtyard of the new palace. The gate slammed behind them, and the leader turned to his men.

"You're dismissed. Leave him here."

The soldiers complied, and when the two were alone, the commander crossed his arms and glowered at his prisoner. Jamin stretched his arms, cramped from the grip of the guards.

"We have unfinished business," the warrior snarled. "You attacked one of my men during the riot."

Jamin raised his eyes, and anger rose in his own throat. "I protected my uncle. Your soldier struck him with his spear and was ready to hit him again. He's an old man and was unarmed. He was no threat to you."

The seething commander took a step toward Jamin. "Listen, whelp, if you—"

"Anardu, that is enough." The voice froze the soldier.

A tall man in fine robes stood behind the commander.

The warrior turned to face him. "Yes, my lord. I only—"

"I know. I think your man did survive, though, did he not?" Ahuduri raised an eyebrow.

"Yes, my lord."

"You may leave us now."

Anardu bowed, threw another hostile look at Jamin, and stalked away. Jamin and the official stood and regarded each other. Jamin recognized him as the legate who interrogated Jonah at the Nabu's temple, and then had him arrested.

Suddenly Jami understood. He was to be punished for putting his shoulder into the guard on the temple steps. They had forgotten him in the melee with the High Priestess, and in Jonah's arrest. Now it was his turn. But the man who stood before him did not appear to threaten. It also seemed odd such an elevated official would dismiss his guard to be left alone with a prisoner who had already shown himself capable of violence.

Ahu-duri broke the silence. "Come with me." He turned and moved up the paved pathway. Jamin hesitated, then fell into step behind him.

They rounded a corner and approached a group of three other men, one of whom Jamin recognized as the city magistrate. The other two were probably scribes. One held a softened clay tablet and reed stylus, the other a waxed wooden writing pad and a similar stylus. Another group of men crowded the end of the path near a doorway of the palace.

The official eased himself onto a large cushion near the scribe with the clay tablet. Jamin remained on his feet.

"This man, my lord?" The magistrate—Iqisha, if Jamin remembered correctly—raised an eyebrow.

Ahu-duri nodded and appraised Jamin from his seat. "I have reason to believe he would be a good choice, especially given the current situation."

Jamin fidgeted in the ensuing silence.

After a moment, the official continued. "Young man—Jamin, I believe it is?"

"Jamin ben Obadiah . . . my lord."

"Jamin ben Obadiah, you have a unique opportunity to serve your king and your kingdom. For reasons I will not go into, I have been empowered by King Adad-nirari to designate a substitute king to serve in his stead for the period of one hundred days. I have selected you.

You will begin preparations immediately for the installment ceremony, which will take place in three days."

Ahu-duri paused and watched impassively as the scribe with the waxed board recorded the decision.

Jamin rocked on his feet. His mind melted into a blur.

The vizier turned to the second scribe. "Prepare a decree naming one Jamin ben Obadiah as the *ugu lugal*. I will seal it and dispatch it to Kalḫu."

"Yes, my lord." The scribe lowered his stylus to the damp clay.

Jamin's head swam. He could hardly breathe. *Substitute king?*

"You are dismissed." The official's voice barely penetrated the ring in his ears. "Do not leave the city. Return here at the sixth hour three days from today. I am certain Anardu would be pleased to retrieve you, should you fail to appear."

Jamin's feet rooted in place. He stared straight ahead and struggled to swallow through a dry throat.

The official's voice barely penetrated the numbness that overtook his mind. "I said you are dismissed."

Rizpah stared at her husband's contorted face. "Hiram! What—"

"What are you doing here?" Purple veins pulsed on Hiram's neck.

Ianna pressed against the wall.

The irate elder took a step toward the girl, and Rizpah stepped in front of him. "Hiram!"

"Get out of my way! Why did you let her in? *Her,* of all people?" He hovered, his beet-red face a hand's width from his wife's.

She refused to back down. "Who, 'of all people'?"

The fire in his eyes burned into hers. "That . . . is the High Priestess of Ishtar. She is the reason Jonah is in prison."

Rizpah twirled to face the young girl against the wall. "Ianna, is this true?"

Ianna cringed and lowered her eyes.

"Of course it's true," her husband sputtered. "Do you think I could mistake something like this?"

Rizpah turned her head. "Hiram, let me speak to Ianna. There is more to this than either of us knows."

"What's to know? She's a vile harlot, and I will not have her in my house!"

Ianna flinched at the insult. She rose unsteadily to her feet and lifted her hood over her head. "I'm sorry. I will leave. Please forgive me—"

Rizpah laid a hand on her arm. "Sit down, dear. You aren't leaving."

"Dear?" Hiram blustered. "What are you saying? I want her out—"

"Hiram, enough!"

His wife's challenge brought him up short. He glared at her.

Rizpah's hand held Ianna with warmth, but her eyes gripped her husband with ice. Her words came low and steady. "Ianna and I have spent a long time talking, Husband. Over tea."

"Tea? Rizpah—"

"Yes, Hiram, over tea. And with the fullest measure of hospitality for which our home has become known." She raised an eyebrow. "I invited Ianna into our home, Hiram. You will act accordingly."

Hiram raised his own eyebrows at his wife's usurpation of his authority. He stared at her resolute face, then at Ianna, who had just settled back onto the mat and lowered her hood. He prepared another tirade but choked back his words when a tear rolled down the young girl's face. He threw a helpless look back at his wife.

Rizpah crossed her arms.

Hiram's chest settled with a slow exhale, and he turned away.

Rizpah returned her attention to Ianna. She eased herself down next to the girl and took her hand into her own. "Ianna, would you please explain?"

Ianna sniffed back a sob and looked to the soft eyes of her hostess. She eyed Hiram, who stood by the door with his back to the women.

"Your husband is right. I am the High Priestess of Ishtar. But I don't know why. . . ."

The daylight outside became dusk, then darkness, as Ianna related her story. She told of her newly discovered heritage and her father's abandonment of his faith. Sometime during her tale—she wasn't sure when—Hiram had lit two oil lamps. He had set one on a shelf by the door and the other on the floor by a side wall. She stared at her feet and watched their shadows dance in the flicker of the lamplight.

Once, when she did look up, she was surprised to see Hiram seated on the floor. His head rested on his arms, which were folded across knees drawn up against his chest. Their eyes met for an instant, and he nodded to her. She dropped her gaze and continued.

Ianna omitted Jamin's visit to the temple from her story. It was a most important part to her, for it was the first she had heard of *Elohim Adonai*. But she feared Jamin may not have told them of their encounter, and she believed the story should come from his lips, not hers.

Ianna's tale mesmerized Rizpah. She stroked the back of the girl's hand with her fingertips as she spoke. When she revealed her Jewish heritage, tears sprang to Rizpah's eyes and confusion to her mind that God would allow a child of the Promise to assume such a wicked heathen office. Yet He was God, and He knew all. Perhaps there was more to this than she understood—of course, there had to be more.

The hostess in Rizpah reminded her of the fact that they'd not eaten, and that the girl must surely be hungry. But she wasn't about to interrupt the story for the sake of food.

She studied Ianna as she spoke, struck again by her beauty—and the sadness behind it. *Such a waste. But she is still young. Perhaps there is yet time.*

It took a concerted effort for Hiram to subdue his emotions. The heat in his forehead threatened to burst into flames at any moment, fanned by his heaving lungs. The news of Jamin's arrest slipped from his mind in the confrontation with the High Priestess.

He stood with his back to the women, at a loss for what to do. Slowly, Ianna's words penetrated his burdened mind, and he found his heart begin to soften at her tale. As the twilight deepened, he trimmed two lamps while he bent his ear to her every word. He set one lamp by the front door and the second lamp by the wall, then slid to the floor beside it. He faced the girl for the first time since Rizpah had silenced him. Hiram studied her face and her tone as she spoke. He searched for any sign of deceit or manipulation in her words or her tone. He detected neither. Her soft voice soothed the harshness of the story she told. She minced no words, but neither grew crass in her description of life at the temple.

His reaction to the news of her Hebrew birthright affected Hiram much as it did his wife. He shook his head in wonderment at what *Adonai* could be doing. The threat of Nineveh's destruction, the imprisonment of His prophet, Jamin's arrest, and now the presence of a child of Abraham on the dais of the High Priestess of Ishtar—it was too much. He felt so small, so inadequate as an elder of his people, as he now came face to face with the stark revelation of God's plan as He unfolded it.

Hiram had no answers, only questions. He, like his people, was forced to watch and wait on God's word and His timing. The elder pursed his lips. *Such is faith.*

Ianna finished her story with Hulalitu's confession. She offered no opinions, no conclusions, only the facts. She let the words speak for themselves, for better or for worse.

Suddenly, her eyes widened. "Oh, my. The temple. There are rituals. I must go."

She pushed to her feet and drew her hood back over her head. Rizpah and Hiram rose with her.

Rizpah touched her arm. "Are you sure you must go back? Is there any way you can leave the temple, now that you know your heritage?"

Ianna shook her head. "No High Priestess has ever left the office in any way other than death. I'm not even sure what they would do if I tried."

Hiram approached her. She flinched as he took her arm, then relaxed at his gentle touch. His eyes were warm, but a glint of caution lingered.

"There must be some way."

She flashed a nervous smile. "Perhaps there is. I'll see." She set her jaw. "I would rather die than stay there."

Ianna's words pierced Rizpah's heart. "Surely that won't be necessary."

Hiram and Rizpah saw Ianna to the door. Rizpah hugged her and Ianna flashed a grateful smile, then turned to go. When her cloaked figure disappeared down the street, they closed the door.

"What brought her here? How did she find us?" Hiram asked.

"She told me she inquired about the prophet, where he lived. It was not difficult from there."

Hiram nodded. His mind flashed back to Jamin's face on the steps of Nabu's temple when he saw the High Priestess. He could understand how the girl's beauty had captivated his nephew. He considered telling Rizpah about Jamin's feelings for Ianna but thought it best to wait. The evening was already heavy with more news than he thought they could digest. Besides, she needed to know about Jamin's arrest.

"Rizpah, there was a scene at the Council meeting today. Soldiers—"

A crash against the door stopped him.

A hoarse voice penetrated the wooden panel. "Uncle Hiram. Aunt Rizpah. It's Jamin."

Hiram threw open the door and his nephew stumbled in.

Thirty-eight

Nineveh, the Royal Palace
Sixteenth Day of Du'ûzu

Jonah rolled onto his back and stared through the gloom at the shallow, predawn gray that filtered through a narrow cleft in the wall. A lesser light fought to illuminate his weary heart.

Is this why was I sent here? To die in an Assyrian prison? He gave up his search for answers to these and myriad other questions floating just within reach of his mind.

Countless times that night his hand went to his chest, and panic gripped him each time he felt an empty space where the medallion had rested for so many years. He squeezed his eyes against the persistent image of the heathen priestess fingering his heirloom, her smugness, the glint in her eye. Regardless of his efforts to push it away, her face hovered and taunted him in the murky dusk.

Exhausted after two wakeful nights, Jonah curled onto his side. His body shook in a spasm as his skin pressed against the cool dirt floor. His light robe, woven to dispel the heat of the open desert, afforded little protection against the dankness. He shivered again. How could the ground be so cold, yet the air so tepid? Nothing made sense. Nothing in Assyria—*cursed Assyria!*—made sense. Although addled and restless, he could feel the fatigue that weighed his eyelids and pressed them down beyond his resistance. He tossed just beneath the surface of consciousness.

A scrape disturbed his restless slumber. He opened an eye and blinked into a ray of daylight that streamed through the cleft. The air was warmer, and the floor had lost some of its bite. He turned his head as the noise grew. The scrape became a rattle at the low door of his cell.

The panel ground on its hinges, and an unseen hand pushed it open.

"He's in here."

"Thank you."

The first voice was gruff—the jailor's. The second voice was soft and breathy—a woman's.

Jonah pushed himself up. He squinted into the dim light as a figure ducked through the low doorway.

"Bang on the door when you're finished. Have fun. I know he has no silver." The jailor guffawed and slammed the door shut. His footfalls receded down the corridor, and all went quiet.

An awkward stillness hung in the air. Neither the figure nor Jonah moved.

After a moment, his visitor stepped toward him. The weak light revealed a woman, her face framed in loose wisps of graying hair. She remained silent while she studied Jonah's face.

Jonah furrowed his brow and edged away from the strange woman until his back met the clay wall. *What is this?* His forehead grew warm.

She broke the silence in stilted Hebrew. "Are you . . . the man from Israel?"

Jonah didn't respond.

"My name is Hannah. I have something for you."

He pushed back against the wall. "I'm not . . . I don't want anything."

"I think you do." She took two paces forward and settled to her knees in front of him. She reached out her hand.

"Stop! I don't know what you want, but—"

A glint of metal flashed as Jonah's medallion dropped from her palm. Suspended from her fingers at the end of its leather thong, the amulet twisted in the air and splayed brilliant gold from its polished surface in the narrow ray of light.

"How did you get that? Where did—"

She extended her other arm. An identical medallion fell from it and swung on a silver chain. The golden ambiance, now doubled, permeated the small room and almost blinded Jonah's light-deprived eyes. The two discs danced together in the morning light, as though they rejoiced in their long-awaited reunion.

Jonah stared at the pendants, unable to move.

Hannah extended Jonah's medallion and eased it into his lap. She released the thong and sat on the dirt floor. She lowered the twin pendant onto her own lap and curled her legs beside her. Her gaze never left his face.

"I have the same question for you. Where did you get that medallion?"

Hannah's eyes darted over the gaunt figure against the clay wall. As her eyes accustomed themselves to the dim cell, she surveyed his face. He was pale, his eyes a shade she couldn't describe, but not dark like she would expect in a Hebrew. She sensed his discomfort, but there were answers she needed. She hoped this would not take long.

Jonah's eyes flicked to hers. "It was . . . long ago."

She nodded.

"I found it after a battle. In the Valley of Jezreel." He cocked his head. "You speak Hebrew. Do you know Israel? Have you heard of Jezreel?"

Hannah's mind conjured the image of the valley where her beloved husband, Abim, must have died. She hoped it was a beautiful place. "I have heard of it from my parents. I am a . . . Jewess." It felt odd after all these years to acknowledge her heritage. "My family was taken in an exile many years ago. We have a Hebrew community here in Nineveh." She averted her eyes. "Although I know little of it."

Jonah nodded.

"Why are you in Nineveh?" she asked suddenly.

"You don't know? I thought the whole city knew."

"I've spent little time outside my house since Ianna left. Even less since Mordac . . . since Mordecai died."

"Ianna? Mordecai?"

"My daughter and my husband." She blinked the moisture from her eyes. "I heard rumors of unrest but paid little attention."

Jonah lowered his voice. "I was sent by *Adonai* with a message to the city to repent, or face destruction."

"You are a prophet?"

Jonah's nod lacked enthusiasm.

She frowned. "I heard of an Israelite being imprisoned, but I didn't know why. I have heard of no such message."

"The authorities did not receive it well."

"Yes, that I heard." She hesitated. "My daughter, Ianna, is the High Priestess of Ishtar."

Jonah jerked his head up at the strange woman. A Jewess, the High Priestess of Ishtar? A child of the Promise served the most vile of heathen goddesses? This was unthinkable. He was too well aware of the idol's influence. Her tentacles ensnared pagan cults in different guises throughout many lands. In Sumeria she was Inanna; in Phoenicia she was known as Astarte; in Cyprus she became Aphrodite; and even in his own beloved homeland, she was the Canaanite Ashtoreth, consort of the most despicable of false gods, Ba'al. But a Jewess as her High Priestess? How could this be? The notion pulled his mind back to the scene in the temple square.

He thought of the elders who helped him deliver his message and their abuse at the hands of the gentile Assyrian mob. He lifted a silent prayer that none were seriously injured. The elders had been the only ones, it seemed, to accept the message—and not even all of them had.

Then another thought struck him. Was he sent to Assyria to minister to his own people in exile, not to the heathens? Could it be that *Adonai* might not destroy the city, lest He destroy some of His chosen ones also? Perhaps he was to deliver a message of hope, even to lead them back to Israel before the destruction. Then God could have His way with Nineveh. At last, something his heart could grasp! He was a messenger of hope to the Jews of Nineveh—just like he had been six years ago to Samaria. The attractiveness of the idea obscured the angel's words that he was to preach repentance to the whole city, not rescue a part of it.

But as quickly as his heart soared, it spiraled back to earth. He was still in prison. How was he to deliver any kind of message, to lead anyone away, while in prison? He fought to reclaim the lost hope.

"There is a story." The woman broke the silence as though she read his thoughts. She gazed plaintively into his face. "Do you want to hear?"

Jonah began to retort that he had no interest in the story of an apostate Jewess—especially one who put him in this filthy Assyrian prison—but the look that clouded Hannah's eyes choked back his words. His heart quivered, and then, curiously, settled into a gentle rhythm. When he finally found his voice, it came in little more than a whisper.

"I seem to have little else to occupy my time."

Ahu-duri studied the tablet bearing the edict of the *ugu lugal's* selection. He brushed his finger over the seal imprint and nodded his satisfaction before he handed it to the courier.

"This must be delivered to the king as quickly as possible. Tell him I will return to Kalḫu after the installation ceremony."

The courier bowed, then slipped the royal missive into a leather case and departed.

The vizier turned and ambled to his cushion. With a sigh, he stretched out and hefted his wine cup. He upended the vessel above his mouth and let the dregs run down his tongue and into his throat. Kaheri's voice startled him, and he hacked at several drops that diverted down his windpipe.

"What is it, Kaheri?" he croaked.

"A thousand apologies, my lord. There is a visitor. A woman."

"Yes, yes. See my sister in."

Kaheri cleared his throat. "It is not your sister, my lord. It's the High Priestess of Ishtar."

Ahu-duri rose to his feet as quickly as the heat rose to his face. "I'll see her in. Bring wine and fruit. Quickly."

The vizier hurried to the courtyard gate. Protocol demanded he admit her personally, a rule he was more than pleased to observe with this priestess.

Two soldiers fidgeted next to the portal. They stole glances at the petite beauty who waited outside the gate. Through the portal, the vizier saw the High Priestess adorned in all the finery of her office. He also noticed that, despite the ornate regalia, her silky robe did not detract from her figure. Quite the opposite.

"Open the gate!" he barked. "Do you not know who it is?"

The guards scrambled to their task, then stepped back against the garden wall. Their eyes widened at the regal priestess as she stepped into the garden. Two attendant priestesses in scant blue tunics followed.

"My lord."

"High Priestess." Ahu-duri bowed and hoped his face did not betray his warm forehead. "Please come in. Join me in the garden." He gestured for her to walk at his side.

Ianna nodded and took her position on his left. As they reached the turn in the path, she turned toward her escort. "Wait here. I shall not be long."

The priestesses bowed and stepped to the side of the path. They glanced back toward the two gawking soldiers and shared subdued smiles. Kaheri arrived with the wine and fruit as the vizier and his guest arrived at the cushion. He set the food and drink on the low wall, then retreated to the palace.

Ahu-duri offered Ianna his seat. She nodded demurely. Ianna eased herself into the vizier's seat, shoulders erect. Her slender fingers rested lightly on her lap, and her curled legs formed a gentle angle beneath the sleek fabric of her gown. The royal emissary fought to keep his eyes on her face. He settled onto the low wall of the garden plot.

"To what do I owe this unexpected, but quite pleasant, surprise, High Priestess?"

Ianna smiled, her voice softened with a practiced breathiness. "I wanted to call on you at least once before you returned to Kalḫu. It seemed proper, as you represent the king himself." She lowered her gaze, then flicked it back up to his.

"Yes, I . . . I am glad you thought to do that. It is always a pleasure to receive so . . . so exalted a personage such as yourself." *Personage?* Ahu-duri groaned in the back of his mind, which was quickly turning to mush.

Her coy smile broadened. "It has been an eventful trip, has it not?"

"Yes. Yes, quite eventful. Very much so. Eventful." *Stop it! What is the matter with you?* Ahu-duri cleared his throat and forced a smile.

Ianna averted her eyes to the oleander bushes that lined the garden wall. She lifted her cup of wine and cradled it between delicate fingers. The tip of her thumb massaged the lip of the vessel while she dipped her head, apparently lost in thought.

Ahu-duri stared at the cup.

The thumb stopped just before his breath did. Ianna cocked her head and dropped her voice to a whisper. "You handled the crowd in the temple plaza masterfully. Thank you."

His brain melted. A moment passed—at least, he hoped it had only been a moment. *Say something! Preferably something intelligent.*

"Of course. Yes, it was . . . tense for a moment." He recovered. "Your presence was the key, though, I'm sure, High Priestess. You drew the crowd's attention away from the foreigner." *Oh, did you* ever *draw attention. . . .*

She looked down with a slight shake of her head. "No, not at all. I merely reported the information you needed to arrest the man."

"Oh, you did much more than that, I assure you."

Ianna raised her eyes. She set the cup down and turned to face Ahu-duri. "Speaking of the prophet, I've been thinking."

"Yes?"

Her face grew thoughtful. "His message, in spite of its harshness, intrigues me. I wonder if I might be free to speak with him, to learn more about the intention of his god. Mother Ishtar should be made aware."

Ahu-duri nodded. "Certainly. I could arrange a visit for you in his cell."

She sat back. "Oh my, no. I couldn't do that. It wouldn't be at all proper for me to enter the prison." She pursed her lips and frowned, as though she tried to work through the dilemma.

The vizier reddened at his faux pas. He scrambled to repair the damage. "Of course. Stupid of me. A thousand apologies for even suggesting it. I could bring him here for an interview." He relaxed as the smile returned to her face.

"Possibly, but I hoped to question him where I would have the advantage. Perhaps at the temple?" Her expectant eyes lifted to his.

Ahu-duri frowned. His mind raced through the practical considerations of her request. He thought of the detail of soldiers required to escort the prisoner, ensure the High Priestess's safety, and then return him to the prison. Then there was the commotion the prophet's appearance in public might arouse, and the irregularity of the soldiers' presence within Ishtar's sacred shrine.

"High Priestess, I would worry for your safety. I'm not sure—"

"I'm not concerned, my lord. In fact," she paused, "I question whether the prophet presents a threat anymore."

He raised an eyebrow.

She continued. "The crowd has dispersed from the marketplace. Calm returns to the city. Perhaps his release would quell any further unrest from his supporters. He could be forbidden to preach openly again, or even be banished from Nineveh. With him imprisoned in the city, he may become a rallying point for his followers." She shrugged.

He frowned while he considered her words.

She glanced up again. "Of course, that would require a pardon. I suppose you would have to petition the king for such a thing."

Ahu-duri drew himself up. "High Priestess, I carry the king's seal. I have leave to act with his authority in all matters here in Nineveh."

Her eyes widened. "You carry the king's seal? Oh my, I had no idea you were so . . . empowered." Her cheeks flushed.

Ahu-duri straightened his back. "The king and I are very close."

Her gaze flickered to his, which sent a new wave of heat to his forehead. Her voice grew husky. "You have the power to pardon? You could really do that?"

Renewed confidence reverberated through his voice. "I can." He lifted his head. "And I will. It will be done today. I'll have him escorted to the temple this afternoon. My soldiers will remain outside while you interrogate the prophet. Their presence will deter the threat of any crowd that might gather, and they can take charge of him again when you have finished and escort him from the city."

Ianna beamed at him.

The vizier dared a prolonged look into the High Priestess's exquisite almond eyes. He sensed the draw his powerful position held for her. He also noticed how quickly she averted her eyes, clearly to avoid betraying too much admiration—perhaps, attraction? He smirked inwardly. Yes, attraction. It was all over her face.

Ianna bowed respectfully to Ahu-duri, then exited the garden. She assumed an imperious stride up the road, well aware that his gaze lingered on her from behind. Fortunately, her *naditu* escort remained dutifully behind her. They would not notice the subtle smile spread over her face, or the mirthful tears fill her eyes as she recalled the final look on the smitten vizier's face. It was all she could do to subdue her laughter. The twinge of guilt she felt at such blatant feminine manipulation suffocated under the elation of its success.

Jonah would be free by nightfall.

Thirty-nine

Nineveh, the Royal Palace
Sixteenth Day of Du'ûzu, the Tenth Hour

Jonah mulled over the tale Hannah told him that morning. She had spent half the day in his cell, as nearly as he could reckon it. They shared stories of their families, of their years growing up. She told of how difficult it was to live a denied heritage, to try to meld into a heathen society and never quite succeed. He described the verdant hills of northern Israel, the Land of Promise, of his family's tannery near Gath-hepher. He related the events of his journey to King Jeroboam's court six years earlier and explained that the cleft in the face of his medallion came from the tip of a guard's spear. Her face shone, and she appeared rapt with his descriptions of his homeland, his life, and especially his call as a prophet. She interjected questions several times, very good questions, he thought. Jonah was pleased, even enthusiastic, to answer them. Her smile came more easily as the morning wore on. He realized with some surprise that his did, too. He became oddly comfortable with this stranger—a woman, no less. The oddness didn't strike him, though, until she left.

When Hannah departed, it was with reluctance, he sensed. She left his medallion with him and promised to return with something to eat. Jonah slipped the leather thong back over his head and tucked the precious amulet under his robe. The rest of the day was lost in thought over this woman and her story. But he soon found his thoughts dwelling more on the woman than her story, and that perplexed him.

Jonah's reverie broke as his cell door ground again on its pins. He pushed back against the wall.

"Come out. You're leaving." The guard's raspy voice grated

through the opening.

Leaving?

"Come on! You've got your own escort, you do. Out!"

Jonah pushed to his feet. He shuffled to the door and peered through. *Escort?*

A hand reached through the doorway and grabbed the front of his robe. It yanked him through and shoved him down a short corridor. End the end of the passageway, Jonah stepped into the bright daylight and shielded his eyes. He arched his back, the first time he had been able to stand erect since he was thrown into his cell. When his eyes became accustomed to the brightness, he discovered himself in a large walled courtyard with an enormous structure on his right. Scaffolding gave evidence of a building under construction.

He looked over his shoulder and shied back at the sight of three armed soldiers by the wall. One of them beckoned to him with a finger.

"Follow us." The warrior pivoted and strode toward a gate in the courtyard wall. The other two soldiers moved behind Jonah and nudged him on the back to follow.

He stumbled forward on stiff legs. They passed through the gate onto a narrow road and turned right. As they marched up the street, his surroundings became more familiar. He peered over the shoulder of the lead guard and saw the road open into a broad plaza between two large buildings.

Temples. They were taking him back to the temple square!

"Where are we going? Where are you taking me?"

They ignored him until the group came abreast of the larger temple on the right. The soldier turned around. He jerked a thumb toward the portico.

"This is it."

Jonah stared at the Temple of Ishtar.

The soldier grinned. "You have a fancy audience waiting for you. I hope you bathed."

The other two guards chortled and pushed him toward steps that led up to the columned veranda. Jonah tripped onto the second step and looked back. The three soldiers stood abreast, their arms folded. The leader narrowed his eyes and jutted his chin toward the porch.

Jonah turned to see a stocky woman in a blue tunic by the nearest column. She motioned to him to follow her, then turned and disappeared into the shadows. He swallowed, threw one more nervous look at the guard detail, then trudged up the steps.

He passed into the shade of the porch and saw the priestess poised by a massive doorway. She nodded again, then slipped into the building.

Jonah stepped through the doorway and squinted into the dim interior. The woman beckoned and turned down a long corridor. They rounded a corner to the right and she halted next to a large door. She rapped lightly, and Jonah heard a muffled reply from within. The priestess eased the door open, stood aside, and motioned him to enter.

Jonah edged into the large chamber and stopped short at the sight of a large statue of Ishtar. He flinched when the door latch clicked behind him. The click echoed to silence and a heaviness of more than stuffy air pressed down on him. He started to turn back toward the door when a movement caught his eye.

From beside the pagan statue, the High Priestess of Ishtar, the woman whose words condemned him in the temple plaza, stepped forward. She wore a plain silken robe, the ceremonial cap and staff absent.

Jonah's throat went dry when the priestess took a step toward him. "What is this? What do you want?" His eyes darted around the room.

"Please. Don't be alarmed."

He drew up at the words. He knew that voice, and it didn't belong to the High Priestess.

Hannah?

Hannah appeared beside the statue from where the High Priestess had emerged. She placed her arm around the young girl's shoulders, and it came back to him that the High Priestess was her daughter.

Jonah swallowed, at odds between Hannah's warm familiarity and the cold sterility of the temple. "I don't understand."

Hannah and her daughter exchanged glances.

"My daughter—Ianna—had you released from prison."

"But how? Why?"

Hannah whispered something into her daughter's ear, then nodded at the reply. "The how is not important." She smiled and squeezed her daughter's shoulders. "The why is very important. Ianna has learned of her Jewish heritage. There's much to explain. Perhaps later. For now, we must get you out of the city."

"Out of the city?"

"Yes. For your safety."

"But what of my commission to preach? The reason I was sent to Nineveh?"

Hannah shook her head. "I don't know. I only know you're in danger of being taken again by the soldiers or mobbed by the people if you remain. You've delivered the message. It's time for you to go."

Jonah frowned. "But it's all turned into such a mess. In fact, my whole trip has been disastrous since I left Israel. Why would—"

"Jonah, I don't have the answers to your questions. *Adonai* knows and we must trust Him. I only know we must leave. We'll go after dark."

"Go where?"

Hannah whispered to her daughter. Ianna nodded.

"My daughter and I agree. The gates will close at dark, so there's no chance for you to leave the city tonight. But it would also be dangerous for you return to the house where you were staying."

"With Jamin?"

Hannah creased her brow. "Jamin?"

Jonah nodded. "Jamin ben Obadiah. It is the name of the young man who helped me. He lives in the artisan quarter with his Uncle Hiram and Aunt Rizpah. His uncle was the old man the soldier attacked on the steps of the temple."

Hannah spoke again to Ianna. Jonah saw a change come over the face of the High Priestess as her mother spoke the name "Jamin." Her eyes seemed to brighten, then she looked down at the floor, as though deep in thought. Hannah had already turned back to Jonah and her daughter's reaction apparently escaped her notice.

"The only safe place for you is . . . my house." Her cheeks

reddened, and her eyes faltered for a moment. "For now, that is. We can find you a change of clothing among my late husband's things. Then we can decide the best way to get you away from Nineveh."

When Ianna lifted her eyes again, Jonah said to her, "I . . . I should thank you. Although I still don't understand."

Ianna's gaze flicked to her mother, who whispered a few words to her.

Hannah looked back to Jonah with an apologetic smile. "I'm sorry. Ianna does not speak Hebrew. We—" her eyes misted and she glanced back at her daughter—"neglected the language of her people, as we did so many other things during her childhood. Perhaps we can correct that after today."

Jonah nodded at the young girl. She returned the gesture.

Twilight crept into the chamber while Hannah related what she knew of Ianna's visit with the royal official. She and Jonah sat on tufted cushions next to the wall, their heads close in the quiet of the room. They passed the hours until darkness with more stories that filled the gaps from their earlier conversation in the prison cell. Jonah again found himself strangely at ease with this woman. The convergence of their pasts, evidenced by the twin gold medallions, lowered barriers that would otherwise have set his nerves on edge—which was their normal state anytime he was around a woman outside his family. He studied her face and felt she should look familiar to him, that he should somehow already have known her.

Hannah's tone was soft and her language informal, yet not presumptive. It was as though she sensed a kinship with him, as well. The social impropriety of their closeness in such an intimate setting would have weighed on him at any other time. This evening it never crossed his mind. They huddled in the waning light, drawn together by spiritual weightiness of the pagan temple and the physical danger to Jonah.

Jonah began to wonder if there might be more that drew him to her. The feelings she aroused were unfamiliar, but not unpleasant. The closeness of her face pricked a sensual notion in him, but, unlike other times in his life, he didn't fight it.

Ianna had left earlier to attend to rituals. It was important that the evening activities proceed as usual, that nothing seem out of the ordinary. When the time was right, she would send for them. What would happen from that point, he had no idea.

A click at the door startled them. The priestess who had escorted Jonah to this room appeared in the doorway, a torch in one hand and two bundles cradled in the other.

Relief flooded Hannah's voice. "Hulalitu. You startled us."

The *naditu* smiled her apologies. "I have clothes for you to change into and a pouch of food for the prophet. There are *ishtaritu* rites tonight. You will have to dress the part not to be noticed."

Hulalitu slid the torch into an iron holder affixed to the wall, then pulled a hooded cloak from a bundle and handed it to Jonah. From the same bundle she produced a light blue tunic.

"I can't wear that. It symbolizes everything I hate. I won't—"

The *naditu's* raspy voice cut her off. "You must. There is no choice. It's the only way to pass without notice." Her eyes softened. "I know it is distasteful to you. But perhaps what the goddess uses for evil, your God will use for good."

Hannah cocked her head at the pagan priestess's words, much like those of the patriarch Joseph's message to his brothers in Egypt so many years earlier. It struck her how easily such profound truth passed the lips of the uninitiated—perhaps unintentionally, but then, perhaps not. She stared at the garment draped over Hulalitu's outstretched hand. Then she nodded and accepted the tunic.

The priestess stepped between Hannah and Jonah, who had pulled the cloak on over his soiled desert robe. She faced him and put her hands on her hips, an eyebrow raised. Jonah looked at her in puzzlement. Hannah's face, tinged pink, peered over Hulalitu's shoulder with an awkward smile.

"Oh! Yes. I'm . . . excuse me." Red-faced, he turned toward the wall while Hannah disrobed. After a moment, Hulalitu tapped Jonah's shoulder that it was proper for him to turn around.

He turned just as Hannah gathered her hair from the neck of the tunic.

The sheltered prophet's breath caught short at the transformation in his new companion. Hannah paused in the flickering torchlight, and a self-conscious look overtook her face. She averted her eyes from Jonah's. The tunic's flimsy material clung to a mature, well-proportioned figure, and did nothing to disguise its wearer's curves. Shoulder-length, silver-streaked hair flowed with a graceful softness onto her shoulders, themselves partially bared by the loose neckline of the enticing *naditu* garb. Jonah swallowed. He began to wonder who this woman was and where Hannah might have gone. The shapeless garment she had worn up to this point would not have sparked even the most visceral of instincts in the worst of men. But now . . .

Oh, my.

A guttural cough broke his stare, and he drew back, his face scarlet under Hulalitu's glare. Hannah cleared her throat, her face its own shade of red, but her lips unable to resist a slight smile.

Hulalitu retrieved her torch and motioned for Jonah to pick up the pouch and garment bundle. "It's time. Follow me. You can't be seen coming from this chamber. The way is dark and narrow, so stay close to me."

Jonah raised an eyebrow at Hannah, who translated the *naditu's* instructions.

The priestess led them around the dais. She slipped the torch into a holder on the back wall and ducked behind the platform. Halfway along the wall, she dropped to her knees and pressed her fingers against the wall. An opening appeared, and she disappeared through it.

Her followers shared a quick look, then followed Hulalitu's example. Hannah went first and Jonah followed, consciously keeping his gaze elevated. Once through the portal, he pushed to his feet and found himself in a dark tunnel. He turned to the left toward the scuffle of feet and struggled with his bundle as they sidled along the narrow passageway. After several paces, Hulalitu stopped. They heard a scrape, and a dim light glimmered through another low portal in the wall. The priestess's sturdy figure filled the space and then disappeared.

Hannah and Jonah emerged from the passageway and stepped around a heavy tapestry into a small chamber. The room was empty but for a bed mat and a small cup filled with what appeared to be wine. Hulalitu had already crossed the floor and was by the door. Jonah adjusted his load and followed.

The *naditu* turned toward them. "Listen carefully. I will go ahead of you. Stay close enough so you can see me, but not so close that others will suspect we're together. Jonah should put his hood over his head."

Hannah turned and relayed her words in Hebrew. Jonah complied.

Hulalitu added, "Now, take his hand in yours."

The false *naditu's* cheeks flushed. She hesitated.

The priestess frowned. "Quickly. And don't blush. That *never* happens here."

Hannah nodded and turned to meet Jonah's puzzled look. She smiled, then held out her hand. He looked at it for a moment, then extended his arm. The soft warmth of Hannah's hand drew cold sweat to his. His own blush was hidden beneath the hood.

Hulalitu nodded her satisfaction. "Now, act natural."

Hannah raised an eyebrow.

The priestess tried to suppress a smile. "Well, as much as you can."

With that, Hulalitu stepped out and strode with purpose down the corridor.

Hannah and Jonah followed Hulalitu at a safe distance. They picked up their pace when she disappeared around a corner at the end of the hall. When they reached the corner, they nearly collided with a young girl in a white tunic leading an older man down the passageway. Hannah stepped aside and drew Jonah out of the way. She hesitated, feeling a fresh wave of heat rise to her forehead as the girl guided the man into the first doorway to the left and slid a cloth across the opening. *Was this what it was like for Ianna? My Ianna?*

A nudge from Jonah broke her thoughts, and she looked down the corridor. Hulalitu was no longer in sight. She stepped off at a quickened gait, her hand still clasped in Jonah's. At the end of the hallway, they found a large antechamber where women in tunics of various colors milled about. Hannah stopped. Her gaze darted around the room in search of Hulalitu's thickset figure. A wave of fear surged up her spine. Her throat constricted at the thought of becoming lost in the temple. She calmed when she spotted the *naditu* by a large door on the left wall. The priestess conversed with two other women. She ignored the couple paused at the entrance of the corridor.

Hannah knew they would attract attention if they stood there for too long. She decided the large door must lead outside, so she tugged on Jonah's hand and stepped off with assumed confidence.

"Stop!"

Hannah froze. Jonah bumped into her from behind.

A tall woman dressed in a blue tunic with gold trim bore down on them from across the room, her eyes narrowed at the counterfeit priestess. She blocked their path. "What are you doing?"

Forty

Nineveh, the Artisan's Quarter
Seventeenth Day of Du'ûzu, the Second Hour

"There has to be something we can do." Rizpah dabbed at her red eyes.

Hiram shook his head. "We've been through this. There's nothing."

Jamin slumped in the corner of the room. He hadn't left the house since returning home the evening before. His mind still reeled from the impossibility of the royal pronouncement. Hours ago he stopped asking himself why, of all the people in Assyria, they chose him. How did they even know he existed, and what had he done to deserve this? The questions were as moot as they were unanswerable. It was evident that they knew who he was, that they did choose him, and that he must have done something.

The thought weighing most heavily on him was that of his parents in Aššûr. Would they find out? Could he send word? If he tried to leave the city, he would endanger not only himself, but also his aunt and uncle. The royal official had been clear on that point.

He leaned his head back and sighed. The installation ceremony was in two days. He had no idea how to prepare for it; indeed, there was nothing he could do to prepare. All he could do was wait. Just wait.

"I asked you what you're doing." The senior *naditu* glowered at Hannah.

Hannah stammered, but nothing came out.

"I sent her, Shalla." Hulalitu's husky voice arced over the priestess's shoulder.

Shalla spun around. "You? What have you to do with this, Hulalitu?"

The *naditu* met Shalla's glare. "I heard of a disturbance in the Hall of the Ishtaritu. I sent Hann—Hani to investigate. This man—" she gestured toward Jonah—"became violent. He needed to be removed."

Shalla glanced at the stooped figure behind the flustered priestess. "Him?" She turned on Hulalitu. "He became violent?"

Hulalitu didn't flinch. "Yes. Hani was able to calm him. It's not the first time this . . . intruder has entered the Hall of the Ishtaritu." She dropped her voice. "He has a problem in the head."

Shalla raised her eyebrow. "It doesn't matter." She pointed at Hani. "You know the *naditu* do not interfere with the *ishtaritu* ritual. Mother Ishtar will protect her devotees."

"In this case—"

"And who is this 'Hani'?" Shalla scrutinized Hannah. "I have never heard such a name among the *naditu.*"

A sharp voice jerked Shalla's head around.

"She is here at my behest." Ianna stepped to Hulalitu's side. She blazed her fiercest look at the senior *naditu*.

Hulalitu and Shalla stepped back and bowed their heads in the presence of the High Priestess. Hannah took their example and did likewise.

Shalla's face stayed down well short of the amount of time custom prescribed. She jerked her head back up, the fire in her eyes now directed at Ianna, her perfunctory courtesy coated with a heavy frost. "Greetings, High Priestess. How good of you to grace us with—"

"Thank you, Shalla." Ianna's icy voice matched the senior *naditu's*. "What seems to be the problem?"

"High Priestess, I'm sure you are aware of the rules that govern the *ishtaritu* rite." She barely covered her sneer with a lowered head. "Despite the unusual circumstances that surrounded your own."

Ianna ignored the jab. "Of course, Shalla, and I am most grateful at your diligence to remind us of the most obvious of temple protocol." She took the moment Shalla's head was bowed to signal Hulalitu with a jerk of her head. She glanced at Hannah, then at the door.

Hulalitu sidestepped to her right and tried to make eye contact with Ianna's mother.

Shalla lifted her eyes. "Thank you, High Priestess, for understanding how important it is for *someone* to maintain discipline in the temple."

Hannah caught Hulalitu's eye. The priestess glanced at the door and tipped her head. Hannah's eyes widened. She squeezed Jonah's hand to alert him.

Ianna shifted to her left. The senior *naditu* adjusted her stance to face the *Entu*, which put her back to the temple entrance. Hulalitu jerked her head, and Hannah pulled Jonah toward the door.

Ianna's sarcasm sliced the air. "And, of course, *you* are just the person to do that."

No one in the quieted crowd of priestesses noticed Hannah and Jonah slip out. All eyes were glued on the confrontation between the senior *naditu* and the High Priestess. Hannah chanced a glance over her shoulder when they reached the outer portico and caught a smile on Hulalitu's face just before the door closed. She wondered how she would ever be able to repay the priestess for all she had done, and for the peril she now faced for it.

The faux priestess gripped Jonah's hand while she scanned the porch for her bearings. She had always avoided the temple square, which now left her uncertain how best to escape it. A squeeze from Jonah's fingers pulled her attention. He tipped his head to the right. She took his cue and moved along the porch. They passed another *ishtaritu*, leading her partner toward the door. Hannah and Jonah descended the steps and rounded the northern corner of the building.

Jonah's muffled whisper came from under his hood. "I think we cut straight across the square. That should put us in the upper residential quarter."

She nodded and set off across the plaza, past the fountain and into the shadows of another building. Jonah pulled back on her hand and she stopped. He slipped his hand from hers and in the darkness she heard him rummage through his bundle. She felt him press a bundle of cloth against her arm, and recognized the coarse material as that of her own robe. Only then she realized she was still clad in only the tunic, which would be sure to draw attention beyond the temple square.

Hannah smiled to herself as she drew her robe over her head. Her cheeks reddened at the realization that she had enjoyed the sensual freedom the sheer tunic lent her. The weight of her old garment almost stifled her now.

"I thought it best. You know . . ." Jonah's tentative voice was clearer. She realized he must have pulled back his hood.

Hannah's smile broadened at the awkwardness in his tone. Her forehead prickled with an unexpected giddiness as she flashed back to his expression when he first saw her body give the delicate material its shape. Hannah couldn't remember the last time Mordecai had appreciated her with his eyes. She felt herself swept up in an urge that surprised her, but that she felt no desire to resist.

There, in the darkness, she found Jonah's hand and took a step closer to him. She leaned forward and brushed his cheek with her lips.

"Thank you."

The kiss paralyzed Jonah. He didn't flinch, which shocked him. He felt no shame, no condemnation at what he would normally have considered a brazen gesture. That also shocked him.

Hannah's soft breath against his face and gentle whisper in his ear flushed his head not with the heat of indignation, as he would've expected, or even embarrassment. This was an entirely new feeling, a sensation different than any he had experienced before. It also aroused a response he'd never felt before, but one that he was powerless to restrain.

Jonah released her hand. After a moment's hesitation, he reached out to her. When his fingers brushed her cheek, they lingered for a moment. He gently traced her jaw to her chin with his fingertips.

He didn't recognize his own throaty voice. "You're welcome."

Hannah drew back after the kiss. It felt so natural to her, but there was no response from Jonah. When he released her hand, she stiffened, suddenly embarrassed she had overstepped. What was she thinking? Maybe he was married. She had never acted so brashly toward a man. What kind of woman would he think she—

The tender stroke of his fingertips across her cheek startled her. As his unseen hand traced her cheek line, tears sprang to her eyes. She tried to remember when she had felt so gentle a touch from a man.

His husky words stopped her breath. As his hand paused at her chin, she brought her own up and cupped his fingers against her face.

Time stood as still, as did they. Neither knew how long they lingered in each other's arms; neither cared. The embrace was completely new to Jonah, vaguely reminiscent to Hannah. The raw peril of what they'd just been through faded for them both. Across the plaza, the flurry of activity at Ishtar's temple ebbed as the crowd of men dissipated. Soon the night was quiet.

"We should be going."

"Yes."

They remained.

Forty-one

Nineveh, the Privileged Quarter
Seventeenth Day of Du'ûzu, the Third Hour

Hannah veered onto a narrow side street. When they crossed into the residential quarter from the temple square, she led with renewed confidence. The road took them past a loop of the Tabiltu River, where she turned along a footpath that skirted the water's edge. The ambient torchlight from the temple plaza dimmed and left only a silvery half-moon to light their way. This path was familiar to her, though, and the subdued light presented no problem. Many an afternoon over the past few years found her along this embankment, where she fretted over the gap in her marriage and the uncertain future of her daughter. Now she fretted over the uncertain future of—her new love?

She shook her head. How could feelings like these blossom so quickly between two people? Perhaps their maturity granted a perspective that cut through the foggy infatuation into which youth so often stumbled. Or maybe their advanced age simply reminded them that they had less time to dither.

She smiled to herself. Who cared? The point was, two mature adults had discovered love and were ready for what it had to offer. Her mind floated on air, hopeful for the first time in years.

I feel so light. So peaceful, but excited.

She was certain from their embrace that Jonah felt the same way.

I'm a mess.

Jonah stumbled along and kept a lame grasp on Hannah's hand

while his brain pinged in all directions. He was convinced no man in history was less equipped for the emotional state he found himself in. Restless energy he didn't know he possessed surged through his body, but his mind had no idea what to do with it. Was this love? He supposed it to be, but he wasn't sure. He always thought love to be a serious endeavor, something two people set their minds on and worked hard to nurture. So then, what was this silly grin on his face?

His mind reeled from his first embrace with a woman not his relative, the first approach of romance that didn't collapse his senses. He still didn't understand it, but to understand became less important the longer her hand remained in his. All he could think of was that kiss. Then that hug. His cheeks burned at the memory, but in desire rather than embarrassment.

A curious sound wiggled between his lips. He frowned. Was that a giggle? Of course not. He didn't giggle. Never had. Must've been a chuckle. *Why am I chuckling?*

Her voice penetrated his thoughts. "Did you say something?"

"Hmm?"

Hannah slowed and turned her head. "I thought I heard you say something."

"Did I?"

She stopped. "Jonah, what's wrong?"

"Wrong?"

She leaned forward and squinted at his face through the pale moonlight. "Why are you smiling?"

Come closer; I'll show you. Was that another chuckle?

"You're . . . you're giggling!" She stared at him.

"Chuckling. There's a difference."

"Jonah—"

His lips covered hers. He couldn't help it.

Oh, was there ever anything so glorious? *Why did I wait so long?*

Hannah stiffened, and a muffled cry puffed her cheeks. He gripped her shoulders, not too tight. She pulled back, not too hard. Slowly, he felt her relax. She settled into his arms, and her breath matched his. The world slowed as his lips grudgingly released hers.

A twinge of panic pricked his forehead. *Now what?*

Her voice was small. "Jonah?"

A rush of heat enveloped his brain as it occurred to him what he'd done. "I'm . . . I'm sorry. It's just . . ." A forced swallow interrupted his words.

Her face shone softly in the moonlight. He had never seen anything so beautiful in his life. It took a moment for him to realize she was smiling, too. "Hannah?"

"Yes?"

"I love you."

The words startled him. These were words he had reserved his entire life only for family. Odd, though, that now they tripped so easily from his lips—and how good they felt. He prayed they felt good to her, too. He dropped his gaze when a sudden fear of her response gripped him.

Her voice came barely above a whisper. "I love you, too."

His head jerked up. "You do?"

"Yes."

"Why?"

"What?"

"Why? Why do you love me?"

"Jonah, what do you mean—"

"No, really. Why would you love someone like me?"

"Jonah, we don't have time for this."

"We'll make time. You don't understand. This has never happened to me. I have to know—"

Hannah's touch on his cheek cut off his words, his breath, and, for a moment, his heartbeat.

"Later. We must get to the house. It's not safe in the open."

He sucked in a deep breath. "Yes. All right. But we have to talk."

She nodded. "Later."

Her hand grasped his, and she turned back along the path.

Hannah stopped at the convergence of a side road and the main street that cut through the center of the district. She guided Jonah into the shadows. "Wait here."

After a few moments—an eternity to Jonah—Hannah returned and took him again by the hand. They rounded the corner and hurried down the street. She stopped at the third house on the left, lifted the door latch, and they slipped inside.

Jonah was breathless. His head still swam with anxiety, physical exertion, and love. Hannah released his hand, and he struggled in the darkness to calm his breath. He heard the shuffle of her sandals, then the sound of something scrape along the floor. He jolted when he felt her hand again slip into his.

"Stay close to me. I don't want to light any lamps. It's late, and the light may attract attention. I'll take you to Ianna's niche. You can sleep there tonight."

Jonah nodded, still submerged in his thoughts.

"Do you hear me?"

He nodded again.

Her voice finally cut through his daze. "Jonah, it's dark. I can't see you. Say something."

In spite of the late hour and the strain of the evening's events—or perhaps because of them—Hannah's succinct revelation of the obvious snorted a laugh through Jonah's nose. The snort released an involuntary flood of laughter. He plastered his hand against his mouth. The hysteria lasted only a moment, but it left him with watered eyes.

"You're tired, aren't you?" She giggled.

He nodded again, then squelched another snort.

"I love you," she murmured.

Forty-two

Nineveh, the Temple of Ishtar
Seventeenth Day of Du'ûzu, the Eighth Hour

"You can't go in there!" Thura's shrill voice penetrated the door of the High Priestess's chambers.

"Move!" A smack punctuated the command, followed by a shriek.

The door flew open, and Shalla glowered on the threshold. Thura sat on the floor behind her with a hand pressed to her reddened cheek. The senior *naditu* strode through and slammed the door behind her.

"Do please come in, Shalla." Ianna raised an eyebrow.

"Thank you, my High Priestess." The sarcasm dripped from the priestess's lips like rancid olive oil. The senior *naditu* stalked to the foot of the dais and stopped two paces in front of Ianna. She leaned her long torso forward in an obvious attempt to intimidate her diminutive rival.

Ianna tapped the palm of her hand with the scepter, her face impassive. "To what do I owe the pleasure of this . . . unannounced . . . audience, *naditu?*" Ianna stressed the last word and stifled a smile at the bulge it brought to the veins on Shalla's neck.

"You have violated the sacred rites of the Mother Goddess for the last time." Shalla's chest heaved.

"Oh, my." Ianna pursed her lips. "Violated is such a harsh word. Well, Shalla, since we appear to have abandoned any sense of protocol—and decorum—please, feel free to speak your mind."

Shalla's body shook. She sputtered, "Since you became *High Priestess,* you have dishonored the holy office like none other before you."

"Dishonored." Ianna nodded. "I see. Please go on."

"You have foregone attendance at rituals, disregarded all advisement—"

"Only yours, Shalla," Ianna corrected.

"—and failed to enforce temple etiquette. Discipline is nonexistent among the lesser priestesses."

"Lesser meaning anyone but yourself."

Shalla appeared on the verge of a seizure. Ianna wondered how red a person's face could actually become.

"And last night was the final humiliation. You deliberately and publicly desecrated the sacred *ishtaritu* ritual and permitted—no, aided—the escape of those who committed the travesty with you."

"Oh, dear. I am a mess, aren't I?" Ianna clicked her tongue and shook her head.

Shalla exploded, "This cannot go on!"

Ianna glanced back up. "Whatever shall we do?"

Shalla gritted her teeth. "I don't know how you positioned yourself to become High Priestess. I don't know what you did or said to Issar-surrat that coerced her to petition the king on your behalf, but I intend to find out."

Ianna suddenly grew tired of the game, the intrigue, the charade of empty religiosity. The walls of the room closed in and squeezed the air until she thought she might suffocate. Her robes and cap pressed down until she feared she would collapse under their weight. She suddenly extended the scepter toward Shalla. "Here, hold this for a moment, would you?"

The senior *naditu* froze. She eyed the symbol of ultimate power, torn between her consuming desire to possess it and the knowledge that no one but the High Priestess was permitted to hold the relic. Her voice wavered. "You know I cannot do that."

"No, really. Here."

Ianna grasped Shalla's hand and thrust the sacred staff into it. She pivoted and strode a few paces to the side. When she turned back toward the *naditu*, she would have laughed, had the sight not been so pathetic.

Shalla stood as rigid as Ishtar's statue poised a short distance away.

She stared at the rod as though it might consume her hand, or that the Mother Goddess might strike her dead on the spot.

Ianna surveyed the paralyzed *naditu*. A sheen of perspiration glistened on her forehead, and her hand quivered. An odd feeling of pity arose within Ianna, and she shook her head. So much delusion, so much self-induced terror at a deity chipped from stone. In Shalla, she witnessed how delusion could lend power to the inert and ascribe fearsomeness to impotence. The creators became the creation's slaves, so fervently did they crave the innate need to recognize and serve a power beyond themselves. They were lost. Shalla was lost. A captive of her own misplaced devotion.

Shalla had nothing to fear from the goddess's divine wrath. Mother Ishtar would do nothing.

Ianna's voice was hushed, its former sarcasm blunted to irony. "Oh, dear, I appear to have broken another rule."

Shalla's wide eyes swung toward Ianna's.

The High Priestess stepped back to the senior *naditu* and gently lifted the staff from her stiff fingers. She gazed into the priestess's ashen face and whispered, "Go now, Shalla. It won't be long."

Forty-three

Nineveh, the Artisan's Quarter
Eighteenth Day of Du'ûzu, the Ninth Hour

Hiram couldn't believe his ears.

"I tell you, the people are fearful. Word of the prophet's disappearance has spread throughout the city." Yitsak, an elder of the Council and one of Hiram's closest friends, waved his arms in the air. "Those who refused to believe the prophet's words believe the words of the soldiers who delivered him to the Temple of Ishtar. They waited, but he never came out."

"Do they think Ishtar had something to do with this?"

"At first, yes. But the High Priestess has assured her council that the goddess had done nothing. She reported that one moment she was with the prophet in the great hall, and the next moment he was gone. The priestess who took Jonah to the shrine room testified the same." Yitsak lifted his shoulders. "He was gone. Just gone!"

"Like Elijah?" Hiram wondered.

The elder shrugged. "Well, nothing so spectacular as a chariot with fire, but he's just as gone."

Hiram shook his head.

Yitsak continued. "It's been two days, and there's been no sign of him. Our people watch for the angel of death to descend on the city. They believe *Adonai* has spirited His prophet away to escape the destruction. Many have donned sackcloth and sprinkled ashes on their heads. They fast and pray that God will yet have mercy on Nineveh."

"What of the Gentiles?"

Yitsak shook his head. "That's the amazing part. They approach the elders everywhere and ask what to do, how they should respond."

Hiram was startled. "What do the elders tell them?"

"To do as the Jews do. They are to show their repentance before this all-powerful God, even if they don't understand why, if they want to avoid His fury. Many have followed our people's example of sackcloth and ashes, and sought their hearts for what has angered God."

Hiram allowed himself a tentative smile. "Then . . . then it could happen."

"Hiram?"

He grasped his friend's shoulders. "Don't you see, Yitsak? *Adonai* has sent out His word, and now it bears fruit. Repentance. That is what Jonah preached. That was the message God gave him. Only none of us really believed the city would listen."

Yitsak nodded. "You're right. Our faith in His mercy has been as weak as the Gentiles' desire to know Him." His voice tightened. "Do you really think this could happen? Could the whole city repent?"

Hiram's smile broadened. "What did you just say about our faith, Yitsak? Of course the whole city can repent, if *Adonai* is in it. And I begin to believe He is in it, and that it will repent."

"What do we do?"

"More of what we're doing now. Spread the word through the Jewish community to follow their brethren's example, to fast and pray. Have them tell whoever will listen to do the same. We will all don sackcloth and ashes. We've forgotten that God has commanded the whole city to repent, and that includes us." Hiram lips thinned, and his voice lowered. "We thought ourselves immune from repentance because we're children of Abraham. But we're not exempt—in fact, the opposite is true. The Law to us has been entrusted not to horde, but to share. We're to set the example, to spread the news. We are to teach the nations of the Law and the Giver of the Law—starting here with Nineveh."

Yitsak's voice lowered. "The prophet gave the city forty days."

Hiram nodded. "I've been counting. That only gives us fifteen more days from when he arrived and met with the Council. We must hurry, my friend. There's not much time."

𝆕 𝆕 𝆕

Ahu-duri lounged and fanned himself with a clipped palm frond. Just before sundown, he would officiate the *ugu lugal* ceremony. His soldiers kept a quiet eye on the artisan's quarter to ensure Jamin ben Obadiah did not attempt to leave. Invitations to attend the ceremony went out to the noble class. The ritual would take place in the garden courtyard, not far from where he sat. Then the substitute king would take up residence in the partially completed palace. From there he and his queen would assume reign over the kingdom for one hundred days.

The queen.

She had been a niggling detail for him from the start. It was unfortunate the young Jew was not married. It was not necessary, though, that his queen be his common wife. But they did need a queen to take Sammuramat's place, and he was nowhere close to finding one.

Ahu-duri's thoughts then turned to where they had lingered for the past couple of days. His encounter with the High Priestess would not leave him alone. He cursed his high position that disallowed him to partake of the *istaritu* ritual while in Nineveh. But the *Entu* was a different matter. Her exalted position not only put her on a social plane equal to his, but confidentiality and privacy of a meeting could also be assured. The question was how to go about it.

He had no doubt she was enamored with him, despite their age difference. That much she made clear at their last meeting. All he needed now was the opportunity. It would be awkward for him simply to appear at the temple. He contemplated a disguise of some kind, but he was too well known. Only with her complicity could he hope to arrange a tryst—dedicated to the Mother Goddess, of course. He had planned to leave Nineveh following the installation ceremony, most likely early the next morning. His departure could be delayed, though, and he was under no obligation to explain why. There remained only one chance to speak to her without going to the temple.

He had ensured there was a special place of honor reserved for her at his side during the ceremony. It was only appropriate, of course. He was the senior royal official, and she was Nineveh's preeminent spiritual figure. Iqisha would just have to understand why he would be relegated to third position. The commotion that was sure to follow the ritual would provide the best opportunity to inform her of his availability—and his desire. She would know what to do from there.

Jamin hugged his aunt and uncle. He had done his best to encourage them, but the effort fell flat. He was adamant that he go to the palace unaccompanied. It would be difficult enough to enter the palace gate without tearing himself away from loved ones, too. Hiram protested that they were family, and they couldn't just watch him walk away alone, but Jamin wouldn't hear of it.

Aunt Rizpah's eyes had not dried all morning, her normal prattle silenced since breakfast. Fury and helplessness locked Uncle Hiram's jaw. He felt responsible for his nephew's presence in Nineveh, and now it had led to this. All they could do was promise to get word to his parents in Aššûr, although neither of them knew what to say, or how to say it.

"I must go. Perhaps *Adonai* will yet intervene." Jamin attempted a smile, but it died on his lips.

Aunt Rizpah turned away amid a fresh wave of sniffles.

Uncle Hiram grabbed his wrist. "We will pray."

Jamin stepped out the door. The latch clicked, and he was gone.

Ianna, clad in the most glorious raiment the High Priestess of Ishtar's wardrobe had to offer, sat on an embroidered cushion while Hulalitu ran an ivory comb through her hair. The regal necklace of her office hung around her neck. The ceremonial cap and staff laid on the mat by her side. Everything was ready, except the High Priestess herself.

Her gaze was distant, her thoughts far away. Since she received the vizier's invitation to the ceremony, her mind searched frantically for a way to decline, but there was none. News of the substitute king's selection had become lost amid the drama of her mother's and Hulalitu's revelations, then Jonah's release from prison and escape from the temple. She had nearly forgotten the reason for the royal entourage's presence in the city until word arrived this afternoon that her attendance was expected. Although she knew of the *ugu lugal* custom, she knew nothing of the installation ceremony. She assumed she would have no part; surely she'd have been told if she did. And then there was the matter of the young man, Jamin.

Jamin.

She was unprepared for the effect his name would have on her. When her mother whispered it to her in the cella two days ago, a warmth had spread down her cheeks. Her thoughts had been on him often over the past several weeks, more so since they locked eyes on the steps of Nabu's temple. Now her thoughts were seldom elsewhere.

Jamin.

Such a simple name, and how easily it rolled off the tongue. He was the first man to speak love to her. His love and that of a strange God—her God. Despite everything Jamin's aunt told her that evening over tea, there was still so much more to know, so many more questions. It warmed and puzzled her how a common ancestry and faith now connected her to the impetuous young Jamin.

The ethereal voice that plagued her the evening of her ascension to High Priestess had probed her twice since she cast it before God. It fought to grip her brain in its prickly shell and whisper its venom in her ear, but it snapped away at the mention of *Elohim Adonai*. Ianna mouthed the name of God over and over again. She thought of another voice, a quiet voice that revealed this God to her when she needed Him most. But, along with her new God, stood the young man.

Jamin.

Elohim Adonai.

It also struck her curious how both Jamin and *Adonai* crystallized in her mind the moment she learned their names. She remembered the story of a god who withheld his name from the other gods in the belief that anyone who knew it would gain a measure of control over him. And didn't her own father hide their family's true names and assume ones he believed would garner them more acceptance by their neighbors? A mirthless smile came to her lips. Her father was right in all his wrongness. A simple name could mean so much.

If the voices who served Ishtar could not stand before *Elohim Adonai*, then He was mighty indeed. One worthy of devotion, worthy to be served, worthy of—her love.

Elohim Adonai.

Jamin.

Her head cooled, awash in peace the moment she could call them by name. Then she looked around herself, and the peacefulness ebbed.

She was still here. In this temple. In this gown. She was trapped as the preeminent servant of a goddess she despised. Ianna wondered if there would ever be a chance to escape. One thing she did know. She could not go on this way.

For two days now, Jonah remained hidden in the house away from the windows, out of sight. He felt caged, hopeless, impotent, and he didn't like the frustration it stirred. The melee in the temple square played itself over and over again in his mind. The elders had tried to carry the message, to warn their Assyrian neighbors, but were only beaten for their efforts. Nineveh was beyond hope; now he was certain of it. The city deserved the destruction *Adonai* was sure to deliver, and, in his restlessness, he believed the sooner God acted, the better.

An overwhelming desire to express his love for Hannah added to his restlessness. His insecurity with such new and raw feelings confused him. He stifled the sensual urge out of respect for her, but it didn't lessen—quite the opposite. He'd lay awake, restive with desire and guilt every time his mind strayed to where she lay in the darkness a short distance away. And those times were many.

Hannah spent most of the day away from the house. She sought ways to get Jonah out of the city, but not with enthusiasm. Her head understood the need, but her heart did not. She spent much of the night awake, aware that Jonah tossed on his sleep mat across the room. She wondered if she should feel guilt over the speed with which she shifted her love to Jonah so soon after her husband's death. Similar thoughts had assailed her as a young woman when she lost Abimelech, then entered Mordecai's house immediately upon the family's acceptance of his brother's death. But it was the way of her people, and her husband had left no legacy to sustain her, so poor were they. Fortunately, Mordecai prospered as a silversmith and he left substantial resources to her after his death, resources she could now apply toward Jonah's safety.

Her deep attraction to Jonah was the greatest mystery. Was it fascination with his calling as a prophet? Perhaps it was the tie to her beloved first husband through the gold medallions. She hoped not. She thought not. No, she was sure not. Jonah was innocent, even naïve, in many respects, but there was a steadfastness and strength of noble purpose in him that Mordecai had lacked. Jonah's love appeared pure, almost childlike in its abandon, and it enthralled her. There was no guile, no presumption, no expectation. Most of all, he respected her, a trait immature in her marriage to young Abim and absent in her relationship with Mordecai.

So her heart fought with her mind over the need to lose the man she had come to love.

Jonah leaned against the wall in Mordecai's work area, his head bowed in thought. Hannah sat on a mat across the room. She broke the silence. "I think it's the only way."

Jonah looked up. "I never thought to look that direction."

She nodded. "Neither did I. I looked only westward, to Israel and your home. I forgot the Ninlil Gate on the eastern road is being rebuilt.

The door has not yet been hung, so they can't close it at night. There are guards, but if we leave just before sunrise, when the night watch is tired and while they prepare for their relief, we might be able to slip through unnoticed."

"It sounds risky."

"Perhaps, but I think it's the only way." Her voice dropped. "We should try tonight."

Forty-four

Nineveh, the Royal Palace
Eighteenth Day of Du'ûzu, the Eleventh Hour

Jamin loitered on the road a short distance from the palace gate. When he entered that courtyard, life would never again be the same. He tried to reconstruct the events that led to this moment, but there were too many gaps. He still had no idea how he had come to the notice of the royal official. He could only suspect that this was punishment for his attack on the soldier on the steps of Nabu's temple. But this ritual was not supposed to be a punishment, was it?

He had heard of the *ugu lugal* tradition but knew little about it. The substitute king was to either avert or bear the brunt of the gods' displeasure in the true king's stead. There would be a part of the ceremony where the evil *ittu*—whatever the omens had been, he still didn't know—would be transferred to him in the presence of the Sun God, Shamash. There would be further rituals during the one hundred-day reign in which he may be expected to read other omens, or divine other unknowable things, but he had no idea how he would do that. He didn't believe in pagan omens. He didn't believe in Shamash. He didn't believe in any of this.

Other worries plagued him over the past three days since his summons to the palace. What would happen if he couldn't read *ittu?* How much authority, if any, would he actually wield? Would there be advisors to tell him what to do? Most of all, where was *Adonai*, and how could He allow this to happen to one of His own?

The next twenty paces would be the longest of his life. Yet he knew he must take them. If he fled, he would imperil his relatives—and perhaps the rest of the Hebrew community.

Jamin shuddered and took the first step forward. Then he faltered. As he steadied himself against the wall, a clear voice, one that seemed to come from everywhere—or nowhere at all—spoke.

"Do not fear the road ahead. The Lord is with you."

"Lord?"

"All is well. Adonai sees and hears. He will comfort you."

Jamin closed his eyes. His head cleared, and he lowered his hand from the wall. At first, he wasn't sure if he really heard a voice. Perhaps it was only his imagination, delusion brought on by sleepless nights. But the peace that flooded his heart as the voice spoke convinced him it was real. He knew he could not delude himself into such tranquility from the despair he felt only a moment ago.

"Lord? If you are in this, I will go. I don't understand it. I don't understand anything. Still, give me the strength to serve."

"You will not be forsaken."

Jamin took a deep breath. With renewed hope, he set off toward the palace.

Ianna shook the folds of her gown and straightened her hair over her shoulders. She knelt to retrieve the High Priestess's cap and scepter from the mat.

"High Priestess?"

Ianna looked up. The *naditu* fingered her ivory comb and studied the petite *Entu.* Worry creased her brow, but no question came.

Ianna smiled. "You may go now, Hulalitu. I'll be along shortly."

The priestess nodded. She set the comb on the brazier stand and moved to the door. With one more look over her shoulder, she slipped out.

Ianna stared at the staff in her hand. An apprehension she couldn't explain overcame her, and tears welled up in her eyes. She blinked them back.

"Do not be afraid. Elohim Adonai is with you."

Yet, despite the quiet voice, she couldn't shake the sense of dread that nagged her. Her chin quivered and her resolve faltered. "I'm scared. I don't know why, but I am."

"GO, CHILD. YOU WILL NOT BE FORSAKEN."

She closed her eyes and drew a deep breath. A gentle rap came at the door.

"Enter." Her voice was quiet.

The door opened, and Thura stood at the threshold. "High Priestess, your escort awaits you for the ceremony."

"Very well. We shall go."

Ianna straightened her shoulders and strode to the door. She glanced back into the room, then stepped into the hallway.

Thura closed the door behind her.

Ahu-duri finished his instructions and waited for the young *ugu lugal* designee to acknowledge. Jamin stood in the antechamber of the palace, vaguely aware of what the vizier had said. The door to his left opened into the courtyard where the ceremony would take place. He could hear the hubbub as people arrived for the ritual. He was relieved there was nothing for him to say. The royal advisor would lead him through the process. He needed only to listen and obey.

"Remember, after the gold necklace is hung around your neck, the royal robes will be placed over your shoulders. Be prepared to accept the scepter at that point." Ahu-duri cocked his head. "Do you understand?"

Jamin nodded.

"Good. We are ready to begin. The guests have arrived, and they are being instructed even as you are now." He circled Jamin and looked him over one last time. "The ceremony is not a long one. I will address the assembly at the conclusion. There is only one detail we have not yet settled, but you need not worry about that."

Jamin raised an eyebrow, but the vizier ignored him.

289

"You will be escorted when it is time. Remain here until then."
With that, the official turned on his heel and left the room.

Ahu-duri assumed his most imperious stride as he approached the crowd. His gaze flicked left and right to satisfy himself that all the details he'd arranged were in order. He viewed the entourage from Ishtar's temple at the right of his own center position. His pulse quickened at the figure of the High Priestess in front of a passel of blue-clad priestesses. He recognized his sister, Hulalitu, at the High Priestess's left. He avoided making eye contact with the *Entu*—as difficult as that was. Aloofness might accentuate his importance and impress her all the more.

Kaheri followed, ready to receive any last-minute instructions. As Ahu-duri entered the circle, the aide peeled off and remained at the head of the pathway.

The vizier halted at the center of the improvised amphitheater. He held his head high and scanned the hushed assembly. His eye lingered a moment on the High Priestess to assess her interest, but her face betrayed nothing. He frowned inwardly. Her eyes canted downward, seemingly disinterested in the ceremony. He cleared his throat and dipped his head toward the gathering.

"You are all most welcomed. As you know, King Adad-nirari has commanded an *ugu lugal* ceremony due to recent *ittu* that bode ill dispositions on the part of the gods. He has honored Nineveh as the venue for the substitute king's reign. One of your own has been selected as the substitute king, which further honors this great city."

He paused to judge the effect of his words. The crowd remained quiet. He saw the set look on Iqisha's face and bristled at the distinct lack of enthusiasm in the magistrate's demeanor. That, he decided, would not serve Iqisha well in the future. The High Priestess's eyes remained downcast.

"Let us proceed."

The vizier strode to his position and nodded at Kaheri. The aide spun and hurried toward the palace. In a few moments, the *ugu lugal* appeared, flanked by a palace steward, two scribes, and two soldiers. Kaheri led him to the spot from which the vizier had addressed the crowd. He halted Jamin there and returned to his post.

Jamin stood in the midst of the assembly, strangely calm. He raised his eyes and looked at the royal official, his face impassive. A splash of pastel to the vizier's right caught his attention, and he shifted his eyes to where the retinue from the Temple of Ishtar stood.

His heart jumped when he saw the *Entu* raise her face. He saw her eyes widen with recognition when they met his. The depth of her stare pushed everything else into the background. He thought he heard the official speak, but the words were lost in the girl's look. He couldn't turn his eyes away even if he wanted to. They held each other's gaze.

Then someone looped a chain around his neck, and it fell against his chest. A heavy embroidered robe dropped onto his shoulders. Something—he supposed it to be the scepter—was pressed into his hand. Still, his eyes were on Ianna.

Another muffled word, probably by the official, and two hands grasped his shoulders. They turned him toward the west, where the sun hung low over the courtyard wall. Another voice uttered an incantation to Shamash, and the assembly responded with something, he didn't know what. His eyes remained focused on the object of his love.

His stupor finally broke when the vizier stepped forward and addressed the people in a loud voice.

Ahu-duri followed the prescribed ritual for the *ugu lugal* ceremony quickly and with precision. He frowned at the apparent distraction on Jamin's face, then grew even more irritated when it became obvious who was distracting him. He glanced to his right, when Kaheri looped the neck chain over Jamin's head, and he narrowed his brow at the steady look the High Priestess held on the young Hebrew.

He announced the bestowal of the scepter, then nodded to the priest of Shamash to begin the transference of the evil omens onto the substitute king. His annoyance grew when Jamin's gaze did not follow everyone else's to the western sky but remained fixed on the High Priestess. The priest finished his recitations, and Ahu-duri decided to end the ceremony as quickly as possible.

He stepped forward and addressed the crowd. "With this, the *ugu lugal* is installed. People of Nineveh, your king stands before you."

The assembled witnesses bowed to the new temporary king.

Ahu-duri continued. "There remains only one act to complete. Our king is without his queen to stand in the place of the Queen Mother, Sammuramat. A suitable wife will be found and wedded to the substitute king at the soonest opportunity. Until then—"

A quiet voice cut him off. "I will take the place of the queen. I will marry the substitute king."

Ahu-duri spun around.

Forty-five

Nineveh, the Privileged Quarter
Eighteenth Day of Du'ûzu, the Twelfth Hour

Jonah stuffed his few provisions into a bundle. Hannah was at the marketplace to procure dried fruit, meat, and flatbread for his journey. Tonight they would try to get him out through the Ninlil Gate, but where he would go from there, he wasn't sure. He hadn't thought about what to do when his mission was over, or how he would get back to Israel. He assumed he would return along the same route he used to the city, but he hadn't anticipated the river travel from Aššûr. That would require advanced arrangements, and there was still the issue of his lack of familiarity with the Assyrian tongue.

Jonah was caught between the urge to leave Nineveh far behind and the desire to see what God planned to do to the city. The refuge in Hannah's house put him out of touch with the Jewish community, so he had no way to gauge the mood of the people. Hannah's forays were focused on a way to escape the city; indeed, this was her first trip to the marketplace since they fled the temple. There was no question in his mind, though, that the city was doomed. He couldn't conceive of a repentant Assyrian, let alone an entire city of them. If God would destroy Nineveh was not the question. It was how He would destroy it.

A bump in the front room interrupted his thoughts. He leaned around the wall and saw Hannah burst into the house. She dropped two small bundles by the door and hurried into the back room. A smile spread over her face.

Jonah cocked his head. "Hannah—?"

She dropped to her knees and embraced him. "Jonah! You've succeeded!" she whispered in his ear, her voice barely able to contain her excitement.

He didn't try to break the hug. "What? What are you talking about?"

She sat back and took his hands in hers. "Nineveh. It's . . . we're repenting!"

He shook his head. "What do you mean?"

"The whole marketplace is agog. Your disappearance from the temple is seen as a miracle. People believe this great vengeful god has spirited his prophet from the city in preparation for its destruction. People crowd the Jews everywhere. They ask who this god is and how to appease him."

Jonah stared, his mouth agape.

She laughed. "Don't you see? Your mission here for *Adonai* has been for good. If it continues at this pace, the whole city will repent well within the forty days."

Repent? Assyria? Nineveh? Impossible!

"Jonah, what's wrong?" Hannah's smile faded.

"Nineveh isn't supposed to repent. It's supposed to be destroyed." His tone was flat.

Hannah leaned back. "Of course, it's supposed to repent. That was your message."

Jonah shook his head. "But there was no chance of that. Assyria is too evil; Nineveh is too evil. It was to be obliterated."

She set her jaw. "I am Assyrian, Jonah. My friends, what few I do have, are Ninevites."

He returned a blank look. "You're not an Assyrian. You're a Jew."

"Yes, Jonah. An Assyrian Jew. This is my home. These are my people."

"But it wasn't supposed to happen this way."

She frowned. "Do you mean you want the city destroyed? You want all of these people—all of us—to die?"

He jerked his head. "No! Not you, of course. Not the Jews, just the Assyrians."

Hannah rose to her feet and folded her arms. "Jonah, you're not listening. I am an Assyrian. If God destroyed Nineveh, all of us would die with it. The elders, their families, my daughter, and I. Everyone. Surely that's not what you wanted. Please tell me that's not what you wanted."

Jonah looked up, his mind in a whirl. "I—"

Her eyes flashed. "You do, don't you? You came here in hopes of destroying us, not saving us."

He scrambled to his feet. "Hannah, I—"

She stepped back, her hands raised. "You need to go. Tonight. I'll see you to the Ninlil Gate. I don't care where you go from there." She turned and left the room.

"Hannah—"

※ ※ ※

Hulalitu choked. "No!"

Ahu-duri stared, his mouth agape. "You . . . you cannot do that!"

Ianna's face was expressionless. "I will invoke the Royal Marriage. The High Priestess of Ishtar can marry the king."

He shook his head. "The Royal Marriage is a ritual for the new year, when the High Priestess and the king come together for a night. It is not a true marriage."

Her voice was low. "And he is not a true king, is he? He is only a substitute king. And this is only for a season, is it not? One hundred days."

"He . . . he is a true king, for as long as he reigns," the vizier stammered.

"Then he has the authority to accept me as his queen." Ianna stepped forward and stood toe to toe with the flustered legate. "Doesn't he?"

"I . . . he—" Ahu-duri threw a panicked look at Jamin.

Ianna turned and followed his gaze. She lifted her gown from around her feet and strode to Jamin, where she stopped a single pace from him. She searched his eyes. "Do you want me?"

Jamin's words rushed out in a forced whisper. "I . . . but . . . I can't do this to you!"

Ianna took another half-pace forward and looked into his face. Her whisper matched his. "I can no longer serve Ishtar. You are now my king. Your people are my people, and your God is my God."

"But you know what—"

"Yes, I know." She leaned forward. "You once professed your love for me. I now confess my love for you. I would rather live with you for a hundred days than to live without you for a hundred years." Her face was a mere hand's breadth from his. "I love you. Please, take me as your wife." A tear moistened her cheek.

He swallowed, then shook his head. "I love you too much to let you do this."

"CHILDREN, IT IS TIME. RECEIVE EACH OTHER."

Ianna jerked her head at the voice. She looked into Jamin's eyes and knew he heard it, too. Her eyebrows raised, and a gentle smile touched her lips.

Jamin closed his eyes. *Why? Why this way?*

"YOU WILL LEARN IN TIME."

He released a slow exhale and opened his eyes. His voice shook with countless emotions. "Yes. I take you for my wife."

Jamin took Ianna's hand in his, and together they turned to face the vizier.

Forty-six

Nineveh, the Privileged Quarter
Nineteenth Day of Du'ûzu, the Second Hour

Jonah stared into a murky darkness that matched his countenance. His mind was full and his heart heavy. Hannah had not said a word since their earlier exchange. She had only retrieved the two bundles of food, dropped them in front of him, and gone to her sleep mat. He could hear her steady breathing through the light scrim that covered her niche.

The news of the city's repentance confused him more than addled him, but he had communicated that poorly. And he'd never seen someone change demeanor as quickly as Hannah had. Her sudden coldness dropped the ache in his heart to a knot in his stomach. There seemed to be no way to let her know what he felt, how complicated this was, how difficult just the idea of coming to Nineveh had been. None of that mattered now. The euphoria of this new relationship sank more quickly than he had after being thrown into the sea from the *Ba'al Hayam*. None of this was supposed to happen.

The words he spoke to Elihu when he ran to Joppa to avoid this very situation rushed back at him. *"If Adonai sends a message to repent, it means the people can repent."*

But in Assyria? He grit his teeth at his dilemma and his God.

"This is why I fled to Tarshish! This is why I never wanted to come to Nineveh! I knew this could happen, although I never believed it would. You offer mercy where mercy is not due. You show loving-kindness where love is not understood. Your justice makes no sense when You override it so quickly with Your grace. I didn't want to preach to this miserable city. I didn't need a relationship with this confusing woman. Yet You thrust both of them on me, and now I've ruined everything. Why didn't You just leave me alone?"

The voice startled Jonah.

"THE WOMAN IS RIGHT, JONAH BEN AMITTAI. SHE IS A CHILD WHO FORSOOK ADONAI, YET SHE KNOWS HIM BETTER THAN YOU DO. A LIGHT IS MOST VISIBLE WHERE THE DARKNESS IS DEEPEST. WHERE MERCY IS NOT DUE IS WHERE IT IS NEEDED THE MOST. WHERE THERE IS NO LOVE IS WHERE LOVING-KINDNESS YIELDS ITS GREATEST GOOD. AND GRACE WILL ALWAYS ABOUND WHERE JUSTICE IS MOST RICHLY DESERVED. YOU HAVE SO QUICKLY FORGOTTEN THAT, JONAH, EVEN THOUGH YOU EXPERIENCED IT YOURSELF IN THE BELLY OF THE FISH AND IN ATTENDING TO THE WRONGS YOU INFLICTED ON YOURSELF AND OTHERS IN YOUR REBELLION. YOU FORGET THAT MERCY, LOVING-KINDNESS, AND GRACE WERE EXTENDED TO YOU AT THE TIMES YOU NEEDED THEM MOST . . . THE TIMES YOU DESERVED THEM LEAST. WHAT RIGHT HAVE YOU TO BE ANGRY, JONAH BEN AMITTAI?"

"But why Nineveh, of all cities? Israel is Adonai's chosen land, not cursed Assyria! What has the God of Abraham to do with the heathens of this land?"

"DO YOU FORGET THAT ADONAI CALLED ABRAM OUT OF UR IN THE LAND OF THE CHALDEANS, OF SUMER, OF ASSYRIA? DO YOU FORGET HIS INSTRUCTIONS TO MOSHEH WHEN HE LED THE PEOPLE FROM BONDAGE IN EGYPT—THAT HE WAS TO RAISE A SWORD NEITHER AGAINST THE EDOMITES, NOR THE MOABITES, NOR THE AMMONITES, FOR HE HAD GIVEN THEIR LAND TO THEM? ELOHIM ADONAI IS THE GOD OF ALL PEOPLE, NOT MERELY ONE. IT IS THROUGH ABRAHAM'S SEED THAT THE WORLD SHALL BE BLESSED, JONAH, NOT ABRAHAM'S SEED ALONE. HIS DEALINGS WITH THE NATIONS—YES, EVEN NINEVEH—ARE HIS ALONE. IT IS YOURS TO CARRY HIS MESSAGE, NOT TO QUARREL WITH IT."

Jonah rolled onto his side and covered his head with his arms. "No more. Please, no more. I haven't the strength."

"GOD'S POWER IS PERFECTED IN YOUR WEAKNESS, JONAH. IT IS WHY YOU WERE CHOSEN."

Jonah squeezed his eyes shut and pressed his arms to his ears against the voice, but the words echoed through his mind. He dropped into a stupor, then finally a slumber barely beneath consciousness, but there was no rest in it.

A nudge against his shoulder stirred him.

"It's time." Hannah's soft voice floated down from somewhere above him.

Jonah squinted into the dark, but he couldn't discern any shapes. He wondered for a moment if he'd gone blind, so total was the blackness. He groped on the floor for his bundles and staggered to his feet. In the inkiness, he caught the padding of Hannah's footsteps. The footfalls ceased, and he heard a click as the door latch slipped from its cradle. A gentle wash of moonlight widened across the floor as the door opened. Hannah's shape slipped into the glow and paused, framed by the low doorway. His throat tightened again at the sight of her. He wanted to say something, anything, to set things right, but his tortured mind failed his tongue.

"Quickly." Her silhouette disappeared.

Jonah edged across the floor and through the open doorway. Hannah scanned the road in both directions, then looked back and gestured for him to follow. Instinctively, he raised his hand to take hers, but she turned and set off up the street. His heart ached with embarrassment and disappointment.

Hannah led back to the bend in the river, to the path they traversed from the temple square. She turned east, away from the plaza, and picked her way along the shadowed pathway. As they slipped along the silent waters of the Tabiltu in the dim moonlight, Jonah's mind churned for something to say.

"Hannah, I want—"

"Quietly. We're nearing the gate." She tossed the whisper over her shoulder and kept moving.

Jonah plodded behind her, his eyes at the ground in front of his feet. He looked up just in time to avoid a collision when Hannah slowed her pace. The city wall loomed only twenty paces ahead, its dark edifice broken by the Ninlil Gate. She guided them off the path and stopped by a pillar embedded in the wall. Jonah closed the distance and halted behind her.

Hannah's voice barely pierced the night. "The moon is low in the west. When we get through the gate, stay in the shadow against the wall until we spot the guards. Stay close to me."

"I'd like—"

"But not too close." Her flat tone cut him off.

Jonah's embarrassment turned to irritation. Before he could reply, she stepped around the corner of the wall and through the opening. He followed. The Ninlil Gate was wide enough to accommodate the Tabiltu entering the city from the east and a main road that hugged the far side of the river. No guards were in sight. She motioned to him and stepped away from the wall.

The lip of the eastern horizon across the river lay barely visible against the predawn. The wall's shadow stretched away from the city and covered them until they reached the riverbank. Hannah stopped.

"There's a ford just ahead. The season has been dry, so it should be easy to cross."

"Hannah—"

"Later. We need to—"

"Hannah!" Jonah's sharp tone cut the stillness.

She twirled around, her dimly lit face knit into a frown.

Jonah matched her stance but dropped his voice again to a whisper. "I know I disappointed you, and I know you're upset. So am I. But you have to believe that there is more to this than I've been able to explain. Much more. Please give me a chance." A plaintive note crept into his voice. "Please . . . Hannah?" His voice caught.

Jonah took her hand. She stiffened at his touch but did not pull back. He lifted her hand to his face and pressed it to his cheek. The word came as a whisper. "Please."

She nodded. Her voice was soft, but urgent. "All right. But it has to be later. We can still be seen this close to the city."

"But we must talk."

"Yes. We'll talk." She pulled her hand from his grasp and turned.

A few paces later the path dropped level with the river. Together they stepped into the placid water, its current barely noticeable against his bare ankles. The river rose only to their hips before they reached the far side. They topped the embankment and crossed the road, but when they reached the hillside, Hannah stopped.

"I'll leave you here. I need to get back through the gate before dawn, or the guards will wonder what a lone woman is doing outside the city at daybreak."

Jonah looked around. "Where do I go from here?"

"At the top of this rise, there are clearings in the scrub brush and ground cover. Watch out for snakes. You can wait until light to decide what you want to do from there."

"But you're coming back." Jonah peered into her face.

She hesitated.

"Hannah, you said we would talk. I'm not leaving Nineveh until we do." Jonah reached for her again, but she shifted her stance and avoided his touch.

"Jonah, I—"

"Hannah, I don't know how you feel about me anymore, but I love you. I'm not letting you go and I'm not leaving without speaking with you. You promised. I'm holding you to that promise."

Hannah tossed her head and looked away, then glanced back at Jonah. She folded her arms and stared at the ground. "I need to get home."

"I'll be here when you get back. Either you come, or I die here. There's nothing else. I'm not leaving."

Hannah eyed him, but he didn't waver. Finally, she shrugged. "All right."

Forty-seven

The Arabian Desert, East of Nineveh
Nineteenth Day of Du'ûzu, the Eighth Hour

Jonah leaned against a boulder and shielded his eyes from the glare of the late morning sky. He had fashioned a crude lean-to from dead scrub brush and now rested between its meager walls. A sparse covering of leafy branches formed the roof, which allowed more sunlight in than he preferred, but he had no tools to trim foliage or harvest any other greenery. So he hunched in the small shelter against the hillside for what little protection it afforded.

His refuge opened to the west. He knew it would allow the hot late-afternoon sun to spill in, but he wanted a clear view of the city lying on the river plain below. Although he wanted to see what *Adonai* had in store, his mind was not on Nineveh. It was on one of Nineveh's inhabitants.

Jonah fretted over the way he and Hannah had parted. He was not confident she would return, but he was firm in his resolve to stay until she did. If she didn't, he was serious about dying on this barren hillside. So he would wait.

His makeshift shelter betrayed him in its inadequacy when the sun approached its zenith. It was not yet the hottest part of the day, but he already felt lightheaded. His lips were crusted and chapped, his hair matted and plastered to his forehead with dried sweat. He pulled his knees to his chest and draped his arms over them. Time slowed, and still Hannah would not leave his mind. His eyelids drooped.

Jonah didn't know how long he dozed before he became aware of a light breeze against his bare wrists. He lifted his head and squinted up. His eyes widened when they met with green rather than blue. He twisted his torso and looked behind him to see a thick vine stretching skyward from behind a large rock. Tendrils from the stalk wove themselves into the shelter's paltry canopy, and broad green leaves sprouted along tendrils that laid flat and plaited a thick cover against the relentless sun. The breeze filtered around a stem that draped the low entryway of his lean-to. Jonah leaned his head back and closed his eyes. He sighed and breathed in the intoxicating freshness of the cooled air.

A tiny splash of moisture on the back of his hand jolted him. He squinted at the splotch of wetness, hesitated, then lifted his hand to his lips. The liquid was cool and sweet, like nothing he'd ever tasted. He looked up and saw another drop poised to release from a pointy nub on the vine's tendril. Jonah touched his finger to it, and drew it to the tip of his tongue. This droplet tasted even sweeter than the first.

Jonah snapped the bit of foliage from its stalk. More of the clear fluid oozed from the open wound and ran down his fingers. He lifted the piece of stalk, tipped it to his lips, and squeezed a flow of sap onto his tongue. There wasn't a time in his life he could remember when anything tasted so good. A quick scan of the underside of the canopy yield several more tendrils. He snapped off the thin stems and drained their sumptuous contents into his mouth. Several minutes later, he yawned and licked the last of the nectar from his lips.

Content, Jonah slipped into a light slumber.

Ianna tucked the last of her few personal belongings into the bundle. The robe of the High Priestess of Ishtar, her ceremonial cap, necklace, and scepter lay in a neat arrangement on her bed mat. She wore a simple white tunic. The plain garb of the virgin *ishtaritu* initiate enveloped her lithe form as gracefully as it had a few short months ago, before her life had come apart. But the spotless white fabric now carried a significance in stark contrast to its original purpose. This day she would wed, and she would approach her marriage bed as pure as the gown she wore.

She closed her eyes and relived the moments after the *ugu lugal* ceremony, when Jamin had taken her aside into a niche of the garden. He gazed into her eyes, saying nothing, but then lifted his hand and brushed his fingers across her cheek. She trembled at his touch, and his face blurred through a sheen of tears. They stood there silently, for how long she couldn't remember. Then he spoke.

He told her they must be married in the fashion of his people before they came together. It would be a proper ceremony in the sight of God and with the blessing of his family. With no priesthood, the Ninevite Jewish community invested the elders with the authority to conduct weddings. He would call for his uncle and ask him to marry them the following morning. But tonight she must return to the temple; she could not stay with him in the palace.

At first, she protested the notion that they should part. She ached to consummate a relationship that finally felt so good and so right. But a loving look told her he would not bend on this. *Adonai* had brought them together, he said, and *Adonai* would see them through. He smiled with a raised eyebrow and whispered to her how difficult parting would be for him, too. Then they stood and held each other while the sounds of the crowd dispersed from the garden.

Ianna smiled at the reminiscence, aglow with excitement at the man who awaited her. She lifted her bundle and turned to face Hulalitu.

The *naditu's* eyes were swollen. She wrung her hands, at a loss for words.

"Hulalitu, my . . . friend. Have you summoned Shalla?"

Hulalitu choked back a sob at the precious honorific. She couldn't remember the last time anyone had called her a friend. She could only nod.

"And you will go to my mother when I've left? I don't know whether she's heard about the ceremony yet. Please tell her gently."

Hulalitu nodded again.

A rap on the door broke the stillness.

"Enter."

The door opened, and Shalla stepped into the room. She began to dip her head in regulatory respect but balked at the sight of the High Priestess in an *ishtaritu* tunic.

"Come in, please. Close the door, would you?"

Her eyes still locked on Ianna, the senior *naditu* nudged the door closed. Ianna beckoned her forward.

"I know we have had our differences, Shalla. I want to tell you, though, that I always believed you should have been the High Priestess, never myself. My selection was as much a surprise to me as it was to you, to everyone." She paused. "I still believe you will make a good *Entu*."

Shalla shook her head. "I . . . I don't understand."

Ianna smiled. "Issar-surrat, for reasons still unknown to me, arranged for me to replace her. We both know how unusual that is, that the king selects the *Entu* of Ishtar. However, since the precedence has been set, I've had a temple scribe record your name as my successor. I sealed the tablet earlier this morning. With my new . . . relationship with the substitute king, I'm sure he will have no objections. And yes, he is authorized to have you installed as the new High Priestess. King Adad-nirari will have gone into seclusion by now, so he will not be accessible for one hundred days. The position of High Priestess cannot be vacant for a day, let alone one hundred, as you well know. There will be no issues over your ascension. Hulalitu has already begun notifications for the *naditu* council to gather and prepare for your ceremony."

Shalla swallowed. "I don't know what to say. I have never disguised my resentment at your ascension to High Priestess. I have disdained you in private and challenged your authority in public. You could have had me disciplined, even banished from the temple, if you desired. Why this?"

Ianna smiled and shrugged. "What is done is done." She stepped over to the new *Entu* designee and hugged her.

Shalla stiffened at the display of—could it be called affection? Such an act was alien to anything she knew in the temple caste. Slowly her heart softened, and she touched Ianna's arms with her fingertips, still afraid to betray too much. To abandon protocol completely, even after her emotional confrontation with this High Priestess toward whom she had directed so much hatred, was still beyond her. But something stirred within her, and she felt helpless to resist this strange demonstration of warmth.

Ianna pulled away and gestured toward the sleep mat. "The accoutrements of office are all here. It's time I go."

With that, Ianna hoisted her bundle and walked out of the quarters of the High Priestess of Ishtar for the last time. She never looked back.

A knock on the door startled Hannah from her thoughts. She sat on her sleep mat, not having moved from her niche since she awoke earlier that morning. Her head ached over the loss of Jonah. She was furious with him when she discovered his true feelings concerning Nineveh and angry with herself for how she still felt about him. She still hadn't decided whether to return to the hill east of the city. His promise not to leave, even to die, if she did not return, ate at her. It wasn't fair to put her in that position. She felt manipulated but struggled with the knowledge that the manipulation was born of love, not power. He said he had more to tell her, that there was more to the story. What more could there be? He hated her city, her people. How could he love her? Yet she knew he did.

The rap at the door came again.

Hannah rose and went into the front room. She opened the door to find Hulalitu on the threshold. The *naditu* wore a plain robe; the blue tunic was absent.

"Hulalitu, what are you doing here?"

The priestess looked down, clearly distressed.

"I'm sorry. Please, come in." Hannah moved aside.

Hulalitu stepped into the room and turned toward Hannah. Her eyes filled with tears. "I have a message for you."

◢◢◢

Hiram smiled at the couple as they stood under a makeshift canopy in the palace garden. Rizpah stood behind him and dabbed at her eyes. Jamin and Ianna faced each other. A white cloth signifying their union bound her hand to his. The ceremony had just completed, and silence reigned in the presence of the Almighty God and the elders who gathered as witnesses.

There would be no week-long celebration, no dancing, nothing on which to feast. The couple would retire to the palace, the attendants return home. But their joy was complete in each other and in their God. Neither knew what this season of their lives would bring, but neither could have been happier.

"What is happening in the city, Uncle? I have been out of communication it seems forever, although it's only been two days."

Jamin stood in the dim antechamber of the palace. Rizpah had accompanied Ianna to the bedchamber to help prepare her for her husband. She had left strict instructions for Jamin to wait until she came for him.

Hiram's face lit up. "The people receive the message well from the elders and follow their example in repentance." Then his countenance fell. "But word travels slowly, and decisions are made even more slowly. I'm still fearful we'll run out of time before the whole city has been reached."

Jamin dipped his head in thought. "Is there anything I can do?"

His uncle shrugged. "I don't know. I didn't think of it, but you are the king now, for all intent."

Jamin nodded. "I'm still unsure of my authority, but I'll never know where it lies until I test it. The royal official from Kalḫu left early this morning without a word. There is no one to ask."

Hiram raised his eyebrows. "An edict, perhaps?"

Jamin snapped his fingers. "Of course! A proclamation from the king. Nineveh is the only city affected, so word may not even get back to Kalḫu until all has been accomplished."

Hiram stroked his beard. "Can you do that?"

Jamin set his jaw. "I don't know, but I will anyway. After all, the substitute king's purpose is to absorb or avert the wrath of the gods. This is exactly what I'm doing—averting the wrath of the only true God. I'll command sackcloth and ashes be worn by every man, woman, and child—even the livestock, just to make sure. They must turn their eyes and their hearts toward God and seek His mercy. Many have already done so. But time is short. I'll attend to it today."

Rizpah's voice interrupted them from the doorway. "Jamin—I mean, my lord." She smiled. "Your bride awaits you."

Jamin stared at her, and a wave of heat flushed his face. He was so consumed with being a king, he had almost forgotten he was also a groom. The thought of Ianna chased everything else from his mind, and he suddenly felt small and vulnerable.

"Go to your wife, Nephew." A good-natured grin stretched Hiram's face.

Jamin managed an awkward smile. "I'll attend to the proclamation first thing . . . tomorrow."

Forty-eight

The Arabian Desert, East of Nineveh
Twentieth Day of Du'ûzu, the Sixth Hour

Jonah stirred from slumber and swiped at a sharp jab against his cheek. He rolled to his side and yawned. A second poke on his forehead opened his eyes. In his palm lay a sprig of foliage. It was shriveled, hard and brown, a remnant of a dead plant probably blown in on the morning breeze. Its barbed tip dug into his skin when he closed his fingers and crushed it. He squinted toward the roof of his shelter but saw only an azure morning sky. The canopy was gone.

He pushed up, and dead leaves fluttered from the folds of his cloak. The lean-to had collapsed. The luxuriant vine that gave him so much relief from yesterday's afternoon sun was a gnarled silhouette that now cringed against the bright sky. The swollen tendrils that dripped such sweet nectar were now withered thorns littering the pebbly sand around him. Even the shelter's frame of scrub brush lay in ruins, flattened under the weight of the vine as it sagged and disintegrated. He had slept, oblivious to the silent destruction around him.

Jonah muttered to himself. The vine that had provided such unexpected relief yesterday had not only collapsed but destroyed the meager shelter he had fashioned himself. The blessing became a double curse, in that it destroyed what little he already had in its death throes.

As he turned toward the boulder, the sun burst over the edge of the hillock and caught him in the face with the full fury of its glare and its heat.

He covered his eyes against the blinding rays and grumbled, "What has happened? Where is my shelter? Am I just to shrivel and die here in the desert like this cursed vine?"

"ONCE AGAIN, JONAH BEN AMITTAI, YOU PRESUME UPON GRACE. WHAT DID YOU DO TO DESERVE RESPITE FROM THE DESERT SUN? WHEN DID YOU PLANT THE VINE? WHEN DID YOU NOURISH IT AND WEAVE ITS FOLIAGE INTO THE CANOPY OF YOUR SHELTER?"

Jonah's breath caught at the familiar voice. His mind faltered, but then the frustration built up over the past several days overtook him. "I neither asked for nor needed the vine. And now that which I didn't need has taken with it what I do need."

"AND YET YOU FREELY PARTOOK OF THE VINE, DID YOU NOT? YOU REJOICED IN ITS BLESSING, AND NOW YOU CURSE IT IN ITS ABSENCE. YOU TOOK FOR GRANTED THE GRACE AND THE BENEVOLENCE OF ELOHIM ADONAI, WHO PROVIDED YOU RELIEF IN THE MIDST OF YOUR SUFFERING, JUST AS HE DID THE CHILDREN OF ISRAEL IN THE WILDERNESS OF SIN. THEY, TOO, PARTOOK OF HIS BLESSINGS WITHOUT THANKSGIVING, AND CURSED HIM IN THEIR TIMES OF TRIAL. YOU STAND WITH LESS EXCUSE, JONAH, FOR YOU HAVE THE BENEFIT OF THEIR LESSON, YET YOU HAVE LEARNED NOTHING FROM IT."

Jonah's shoulders drooped at the divine chastisement.

"What trial? What am I supposed to have learned? I delivered His message to Nineveh. What more does He want?"

The voice came quietly, its tone softened. "DO YOU REMEMBER YOU ASKED A SIMILAR QUESTION IN THE BELLY OF THE FISH, JONAH?"

Jonah sighed. "I asked what I was supposed to learn, how much longer the lesson would be."

"AND THE ANSWER?"

He swallowed a lump at the memory. "Until I learned to . . . rejoice. I remember being at the Temple with my family. I remember an urge to sing, to exalt the Lord God in His dwelling place."

"AND YOU DID SING, JONAH. EVEN IN THE ENTRAILS OF THE FISH, YOU SANG. YOU REJOICED. YOU GAVE THANKS."

"I remember more."

"YES, YOU GAVE THE PEOPLE OF NINEVEH OVER TO THE SALVATION OF THE LORD. YOU RECOGNIZED HIS SOVEREIGNTY EVEN OVER ASSYRIA. 'SALVATION IS OF THE LORD,' YOU SAID, 'EVEN FOR THE ASSYRIAN.' YOU HAVE FORGOTTEN THAT, JONAH."

Jonah buried his face in his hands. "I have forgotten."

"*AND NOW YOU HAVE FALLEN IN LOVE WITH AN ASSYRIAN.*"

Jonah lifted his head. "Hannah? She was all part of this lesson? God made me fall in love with Hannah to teach me a *lesson?*"

"*NO, JONAH. ADONAI DID NOT MAKE YOU FALL IN LOVE WITH HANNAH. HE ALLOWED YOU TO FOLLOW YOUR HEART, AND YOU FELL IN LOVE WITH AN ASSYRIAN.*"

"But she's a Jew."

"*YES, AN ASSYRIAN JEW, AS SHE REMINDED YOU. AND YOU SAW HER DISAPPOINTMENT WHEN SHE DISCOVERED WHAT YOU HAD FORGOTTEN FROM THE BELLY OF THE FISH.*"

"But she's . . . different. She—"

"*YES, JONAH, SHE IS DIFFERENT. THERE ARE ONE HUNDRED AND TWENTY THOUSAND SOULS IN NINEVEH AND EACH ONE IS DIFFERENT. ELOHIM ADONAI LOVES HANNAH AND EVERY ONE OF THE ONE HUNDRED AND TWENTY THOUSAND MORE THAN YOU WILL EVER UNDERSTAND. HE HAS PROVIDED THEM EVERY OPPORTUNITY TO REPENT, FOR THE WAY HAD BEEN PREPARED BEFORE YOU THROUGH THE LIVES OF HIS PEOPLE, OBEDIENT AND DISOBEDIENT, KNOWINGLY AND UNKNOWINGLY. THROUGH HIS CREATION—THE SKIES, THE EARTH, AND THE BEAST—HIS WILL HAS GONE FORWARD TO PREPARE THE WAY FOR HIS WORD. MAN'S PART HAS BEEN ONLY TO RESPOND.*"

"And the city will repent?"

"*THE CITY HAS REPENTED.*"

"But how?"

"*THAT IS NO LONGER YOUR CONCERN, JONAH. YOU DEPRIVED YOURSELF OF THE BLESSING OF GOD'S MESSAGE WHEN YOU DISTRUSTED IT. IT IS TIME FOR YOU TO GO BACK TO ISRAEL.*"

"Go back? Now?"

"*YES. THERE IS ONE MORE MESSAGE FOR YOU TO DELIVER.*"

"Jonah?"

The hoarse call floated over the rise of the hill and rousted Jonah from his restless slumber. He opened his eyes to an afternoon sun on its final descent toward the horizon. He shook his head, unsure where the voice came from.

"Jonah!"

Two figures appeared over the edge of the outcropping.

"Hulalitu?" Jonah sat up.

The priestess stumbled the last few paces up the incline. Her arms supported a second figure bent at the waist.

"Hannah!"

The priestess eased her companion to the ground.

Jonah grasped Hannah by the shoulders and peered into her face. She stared with vacant eyes, her arms clasped at her waist.

"What's wrong?"

The *naditu* only shook her head. Jonah frowned in frustration when he remembered she could not understand his words.

Jonah held Hannah against his shoulder. She stared ahead, her breath shallow. Jonah questioned Hulalitu again with his eyes, but the priestess concentrated on her distraught friend. Finally, Hannah raised her face to his. She opened her mouth, but a violent sob choked her words.

Jonah hugged her close, grateful to have her in his arms again, despite the circumstances. He rocked her and pressed his cheek to her head. The fragrance of her hair filled his senses, and he closed his eyes. For the next few moments, Jonah immersed himself in her. He felt every sob, every whimper. As her convulsions lessened, he pulled back. He brushed loose strands of hair from her face and looked into her eyes.

"Hannah. Tell me what's wrong."

Her voice quavered. "It's Ianna."

Jonah frowned. "What about Ianna?"

"King Adad-nirari . . . commanded the investiture of an *ugu lugal*, a substitute king."

Jonah frowned. "Hiram said something about an *ugu lugal*, but I don't understand what that is."

Hannah drew a deep breath. "The Assyrians believe that when the gods are displeased, it reflects on the king. To avert divine wrath, a subject of the kingdom takes the king's place, so any divine punishment would fall on him instead of the king."

Jonah nodded. "I see. Like our scapegoat, which takes on the sins of the people. But here it's not a goat; it's a person."

Hannah continued. "The king's emissary chose Jamin to be the substitute king."

"Jamin? But why."

She shook her head and fought back a fresh round of tears. "I don't know."

Hannah sniffed. "They also needed a substitute for Queen Sammuramat."

Jonah just frowned and shook his head.

Hannah looked up at him. "At the *ugu lugal* ceremony, Ianna stepped forward to marry Jamin and take the place of the queen mother."

Jonah paused, then smiled. "She must love him. Isn't this good, if they want to be together?"

Hannah stared at him. "The substitute king and queen reign for only one hundred days."

Jonah nodded. "Yes?"

"At the end of the one hundred days, the rightful king reclaims his throne."

Jonah cocked his head.

Hannah's eyelids squeezed shut. "And the substitute king and queen are put to death."

Forty-nine

Nineveh, the Royal Palace
Twenty-first Day of Du'ûzu, the Sixth Hour

Jamin rolled onto his side. He propped his head onto his arm and gazed at his exquisite bride. Ianna lay on the mat beside him, fast asleep. Her sleek ebony hair splayed over her white pillow and glistened in the early morning light that spilled through the high window of the king's bedchamber. He watched the coverlet across her bosom rise and fall in the gentle rhythm of a carefree slumber. A subtle smile played across her full lips, and her breath came in soft sighs. He wondered what she might be dreaming. He hoped she reminisced the night in his arms.

An eyelid quivered, and her nose twitched. She drew a full breath and stretched her arms above her head. The smile on her face deepened. She opened an eye and squinted into the adoring face of her husband.

He smiled back and whispered, "I love you."

She reached up and touched his face.

He kissed her fingertips.

Ianna's lips parted to speak, but he covered them with his. His arms encircled her waist, and they melted together.

The sun flooded its full light into the bedchamber, which signaled a half-spent morning.

Jamin touched the tip of Ianna's nose with his forefinger. "We will have to get up sooner or later."

A coy smile curved her lips. "Why?"

"Well, I am the king, of course. There are people to rule."

She laughed. "They got along fine without you before."

Her husband's grin softened. "No, they didn't. I believe it's for that reason I have become king."

Ianna knit her brow.

Jamin stroked her cheek. "I believe *Adonai* placed me here. The message of the prophet was for the city to repent of its evil ways. Much of it has, but not all. Today I issue a proclamation that mandates sackcloth and ashes for everyone. The city may yet be saved."

She frowned. "Can you do that?"

His smile returned. "Just watch me."

Jonah caressed Hannah's hair as she lay asleep against his chest. The night had passed fitfully for him, quietly for her. He had never held a woman like this—certainly never for an entire night.

Hulalitu had left in sufficient time to make it back to the city before sunset. Hannah had already fallen asleep from the exhaustion of a sleepless night, and neither Jonah nor Hulalitu wanted to disturb her. So she stayed. Before the priestess left, Jonah shot a questioning look at her, but Hulalitu only smiled and put her finger to her lips. Hannah slid her hand onto Jonah's chest and snuggled her face into his neck, as if she discerned his awkwardness in her sleep. Her breath came soft and slow. Jonah laid back and gazed at the blanket of stars that blinked their watch into the cobalt mantel unfolding from the east.

Visions filled his mind—images of days, months, and even years past. He fancied his brother Boaz's face in a cluster of stars to the north. His astral grin teased his little brother over the woman who lay at his side. The stars morphed into his father's kind and weathered visage that wore a different kind of smile. Deborah, his mother, formed into view beside her husband. Her eyes twinkled through two of the brightest stars.

A patch of darkness to the west became a hollow between massive waves of water. He felt himself falling, falling, finally going black. When his eyes jerked open again, a sliver of moon floated just to the south, its tips turned up into a smile—at him?—surely not. Throughout the night Elihu, Moshe, and even little Leah peered at him through the restless sky. They brought their own pieces of his life once again into focus, though still jumbled.

Finally, the yellow-blue sheen of pre-sunrise edged over the top of his boulder and rescued him from the illusions of the night. Jonah sighed. His eyes burned, the grit trapped against them betraying hours forsaken by sleep. Strands of Hannah's hair were wrapped around his fingers where he stroked her neck and head. He squeezed his eyelids shut and stretched his stiff back against the hard ground.

The movement drew a chopped breath from Hannah. She shifted against his side, the first time she had moved all night. Her fingers drew closed around a knot of cloth from the robe over his chest. She drew a deep breath, and he felt her eyelashes flutter open against his neck. Then he heard a gasp.

Hannah jerked her head up and stared into Jonah's face.

He smiled. "Good morning."

"What . . . what are you doing here?" She swept the niche with a wide gaze, as though to make sense of her surroundings.

"I live here. How about you?" Jonah couldn't help but chuckle at her panicked look.

She shot up to a sitting position and clamped her arms around her waist, her face ashen.

He raised himself on one elbow and touched her on the arm. "It's all right. You fell asleep yesterday evening. You were upset, exhausted. Hulalitu and I let you sleep."

"But . . . I . . . we . . . ," she stammered.

"Nothing happened, Hannah. You slept. Better than I did, in fact." He yawned.

"I don't know what came over me. I should never have—" She sucked in a sharp breath. "Ianna . . ."

Jonah went still. "Yes. You told me."

She put her head in her hands. Jonah sat up and put his arm

around her shoulders. He drew her to his side. Her shoulders convulsed, and she buried her face against his chest. Then she pulled away.

She brushed the tears from her cheeks. "I must go to her. I need . . . to be with her."

Jonah nodded. "I understand."

They pushed slowly to their feet. Jonah brushed sand and debris from his cloak, then retrieved his bundles.

She turned to him. "But you can't come back to the city. They'll see you. I don't know what to—"

"I have to go, Hannah. Back to Israel." He dropped his gaze.

Her breath caught short, but she said nothing.

"The angel spoke again yesterday. There's more for me to do there." He looked into her eyes. "I leave today."

Silence fell between them, and they both looked at the ground, at a loss for words. Finally, Jonah looked up. "I don't want you to be alone."

She flashed a weak smile. "Hulalitu will be at the house. She has renounced Ishtar and wants to serve *Adonai* in whatever way she can. I told her she can stay with me until . . . for as long as she likes."

He matched her smile. "She will make a good Jewess."

Hannah nodded.

Jonah fidgeted for a moment, then dropped his bundles. He stepped closer and lifted Hannah's chin with his finger. "You should go. There is much for you to do." Her face blurred through a sheen of moisture in his eyes.

She swallowed and nodded.

Jonah leaned forward and brushed her lips with his. Her eyes closed, and she slipped her arms around his waist. They held each other, and soft kisses punctuated their embrace until he thought his heart would burst. He drew back, rubbed his sleeve across his eyes, and smiled at her. Without a word, he took her by the shoulders and turned her around to face the city. A final squeeze and his hands dropped away.

༄ ༄ ༄

Hannah stood at the edge of the rocky outcropping. So much had happened in so little time. She knew God was in it, but she still didn't know what it all meant, why it had to be. She knew the city was saved. But she didn't know what to do now with her own life. Issues of cosmic importance—the salvation of a city and the glory of *Adonai*—were resolved. But little human issues still lingered—issues like her daughter, her widowhood, and her life from this point forward. She sighed in the knowledge that she needed to trust Him with those, too, but she didn't know where to start.

A thought struck her. Jonah was a prophet. Perhaps he could—

She turned, her mouth half open with the first question.

He was gone.

Fifty

Israel, Gath-hepher
Twenty-fifth Day of Âbu

Jonah sat on the slope above the family's tannery. Ehud had rebuilt their father's limestone cairn while Jonah was in Assyria. He had leveled the site and cleared away years of debris and undergrowth. His mother's grave lay neat and clean next to her husband's. His eyes roamed the twin monuments, and his mind recaptured the faces of his beloved parents from years less complicated.

Amittai's soft chuckle at one of Boaz's wayward comments echoed through his mind. Deborah's vision brushed an errant wisp of hair from a youthful Jonah's forehead with an adoring look and tucked him under his blanket. The blessings that were his parents loomed so vividly in his mind after his experience in Nineveh. The peace he knew as a child in the Amittai ben Avram household stood in such stark contrast to Hannah's faraway look at what might have been, had Mordecai and she not forsaken their heritage. The emptiness he had seen in her lent a somber reminder of the Judge Samuel's words, *"Everyone did what was right in his own eyes."* To forsake the God of his fathers seemed impossible to him—until he remembered his own rebellion. Had he not also done what was right in his own eyes?

Jonah sighed. *I am so weak, so small. Why* Adonai *chose me to carry His word will forever be a mystery to me. I am truly no better than Mordecai, who considered himself and his desires ahead of God's.*

A hoarse cough startled Jonah from his reverie. He turned his head. "Eli!"

He jumped up and turned toward his old friend. Elihu ben Barak stepped forward, and they grasped wrists.

"Your brother told me you'd be here. I'm not disturbing you, I trust."

Jonah shook his head, unable to shake his grin. "No, of course not. It has been too long, my friend."

Elihu nodded. "I missed your return from Joppa, although Hadassah and Benjamin told me about what happened." He paused. "Little Leah is well, by the way. She has become Hadassah's shadow. They're teaching her the ways of the vineyard. I believe she's going to be all right."

Jonah nodded and smiled as his mind flashed back to the orphan girl he'd brought to Elihu's sister and brother-in-law for refuge from a life of forced harlotry.

"That is good. I knew Hadassah would be the perfect mother for her."

Elihu smiled. "Yes, Leah has completed her. No woman on earth was meant to be a mother more than Hadassah. We thought it a cruel twist of nature that she was barren, but now all that has changed." He glanced at Jonah. "You should visit them."

Jonah looked down. "That would be nice."

Elihu's face grew serious. "That's why I'm here. I thought you might stop to see them on the way to Samaria."

"Samaria?"

His friend nodded. "King Jeroboam asks for you. He wants you to come to Samaria, to enter his service as a court prophet."

"A court prophet? But we discussed that when I was in Samaria, Eli. He knows I am of no use until *Adonai* chooses to speak through me again. I promised to return if such a commission came, but not before."

Elihu set his jaw. "Yes, but things have changed."

"Changed?"

"There is a man from Judah—another prophet, some say—who preaches against what you preached."

Jonah shook his head. "I don't understand."

"This man, Amos, disquiets the people." Elihu went on, his voice harsh. "Amaziah, the chief priest at the shrine at Bethel, reports that Amos prophesied Jeroboam will die by the sword, and that Israel will go into exile. The upstart complains of religious and social injustices—completely without basis, of course. His message runs counter to what you told Jeroboam."

Jonah looked up at his friend. "Does it?"

Elihu frowned. "Of course it does. You prophesied the land would be restored to Israel—" his face broke into a smile—"which is happening. Half of *ha eretz* now lies under the control of Jeroboam. And in Judah, King Amaziah and his son, Uzziah, have embarked on forays to the south and the west. More and more of the Promised Land is recaptured every day. What you prophesied is coming true."

"But, Eli, don't you remember the rest of the prophecy? That the restoration would only be for a season if the people refused to repent and seek *Adonai's* face once again?"

"But they do." Elihu knit his brow.

"No, Eli, they don't," Jonah said solemnly. "On my return from the east, I passed both Mt. Hermon and Mt. Tabor. Not only did I see the old high places, pagan altars and Asherah poles still in place, I saw new ones. In fact—" He nodded over Elihu's shoulder.

The soldier turned around. On a bluff just north of where they stood, an altar of piled rock sat amid a freshly cut clearing. A tree, newly stripped of its bark and scored with signs of the goddess Asherah—known also as Ashteroth, also as Ishtar—rose by its side. Elihu dropped his gaze, then turned back toward his friend.

Jonah's voice lowered. "Perhaps this new prophet is right."

Elihu ground his jaw. "Of course he isn't right. He speaks against the king."

"But he speaks for God." Jonah peered into his comrade's narrowed eyes. "Eli, it's been over six years since I delivered God's message to Samaria. Why does idolatry still flourish in Israel? You say half the land has been conquered for the king, but none of it has been restored to *Adonai*, to whom it really belongs."

Elihu shook his head. "These things take time, Jonah. It was first necessary to reclaim the land for Israel. That is being done."

"Why?"

"Why what?" Exasperation flooded Elihu's voice.

"Why is it necessary to conquer land with armies before you conquer hearts with truth?"

"There are priests for that. Jeroboam is the king. He leads an army."

"Perhaps that is part of the problem, Eli. The priesthood. Didn't you say Amos speaks out against religious injustice, too?" He continued before Elihu could interrupt. "And who do the court prophets serve? The court, of course. The king. If the king shows no interest in the things of God, neither will his priesthood. No, the king doesn't just lead the army, he leads the people. All the people in all ways. This king fails the people."

Elihu's face grew hard. "I won't listen to this. How would you even know the problems that face a king?"

Jonah smiled sadly. "I do know of such things, my friend. I just left a land with a king and a queen who lead their people in the matters that are important, albeit for only a season. The gentile Assyrians of Nineveh have repented, Eli. The chosen people of Israel have not." He shook his head. *"Adonai* has spared Nineveh. Will He spare Israel?"

Elihu glowered. "This is the land promised to the people by God."

Jonah sighed. "It's not *where* the people live; it's *how* they live."

The old soldier spun on his heel and stalked several paces away. He stood with his back to Jonah, his shoulders hunched. Several moments passed before he turned. "So, you won't come back with me."

"I love you like a brother, Eli, and I love this land. But, no, I will not go to Samaria. There is nothing for me there."

Elihu took a step forward. "There is prestige and glory—and the honor of service to your king."

Jonah shrugged. "All of which crumble to dust compared to the honor of service to my God."

Elihu dropped his head and exhaled slowly. He rubbed his eyes, and looked back up. "So, what will you do?"

Jonah smiled. "Go back to Nineveh."

"What?"

"I leave in the morning."

"But *Assyria?* Why?"

"There are people there who need me." His smile deepened. "And there is a person there who I need."

"But your people are here. Your family, your land."

Jonah nodded. "My family knows. They understand."

"But—"

"Eli, if *Adonai* gives me another message to deliver to Israel, I'll be back. Until then, I'll go where I'm needed the most." He shrugged. "And who knows? Perhaps God has already passed my mantel to this— Amos, was it?"

Elihu frowned.

Jonah cocked his head. "If I were you, I'd listen to him."

Epilogue

Israel, the Valley of Jezreel
841 B.C.

Jonah picked his way down the slope. He took extra care after he tripped over a broken spear and nearly pitched over the edge of the ravine. This was no time for clumsiness. The early twilight hindered his search, and he needed to finish before dark. Jehu's army would bury their dead at first light tomorrow. Another glance at the encroaching shadows, and Jonah's hope began to ebb.

He knew he shouldn't be out here. Elihu agreed to let him stay only if he kept to the rear of the battle lines. Jonah had promised not to venture out on his own—just as he was doing now. A prick of guilt stabbed his mind for going back on his word, but not enough to turn back. Elihu was a good friend, but he was too protective. No matter. Jonah had his reasons, and he wasn't going to let Elihu or anyone else dissuade him.

He worked his way to the edge of the drop-off and scoured the desecrated hillside. The sickly sweet odor of spilled blood fueled the bile in his gut, and the sight of raw flesh burned a grotesque image in his mind. It was all he could do to remain focused.

Jonah skirted a rock formation and pulled up short atop a cliff where the ravine walls jutted out onto the riverbed. He braced himself and peered over the edge. To the west, evening shadows crawled down the valley floor, the day anxious to release the horrific scene to the darkness of night. A light breeze picked up and eased the heaviness of the late afternoon air. Below him the Kishon River ambled past the mouth of the gorge, seemingly unaware of the violation so recently committed on its banks. He resumed his search and his eye swept over a prostrate form at the water's edge. Jonah squinted into the shadows, then set his jaw.

He scanned the steep grade for a way down. Several paces to his left, he glimpsed a cleft in the lip of the precipice. A switchback trail cut by generations of goats who had grazed in this valley led down to the riverside.

Jonah stepped onto a rock ledge at the head of the ancient trail and began the arduous climb down to the river. He sidestepped between boulders and slipped on loose dirt and rock shorn up by countless scrubby saplings and shrubs that clutched the face of the cliff. At the bottom, he stumbled onto the pebbly surface of the riverbank. His heart pounded as he hurried to the fallen warrior. He stepped over a dead Assyrian soldier with an arrow in his ribcage and a sword across his body.

Next to the Assyrian, the Israelite soldier sprawled in a small dark pool cut off from the river by a graveled sandbar. He had come to rest on his back, with only his head and shoulders above the glassy surface. An arrow circled with rings of scarlet protruded from his chest.

Jonah slackened his pace at the foot of the sandbar. He stared for a long moment into the ashen face of the warrior, then sank to his knees in the shallow pool. The movement sent ripples across the water and undulated strands of black curly hair across the man's temple.

His greatest fear was realized. Boaz, his brother, was dead.

Jonah squeezed his eyelids closed but failed to stem the flow of tears that surged down his cheeks.

Boaz!

Somehow, Jonah knew he would find him here, like this. He had braced himself for this moment, but not well enough. His trek through the grisly death strewn across the battlefield did not numb him sufficiently for this discovery. Boaz, his brother, his mentor, his friend.

Jonah settled onto the sand beside his brother's body.

"You knew it would come to this, didn't you, Brother? Your quarrel with Father was so pointless, but it gave you the excuse to escape the tannery, Gath-hepher—and us."

The wavelets tickled Boaz's beard, thin wisps of hair that had not yet blanketed his chin. His face was without expression, as Jonah had often seen it after an argument with their father.

"Restless spirit. That's what you always called it, but nothing Mother or Father tried to do was ever enough. Nothing satisfied you. When you sneaked out that night, I knew you weren't coming back." Jonah narrowed his eyes at the memory. "Mother suspected, too, but she never spoke a word. Father's heart broke. He watched for you to return until the disease took him this year. You didn't know that, did you, Boaz? Father died."

Jonah drew in a deep breath, then set his jaw.

"Mother clings to the hope that you're alive. She needs that hope, or she'll soon follow Father to Sheol, I know she will. I can't tell her. I won't tell anyone." Jonah brushed away a tear. "Maybe you've found a girl and have settled down. Maybe someday you'll come back with a grandchild for Mother. Or maybe you're in Jerusalem, where you're learning a trade. Or maybe . . ." He choked back a lump in his throat.

Boaz . . .

Jonah reached toward his brother's still face, then hesitated. The strength left him and his hand dropped onto Boaz's chest. His fingertips tapped against a hard object beneath his brother's tunic. He frowned and shifted the material to reveal a leather thong looped around the young soldier's neck. He pulled at it, and his eyes widened at a gold medallion that slipped through the tunic's collar. He eased the thong from around his brother's head and squinted at it in the dim light. Etched on its glossy surface was a *menorah*. He frowned. *What is this?*

"Jonah!"

His name floated on the evening breeze and nudged him from his reverie.

"*Jonah!*"

Jonah lifted his head and saw Elihu splash across the river downstream. Deep dusk had overtaken the valley and mercifully cloaked the remnants of battle in its gloom. Jonah rose to his feet and cradled the amulet in his hand.

"Jonah!"

Elihu limped toward him along the riverbank.

Jonah tucked the costly heirloom into the pouch tied to his waist and raised a half wave to his friend. He bent back over Boaz's prostrate form.

"Shalom, Boaz ben Amittai," he whispered. "Sleep well."

Jonah wiped a sleeve across his swollen eyes, then set off across the gravel toward Elihu.

"SO IT BEGINS."

Don't Miss . . .

The Journey Begun

Book One
A PROPHET'S TALE

*"When you run away from God,
you break things and hurt people."*
The prophet's own words bent him to the ground.

Israel, eighth century, B.C.

Six years ago, Jonah ben Amittai delivered a message of hope and redemption to his beloved homeland of Israel. Now he's called to the hardest task of all: to bring a message of repentance and hope to Nineveh, a city in the land of Israel's archenemy, Assyria.

Horrified by memories of brutal warfare in his youth, repulsed by his hatred of all things Assyrian, and spurred on by dark forces who have no intention of letting *Adonai's* prophet onto their turf, Jonah flees to the seaport of Joppa. But can he flee the memories of betrayed loyalty, broken friendships, and shattered family relationships? Can he escape the all-seeing eye of *Adonai?*

*The story you thought you knew . . .
A prophet's ageless tale of danger, redemption, and love*

www.brucejudisch.com
www.oaktara.com

About the Author

BRUCE JUDISCH, a Senior Information Operations Analyst for the Joint Information Operations Warfare Center, has been writing for many years.

"*A Prophet's Tale,*" Bruce says, "is a story we *thought* we knew—an ageless tale of rebellion and intrigue, love and faith, and spirits in battle over a destiny of a man. I wrote the series to portray that the actions the Lord calls us to always affect those around us, never us alone. If you've heard the story of Jonah, you may know about the storm and the great fish, but what of the consequences of Jonah's rebellion? What of the broken relationships? The lost opportunities? My motivation for writing this trilogy is to tell the prophet's story in a uniquely fresh, entertaining, and thought-provoking way."

Bruce is the author of *The Journey Begun,* Book One of A Prophet's Tale series, another novel, *Ben Amittai: First Call,* the prequel to *The Journey Begun,* which introduces the trilogy on Jonah, and also more than 18 Bible book study booklets, as well as topical studies on the Seven Churches of Revelation, the Resurrection, and Discerning God's Will.

Bruce holds an MA in Information Systems and Computer Resources Management; an MA in Management; a BA in Russian; and an A.A. in Communications Processing Management.

Bruce lives in Texas and is currently working on a new novel, *Katia.*

For more information:
www.brucejudisch.com
www.oaktara.com